THE SUNSET WAR:
UPRISING

BY
JACE OWENS

To James,
and everyone else who
helped me along the way.

TABLE OF CONTENTS

CHAPTER 1:
THE CATALYST

America will never be destroyed from the outside. If we falter and lose our freedoms, it will be because we destroyed ourselves.
— Abraham Lincoln

Pain... throbbing, consuming pain. Emily's eyes snapped open, then immediately closed again, seared by the lowering sun. Her head weighed more than the entirety of her body, her left arm ached, what happened? How did...

"Fire!"

Eyes flew open again, torso lurched forward, breaths came deep and ragged. Emily knew that she'd made a mistake making such an abrupt motion. Too late now. Trembling, her body hacked and coughed itself into a dizzy haze, she used her right arm to steady herself and felt something soft beneath it. Another wave of memories broke through the fog, gripping her mind as she staggered to her knees, then feet. For a long agonizing moment, Emily just stared at the shredded, bullet-riddled police cruiser in front of her. Catching her breath, with great reluctance, she turned around to face the hellish vision she knew full well awaited her.

Five bodies. Four lay lined against the destroyed SWAT van, with a space between them that she'd just stood up from, the fifth curled up in front of them. All long dead. Emily clutched at her left arm, finding a painful flesh wound, then raised her trembling right hand to the spot her pulsating headache seemed to emanate from. Her fingers glided across a mess of scab around a rough lumpy ridge that ran along the upper righthand side of her skull. Backing up as she tentatively assessed the extent of her wound, Emily blundered into the wrecked squad car, jolting her head around in surprise. The dizziness resurged full force as her vision settled on the rest of the aftermath. The little farmhouse had burned to the ground, all the grass surrounding it blackened and charred. Both of the other patrol cars also pulverized by bullets and burned out, another half dozen blue-uniformed corpses lay scattered across the yard, a couple of them horribly charred along with the grass they'd fallen upon.

Vision became blurry, vertigo took over, she surrendered. She fell to her knees and retched up everything she had left within her, then a violent cough turned her throat into sandpaper. It took all the energy Emily had to avoid collapsing to the asphalt again and never getting back up. She couldn't though, three other lives depended on her. She couldn't break down. Climbing back up to her feet, she felt around for her radio but found none. She made a clumsy stumble over to the gutted van and peered inside to find nothing of any use. Emily compelled herself to examine her butchered comrades, finding them also stripped of all their weapons and gear.

Emily felt her whole body shiver in sickened revulsion at the thought of hostile, callous hands roughly patting her down and tearing away everything that had protected her and made her feel powerful. Now she stood there. Just a woman in bloody, tattered clothes. No gun. No baton. No mace. No armor. No radio. Then it all hit her in a rush. *Radio, the others... Why has no one come?* Feeling at her massive, scabby, weepy head wound, and looking back to the collapsed timber pile that remained of the farmhouse, Emily concluded that all of it had sat this way for a full day at least. The deep pulse of her own heart became the only noise Emily could register in her mind, beads of sweat began sliding down the sides of her face. *Why haven't they come?*

With nothing else she could do, Emily turned down the road and began shuffling back to Sacramento. The closest town, Pilot Hill. Five miles south. The wrong direction. She had to get back home, now. No time for any detours.

#

As she made her way down the desolate rural road, Emily had little else to do but brood, running through theories about how this had happened and why, along with speculations about just which of the nation's various enemies bore responsibility. The one thought she avoided at any cost though: speculation as to the whereabouts of her children.

5

They're at home. They have to be. They'll be at home, or at the station. Try as she might, she could not avoid the one question that refused to stop tapping away in her head. *Why did no one come?* Whatever the answer, her first priority remained getting help for her wounds, which became harder to ignore as the initial burst of adrenaline began to wear off.

The steady drone of a diesel engine pulled her attention around to an old beat-up truck speeding down the wooded country road. Heading towards the city, the same direction anyway, so Emily tried to wave the driver down with her good right arm. The faded blue truck sped onward without even slowing down. For a moment, Emily just stood there in disbelief and watched it blur past. As the truck disappeared over the next rise, Emily resumed her previous stumbling up said hill, the seeds of grim possibility now watered. *Why the hell didn't they stop? Couldn't they tell I'm a cop? Should've noted their plate to report them later...* The drifting wonderings of her haze-addled mind came to a tire screeching halt upon reaching the hill's crest.

An incredible vista of the vast urban sprawl of Sacramento spread out before her westward view. The capital, though far less famous than California's other urban centers, remained no less a mighty metropolis. Quite a view she now realized, but the beauty of the evening scene almost immediately evaporated, replaced by the horror. Several columns of smoke scattered across the city, some small spirals of white steam, others huge towers of thick black soot ascending into the heavens. The smoke lay so thick above Sacramento that the setting sun had distorted into a polluted brown. Despite the time of day, a scattering of lights flickered and fluctuated across the state capital. No building lights, no streetlights, nothing of the kind. Darkness, broken only by fire. The single most chilling aspect of the whole spectacle, the ambiance. A steady orchestra of tattering and crackling emanated from the concrete forest, accompanied by sporadic flashes in the dimming daylight.

Emily stood there for a moment, trying to somehow process what she saw in front of her eyes. Before she really had much of a chance though, a large flash erupted above the southern edge of town followed by a huge tongue of flame, then a deep **boom**. Emily's knees failed, and she once again cursed her still unknown assailants for robbing her kneepads. *This is impossible, isn't it? This kind of shit only happens in movies! Who could do this? The Russians? China?* Then it hit her. *No... they were Americans, but are they responsible for this too?* Before her mind could fall too far down the rabbit hole, she managed to grab hold of herself. *It is possible, it's happening. It doesn't matter how or who or why, not yet. I **have** to get back home.* Emily completed the remainder of her journey with far more care, and made a deliberate effort to stay out of sight. Without any solid information she couldn't afford to take any chances, and now felt somewhat nervous about her previous encounter with the blue truck. *Who could that have been?*

#

The endless spats of gunfire grew more distinct as Emily finally reached the suburban outskirts of Sacramento. Not the rapid tit-for-tat exchanges of a gun battle though, just the occasional crack and burst that seemed to flare out from everywhere. Not until she entered the suburbs though, did the true nature of the thing revealed itself to her. Some of the houses lay pillaged and stripped out, ruined possessions and various pieces of trash and chunks of structural debris littered their yards. Doors and windows all smashed in. Cars as well as piles of tires and trash also blazed, and small bands of people just loitered all about, picking through the leftovers. A few other houses remained covered in huge plastic quarantine tarps. No one was crazy enough to loot those. But some homes seemed to stand untouched, apart from the odd chunk of debris that had migrated across the block. Each undamaged suburban home had only one visible thing in common with its plundered neighbors- a crude red star painted on the door.

Emily ducked into one of the gutted homes after she noticed the shapes swinging from a few streetlamps. She flew up a set of refuse-strewn stairs, into a ravaged bedroom, and struggled to control her breathing. With every step she took, it all just kept getting worse. Her house, not far from here, it couldn't have remained untouched by this chaos. What grisly scene would she find awaiting her? She managed to find a dark green t-shirt and gray sweat pants just about her size among the handful of items apparently not worth stealing. Emily tried in desperation not to think about who this shirt may have belonged to and what fate they may or may not have met, as she ditched the uniform that had become a dangerous liability.

On her way back out, the brutal rattling of an old diesel engine sent her sliding into cover beside the shattered front window. Keeping to the shadows, Emily declined to peer outside, waiting for them to pass into her view. The smatterings of people who had wandered in or near the street wasted no time hopping to the sidewalks, raising Emily's hope for just a moment that perhaps it signaled the appearance of someone on **her** side. Then an old green pickup truck, with a mounted fifty caliber machine-gun and a flatbed full of armed people, zoomed down the road leaving a wake of churned up debris. The truck raced by as fast as it could without dumping its passengers onto the asphalt, paying no regard to the heaps of trash strewn across the road. Most of the riders carried guns, but three were gagged and tied between them on the flatbed. While Emily watched it go, trying in fruitless desperation to make out the identity of the prisoners, another vehicle raced past after it, then another. An old sedan that she could only describe as rust-colored chugged past, a trail of black smoke sputtering out behind it. The sedan, also filled with gun-toting figures, appeared no more distinct. Behind it came a prison bus, all of the windows smashed out, but the bars left in place, gun barrels waiting behind them. The implications made Emily's skin go gray.

All the vehicles shared the same symbol that marked the pristine houses: the Red Star. The only distinctive attribute of the men in the truck? Red armbands.

Emily lost all sense of time and sound as she charged out the back door and down the drainage ditch that separated this row of houses from the next. *It's **them**!? First I thought they were a joke, then a menace, but this? How is this even possible!?* The journey felt like it passed by before her eyes in only a few moments. Her gravest fears seemed legitimized when Emily finally arrived at her previously well-kept suburban home. The front door smashed off its hinges, the garage door torn out into the driveway. Another moment and she flew inside, up the stairs, and into her bedroom.

Trashed, even worse than the last house. Splayed out on the floor her mattress lay gutted, the victim of a search for stashed money. Someone had ripped all the copper out of the walls, leaving them covered in long gashes. Her closet safe-room lay savagely breached. Emily peered into the small armored chamber intensely, ever-so-slightly relieved not by what she found but by what she didn't. No sign of anyone inside at the time. Of course, the looters had robbed all her guns and bullets, as expected. *At least they missed **one**.* She checked Christina's room next to find it equally plundered, same for Zechariah's, but Rob…

Robert's room, savaged but not with the same degree of wanton destruction. No remains of anything broken or smashed, yet also devoid of anything useful. This anomaly barely phased Emily's frantic search though. After checking every closet and cabinet on every floor, Emily had to face reality: her family was gone, but might still be alive. No blood or discernible sign of struggle anywhere, just chaotic pillaging. Her next stop, the station. She had told them to go there in case of an emergency. This now far surpassed the realm of emergency. This emergency, had now become a disaster. Looking for her hammer and then realizing the looters had stolen even it, Emily grabbed a nice hefty rock from the back yard and rushed back up to her room. Not wasting a second, she smashed away at the floorboards in the corner between her bed and the closet. Having pummeled a sufficient hole into them, Emily wrapped strips of torn bedsheets around her right hand to guard against splinters. Then, she pulled two of the boards up to reveal a dusty little space occupied by a rough, featureless, wooden box.

After pausing for only the slightest heartbeat, still in near disbelief that it had truly come to this, but nonetheless propelled by the inertia of sheer will, she gingerly flipped the box open. The container and its contents felt ancient, stowed under the floor for well over a decade. She revived a weapon from a previous era in hopes that it would serve her family now as well as in her great-grandfather's war. Five magazines of .45 ACP, only eight rounds in each though. Not one of her favorites, she never understood why the old men always went on about it. No time for pickiness now though, she'd chosen to stash this one away for a reason. One round could kill or incapacitate, she hoped she wouldn't need to use any. Wrapping the old gun's holster under the sole blue jacket that had survived the scouring, Emily left her home behind. Forever.

The county sheriff's department, though the closest to her house, lay almost a dozen miles away, more than far enough for the scale of the catastrophe to reveal its whole extent. The sun now gone, the only sources of illumination left came in the form of countless and varied fires. At least two raged on every street. As Emily slunk down the increasingly crowded sidewalks, it all only continued to decay the deeper into the city she ventured. Dozens of bodies hung from lampposts, at least one on each, while others swung from trees, billboards, and bridges. Some clearly cops, many wore some kind of uniform. The rest wore suits, jackets, button-ups. Nice-looking clothes. Heads, chopped off and heaped into piles that rested beside intersections like totems of hell. No one around her seemed phased by any of this carnage. Either they busied themselves picking through the abandoned structures, or they too headed someplace else keeping their own heads down so as to go unnoticed.

Then, she saw the others.

Standing guard or walking about, they wore normal civilian clothes with the odd item of military surplus here and there, especially gas masks, coming from a slew of different nations and eras. Carrying a wide variety of assault rifles, shotguns, bolt-actions, and submachine guns, they shared no standardization whatsoever, save for the blank red armbands they all wore. Upon close yet very covert examination, Emily saw they could hardly even qualify as armbands. Really just strips of red fabric tied in haphazard fashion around either upper arm. In addition to the armbands they also wore, bandanas, shirts, and other random articles of red clothing to mark them rebels. She considered trying to somehow corner and interrogate one of them, but they seemed to exist only in large groups, at least five or more. Instead, she just plodded onwards, head firmly kept to the ground. Emily suddenly felt relieved to have ditched out of her tattered police uniform, dressed in looted clothes. They would've hung her from one of those lampposts before, now none of them gave her a second glance. Her injuries attracted no special notice either. Other wounded unfortunates hobbled about and groaned everywhere.

A loud metallic clattering and the roar of a mighty engine pulled her attention around to a sight she though would make her heart give out right then and there. Another rusted-out jalopy cruised down the cluttered street, its doors removed and both occupants waving their arms and shouting for everyone to clear a way. Behind them followed a true game changer. An M1A1 Abrams main battle tank crawled across the tarmac, crushing garbage, chunks of buildings, and grisly remains without notice. It seemed normal enough at first, save for a trio of scorch marks on the turret front. Until it rumbled past, revealing the lone, spray-painted red star plastered on the side of the hull. The two crewmen manning the fifty cals in their respective cupolas also appeared at first as perfectly normal national guardsmen, until their red armbands became visible, along with the lone red stars emblazoned right on the front of their helmets.

Insanity. Emily's world continued to crumble beneath her feet. Slipping into a backstreet, she ran. Ignoring the agony in her arm and brain. Everything just continued disintegrating.

At about the time Emily arrived in Nimbus Industrial Park, she heard the first cannon shell. She urged herself onward with what little remained of her reserves, until she happened upon a potential goldmine hidden deep in the back alleys, an abandoned police cruiser. She eased inside, visually scouring the interior, finding only another murdered comrade and a pockmarked windshield. She tried the ignition, which still had the key in it, but nothing at all happened. Then, the distinctive racking of a shotgun assaulted her left ear.

"Looking to pick over our dead, you fucking vulture!?"

Emily froze, knowing that death awaited if she made a wrong move. That voice though... "Scott?" Silence for a few moments. She turned her head to face down the barrel of her coworker's weapon. His face widened in genuine shock and his aim wavered. The blonde-haired green-eyed young man looked like complete hell.

"Dawes? You're alive?"

With an annoyed huff, Emily batted aside his shotgun with her good arm, sliding back out of the useless vic. "No thanks to any of you! You just left me at that goddamned farmhouse!" Emily knew her words harsh and unreasonable, but she hadn't met anyone she could talk to since waking up. And Scott had just jammed a gun in her face. "What are you doing here anyway? Shouldn't you be defending the station?" She brushed past her bewildered colleague towards the edge of the last cluster of warehouses, to where she could actually see the station.

"Farmhouse? Wha- wait Em, don't!" Before he could stop her, she crept to the edge of the warehouse and peeked around the corner. Then she wished Scott had managed to catch her.

An uncontrollable blaze consumed the entire station. A few scattered figures hosed down the building in an iridescent stream of liquid flames, flowing out from crude launchers strapped to their backs. No less than half a dozen tanks ringed the structure, their barrels leveled. Without warning, one of the tanks blasted a shell through a shattered window and into the interior, causing that section to collapse. Emily felt her heart stutter. Before she could draw her old gun and start firing at anyone and everyone, Scott jerked her back behind the warehouse.

"God, what are you, **nuts**!?" he hissed. "Forget about it, it's too late for any of them!" At first she struggled against his pull, but quickly surrendered. "We've got to get the fuck out of here befor-"

"Zechariah, Christi, Rob…" Tears welled up in her eyes, no matter how hard she tried to keep them down. Scott's face became twisted in confusion.

"Who?" Scott pressed.

"My kids! My three kids! I told them to-" Emily stammered. Scott slung his shotgun and grabbed Emily by both her shoulders, staring into her eyes.

"Em, listen to me. There were no kids in that building. Your kids weren't in there! We have to go, now, or we are both going to die." He spoke with a slow and deliberate voice, providing just the anchor of reason that Emily so needed.

"There weren't any kids inside?"

Scott's expression softened. "No. No kids." He let her go, and she moved away from the corner and back down the service road.

"Do you have a car?" she managed to ask.

"No, I was going to use that one you were poking around in. Is it-?"

"Dead," Emily confirmed. She began running the possibilities through her head of where else her children might have hidden. The sole possibility that remained, the one other family member she had in the city. Her mother. Only after this conclusion materialized did Emily's thoughts come back around to the unfortunates still trapped in the station as it dissolved to ashes. She halted, about faced, and grabbed her surprised fellow officer by his shirt with both hands, despite the pain.

"Scott…" Emily uttered through gritted teeth, staring into his very wide and concerned eyes. "What the **fuck** is going on!?" she hissed. His eyes jerked around for a moment in confused desperation before returning to meet Emily's fiery blue irises again.

"I- I don't really know. Nobody does." He admitted. Emily felt numb again, wondering if perhaps she were actually dead. Or maybe in a nightmare that she hoped she would wake up from. "A couple days ago all the power just blinked out and since then we've all been locked on a railroad to hell. They just started hitting us everywhere and didn't stop. We tried to call in the national guard to help us get things under control and they opened up on us instead! It's gone from bad to severely fucked."

Emily let this all filter into her mind. *How could the power just go out?* "Who? Who's behind all this?" she pressed.

"We know the Reds have taken charge, at least nominally. As for starting it all, I don't think any of them are actually behind the power. Every soul out there who hates our guts just saw the same opportunity and took it."

So it is them. The Reds. The Reds are running the show after all. Emily felt sick inside. She had clung to the possibility that Sacramento simply descended into disorganized anarchy. But if they had actually taken charge, then this had graduated from a mere riot to something else all together. And at the rate things continued to deteriorate, Emily didn't want to wait around and hope that cooler heads would prevail.

9

Different things ignite madness in different people's minds.

Paul felt certain that only endless boredom could drive him off the cliffs of reason. If not that, then endless boredom while trapped in endless darkness, with an endless soundtrack of moans, groans, and shouts from outside. And, of course, the mumbled ramblings of the newest of his four cellmates. They all snored away in the bunks around him.

Not Maniac Jesus though.

There he sat in a lotus position, right on the floor in front of the lower mattress. Paul washed off his face with a stained rag, approaching the seated man.

"Hey man, you claiming the bottom bunk?" He asked in a slow voice.

"If your asking for it, then it is yours, brother." The tattered man responded.

Paul grunted, "Well uh, all right then. Thanks."

Normally getting ahold of the bottom bunk represented a major ordeal. Bribery, manipulation, and threats were all expected. But not this time. Without another word, Maniac Jesus clambered up to the top rack, where he sat down and began to… meditate? Pray? Paul couldn't be sure. All he knew: the authorities had decided to incarcerate this character along with some the most dangerous "criminals" in the whole South. *But why?*

To Paul, he seemed just a strange, frail man. His green eyes wide and wild, but neither hostile nor aggressive. No hint of the despair that would set in once he realized he would die in this hell, nor the grim determination that sometimes grew out of melancholy. The determination to survive. That made him new. Whatever he'd done on the outside made the Big Man awfully mad. Mad enough to send him straight to max sec, and from what Paul could see in those eyes, the guy had barely gotten started. Or at least, so he thought. No one escaped, and those who did never made it far. But Paul had long since given up on trying to relieve his fellow prisoners of their pleasant delusions, far better to allow them to realize it for themselves and help them cope if needed. Others tried to exploit anyone and everyone, but not Paul.

Bad enough trying to exist in this shit-hole when the power functioned, but now? Hot, smelly, and pitch dark. Sometimes a guard would patrol down the hall with a candle or an gas lantern, providing a few moments of illumination before it once again faded. Each time a guard passed, a number of other prisoners would ask, plead for, or demand information about why the power remained out, and why they remained on lockdown. Each time, they went unaddressed, any hand or arm that passed beyond the bars got batted away with the club. Paul knew of few things that could knock out the prison's power. Someone would have to cut its grid connection, and damage or destroy the backup generator. In other words, some pretty serious sabotage. At least he thought so at first, but then it had lasted into the next day, then the next day, now three dank and exhausting days without any power. Everyone still confined to their cells. Three full days, now coming up on a fourth. One would've thought that if a saboteur did it, they've long fixed it by now. At first they used flashlights, but then they switched over to gas lanterns and candles. Which meant, they had run out of batteries, or hoped to save what little remained.

His mind once again became drawn to the ramblings of his cellmate, who looked like a sort of Maniac Jesus. Paul still couldn't make out any of the specifics, but the rhythm made them sound like meditative chants of some sort. Paul envied him to an extent, probably kept the guy's thoughts off the miserable lot they had all drawn. Having no chants he could recite to ease his nerves, he decided to do something he hadn't successfully tried yet, communicating with his cellmate.

"Hey man, whatchu goin' on about up there?" Paul asked without giving off any sense that he really even cared. Yet the only reply he received… an uninterrupted continuation of the chant. Paul sighed. "Look man, if I you don't start talkin' to me, I may just assume that you've lost your shit. Would you wanna be stuck in a dark, dank-ass cell with a guy who's lost his shit?" More chanting. Paul grunted in annoyance but before he could press on, he heard a loud pop from outside. Then another one, another. Soon the crackling became impossible not to notice, and the chanting on the bunk above ceased.

Sharp clacking of boots and jangling of keys echoed through the hall as two guards sprinted past. The popping and snapping sounds became louder and more frequent, then they tapered off, before beginning anew with greater fury. No mistaking the sound now, Paul had spent too much time in Afghanistan not to know. Gunfire. Lots of it. The shifting of legs above him drew his attention. *Oh, so now he's interested in the mortal world? Just in time for us to die.* A soft, quiet voice somehow managed to reach his ears through the distant yells and cracks.

"What were you before this place, brother? Why did they seal you away in here?" Paul blinked, annoyed at the presumption of the weird guru, but having no real reason to not answer.

"I was in the army. Couldn't hold down a job after I got back. Heh, I got thrown in here because I punched out an off-duty cop in a bar fight." Again the gunshots became louder before again fading, until once again they exploded, this time inside the building. A limping guard lurched down the hall off to the right, the opposite direction from before. *Great.*

"It pains me deeply to say this brother, more than you believe, but you will have a purpose once again." Paul felt his eyebrow raise.

"Oh yeah? You sure we aren't about to get fucking killed?"

"I am." Maniac Jesus' statement came not with pride or arrogance, but a kind of grim assurance. This piqued Paul's interest. He decided to take a slight chance, after all he had nothing to lose.

"You know why the power's dead?" A long silence followed.

"No. But I do know what it means." *Oh?* More clacking of boots away from the entrance. Paul waited on his bunk to watch the guard run by as best he could.

BANG!

Shocked out of his cynical passivity, Paul just managed to avoid smashing his head against the upper bunk frame. He arrived on his feet just in time to watch the shape of of a very dead guard slide to a stop on the harsh tile. The motionless form became revealed as a guard by an approaching beam of light, along with a spreading pool of blood around his neck. Paul closed his eyes and breathed in deep, not sure he wanted to know the answer. A chorus of footsteps outside the cell, the metallic racket of a key jammed into a slot, and the dull screech of the door sliding open.

"Freedom." Eyes slid back open, met by a crowd of masked and armed figures waiting in the gloom.

#

Alexander had never loved the 98 percent of his job that revolved around virtual inactivity, until now. Hardest tour yet, and the most demoralizing. No change, no progress, no end in sight. Bad devolved to worse— half the region trying to kill them and the other half wanting nothing to do with them. But now? Now things lay in tatters. In their infinite wisdom, the oligarchs had decided to pick a fight with half the world, and cause the other half to turn its back. Now, the Insurgents came better equipped than ever, in greater numbers than ever, and with more daring and determination than ever.

He just left a briefing with his superiors explaining to him that they still had no communications with home. *Perfect.* The Brass had no information. In fact, all of their systems that had anything to do with satellites were just dead. The only theories anyone had revolved around some sort of mass cyber-attack or, God forbid, a plot by the Chinese and the Russians.

Chinese. Russians. Iranians. Saudis. Jihadists. So very close to so many enemies, so very far from home.

Alexander knew full well the men under his command also felt seized by lethargy and despair. This paralysis festered away at the very heart of the army like a cancer, harder and harder to ignore with the passing of time. Each of their minds seemed fixed upon their own ETS, PCS, DEROS— anything to get back home. It felt far different than anything Alexander read about in his history books, or even anything his old man told him about. No one wanted anything more than simple survival. No one held any higher motivation. Many had only taken the job so their families could afford a decent living, and no one intended to die for the objectives or masters which had sent them here.

The telltale sound of a tent flap folding back drew Alexander's attention from the written copy of the report, which included official congratulations for his promotion. Sure enough, his old friend Derrick Maxwell stood there saluting him with a smug smile on his face. Alexander sighed in defeat, reached into his pocket, dug six 20s from his wallet, and hurled them at Derrick in mock contempt. His old comrade caught the wad easily enough, shaking his head as he counted the bills.

"Tsk tsk… Should've tried harder to avoid the spotlight, Captain Harris, sir!" Alexander chuckled and shook his head, turning to a plastic cooler on the ground.

"Oh believe you me I tried my best, lieutenant, but the all-seeing eye of our glorious leaders will allow no talent to go unexploited." He pulled out two of the cans of beer he'd bought off a helicopter pilot returning from RnR in Germany. He extended a can to Derrick which he accepted with a wide grin, and came to a seat on Alexander's bunk. Alexander leaned back in his cheap office chair, putting his feet up on his desk, and popping his own can open. Each man took a long, desperate drink. Then, they sat in silence for a while. Not an awkward and uncomfortable silence, but an exhausted and lost silence.

"Look man, things can't go on like this." Alexander's eyelids slid closed, he rubbed his shaved and aching head, looked down at his sweat-coated brown hands. Now even more of the army's problems would become his problems.

"I know." What more could he say? Endless harassment, lack of information, constant misdirection and lies. They had all reaped their toll. But, what could he do about it? Derrick pressed on though, he had to. The tent roof shuddered for a bit as a helicopter hovered by overhead, blanketing the air in the deafening wail of a rotary whirlwind. Once it passed and audible communication became possible again, Derrick spoke up despite the sand in his eyes.

"Damn flyboys," he muttered.

"We had another squad just disappear yesterday. Without sats or drones the air crews are being pushed to the limit just trying to keep enemy air at bay, let alone watching over our guys."

"I know." *It can't last.* **Something** *has to give…*

"Any word on home? On our families?" Derrick knew better than to ask. Alexander met his gaze. Derrick sighed. "Eh, was worth checkin'."

He took a long swig from his can. Alexander once again cursed his "superiors" for their utter failure to create any plan of action in three days of complete silence. For their refusal to extend the troops even the slightest consideration by telling them something, anything about what the hell had gone on back home. Nothing. Just, *"Hold fast and keep the men together captain. We'll know more soon enough."* Funny, after the blackout they had said the same thing.

"What… is to be done?" Alexander wondered aloud. Derrick looked up from his beer can, the solemn resignation on his face twisted into curiosity, then contemplation.

At that moment, a flash of light—almost supernatural in scope— spilled into the tent from every open crevice, as if some cosmic camera had just taken a photo outside. Derrick and Alexander shielded their eyes with their forearms and grunted in stunned annoyance. Then it was gone.

The two comrades stared at one another for just a moment, until they got blasted off their seats by what felt like a moving wall. Engulfed in darkness and the mild chemical smell of army canvas, Alexander jammed his hand around for the multitool on his belt. Ears ringing, Alexander managed to cut a small hole in the collapsed tent fabric and tear it into a large enough gap that he could escape through. Dragging himself out onto the baked sandy soil, Alexander just turned back to help Derrick only to watch his friend follow right behind him through the improvised door. As his hearing began to return to normal, Alexander staggered to his feet and took a look around struggling to regain his equilibrium.

The two men saw every tent in camp flattened, all manner of metal prefabs and a water buffalo had been knocked over, soldiers' possessions and paperwork now scattered and fluttered across the camp like the aftermath of a rock concert. Soldiers sprinted to and fro, clutching at their eyes or ears, or just wandered, devoid of any direction. So overwhelmed by the theater of hectic chaos playing out in front of him, Alexander did not, until he felt a hand on his shoulder, notice the cause. Alexander turned himself around to face Derrick, who wore an expression of absolute horror, something which Alexander never witnessed in his comrade before, and drove an icepick into his soul. Fighting against every bit of sense he still possessed, the young captain followed his friend's dismal gaze, and felt his whole world evaporate beneath him.

In the southwestern skies above Kuwait City, a mushroom cloud billowed up from the dusty mass above the city and ascended upward. The rising sun almost blocked out by the great pillar of soot, sand, and ash, the base of the terrible column illuminated by a lake of fire. Alexander, for the first time in two decades, was lost.

CHAPTER 2:
PATHS TO SALVATION

You only lose what you cling to.
— The Buddha

Many events in the history books bore resemblance to the tragedy now playing out before Yujing in the streets of D.C. below and around her. None quite captured the sheer pulsating wrath of the chaos, the weight of pain, terror, and death in the air. The endless ambiance of industrial death and rabid flaming decay in the face of the spreading inferno. The masses of people who flowed through the streets all headed in the same direction, The Mall. Yujing hadn't seen any law enforcement in over two days, just looters and the two rival hordes of revolutionaries.

They called themselves the Brotherhood of Patriots and the Popular Front respectively. The Brotherhood wanted a conservative libertarian government to take the place of the old, while the Popular Front wanted a more socialist system implemented. She had discerned all of that from the wounded coming and going in and out of the hospital. This was what she did as a reporter for the BBC. The names of those involved, the details of their motivations, and what exactly sparked the violence between the two remained a mystery for now. Not to mention what sort of anarchy had erupted elsewhere across the country. If D.C. had already gotten this bad, Yujing didn't want to imagine what the West Coast must look like.

Her native city of Hong Kong suffered through its own period of terrible upheaval, but nothing like this, even in the most desperate times. She tried not to think about home much, hoping her parents possessed the sense to just keep their heads down until she got back. If, she could even make it back. She hadn't heard **anything** about the states west of the Mississippi let alone her home. For now, she needed to focus on the present, the world-moving events that swirled in the streets beneath. Reading about these sort of things often made them sound like a logical sequences of events, a march toward the inevitable outcome. In reality though, everything was chaos. Who could know the outcome? Only time would determine the victor. Until then, Yujing would be there to ensure nothing went unrecorded. Until then, Yujing saw it as her duty, to not only stay alive but to chronicle all of the horrors and glories. She'd already heard lies without number, and her greatest challenge—below not getting killed—would be keeping an objective outlook. Serving the truth. *If that's even possible.*

#

Paul felt for the first time in his life as though some cosmic hand had dragged him away from certain doom. The etherial glow of improvised torches bouncing off concrete and steel as a chorus of footsteps clattered all around him. He followed his former cellmate through the brutal concrete corridors of— whatever name "The Man" had slapped onto this particular den of misery— with a sort of surreal compulsion. Clad in a wide range of ragged clothes and mismatched military gear, the procession emitted an aura of inevitability as it steadily closed on the yard. Paul's new friend led them all with an intensity animated not by arrogance or presumption, but a sort of grim resolution.

Freedom. That's what he'd said. Paul had no way of yet knowing what this guy meant by that word. He wouldn't need long to find out.

The yard, a lone open-air space enclosed by huge walls of concrete, bustled in loud and confused motion. Prisoners piled in from the various wings in a continuous stream as armed men and women attempted to corral them into groups. Paul saw uniformed personnel— who he assumed to be the guards and staff— isolated into one group on their knees and surrounded by more armed people. Several familiar faces among the guards now absent.

Finally standing in what could with some charity be called a well-lit area for the first time in days, Paul could now get a decent look at his "liberators." A motley bunch. Many wore the obvious garments of the militias, U.S. Army gear and weapons emblazoned with coiled snakes, Confederate battle flags, and of course the cross in its many, many forms.

The rest, who in fact made up the majority, consisted of a wide assortment of characters from rednecks to urban poor, united only by the brown sashes they all wore around their waists and scarfs around their heads and necks. Men and women, young and old, gorgeous and hideous, all stood in wary watch over the captive guards and the steadily growing mass of prisoners.

Impossible to describe the thoughts and emotions swirling around in every prisoner's head. Confusion, curiosity, jubilation, uncertainty, fear. You could feel it all in the air, in the words they all spoke. Paul couldn't escape it either. Who were these people? Would they really let *everyone* go? They'd already made themselves enemies of the state, so why not go the extra mile?

At around the same point that Maniac Jesus veered off into the guard tower that overlooked the yard, the closest thing Paul had to a friend in this place approached him. Mason stood a full six feet tall and looked able to bench press a truck. Not much to do in prison other than chores, work, read, or lift weights, and Mason particularly enjoyed the last of those options.

"Hey man, s'goin on? You know that guy?" His voice reverberated deep within the earth. Paul shrugged.

"Nah he's just my new cellmate. Or I guess he *was*. No idea who he is though. Just sorta rambled somethin' about God," he answered. Mason's eyebrows rose up.

"Somethin' about God huh?" Mason inquired. The apathetic veteran rolled his eyes.

"I couldn't understand him, dude. He was whispering and shit. Until these guys came and got us out." He craned his head towards the militia. "All he told me was that he didn't know why the power's out, but that it means freedom." Mason's eyes widened at that.

"No shit, for real? You think he means freedom for us, or just him?" Paul turned up to the guard tower, where his cellmate had finally reached the top, and had extended his arms, waving for silence. He turned back over to Mason.

"Looks like we're about to find out."

The mild bedlam of the yard simmered down until only scarce whispers remained. The ragged, bearded man took a deep breath, and began to speak.

"My friends, my fellow citizens, fellow sons and daughters of the South. Each of us stands here today in this terrible place for the same reason. Our national government has long since abandoned it's stated goal of defending the rights and liberties of it's citizens. What rights do we still possess that cannot be ignored? What meaningful liberties are we still allowed to exercise?" A murmur of general disgruntled agreement bounced through the room. "Our nation has become nothing more than an insatiable siphon, that exists only to funnel the wealth of the whole world into the wallets of a despotic and uncaring oligarchy! We slave away either at our work posts or in concrete tombs like this place, while they live in untarnished luxury! My friends, this disaster is, in truth, a blessing from the Lord! He has struck our great enemy deaf and blind, given us the chance we need to brake the shackles of the new pharaohs! The time to fight is now!" Another wave of affirmation. "Join us, or go free. The choice is yours. But if we fail to cast off our enslavement at the hands of the forces of Death, there will be no future left for our children."

#

As the ringing in Alexander's ears faded, he realized that apart from a few pained cries and groans, near silence enveloped the camp. Tearing his vision away from the dreaded cloud, he saw that everyone who could still see remained locked on the surreal spectacle unfolding above the city. Some stood there stunned, their faces blank in horrified disbelief. Others forced themselves to resume searching for a friend, comrade, or even lover elsewhere in the base. Some had tears rolling down their cheeks, looking broken or half dead.

With Derrick right behind him, Alexander stumbled his way over to the collapsed commander's tent. Slicing his way inside with some care to avoid accidentally gutting someone, he poked his head inside to discovered it empty. He pulled his head back out of the crumpled tarp and looked around for his superior, until Alexander finally spotted him out fifty feet away. Colonel Baxter stood still as a mannequin, his gaze firmly fixed on the great black plume rising into the heavens. A mess of panicked humanity swirled around him like a force of nature, as the shouts and commands from

15

a handful of iron-willed sergeants and lieutenants attempted to organize the chaos in a borderline futile effort. Alexander placed a hand on the colonel's shoulder to get his attention.

"Sir?" Nothing. *Not a good sign*... Alexander walked in front of the colonel to see his face, and felt his own go bit numb. Baxter had gone deathly pale, green eyes twitched, mouth hung open. He looked stunned, in utter disbelief. Sweat, streamed down his face.

Alexander hadn't known the man for long, but he hadn't thought of Baxter as a coward. Nor did he now. Still, this response came about as close to the opposite of what Alexander needed from the man as it could get. **Someone** needed to take action. Alexander, no expert on nukes, still knew which way the wind blew in from the Persian Gulf, and fallout would soon manifest as a very real threat. He shook Baxter' shoulder firmly.

"**Colonel!**" Baxter turned to Alexander, as though looking through him.

"Captain? Harrison?" He sounded adrift, seeking some connection to the real world, as though lost in some horrible dream. Alexander didn't know what else to do at this point so he pressed on.

"Colonel! What are your orders sir!?" he shouted over the commotion around them.

"My... my orders?" he stammered the question out, the concept foreign to him. *Fuck. He's had it, hasn't he?* This... was not how things were supposed to go. Baxter gave the orders, Alexander carried them out.

"Sir," Alexander said with resolve, "we need to move the unit eastward to the National Guard depot. We're in the path of the fallout!" Alexander's command seemed to reactivate some part of his scattered mind.

"Fallout... that was a nuke? A real goddamned nuke?" Alexander took a very deep breath.

"Sir, we need to-"

"Don't you get it kid?" Baxter interrupted, forcing Alexander to pause. "This is the end. No contact with home, no satellites, no orders from high command. They're all gone. This is the end. This is... this is the end!" He turned back to the billowing mushroom of dust, extending his arms upwards, a manic smile having formed across his face. "They did it! Those bloodthirsty bastards finally did it! It's the end! The en-"

WHACK!

Alexander's pistol just about fell from his grasp as he processed what he'd just done. Reluctantly, he looked up from the unconscious colonel to find himself surrounded by a circle of stunned and uncertain faces. Somehow, in this particular situation, he found relief. At least none of them looked ready to go after him for assaulting their superior officer. He hadn't wanted to do that of course, but if the poor bastard went around sending everyone into hysterics, well... he could just forget about getting things back under control. And if he didn't get things back under control, at least a little bit, everything would get *so* much worse.

"Get everything packed ASAP. We're moving east in fifteen!" Alexander looked between faces, but no one moved. Come on guys. "Look, if we stay here we're all going get irradiated to death. So we **need** to get out of here and try to regroup with everyone else." A few soldiers here and there shook themselves from their overwhelming stupor and headed off to pack their shit. "Get the vics ready, load the wounded and supplies up first."

"What are you serious? We'll get covered in fallout." Not the time to dole out harsh punishments for insubordination, not the time to just let it slide either.

"That'll only happen if we stick around here too long!" he answered. A few more peeled off to tend to preparations. Alexander turned to Derrick. "Find Lewis, I need to wrack his brain over this." His old friend nodded and headed off towards the I.T. tents in search of the outfit's resident geek. Definitely the most useful, and least irritating geek Alexander had ever dealt with, and he'd never been so happy to have the guy around. As the crowd of troops and civilian personnel in aprons, jumpsuits, and t-shirts cleared away Alexander heard more than a little grumbling.

"What the hell is going on back home? Is everybody dead?"

"I bet those stupid bastards finally pushed the Ruskies or the Chins into nuking America. Now they're getting around to us."

"How do we get back home? Is there even a home to get back to?"

"We listened to them, we did whatever they said, and now we've all been left to fuckin' die!"

Alexander kept quiet for now, he had no answers after all. He could only really take solace in the knowledge that most of it didn't seem directed at him... for now.

After seeing to it that Baxter got stuffed into the back of a Humvee, Alexander ran over what little he knew and wracked his brain trying to decide what the do next. He knew they needed to leave, now. But where would they go? The first choice: Camp Buehring. But that would place them even further into the fallout's path. The national guard depot provided another option, which would put them closer to both the city, and the front line. Even if the Iranians didn't launch the nuke, they knew about it now. Who knew what response they would send? Alexander realized that with Baxter having snapped, he now stood as the highest ranking officer in the camp. The captains worked at the HQ... probably a sizzling crater now. So, he had command. At least for the moment. *Great.*

At around the point where he had decided to make for the guard depot, a burst of gunfire followed by the immediate revving of an engine sent Alexander sprinting across the camp. Rounding a corner to find himself enveloped in a scalding shower of sand and dust, he could only expel a series of violent coughs as a lone Humvee hurtled off towards what remained of the airbase to the northwest. Iranian ballistic missiles leveled the place months ago, but the rebuild went well, and a few AC-130s operated out of the rudimentary airstrip. The only possible reason to go there? Escape. The problem? The fallout cloud would hit there first.

Once the dust had cleared away, Alexander noticed a figure writhing and groaning in the sand. Before he could move a short, brown haired man with a red cross on his arm slid next to the wounded soldier, and began inspecting the multiple gunshots he'd suffered. *Must've tried to stop them from leaving. Damn fools.* No more time to ponder. Once again Alexander took off down the dusty footpaths between flattened tents, looking for the IT detachment where he hoped to find Derrick and Lewis. Assuming of course that the big man up top had finished making his displeasure known for now. Coming to a skidding halt, Alexander found Lewis getting a bandage wrapped around his head by Dr. Candice Bowman. Derrick grilled him.

"C'mon egghead, how much time do we have to rescue our people close to the blast?" he demanded.

"You can't be serious," Lewis groaned in his usual cynical voice. "Look I told you, either they've been incinerated, or their lives can be measured in hours if they're lucky." Rather than getting annoyed like Lewis and Derrick seemed, Alexander remained focused.

"Go on," he insisted. The programmer coughed and continued. "Camp Buehring will be fried within a day. The guard depot is the only place that's safe. From the fallout anyways."

Derrick nodded. "The Locals will be mighty restless soon."

Approaching the trio, Alexander addressed the injured techie, unwilling to accept complete hopelessness just yet. "Lewis," the younger man turned to Alexander with jaded but listless eyes, "Is there at least a safe distance we can send some scouts? See if anyone else escaped the direct effects?"

Lewis thought for a moment. "If they keep well outside the city they should be fine, at least for a few hours," he conceded. "They'd have to be quick about it though."

"I should go," Bowman insisted. "I can best determine who's savable, and get the vehicles ready to deal with fallout," the doctor explained, a sense of well-hidden desperation in her eyes. Alexander knew full well she had another reason for wanting to go look for survivors, but it hardly mattered. If anything, it would make her more determined.

"Go," he said. "Take as many people as you can talk into following you." She nodded and headed off toward the vehicle depot, having finished bandaging Lewis's head.

"Thanks, Bowman!" Lewis called after her.

"Don't mention it!" she shouted back, disappearing around a corner. Derrick turned to Alexander, a lost expression hanging from his face.

"What are we going to do, man?" Alexander gave his old friend an exhausted grin.

"We're going to round up as many outfits as we can," he answered, turning to follow Bowman to the depot. The

17

programmer and lieutenant tailed behind at a brisk pace, all of them shielding their eyes from a blast of dust-filled wind.

"And after that?" Derrick pressed.

Alexander scoffed. "Hopefully we manage to find someone who outranks us, or has some idea what the hell is going on." Alexander's sole focus remained getting his people out alive. Derrick, however, remained insistent.

"But sir, what if there is no one to take charge? What the hell are we going to do if we can't keep the Iranians in their cage? If the Saudis decide now's the time to move on us?" Alexander came to a halt in realization. He knew Derrick was right. They needed a clear-cut goal to keep everyone together over the next 48 hours. If they couldn't manage that, they all might die. Sooner, or later. He turned to Derrick and Lewis.

"This war is over." A statement. A declaration. Several passing soldiers came to a stop. Even the apathetic Lewis now paid close attention. *Shit, maybe a bit louder than intended?* With no options left, now he continued. "We have no clue what's going on back home, the one thing we do know is that most of the Pacific fleet doesn't exist anymore, and God knows what's become of the rest. All we have left is getting the hell out of this place. If there's no better plan, then the plan is reach Israel, then Europe, then home."

#

Now, only one. Only one place they can possibly be. If they're not... Emily pushed the dire thought from her mind. She had to focus. *Not much further now.* She would hold all three of them in her arms soon, and they could start making their way out of this disaster. A sudden throb of pressure battered Emily's skull, compelling her to cup the not-quite sealed wound and let out a pained moan. Scott looked over from the driver's seat, clearly worried.

"You alright? We really need to do something about that head injury. What happened anyway?" he asked. Emily made something between a growl and a groan upon realizing that in all the confusion, she'd never actually told him.

"I got shot," she bit out. Envisioning the faces of her family, she felt her agony begin to recede. Scott's head flew back over to her, his eyes wild with astonishment.

"You got shot!? In the head!?" The pain had almost subsided now. Emily released a slow and ragged breath. She hadn't even realized how long she'd held it.

"Yeah, and I was the lucky one." For the first time in more than a decade, Emily wished for a cigarette.

A strange grinding whir created by an overhead aircraft sent both officers into a frenzied scramble for cover beneath a tattered awning. Curious as to what could be making the unusual sound, Emily peeked out to find, of all things, a V-22 Osprey approaching the street ahead with its rotors tilted upward. The marines used them almost exclusively, painting the craft in a light gray, but this Osprey was all black without any markings, much to Emily's surprise. She'd never seen one in person before, only in movies and TV. The thing gave her the impression of a looming vulture. After it disappeared behind some buildings, Emily turned back to the unnerved Scott.

"We need to get a look at that Osprey."

"What!?" he hissed. "Why?"

"I want to see who the hell is in that thing, and what they're up to," Emily answered before making her way toward the open street, hugging the walls of buildings as she did.

"Who they are doesn't make much- no, wait! Emily!" Scott tried to splutter in protest but ended up chasing after her with his shotgun at the ready.

As she reached the mouth of a narrow alleyway, Emily closed her eyes and took a deep breath. The grind of the unusual aircraft's whirling rotor blades deafened her while whipping up a prop blast that disrupted the layers of dead leaves, trash, and debris caked everywhere. Emily shielded her face and ears as she checked to make sure Scott had followed, then poked her head out just enough to get a view of the unknown street beyond. *Are they some secret government force? Is the regular military finally getting involved?*

What she found in that street chilled Emily to the marrow. The blacked-out Osprey rested on its landing gear with the back door open as dozens of Reds clustered around, its rotors slowing to a minimal rate, lessening the gale they created to a stiff breeze as the rebels unloaded metal crates and began hauling them onto a string of waiting trucks. In truth it didn't matter what exactly the cargo contained, Emily's imagination threatened to run wild nonetheless. The aircraft appeared pristine, unblemished by the ravages of war, like some fallen angel.

Emily's eyes fell wide open as she watched the frantic Reds scurry away at their task, then she noticed the four well-equipped soldiers overseeing them. Loaded for bear to a standard that would have satisfied the most demanding special forces commander, the four troops prowled around, carrying M4s covered in attachments and wearing goggles with face masks that made identifying them impossible. The soldiers stood in contrast to the horde of mismatched Reds, who regarded them with no small degree of suspicion.

"What's happening?" Scott asked.

"They're dropping shit off to the Reds."

"Who is? Can you tell?"

"Creeps in all black," Emily growled.

"Antifa?"

"Nah, they're some kind of military or contractor types."

"So… they could be just about anybody?"

Emily groaned. "Pretty much."

After the last few crates got removed, all four "men in black" returned to the dual tilt-rotor craft as it spun up to full speed and began slowly ascending into the sky, its rear ramp closing up after them. The Reds took cover behind vehicles and walls, swearing as debris and trash hurtled around everywhere like a hurricane had cropped up in the street. Emily watched with narrowed eyes as the unmarked Osprey banked off towards the Sierra Nevadas. Determination began brewing deep within her, Emily wanted to find *everyone* responsible for this. She turned back down to the street level… and locked eyes with a perplexed Red gunman sitting in the back of an old technical.

Emily's eyes flew wide open and she ducked back behind the wall. "We need to move, now!"

She bolted past Scott and dragged him behind her until he started running on his own, three deep thuds emanated from down the street an instant before a triad of rounds obliterated the corner where Emily had just stood. As they got moving and the roar of a truck engine billowed over the rooftops and down the street, Emily realized that the end of the alley lay out of reach. Her gaze flew back and forth before at last landing on a door which had gotten smashed in. She careened into the open doorway with her pistol drawn, scanning everything the second she arrived inside. For a moment, Emily could only hear her own heartbeat and controlled breathing, then the clatter and scuffle of Scott coming to a halt beside her. Then sheer silence.

The pair stood in the ransacked backroom of a clothing store, amid boxes torn open, their unwanted contents strewn everywhere, every piece of furniture upended. Nothing moved that she could see in the dim place, as the raging fires outside provided the only illumination. After waiting another moment, Emily whirled back around to the empty doorframe, taking position on her lefthand side, and to the right of whomever might enter. Scott took cover next to her behind an overturned table as the screeching of tires made Emily flinch.

They waited.

The rattle of an ancient engine echoed down the alley and into the backroom. Emily's fingers tightened around the grip of her old 1911 as she exhaled all the air from her lungs, sweat coating her palms.

Still they waited… but no Reds came.

Then, Emily heard voices shouting through the mechanical clatter.

"I don't see fuckin' thing! What did you say you saw?"

"Somebody was watching us, man!"

"Ah… Fuck this, we've got to get all this shit outta here. Whoever those jokers were, they can't do anything now."

And just like that, the engine rumbled back up and they peeled out. Emily watched through battered doors and holes in the walls as the technical's headlights sailed past down the road, leaving the clothes shop in near total darkness once again. For a while the two of them just sat there, breathing sighs of relief.

"This… this is insane," Emily said in a voice that shook.

"Yeah. Tell me about it."

"Have you seen anything like that before now?"

Even with the near absence of light, Emily could see Scott shake his head.

"Oh… this is just so *fucking* perfect," she muttered in bitter resentment. *Some secretive G-men pulling strings, just what I need.*

"What should we do now?"

"Oh, now you're asking *me*?" Emily laughed.

"Hey, you're the hotshot S.W.A.T. lady," her former partner joked.

Emily straightened, taking up a more serious demeanor. "You bet I am. Now come on, I saw an abandoned car out front that might be usable."

CHAPTER 3:
WINDS OF CHANGE

Ideas pull the trigger, but instinct loads the gun.
— Don Marquis

Bennigsen had never considered himself a bloodthirsty man, but neither was he a coward. Presented with the choices of submission and slavery, or war and possible death, he made the same decision made by countless men and women before him. But that didn't make what had to be done easier, nor did it alleviate his fears for his family in this chaos. He had hidden them away for now. They were as safe as anyone— in America— at the moment. Bennigsen took a moment to remind himself why he came here. Why he left them in that apartment in Sacramento. Why he'd laid out his life upon the altar of revolution.

A huge mass of humanity clustered around the gate of Desalinization Plant 04, growing and shrinking as new members arrived, and those at the front made there way home clutching packages to their chests. At the gate a large military truck lay parked across it blocking it off to other vehicles, its flatbed loaded with Red Army soldiers grabbing bottled water from crates stacked next to the inside half and passing them out to the surging masses. Desperately outstretched hands snatched up the offered liquid of life and vanished, replaced by others in an instant. Until nine hours ago, a single bottle cost over 35 dollars. Almost a full day's wages for someone lucky enough to still have a job. Now? They cost nothing. Nothing cost anything anymore. The expressions of jubilant disbelief written on all their faces made all the risk and plotting worthwhile. All of it. Those faces, those people felt for the first time in as long as they could remember that they mattered. That someone actually gave a damn. That no one would leave them to die.

A panicked scream off to Bennigsen's right drew his attention to a ways down the street from the plant where a trio of Red Army men and one woman thrashed a crumpled figure on the pavement. One of them had thrown a rope over the adjoining lamppost, and busied himself tying a noose. Bennigsen sighed. When the Assembly found out about the lists of sanctioned zones and target names, the long awaited showdown between the old movement leaders and the Red Cabal would come at last. Lighting a small joint for his nerves, Bennigsen couldn't help but grin in the knowledge that his comrades now stood more than ready to win that confrontation.

They had the gangs. They had the guard. They had the masses in the street. They even had all the drones, eventually they'd have the robots too.

And who did the Assembly have? A few rogue politicians, bankers, bourgeoisie, and lawyers. Constituencies in the process of getting, as Singh had said, "put to the sword" by the vengeful populace. The agitators had deliberately placed them right alongside the corporates, the cops, and of course the politicians, with the full intention of removing them from the equations of power. In addition to being told that they did in fact matter, the people had also been told that it was now okay to go nuts. At least, on certain people, places, and things.

His own death, no longer really concerned Bennigsen. Either they would win, or they wouldn't. The only real worry left, the fate of his mother.

He'd tried to convince her to stay at home, to take some time off like she'd always talked about. But no. She had to feel that damned sense of duty that always blinded her. "Too dangerous out there to walk now," she'd said. *That was the idea.* No way to find out what happened to her for now. But it still ate at the back of his mind.

"Comrade Bennigsen." His head turned to the exit doorway of the plant, where stood a Hispanic man in his early thirties, a Kalashnikov slung across his shoulder beside the red bandana tied around his sinewy bicep. The expression he wore appeared near tranquil, a stark contrast with the scattered bits of dried blood spattered across his face. Carlos he called himself, one of Singh's guys. Loyal, quiet, yet… imaginative. And, dare he say it, driven. Whatever his past or "quirks," Bennigsen valued his presence and skill a great deal. Even if the ease with which he aided in the organization of death unnerved him ever-so-slightly.

Beside Carlos stood a white woman in her early twenties wearing the plain navy uniform of the plant workers, plus a red rag tied around her left arm. A pair of tortoiseshell glasses sat on her freckled nose over fearful terracotta eyes. She appeared far less at peace than his comrade. Who could blame her? She shifted on her feet, keeping her eyes to the ground. "This girl here," Carlos arched his head backward towards the worker who flinched. "Says they need loads o' gas to keep the place runnin', and they don't have much left. We gotta get the power back on, or get 'em more gas, man." Bennigsen listened to Carlos's smooth voice and nodded, rubbing the shaved stubble of his chin. He turned to the worker.

"You'll get your gas. How much longer will the plant keep operating on what you have?" The girl looked up from the ground surprised, for some reason, that he would address her as an individual. The poor girl gave a quiet and nervous answer. An answer that caused Bennigsen to roll his eyes as it became drowned out. A denunciating screed of a Red Army agitator outside the fence, and the subsequent howls of the rallied crowd. "I'm sorry, what was that?" he asked again, a bemused expression on his face. The woman's face scrunched up. She cleared her throat, and spoke again.

"We have enough fuel to run the generators for six more days," she stated. Bennigsen crooked his head.

"Six huh?" His eyes narrowed. That sounded like a lot to have just have lying around. Especially these days. She gulped, then sighed.

"We knew that someone might try to shut the plant down in order to foment unrest. We didn't think it would come to this..." Bennigsen took a deep draw from his joint, then allowed the smoke to billow out from between his lips.

"Well, it has. And so long as you keep doing your part, you have nothing to fear from us and everything to gain." She looked at him with an arched eyebrow, and Bennigsen laughed. "Don't believe me? Congratulations! You've just been promoted, uh..." Her eyes widened as Bennigsen fished the folded manifest of the plant's workforce out from his coat. He compared the barcode number on the left side of her uniform to the list of highlighted names with: "subservient personnel-DO NOT EXECUTE" written off to the side. After a moment he found her number. 8471834-Tracy Stone. "Tracy! You're now in charge of running this place, at least for now." His mouth had not closed for a full second before Tracy's own began sputtering about how she felt totally inadequate for such a position, but he waved it all off. "Listen sister, it's either you or some other random character who has some clue of what they're doing. Seeing as all your direct bosses have been... uh..." He turned back to the trio of Reds to find the last supervisor spasming and clutching at the crude noose around his neck, whatever sounds he made drowned out by the oblivious crowd. "Let's go with, laid off? Anyways, all you have to do in order to avoid their fate is one- Keep the place running to the best of your ability, and two- Just hand out the water for free to anyone who needs it," Bennigsen explained, raising two fingers in turn. "Understand?"

Tracey gave a series of furious nods as an answer, and Bennigsen nodded and grunted in approval. "Good. Like I said, you'll get your fuel. And anything else you need. All right, I'll let you get back to it."

"Thank you," she said, almost breathless. Bennigsen shook his head slightly after she had gone back inside, leaving him with only Carlos and the mob on the ground level below.

"Tsk, poor girl probably thought we were going to hang her too." Turning to look Carlos in the eyes, his small smile vanished. "What is it, somethin' else?" The ex-sicario closed his eyes and gave a single nod.

"Boss wants to see you in City Hall. Says it's important." Bennigsen started on his way back inside, down the inner stairs, and out towards the old jeep that he'd designated as his "staff car."

"Dammit Javier, why wasn't that the first thing you told me?" he demanded in mock irritation.

"Take it easy man," Carlos answered with a smile, following close behind "He said to finish up your business here first."

"We are finished here." Bennigsen discarded the spent stub of his joint into an already burning trash bin as the pair walked out. They passed dozens of workers trying as best they could to focus on doing their jobs, and not on the new management currently prowling around with assault rifles and rummaging through everything. A couple of guards lay slumped against the inner side of the plant's fence, the only ones stupid enough to try and fight back. The others had either gone home or now sat in trucks outside, destined for induction into the Red Army.

As he slid into the rear passenger seat of the jeep, Bennigsen reminisced upon how depressingly easy they'd found it to just show up, demand control, chop down the one manager and two guards who refused to comply, and then just take over in the name of the Revolution.

The old junker lurched inland, away from the coast, away from San Jose, back to the state capital building in Sacramento. Red Command had taken the area over as their central control point with great speed, though it wouldn't remain such for long. Even though the Red Army had taken all of the major cities, broader organization remained nebulous. Everyone knew more or less who stood at the top of the rank pyramid, but everything beneath it remained murky. The capital represented power, a place to go and find help, to get orders. When they did so, they would find Red Command ready to assist them in any way they could, or just tell them what to do. And for all the fighting in the streets, the building itself had fallen with barely a fight. Abandoned by its previous occupiers.

Things would rarely come so easy in the future, this he knew. Yet, he'd never quite grasped Subutai's willingness to bend and incorporate groups from all over, until now. Until now, he'd thought the best ideas would win in the end once everything laid bare in the light. Not so. He'd never considered himself an idealist, until he watched half a dozen cops get torn limb from limb by a vengeful mob. Since then, one barrier after another had eroded to nothing. *Oh well...* The only alternatives to pressing on all involved either total ignominy and disgrace, or a horrible, torturous death. *And what kind of choice is that?*

Carlos swerved to avoid an upturned armored car, a small gaggle of children jumping and playing around on top of it. Bennigsen sighed, no going back for him now. Pandora's box had burst open. No doubt some would still try and seal it shut, but Bennigsen flattered himself in the knowledge that he would not be among them. Once he'd met with his family, told them everything, he would meet with Singh and get started anew with a clear head. This wild journey to a new world had only just gotten started.

#

Weaving through the streets of inner Sacramento had never been such a harrowing experience. Not even when flying after a suspect at seventy miles an hour. Emily felt a deep longing for the days when Sacramento's shitty traffic served as the greatest obstacle to reaching her mother's apartment, and the only reason for doing so being a rare holiday visit. A light clattering sound drew Emily's attention to the car door's armrest. Her hand trembled of its own accord, making her short fingernails rattle against the fake wood. Emily pulled her right arm off the door and clutched it in her left hand, trying to soothe its nerves and tendons.

She looked over to Scott, thankful to see only the blond-haired back of his head. If he'd noticed her sound or movements he gave no outward sign, fixated on the streets ahead. Emily didn't want anyone worried about her. She wanted to know the fate of her children, and get them back. There would be time for tears later.

As the car glided deeper and deeper into the inner city, the numbers of people in the street became greater and greater. Red banners flowed with the wind everywhere, draping from windows, lampposts, overpasses. Far fewer corpses littered the streets here than in the suburbs, despite the signs of battle all around. Craters blasted into the asphalt, pieces of walls chiseled away by small arms fire, scattered vehicles gutted by flames. And yet, the atmosphere had shifted dramatically. It now resembled one of celebration and purpose. Groups of people worked to clear the roads of debris, smash their way into locked buildings and collect valuable supplies. Armed rebels stood guard everywhere, on street corners, rooftops, and in windows. Others marched down the streets in great columns, carrying banners that read things like, "Judgement day is here!" or "Untouchables, Rise!" and "The past is dead!" The most commonly carried though, read "Long live the wild west!" and "Death to the oligarchs!" in big red letters on black banners. The enormous mobs carrying these grim messages required a wide berth, headed off to wherever the invisible hand of their mysterious all-seeing, all-knowing masters had pointed them in. Scott released a deep sigh after darting into a side road and between some buildings.

"Christ, this just keeps getting worse! I mean, I knew times were bad. But this…"

"We should've known," Emily grumbled. "We knew things couldn't go on like they were, and we still did nothing. Nothing but kick down." Scott turned to her, a concerned glint in his green eyes.

"Well, what else could we have done? Joined the Reds?" he demanded as a half joke. Emily sighed, leaning back in her chair, closing her eyes. *That certainly would've helped.*

"Could've listened to Rob. Taken the week off…" Then, she stopped. *He did say that. He did say I should "take the week off"*… Emily swatted the thought away. Rob, one of the smartest people she knew, could see things kept getting more dangerous, and he just wanted her safe. *Yes, that's why he did it.* The gentle squeal of the car's brakes jolted Emily away from such self reassurances. They had arrived behind her mother's apartment building. The last place Emily could think of where her children could have holed up.

"Alright, we're here. You want me to…?"

"Stay with the car, keep it ready and safe," Emily instructed, climbing out of the old sedan. "I'll be quick as I can." Scott handed her his flashlight and nodded.

"Will do. Be careful, Em."

Emily smiled down at him from outside the car. "I make no promises."

Keys clattered into the lock, and the outside door creaked open. Emily slid inside to find herself at the bottom level of the stairwell. Darkness. Save a faint flickering light about halfway up the vertical shaft between stairwells. She clicked the button of Scott's flashlight, then ascended the first step.

The meagre handful of denizens Emily encountered paid her no mind at all, and that suited her just fine. Smoking, shooting up, shuffling about from place to place, and spreading wild rumors gave them all more than enough to concern themselves. Shouting and music billowed from the walls, the pounding drum of people running around upstairs. Emily avoided all eye contact, while doing her best to not look like it.

Finally arriving on the sixth floor, Emily exited the stairwell to find a pair of Reds nailing up a poster in the hallway. A third man, carrying a submachine gun of some kind strapped around his shoulder, stood guard behind the other two as they busied themselves. The dead-eyed man regarded Emily for a moment, looked her up and down, then returned his attention back to the materializing propaganda. The poster featured no words, instead it depicted a singular red star with a golden sunburst emanating outward. A simple city skyline — complete with smokestacks, high-voltage power lines, and cultivated green hills — dominated the bottom of the poster. A trio of white bird silhouettes soared between the star and city, giving the whole image a sense of reality and presence despite its stylized nature.

Emily found herself taken aback by the abstract symbolism on display, leagues ahead of the juvenile propaganda slogans that bombarded her in the past. One of the Reds putting the poster up, a middle-aged black man, turned in Emily's direction when she walk past. He nodded, then went back to his work. Emily contained a deep breath, and slipped by the working rebels.

Halfway down the hall, she dodged a boy zooming past on his skateboard, sounding like a roller-skating rink in a tunnel. *Almost there…*

Upon arriving in front of room 405, Emily came to a gradual, stuttering halt. Her heartbeat became the metronomic soundtrack of her mind. *This is it.* The trepidation started to overwhelm her. *What if they aren't here? What if no one is here? What if my kids aren't here, but she is…* Emily gritted her teeth, far too late now. She had to know. Taking a deep breath, Emily took the plunge, and knocked on the blue wooden door three times.

For the better part of a minute, Emily stood there. Motionless, her eyes fixed on the tiny peephole. For almost too long, no sound came from within the apartment. Then, a faint clatter. Emily felt beads of sweat materialize all over her scalp and face. Footsteps crept up to the opposite side of the door. Emily felt her jaw clamp together. First the deadbolt, then the knob clacked, the door swung open to reveal the teary-eyes of her fifteen-year-old girl.

"Mom!?" Christina exclaimed in thrilled disbelief. Emily scooped her eldest daughter into her arms, ducked inside the apartment, and bumped the door closed all in a single motion. Every effort she had poured into warding off emotion collapsed all at once. She kissed Christina's forehead and held her close, ignoring her own pain, the girl's pair of long thin arms coiled around her neck.

"Oh, sweetheart! I'm so glad you're okay!" Emily's tears flowed as she allowed every muscle in her body to succumb in exhaustion.

"Mama!" A pair of small feet rushed over to Emily as she released Christi and brought her own knees down on the cheap shag carpet. By instinct, Emily extended her arm and embraced her eight-year-old who wrapped himself around her waist.

For a long moment Emily just wallowed in the sheer relief and exuberance of it all. Hugging, kissing, reassuring her children. The crushing weight of uncertainty and terror dissolved away like a castle of sand in high tide. For a long moment, all the terror and chaos still happening outside didn't matter. Emily couldn't remember the last time she had felt such pure joy. Maybe when Zechariah was born, but even that didn't feel the same. She felt born again.

"Oh my God! I thought you were dead!" Christi admitted, a tinge of shame in her voice.

"Where were you Mama? Why didn't you come home?" Zechariah asked through sobs.

"It's okay! It's okay sweetie… Mama got hurt but I found you! I found you!" Emily began to collect herself enough to notice the absence in their group. The missing piece.

She looked up from her two youngest, expecting to find the smiling face of her eldest son waiting for her, looking down on the three of them in that way he always did. But there was no one. The creak of a door in the depths of the apartment, the bathroom, and a pair of heavy steps began making their way towards them. Emily felt her smile melt a bit. Her mother, Heather, plodded into the room with a shocked expression on her aged face.

"Oh my Lord, Emily! Where have you been!? What happened to your head!?"

Emily groaned a bit as she returned to her feet. "I got shot, Mom. Where's Rob?"

"He left! He's been gone for more than a day," Christi answered.

"He went to find you." Her mother elaborated, "I couldn't stop him Emily, I tried."

Emily drew in a very deep breath and released. *It always has to be something. No time to second guess though.* "Start packing. We need to get out of here. Scott's downstairs with a car," she commanded, summoning her best motherly tone.

"But Rob told us to wait for him," Zechariah pointed out. Emily gazed down at her son to find him looking back up at her with scared, innocent eyes.

"Yeah! He said to stay here, even if you came back," Christi added.

Emily's eyebrows rose. *That could be a problem…* A key jammed into the deadbolt, and before Emily could even process the sound and react, the apartment door swung open. There, frozen in mid step, stood Rob, in a long brown trenchcoat and a green visored cap with a red star pin smack on the front. He stood locked in place with saucer eyes like he'd just been caught sneaking back in after ducking curfew. Emily started to feel light-headed, her vision became fuzzy.

#

Alexander figured he would have another decade or two before he needed worry about this level of responsibility. Yet, here he stood, amid a sea of fellow junior officers, witnessing an absolute shit show. An endless circular argument about whether or not to leave, where to go, how to get there, repeat. Alexander only wished for one thing, and he didn't get it. No superiors to hammer out the madness. The best he could hope for: gather enough men behind him that they could actually make it to Israel. That seemed, at least for now, the best way to get on the long, treacherous road back home. Trouble was, Alexander remained unsure how exactly to do this.

He just didn't possess the authority or recognition of the old guard, but so far as anyone could tell, the old guard all got killed in the blast. In what had to have fulfilled the wildest dreams of those who deployed the weapon, it went off just outside LFI HQ while the brass met to figure out what to do about losing all contact with home. Now it fell to them

25

to decide what to do next, with the added bonus of an ever encroaching chaos on the horizon. No one really wanted to stay, almost everyone had the goal of going home. But how this could best be done exploded into a point of major contention.

"You can't be serious! It's suicide…" Captain Warwick protested.

"Unfortunately, it's the best chance we have." Alexander stood firm. "Without satellites we'd just get lost in the desert. And thanks to the nuke, we wouldn't be able to change our minds."

"Going along the rivers will take us near populated areas. Areas that are already losing any sense of cohesion. Iranians and Saudis will be turning that place into one huge battlefield within a week if they haven't already," Sergeant Major Escobedo pointed out. "We'll need help."

"Of course." Alexander agreed with a single nod. "We need people to fan out and round up as many units as we can find."

"Sure. Who else are they going to listen to? Other than themselves, that is…" Captain Nakamura rubbed the back of his neck.

"You had some guys take off too?" Alexander asked.

"Yeah, a few grunts decided to go full "*Mad Max*," and took off in a tank. God knows what the hell they've done since then. Or what they **will** do."

"They'll get fucking killed is what they'll do," Escobedo stated. "Especially if we see them again."

"What about the contractors? The translators?" Warwick asked Alexander, changing the subject.

"Well, they want to get back to the world, right?" he asked.

Warwick nodded and sighed. "Oh yeah. They do, but most of them can't fight…"

"If they want to come then they come. Nobody gets left for dead," Alexander declared.

Escobedo gave a firm nod. "Damn right. It'll be risky sure, but we ain't leavin' anyone to die in this hell."

A murmur of affirmation made it's way around the plastic folding table.

"Do we have to pass through the most dangerous place in this hell to escape it though?" Nakamura posited with unease. Alexander sighed. *Can't bring anyone into that hell who isn't really up for it.*

"Anyone who really wants to try the desert and die of thirst can go through the goddamned desert," Alexander conceded in near desperation. Regretting it at once, but without any alternative. "We just need to get the hell outta here…"

"So we're really doing this? We're really going to mutiny and just march off to try and somehow get home?" Warwick asked in exasperation. He didn't seem angry, just shattered. Searching out some confirmation that he hadn't lost his mind. Yet his question ushered in a hushed silence as everything came back into perspective.

"Well, if anyone is uncomfortable with semantics, I'm not sure there's anything left to mutiny against," Alexander pointed out before taking a long drink from his canteen. It did nothing to lighten the mood, but it did help dismiss some of the lingering uncertainty.

"Well then how do we know there's any home to go back to?" Nakamura wondered aloud.

"What other choice is there man? Stay here?" Alexander pressed. "It'll be crazy dangerous, and a lot of folks will end up dead. But if we stay here? We're all dead."

Escobedo grunted, grabbing his wide-brimmed hat from the table and fixing it to his shiny, bald head. "Then there's no more time to waste." He made his way to the tent flaps, leaving everyone else to accept what now needed to happen and get to work.

Stepping out into the oppressive heat, Alexander rubbed the growing stubble on his chin. A pair of supply trucks rumbled by, clouds of dust billowing up behind them. Groups of marines, guardsmen, and army troops milled around, chatting amongst themselves in a far more covert manner than usual. Wild speculation still ruled the day, and until Alexander held some solid information in his hands that could ease their minds, any effort to clamp down on the chatter could be counterproductive. At least it kept some of their minds away from how screwed they all were. The rustling of canvas behind him announced he'd been followed.

"Harris!" Warwick's voice. Alexander squeezed his eyes closed for a moment, then turned to face his fellow captain, doing his best to feign patience. "Look man i'm sorry if I-, I mean I didn't mean to take a stand against ya I just… Goddamn, this is all just so fucked!" He removed his cap, rubbing his hand across his sweaty shaved head.

Alexander's expression softened a bit and he chuckled. "Hell yeah it is," He cocked his head, "Are you really heading off into the desert?"

Warwick groaned and shrugged his shoulders "I don't even know man, I'm sure somebody will want to. I just want to get outta here without my ass bein' blowin' up ya know?"

Alexander nodded his head. *At least **he** isn't looking to turn this into a battle over authority. For now…*

"But I have to ask," Warwick interjected, "what do we do about Baxter? And, don't take this the wrong way, but who **is** in charge? You? I mean, what if we run into some brass that decides to—"

Alexander put a hand on Warwick's shoulder. "Take it easy man, we'll cross that bridge if we blunder into it. And yeah, until we find some higher-up or everyone decides they hate my ass, I'll keep them all from killing each other." After a moment Warwick smiled, then laughed. Alexander, despite himself, started to laugh too. It only lasted for a few minutes—two captains standing outside of a tent, laughing their asses off at nothing. Under normal circumstances, the passing troops and personnel would've become concerned, to say the least. But now? They only spared a few brief glances, far too consumed with their own problems. Finally the two men worked through their collective bout of giddiness, returning to the grim present.

Warwick sighed. "I'll get my unit ready to move out. When do we start?"

Before Alexander could respond, the roar of a Humvee's engine drew their focus towards the camp's eastern gate, where a trio of the vehicles had just zoomed inside and slid to an abrupt halt. Before they even stopped, the doors had flown open and soldiers poured out. A tall black man with a voice like a speaker system emerged from the passenger side of the lead Humvee.

"We got casualties here! The fuck's the hospital at!?" he demanded of no one in particular, already working with others to lift someone on a makeshift pancho stretcher out of the vehicle. A swarm of soldiers descended on the Humvees, carrying their comrades over to the medical tent. All three vics had bullet holes, shattered glass, brass casings glinting all over the floor.

"Now," Alexander answered at last, shooting a emphatic look at Warwick.

"Sounds good." Warwick headed off, his footsteps merging with the bedlam of the compound. Alexander felt his eyes become transfixed by a large splotch of blood on the inside of the Humvee's open door. The thick red liquid dripped down to the steel door's bottom, then pooled on the sand below. Alexander had seen blood before. But it felt different somehow. Throughout his career, Alexander felt assured by the vast machine of the U.S. military at his back. However negligent it might've been at times, it still ensured that everything would **mostly** work. The machine would replace lost men and take away the wounded, rebuild destroyed machines, spit out orders, set new objectives. Not anymore.

Alexander knew if any vehicles get destroyed, they would replace them with whatever the hell they could find. Any information needed he would have to acquire himself. Any wounded had to come along on this insane exodus, and coming across any medicine during said journey seemed quite unlikely. Any man lost, was a man lost. No one would reinforce, resupply, or even assist them in any way. Not now. Now, the machine sat as a pile of burning wreckage. Now, there was nothing. Nothing but him.

"Do we have a new objective, sir?" Alexander turned to find Derrick standing behind him, with a nervous looking gray-clad civilian at his side.

"Fuck yeah. We're heading into Iraq. Once everyone is packed up, and everyone willing to follow has formed up." Alexander nodded toward the unknown figure, "Who's this?"

"7th battalion S2 intel officer, Major Nathan Price at your service," the man spoke up, stepping forward and tipping his gray field cap. A younger black-haired man of ambiguous ethnicity, Major Price seemed like a reserved character. None of the arrogance his like usually exuded, a change Alexander could appreciate.

"He was gonna brief Baxter about somethin', but the bomb went off while he was on his way," Derrick added.

"S2 huh? You here to take command then?" Alexander hurled out to get it done with. Much as he hoped, the skinny spook shook his head with enthusiasm.

"Oh no!" he assured, absently spinning his West Point ring in his hand, "I just want to get back to America, same as you. I'll help in whatever way I can."

Alexander pursed his lips and nodded, narrowing his eyes, rubbing his chin, doing his best to oversell his scrutiny of the man. "Well, what way can you help?"

"I can see to it that you have some idea of what's waiting for you out there, seeing as how all our satellites are toast, and choppers flying around will be dead-giveaways as much as they'll be targets." His answer came with confidence, and perhaps just a bit of indignation.

Alexander grinned. "Well alright, welcome aboard, Major. What do you need to get started?"

"A few good men, a translator, and a local vic," Price rattled off.

Alexander nodded to Derrick, who returned the gesture and headed off. Intent on getting started by finding a couple decent men and a decent vehicle. Something functional anyway. Taking a step closer to Price, Alexander fixed him with the most serious expression he could manage. "So, what exactly did you need to tell Baxter?"

Price took a deep breath, eyes jolting around. Clearly, this violated a whole steaming heap of regs, and it took him a moment to power through his instinctive reservation. "The Iranians are invading Iraq, and the Saudis have sent reinforcements to their own forces already there."

Alexander sighed. "They knew this before the bomb?"

Price nodded. "We didn't know how they intended to keep us sidelined, now we do."

Bad news. If they didn't escape the region, their force would get swept away in a tsunami of chaos. Far faster, and in a far bloodier manner than Alexander had feared. The unmistakable chopping of helicopter rotors dragged Alexander's brown eyes to the moonlit sky. "Ah, shit..."

A pair of Apaches arrived overhead, coming down to land within the compound in rapid fashion, blasting a wave a dust through the "streets." Touching down in a place that looked at least looked like it could be big enough, their arrival served to amplify the general mayhem as everyone rushed to hold down tents and piles of gear. The rotors had barely started spinning down before the angry shouts started flying and the pilots became surrounded by an angry mob.

"We've got no time to lose." Alexander placed a hand on Price's shoulder, guiding him toward the vehicle depot. *Step 1: send the spook on his way. Step 2: save the damn flyboys.* "C'mon ring-banger-man, lets go find you a chariot worthy of being our eyes and ears," he turned toward the waiting command Humvee where a young man stood bent over the open engine compartment. "Driver!"

The brown-haired-20-year-old jolted up from the engine, looking around in frantic motion. "Ye-yes?" he stuttered in confusion.

Alexander smiled with a little eye roll. "We're leaving soon, get ready to roll out."

"Uh... ready when you are sir!" He slammed the hood back down, and bolted around to the cab.

#

"Will y'all keep quiet!? We're tryin' to hear the radio!" Judith called to her two kid brothers from the kitchen as they tore through the living room.

"Oh, just turn it up, sweetheart," her mother chided.

Judith did, and the governor's voice came through with more gusto.

"...ith the chaos erupting around us, our supposed countrymen turning on one another like wild animals, and filling the streets of their cities with blood, we are left with no other choice. Living in freedom and continuing our obligations to the United States, have become mutually exclusive ideals."

Judith felt her heart catch in her throat. Both her parents and younger sister sat glued to the dusty old radio. She hoped her two older brothers, Zack and Dean, also listened to this very broadcast, wherever they'd ended up.

"And so it is by the will of the people of Texas—and I believe God himself— that I announce to the world our unalterable decision... to secede from the United States of America."

Judith heard her mother gasp. Her father remained silent, but neither she nor her sister felt so reserved.

"Yes!" Judith cheered with a loud clap.

Haley groaned. "Finally! I thought we'd all die first."

Their mother sounded less jubilant. "What does this mean, Charles? Are we at war now?"

Charles grumbled in bitterness. "We've been at war for months now, dear. Seems Austin has finally caught up with it."

Judith then stood up from the table, drawing all eyes to her. "I'm gonna join the national guard!" she declared.

For a moment, everyone remained stunned in shock, until Charles ran calloused hands through his sweaty grizzled hair and spoke. "Sweetheart, we've already talked about this."

"No, we talked about it before. This is now! We know what we'll be fighting for now, there's no reason to worry anymore."

"There's a whole heap of reasons to worry!" her father retorted. "I'm not about to let you go out there and get yourself killed!"

Judith became flustered. "I'm a grown woman now, Pa! I don't need your permission."

Her dad coughed. "Damn it, Judith I only—!"

"Charles, could I talk with Judith for a moment, please?" her mother asked in a concerned tone.

He sighed, "Alright Rose, I could use some fresh air anyways." He made his way outside, cigarette pack in hand, much to the loving consternation of his wife.

Rose stood up, taking Judith's hand as Haley turned down the radio so as to keep listening.

"Judi, sweetheart, I know how passionate you are about this, but please... Just give it a little more time. With the boys gone, we need all the help we can get."

Judith felt her temper peter off a bit.

Her mother continued. "But it's more than that, with the boys lost out there somewhere, we couldn't lose you too!" She held Judith's cheeks in her hands. "Please, just wait a little bit longer? At least until we know what's happened to them?"

Judith couldn't argue with that. "Fine, fine. I'll wait till we've heard from 'em."

Before they could continue, Haley jumped in. "Ma, who **are** the communists?" she asked in innocence.

Their mother huffed. "Very bad people, sugar. Why?"

"Governor Whose-it says they rule the west coast now," Haley answered.

Judith snorted. "Just now? Yeah right! More like they've finally shown their true colors."

Her mom looked mortified. "Sweetie please, please don't go off and get killed by some California commie!" she pleaded.

"Mama, I ain't gonna get killed by sum commie son-of-a-bitch. It's the Feddies we've gotta worry about! Besides, the Californians are all the way out on the coast. They'll probably get squashed before they make it anywhere near us," she proclaimed with confidence.

"Oh that's no better! Just please, think this over real hard, Judi?"

"I **have** thought it over, Ma. I can't just let the guys and others fight for ma freedom while I'm stuck here raisin' hogs and drivin' cattle!" Judith vented in exasperation as she plopped back down.

"Oh sweetheart, we **are** helpin' the fight for freedom! Without us, the National Guard and all the folks in the cities would starve," her mother insisted.

"I know Ma, it just ain't the same."

CHAPTER 4:
THE NEW WORLD

I must create a system or be enslaved by another man's.
— William Blake

"What is it exactly that you guys are hoping to accomplish by doing this?" Yujing asked.

"Simple. We intend to drive them Libs out, and clear the way for a new government to get elected in," came the confident reply. "By the way, your English is so good, you almost sound British or somethin'."

Yujing cringed on the inside, but showed no sign of it. "Thank you. Do you believe that you will be able to achieve that with the forces you have in the city?"

A wide grin full of silver teeth. "Yes ma'am, we do." A series of sharp crack and snaps sent everyone ducking. A few rounds chipped some concrete from the building behind them. A long burst from the M60 on the Brotherhood barricade further down the road returned the favor. Another explosion out of sight, not too big, most likely another pipe bomb. "You should probably go now, miss. It looks like they won't be leaving the hill without a fight!"

Yujing saw no reason to argue. She ducked into an alleyway as a stream of bullets tore into the concrete walls leaving a cloud of dust behind. The "Libs" in the capitol area consisted of national guard and the capitol police, who the left-leaning Popular Front had refused to help after deciding to abandon the region instead. But none of that seemed to matter to the Brotherhood. Yujing dug out her stack of U.S. road maps from her coat pocket, and started working out how she would escape the city. *Hopefully, my luck will hold out just a bit longer.* She slid into a corner hidden out of sight, the gunfire flaring around her once more.

Once she regained her bearings Yujing's attention gravitated towards a bizarre helicopter-like whir coming from somewhere overhead. Yujing peered with great care around the corner of a battered high-rise hotel and found, much to her intrigue, a blacked-out dual tilt-rotorcraft hovering over the Jefferson Memorial. The stranded reporter wracked her brain in frantic determination. She knew these aircraft were used by the US military's naval forces, since she'd seen plenty of them on Taiwan, but never before had she seen one painted all in black.

The thing bobbed up and down ever so slightly as it levitated in place, it's position an almost perfect one for observing the street war between Brotherhood and Loyalist forces raging up and down the National Mall. Yujing hoped to heaven that whoever was watching from inside couldn't see her, and if they could, she hoped they didn't care. She spent what felt like almost a full minute scanning in futility for any symbol or insignia on the night-black aircraft until, at a whim, it banked off to the left, angling its twin rotors forward, and hurtling off in the direction of the most important building in the entire United States.

The White House…

Yujing wanted nothing more in that moment than to chase after this mysterious aircraft and try to get a look at what could be taking place inside the President's home, but she knew that amounted to near suicide. All her answers would have to wait for now. She only knew the appearance of these unknown flying machines heralded even greater chaos. With the ambience of gunfire and explosions all around her, Yujing started making her way towards the Potomac River.

\#

The large oak doors gave a bitter creak as the guards on each side pushed them open, allowing Bennigsen to enter the smoke-hazed room beyond. The sweet smell of burning cannabis filled his nostrils as he made his way over to the large wooden desk that sat in front of a great window overlooking the streets outside. Standing at that window, puffing on a steel pipe in his hand, stood a man in black, a long greatcoat and field cap. As he exhaled, a plume of smooth white smoke spiraled over the visor of his cap, merging with the hovering cloud that dominated the whole office. The imposing figure made no other movement to indicate that he'd even noticed Bennigsen's entrance, even though he most certainly had.

The young political officer wandered over to the commandeered governor's desk, paused in curiosity, and scanned over its contents. Maps, speeches, messages, lists of names, lists of materials, mass quarantine procedures… new laws. Bennigsen felt his eyebrows rise. He knew Singh had plans, but not to this extent. Only then did he notice that the left of the two chairs in front of the desk hosted an occupant. Tied to the chair with steel cables and gagged with a strip of duct tape — the chair itself screwed to the floor — sat a man who Bennigsen recognized even in his bloody and battered state. Douglass Samuels, the hated chief of police of Sacramento. Though voiceless, the chief's eyes made it clear he recognized Bennigsen too. They darted between Bennigsen's face and Singh's back, pleading for help. But Bennigsen felt no compulsion to do anything to help this *rat*. If he loved his oligarchs so much, he should want to die in the name of their glory. Besides, this whole mess resulted more from *his* senseless brutality than anything the Reds did.

"Ah… Bennigsen!" The deep, earthy voice pulled his attention around 180 degrees, "I was wondering when you would find your way here." The two young men each wore glasses—Singh with round wire spectacles while Bennigsen had something more like what Clark Kent might wear. Though each stood at an average height, Singh's gaunt features made him look emaciated next to Bennigsen's bulk. As Bennigsen ran his fingers through his sandy brown hair, Singh did the same through his own greasy jet black mane. Bennigsen's light blue irises narrowed just a little as they met with Singh's own jade eyes.

The often unseen leader of the Red Cabal did not betray his true emotions often, so when Bennigsen saw his mentor's lightly-bearded face wearing a look of genuine satisfaction, he took notice. The two comrades clasped hands and embraced, patting each other on the back, Singh gesturing him to take a seat in one of the two chairs in front of the desk. "How are things going in San Jose? How long will it take to get the desalinization plants up and running again?"

"They're up now, comrade. Turns out the company actually thought **we** might use an EMP to wipe out their microchips, so they kept new chips in Faraday cages nearby." A confused grunt emanated from the tied up chief beside Bennigsen, "We just told the people who worked there to install the new ones," he finished, turning around to the restrained police chief.

"Our guest here thinks we **are** the ones who knocked out the power," Singh explained in a bemused tone, pointing a pair of fingers like a gun at the restrained chief. "Rip his gag off would you? I needed a little break from his whining."

Bennigsen turned to his left and asked, "Did we?" He tore the tape from Samuels' mouth, causing the man to briefly cry out in pained surprise.

"Ahh! You assholes!" he yelped.

Singh closed his eyes, shaking his head three times. "No. We didn't." A simple statement of fact, no insistence behind it, even a bit of remorse, as though Singh wished he **did** possess that kind of power. But really, what man in his position wouldn't? "Best working guess right now is the Chinese did it, or the Russians, or maybe it was both. It doesn't really matter. All that matters is that you can go out there, look people dead in the eye, and tell them that 'no, the Red Army is not responsible in any way for the power grid getting completely bricked,' while being entirely honest about it. And isn't that the best kind of propaganda? The kind that is technically true?" He finished with an outreached hand and an expectant look.

Bennigsen shrugged. "It's gotta be better than total bullshit." A gunshot cracked just outside, all three men flinched. "How much longer will this go on?" Bennigsen asked. Singh groaned and leaned back in the luxurious office chair.

"Yes, how much longer?" the raspy voice of the chief added.

Singh ignored him. "If it were up to me, it would've already ended. We've got important things to take care of before somebody else does. Getting everyone pointed in the right direction is our main goal right now. That, and establishing contact between all the coastal cities." He turned back around to face the large window, covered in the flowing light patterns of fire outside. "Right now, we're just wasting time and burning bridges. And we can't have that, can we?"

"What direction do you want me pointed in?" Bennigsen asked.

"Hmm…" Singh contemplated for a brief moment, "You say not all the cops have to be murdered?" The sheer blunt force of the question gave Bennigsen a sense of whiplash, even though he saw it coming. Ever since this whole show started rolling, He'd been trying to convince his fellow revolutionaries that they didn't need to kill **all** of the police, just the ones who proved incapable of seeing reason, if it could be called that.

Before he could articulate an answer, the chief blurted out "What the hell are you talkin' about? You lunatics are really just going to kill everyone!?" Again, they ignored him.

"No, I don't think they all do," Bennigsen answered with care. Singh's feelings, or lack thereof, on the police were well known in the Red Army. It at least partially explained the sheer scale and… *imagination* of the brutality employed against them. To Singh they represented nothing but a massive threat to the Revolution, and three hundred years of baggage he wanted nothing to do with. "If the only option the cops face at our hands is death, they'll just fight us to the bitter end, and we'll have to waste time and lives dealing with them. This way, we at least give another option. One that doesn't let them off or leave them around as a threat, but isn't a guarantee of death… necessarily." In response to Bennigsen's delicate reasoning, Singh hummed. Bennigsen had learned that sound to mean reluctant agreement. The chair turned back around to face Bennigsen and the chief.

"What keeps them from turning against us?" Singh asked in a neutral tone, resting his chin on his hand.

"We split them up like everyone else. Keep an eye on the ones that need an eye kept on them. And… well, they know what will happen to their families if they backstab us."

Singh gave an incredulous stare. "You want me to hold the sword of Damocles over their families' heads to keep them from betraying us?" he asked, unconvinced. "That doesn't sound like a long-term solution."

Bennigsen had to give Singh some credit. *He may be crazy ruthless, but at least he's not actually insane.* "Not explicitly. They know damn well what everyone **wants** to do to them now. Add to that a few examples made of a few particularly egregious figures," he inclined his head backwards to chief Samuels "and I don't think any outright threats will be needed."

"You can't be serious!" the chief blurted out. "You think any of my people will join your commie crusade!?"

Singh's catlike eyes glided over to him in irritation. A silence permeated the room, disturbed only by the ongoing disorder outside. The gray-clad revolutionary released a wave of smoke over the desk, sending the chief into a mild coughing fit. "Yeah," the answer finally came, "Some of them will anyway, and the rest? Well, they won't be a problem for too much longer."

"Do you have any idea how much damage you've done? How impossible it will be for you to repair this, if you even survive the federal response?" Samuels pressed. "Do you know how many enemies you're making? Or how many of your supposed 'friends' will turn against you for it?"

For a moment, the fact that the guy had just tried to narc on him evaded Bennigsen, who could only roll his eyes at the eventual realization. *This guy man…* Singh's eyes bounced over to Bennigsen, broadcasting a message to the effect of, *"Can you **believe** this shit?"* He stood up.

"Well to answer your first question. Of course I'm aware of how much damage we've done. That was the plan." Singh arrived beside to restrained chief, "I don't care about how impossible it is to repair, because I don't intend to repair anything. I intend to destroy it, and then build anew over its wretched ashes." Singh leaned down speaking in a slow, deliberate tone which left no space for interjection, looking Samuels directly in the eyes. Voluntarily or not, the chief backed away from Singh, deep into the pompous armchair. "As for the second question…" walking again, he came around to Bennigsen's side. "The enemies we have made were always going to be our enemies. And more important than that, I know exactly who all of my friends are." He gave Bennigsen's shoulder a couple gentle pats before heading off back towards the great window.

Bennigsen looked over to Samuels with a smirk. "Did you think I'd try to hide who my family is?" he asked, not really expecting to get an answer. The chief just stared off into nothingness, his mouth forming mumbled words with no sound behind them.

"Destroy it… destroy what?" he managed.

"Everything," Singh answered. "The social order, the political order, the economy, culture, everything," he elaborated, surveying the scene outside. "It all has to go, and I didn't even have to get the process started! You guys did all that work for us…" he trailed off, his vision drawn to something on the ground level at the entrance. Singh watched whatever he saw for a good moment before returning to his chair, and grabbing the radio that sat close to his edge of the desk. The radio clicked for an open channel and Subutai uttered two clear, stern words. "Stall her." It clicked again, and after a moment of silence, the unknown receiver replied with two words of his own.

"We'll try."

Singh sighed, leaning on the desk and rubbing his thumbs against his temples. "You know what, Bennigsen, I think you're right." Bennigsen feigned surprise for his friend's benefit. He knew what came next. "After all, the Revolution is about redemption is it not? What good is it to declare that an entire society can be transformed and redeemed, but not every individual? Of course, there are those who will oppose us to their last breaths with every means at their disposal, no matter the merits of our cause or the failings of their own. These creatures, must be put to death mercilessly. But everyone, should at least get a chance, yes? It would only be fair after all."

Bennigsen nodded. "Quite fair. One strike, and you're out." *About what the others got before.* The bitterness came natural now. Any time some lingering tendril of sympathy tried to worm its way into his brain, he remembered the faces. The friends, the classmates, the people who he never knew in any way at all, but whose courage touched something deep in his soul. Those shot, beaten, strangled, dragged off, run over, and just plain old disappeared by his mother's friends. **Damn**, that still stung no matter how much he tried to ignore it. And who held ultimate responsibility for all of that? The chief.

"One strike? Yeah, that sounds about right…" Singh rubbed his stubbled chin as if considering, even though he had already made his decision. "But this man—" he pointed to Samuels, again his fingers arranged like a mock gun "This man has had far more strikes than just one. If I were to even consider letting him live, they might very well hang us instead. Or at the very least, they'd be much harder to control. And who needs that?" He leaned forward, staring right into the chief's soul. "But what to do, what to do…?" Before his fate could be pondered any further, the sounds of approaching footsteps and impassioned arguing growing louder outside the office drew their collective attention. Singh sighed, leaned back into the chair, and brought his pipe up to his lips, gazing with expectation at the big oak doors.

One of them jolted opened, allowing a quite tall, wiry man to slip through and and ease it closed behind him. Stepping into the light, the figure revealed himself as Julian Maxentius, Singh's unseen hand, dressed in a gray uniform that featured only a black star on his cap. Bennigsen knew very little about Julian, save his unapologetic anti-imperial rhetoric and vehement loyalty to the cause. A child of one of LA's worst neighborhoods, and one of the few remaining original members of the "Cabal" which had always guided the Red Army from the shadows. Now, they had far less need to remain in said shadows.

Their goals could almost be called one and the same, both men were intelligent, and both held a penchant for lulling potential foes —and friends— into a false sense of security, into believing they posed little threat. Singh by way of his scholarly appearance and lack of name recognition, Julian by way of his dark brown skin, inglorious background, and accent. In reality both men represented meticulous planners, and between them they'd created the makings of an army out of hordes of angry, dispossessed people. Now, they needed to oversee said horde's transition into a real army, or they would all be doomed.

Julian crossed the office in a few brisk strides, eyes opening wide for a moment as he took a stance beside Singh's chair, and handed his leader a note. "The guard commander's here," Julian announced in his grim, dry voice.

"I noticed," Singh replied, glancing over the message, then folding it back up and slipping it into his coat. "She looked mad…?"

"**Real** mad," Julian confirmed, nodding his head once.

"Hmm. Great." Singh exhaled and passed the pipe to Julian, who accepted it nodding his head in gratitude.

After a tense moment, both doors swung open. An African-American woman in a California National Guard uniform, a pair of prominent black stars on her collar, marched right up to the desk, two gas mask wearing guards followed, their unblinking lenses fixated upon her. The general's eyes fixed on Singh's as she arrived right in front of the desk, between Bennigsen and the chief, neither of whom she even acknowledged. For a while they all just stood and sat there, until Singh leveled a finger at the stoic woman.

"You…" he drew out, "must be Harper, yes?"

Her stern eyes zeroed in. "And you must be Singh," she stated, her tone such that Bennigsen, almost without thinking, placed his hand on the grip of his 9mm.

"That's right," Singh said, his tight-skinned face having morphed into a mask of incredulity. "I'm told that you are displeased with how things have been going thus far?" he prompted. All of this made Harper's eyes shoot open, her lips twist into an indignant scowl.

"You're goddamned right I'm displeased!" she growled. "This was **never** part of the deal! Revenge killings against these morons I get," pointing to Samuels, "but your people are going after everyone that ever wronged them! Everyone who had **anything** to do with the system!"

Julian passed the pipe back to Singh after releasing a waft away from everyone and into the ceiling. Singh smirked a bit and puffed on the sweet smoke. "They're your people now too, sister. And for the record, the pile of heads was not my idea."

"Oh yes! The pile of heads, how could I forget!?" She leaned down onto the desk, bringing her face to within inches of Singh's. He didn't budge. "And I am not your sister. Who the fuck are you people? Have I been tricked into helping a bunch of psychopathic potheads get closer to power?"

Singh returned her accusatory expression with one of incredulity. "We are exactly who we have always claimed to be. And the reason for the pile of heads and everything therein not being part of the deal, is because they were never part of the plan," he admitted. The general's expression relented a bit at that. "I of course, had a **few** names that needed to disappear for all our sakes, but that…" He jabbed a thumb over his shoulder, towards the window. "Not so much."

Harper rose from the desk, still locked on Singh. "You mean, they went and did that themselves?" Her voice heavy with dark realization.

Singh nodded, "Look, I think we can all agree that the rampant murder has gotten somewhat out of hand…" holding his arms out to each of them. "And, that a change of focus is needed."

"Somewhat, out of hand…?" she repeated back in disbelief. "You think that you can just, move past this like it ain't nothin'!?"

Singh shrugged. "You say that, as though there were another choice. I mean, the alternative is to apologize for killing a bunch of people who wanted us dead, and were, by any definition, our enemies." The brown eyes narrowed again.

"And how do you think they will treat our people who get caught now that we've gone all Mongolian?" she challenged.

"The same way that they would've been treated had we all acted like saints," Singh answered in a matter-of-fact tone, without sounding too self righteous. "Come on now, general, surely you of all people understand just what exactly it is we face."

"If you're willing to sink to their level, then what the hell makes you people any better than them?" she shot back, growing more frustrated.

"The reasoning of course. The oligarchs kill anyone who questions or threatens their authority, all in the name of preserving a system that generates profits for them while steadily destroying everything and everyone else. Our goal is to undo that apparatus of exploitation to assure the world's survival… and to seize power." He gazed back at her with

34

those green lenses that lacked any hint of uncertainty. Bennigsen, however, began to question the wisdom of this approach, about the moment that a Beretta M9 flew out of Harper's holster and leveled at Singh's head. Not a second later, two Kalashnikov barrels pointed at the back of her neck, and Bennigsen's glock sat ready to shred her ribcage. An intense moment dragged by.

"What the hell are you waiting for!? Do it already!" the chief urged, causing one of the AKs to be redirected at **his** head.

"Shut up, Samuels," Harper hissed. Bennigsen looked to Singh who, astonishingly, still didn't seem too perturbed by any of this. Though he did raise up his hands in a surrendering gesture.

"Alright, I'm sorry! Not a time for jokes," he admitted. "But in all seriousness, our goal is to create a new society. One in which all human beings are treated as such, where everyone has a purpose and is valued for their contributions to that society, whatever form they might take. One in which the simple right to exist is protected, and where no-one who contributes need ever fear living in depravation. Where everyone has at least a chance to become all that they can be, a **real** chance," he emphasized. "Could our dreams fail somewhere along the way? Of course! But at least we will have tried, as opposed to simply, perpetuating the misery." His gaze drifted to Samuels. "And even if that happens, then at the least we will gain the Western people the seeds of true freedom: a unique identity apart from the rest of the Empire." Harper's eyes widened a bit at that. "And if I must go down in the history books of our enemies, and those who care more for their own self-righteousness than others' well being, as a horrid monster for ensuring that said freedom isn't immediately snuffed out, so be it."

"My God, son, you sure are in love with the sound of your own voice. You want independence... for California?" The Beretta's barrel dipping a bit.

"Not exactly," Singh corrected, ignoring her quip. "As absurd as it must sound to you right now, unlike the oligarchs we do actually give a shit about the lives of the people. I mean Bennigsen here just got back from ensuring that everyone now has free drinking water!" He gestured to his seated friend, whom Harper looked down to for the first time. Her eyes scanned him over with intense skepticism. Bennigsen could only imagine what she thought of the scrawny little white boy sitting in a chair and pointing a gun at her.

"That's right," he confirmed, returning an expression making clear he found her assessment of him meaningless. Unimpressed, but still believing him, Harper turned back to Singh.

"Why should I believe you?" she asked, wavering a bit.

Singh exhaled a cloud of smoke before answering. "Because you have no reason not to. And because the alternative, you killing me, would not only result in your immediate death, but would cause our respective followers to gut each other. So you can forget about curtailing the violence. Oh! And all of this would've been for nothing." A dark silence descended on the hazy office, broken only by the still serene Julian clearing his throat a bit, which made it all seem quite awkward. "Look..." Singh started. "The people have no animosity towards your troops as it is, they're thrilled that you have abandoned the accursed oligarchs and joined them in the great struggle! If they are sent through the streets to rally the people and mitigate the excesses, especially with orders from *us* in hand, I can't imagine they would have too much trouble. We need everyone gathered, equipped, and organized. Neither of us can do that alone." This brutal truth hung in the air for a moment, until the scraping of metal on plastic and a brief click signaled the calming of tensions, but only just.

"Well I hope you're writing all this down for your version of *Mein Kampf*. But I'll cooperate, my people will fan out, and gather everyone in public spaces," Harper acquiesced. "I assume you don't want us dealing out any justice to those who've gone too fa—"

"I will not tolerate such absurd comparisons. Especially those made by a reformed *minion* who *barely* understands them," Singh uttered in a tone so chilling it made Bennigsen's skin crawl and stunned Harper into silence. The gray-clad man then took a deep breath and added, "That being said, you do make a decent point." Another cloud obscured Singh's face for a moment. He looked to Samuels, then pivoted back to Harper, that same assured conviction still projecting from his eyes. "Justice is relative, general. Under Washington it was nothing more than a classist farce, so we must turn it into a universal force of uncompromising finality from which none are immune. Just... don't go overboard. We need these people to fight for us, after all. And I have full confidence that should any of them do something that's just irredeemable or utterly senseless, you will do what must be done to lay out the *appropriate* boundaries."

Harper nodded, the necessary authority now in hand. "We will await instructions from the assembly on where to move once everyone's been marshaled. And we will deal with any criminals according to whatever law the assembly decides upon." With that little turnaround, she spun on her heel and started marching out of the office.

"Um, no no no..." Singh chided, the wooden doors remained closed, their guards motionless, brining Harper to a halt. "We **are** the law. And you will do whatever **we** say." The icy tone with an implicit edge returned full force, but Bennigsen's brief experience with this woman told him enough to know it wouldn't shake her. Sure enough, the stoney general turned right around and marched back up to Singh, who rose from the office chair for the first time since she entered. Pivoting back to the reasoning tactic, he raised a single hand to stop whatever furious retort or tirade she would've unleashed. "You know, I must appear before the assembly, to explain to them what we're going to have to do, in order to not get horribly killed. Why don't you just come with me, general? That way **you** can judge for yourself what you think will make a better vehicle for the people's salvation." Harper's expression shifted to confusion, then surprise as Singh turned to Bennigsen and Julian. "I trust, comrades, that I can leave this matter in your capable hands, yes?" The pointing finger shifted to Samuels. Bennigsen looked at the chief for a moment, then to Julian, before nodding. "Excellent! Come general, there's no time to waste!" In a wild-eyed blur, the young revolutionary flowed past the statuesque soldier and made for the doors. The guards opened them without a moment's pause.

After a brief stagnation, Harper turned back to the still seated Bennigsen, who tipped his hat in a peacemaking gesture. Harper sighed, "Back to business then," the anger that distorted her features now replaced by resignation and confusion. As she turned to following Subutai though, Julian spoke up.

"General, I wanted to thank you for what you've done."

Harper came to a stuttering stop and turned to him. "For what?" she asked, eyes rife with curiosity.

"My little sister was being held in Camp Redding," he explained with a genuine smile, something he displayed even less often than Singh. "You have my family's eternal gratitude, and that of many others."

Harper stumbled a bit, but collected herself. "Yeah I, suppose so..."

"Please do be patient with Subutai, some see him as a desperate measure, but he's the best we got. And don't worry, he doesn't think much of blind obedience. If you don't understand, ask him. He'll tell you. Hell, you get him to respect you and you might even have a shot at changing his mind," Julian assured her.

Harper looked back to the still open doors, biting her lip. "I make no promises... but I'll try." With that, she tipped her field cap to Julian, gave Samuels a disdainful glare, and departed at last.

Bennigsen couldn't help but admire Julian's way with people. Given what Harper just experienced with Singh, and what she surely would see at the assembly, just that little bit of input could be invaluable. *We're all just people. Nothing special or perfect about us.* They all just wanted a better life, better opportunities, a government that actually gave a damn about any of those things. In other words, all the things that the Constitution once promised, but never delivered. Now, even the veneer had rotted away.

"Will you please just kill me?" the exhausted chief's voice beckoned.

Bennigsen swiveled back to face Samuels, fixing him with a gaze of deep examination. *Yep, he's ready alright. Well, time to check on mother...* Bennigsen felt his lips form a grim smile as he glanced over to a waiting Julian, and answered with a single word.

"No."

#

Judith took in a deep breath, released, and pulled. *CRACK!* The empty chili can that Haley had placed on an old fence post got launched and spun into the air. Judith smiled, setting the empty Winchester 1887 down against the fence. The farm girl allowed herself the slight indulgence of pride, 1000 meters out and she'd managed to hit all 18 targets.

"Damn, sis! You sure got this thing down," Haley complimented, taking off her tactical earmuffs as Judith removed the plugs from her own ears.

"I've been tryin' to practice whenever and wherever I can get the chance. These last few years, boy we all knew somethin' was fixin' to go **real** wrong."

Haley fidgeted around like she wanted to say something. Judith grinned and rolled her eyes. "Go on, speak up."

"Does this mean we'll never get to go to Alaska?" her sister asked with a pouting look.

Judith groaned as she slung the Winchester over her shoulder, "I don't know, Hay. It might, or it might not. Can't say for now, and neither can anyone else." She pointed to Haley as they made their way back to the truck. "And any sumbitch who does is a damn liar. Ya hear? This thing won't be over til it's over."

"Will the government try to take us back over?" Haley asked.

Judith remained silent for a moment. "Probably. But they ain't had much luck lately when it comes to bossin' other folks around." She finished with a confident grin.

Haley giggled, then stopped. "I hope the guys are okay."

"Worrying won't do any good, Hay. All we can do for now is pray that Jesus will keep 'em safe,"

"You're going to leave too, aren't you?" Haley asked, not fooled for a moment.

Judith paused midway through loading the rifle onto the truck's gun rack. "Would you hate me if I did?" she asked before at last putting the weapon in place then facing her waiting sibling.

Haley looked down at her feet and kicked the grass. "No…"

Judith felt her lips form a sad smile. "Then, yeah. I probably will," she admitted. Turning to walk around to the driver side, Judith found herself frozen in place, her legs locked together. Looking down, she saw her sister's tiny arms wrapped around her jeans, a mess of dirty blonde hair snuggled against her thigh.

"Promise you'll be careful!" Haley demanded. She was still just a child.

Judith ruffled her sister's hair, and in a concessionary tone said, "I promise."

#

Never in her 22 years had Judith felt compelled to sneak out of her house. The combination of her own desire to not disappoint her parents, along with their respect for her need for independence had always made it unnecessary. With a backpack full of necessities and a couple survival tools, she made her way with as much discretion as she could manage through the short hallway past where her parents slept, into the pitch dark living room, towards the door… Her grandma's old lamp clicked to life, and the space became illuminated by the gloom of an ancient bulb.

Judith's quiet walk came to grinding stop, her eyes clenched shut. Saying nothing, she turned herself around to face just who she expected. Charles sat in his favorite recliner, staring up at his daughter. Judith had anticipated an upset glare of disapproval, instead she only saw his sad, exhausted face. The look of a helpless man.

"You're going, aren't you?" Charles asked.

"Did Hay tell ya?"

Her father gave a sad smile. "She didn't have to, hon." He stood up from his creaking old chair and took slow, tired steps toward her. Judith turned to face him, no longer as worried about chastisement. As Charles made it over to her, the worn-down farmer reached out for an embrace. Surprised at first, Judith accepted the hug, and held held back tears as she squeezed her father's shoulders in return.

"We'll pray for you every day, just like the boys." He pulled back to look into her eyes. "Be safe, Judi." The big man wept in silence, bringing his hand across his face and turning away. "We all love you so much."

Judith pulled her father back, hugging him again. "I'll do my best, Daddy. I promise."

With that, she strode out the door, and onto the night-shrouded streets of her rural Texas town. Judith breathed in the full depth from the cool night air. She could feel the blood thundering in and out of her exhilarated heart. With a

37

triumphant smile Judith ran her hand across the old Colt she'd brought along in her jacket. Then she headed for the only recruitment office anywhere near Fort Stockton. She had brothers to find… and a country to save.

CHAPTER 5:
THE TRIBES

Genuine tragedies in the world are not conflicts between right and wrong. They are conflicts between two rights.
— Georg Wilhelm Friedrich Hegel

Yujing remembered reading a book about the "hero's journey," a narrative device as old as storytelling itself. It more or less laid out the plot of every story in Western literature told since the time of Aristotle. It consisted of several distinct stages, though many variations existed. One thing each of them shared however: the "call to adventure." That about summed up her current feelings on life. Surrounded by American rednecks, religious fanatics, and everything in between, all swarming the urban maze of Richmond, Virginia. Truckloads of rebels, weapons, food, building materials, and debris rumbled by without end, and the cacophonous ambiance of a city in singular motion dominated everything. The people built barricades, boarded and plated up windows. And she stood right in the middle of all of it. The dream or nightmare scenario for any reporter.

Yujing imagined mirror images of this scene now playing out all across America. Each faction dedicated to its own cause, each convinced of their own rightnesses. The man she now found herself interviewing, unlike most everyone she'd spoken to since arriving in the country, seemed to understand this.

"I don't know much about what the rest of America's doin', but I'm pretty hopeful based on what I've seen so far. I mean, I met Conroy in prison, and he didn't seem like the egomaniacal or underhanded type. Kinda looked like a crazy Jesus though." The Southern rebel who identified himself as Paul lit a cigarette, non-verbally passing the next question over to his partner.

"Do you believe that your people here have a real chance of seceding from the U.S.?" she asked.

Mason shrugged his shoulders a bit. "Shit man, I dunno," the big man answered. "Some of these veterans say we all gonna become martyrs. Others think we gonna whip them Feddies good. Either way, It don't matter. I ain't never goin' back."

"Amen to that," Paul chuckled, "goddamn, I could get used to this. And I'm ready to die for it."

Yujing decided to go about asking from a different angle. "The last time the South attempted to secede it didn't end very well, do you think it will go differently this time?"

For a moment both men stood there quietly, then Paul put his free left hand on Mason's shoulder. "Well, last time our ancestors made the mistake of only fighting for the freedom of a few, now it's for everyone's freedom. In Jesus' name of course."

"Yeah, *deus vult,* bitches," Mason said with a smile, silver cross necklace in hand.

"What do you think of the provisional government that's formed in Washington D.C.? Do you see a point in trying to work with them in any way?"

Both shook their heads. "Nah, we might not know for sure what'll become of all this, but that shit is for sure gonna be a fuckin' mess," Mason answered.

"Hell yeah, lefties and fascists fightin' over the throne, ain't nothin' good gonna come of that," Paul added, scratching the bridge of his nose.

"It don't matter if we lose, nothing to do now but fight," Mason said.

"*FUCK D.C.!*" a voice shouted out from one of the passing troop trucks.

Paul smiled and cocked his head, "Yankees ain't never been popular here, ya see."

Yujing, now satisfied, moved ahead. "Have you ever been in combat before, have you fought anyone so far in this war?"

Paul's eyes dimmed just a bit. "Yeah, I served three tours in Afghanistan, one in Iran. Haven't had to fight against other Americans yet though."

"What about you? Have you seen combat before?" she asked Mason.

He smiled. "Yeah baby, I done like 85 tours in Miami Gardens." The two men conspired in a moment of laughter.

Yujing waited for them to finish. "Where is Miami gardens? Is that part of the city of Miami?"

"Yeah, yeah. Gangland baby. Might not be dis, but better than nothing," Mason elaborated.

"Do you believe in Conroy's idea for a rebirth of American Christianity?" Yujing asked.

Paul shrugged. "At least he ain't from a megachurch. Hasn't said anything about the end of the world neither. So for now, yeah. Fingers crossed."

"Yeah man, could be worse."

#

A deep, throbbing ache summoned Emily back into consciousness. Not since high school had she felt so groggy and just destroyed. Muffled, distorted sounds echoed around in her head, unable to escape. She dragged her eyes open, revealing a blurry, dark wall. A concrete wall, a wall blackened and burned. Her eyes drifted closed again. Emily brought her hand up to her sweating head, to her injury. Approaching with great care, her fingers came in contact not with a raw wound, but a cotton pad covered by a band of gauze.

Then the memories came storming back. *My babies, where are my babies!?* Her eyes surged open and she tried to sit up, some of the muffled voices became louder, more urgent. Emily felt a pair of hands on her shoulders, and wrenched around to get a look at their owner. *Scott.* Her muscles relaxed.

"Take it easy, Em," he soothed, leaning her back against the cold and rough wall. "You're alright." The room now came into focus, or rather the cell, illuminated only by candlelight. Four other cops shared it with them, three men and one other woman, while seven others occupied the cell across from their own.

"My kids!" Emily blurted out in a dry, croaking voice. "Where are my kids!?"

"I don't know, Em. I don't know," he admitted. "What happened up in the apartment? Did you find them, were they all there?"

"Yes, yes. They—" Emily's voice stuttered as she noticed a man standing beyond the bars, between the cells, AK in hand, staring right at her. "They were there…"

Scott turned, following Emily's eyes. The Hispanic man outside the bars wore a gray coat speckled with burns and ravaged by cuts, a wide-brimmed cap with a red bandanna wrapped around it sat atop his head. A pair of sharp brown eyes remained locked with hers for a long moment, until the man broke his gaze and slipped away down the hall.

Emily turned to Scott, her face feeling drained. "They got us, didn't they?"

Scott nodded. "I'd love to say that I put up a fight, but they took me by surprise."

Looking over the faces of their cellmates in greater detail, it became clear that Emily didn't know any of these people. Plucked away from a whole slew of precincts, each seemed as uncomfortable as she felt. But another emotion gripped the whole building— fear. Eyes bounced around with unending momentum, voices came out only as whispers, footsteps resonated and silenced everything.

"Hey," Scott's voice brought Emily's eyes back to his bruised face, a faint smile "We'll find them again. They're not dead at least."

Emily nodded her head, breathing in deep, then opened her eyes again, and she froze. Rob stood in front of the cell. Still dressed just as in her nightmare, holding a burning joint, and looking none too amused with anything. Again, Scott followed Emily's pale gaze, shocked to find Rob just watching them.

"Rob? Is that—"

"Yes." Taking a draw from his joint. "Me."

The cell door's lock clacked and a Red carrying a shotgun shoved it open. Rob stepped inside, walking right up to Emily and Scott. The other officers stood up as he entered, halting in place as the shotgun along with three SMGs lined up opposite the bars. Rob regarded them with veiled contempt before arriving at Emily's feet. Kneeling down, he inspected her bandage from afar, before meeting her dire gaze.

"How's the head—bullet—wound?" Rob stumbled out.

Emily blinked. "Terrible," she hissed. "Rob, why?"

Rob's eyes widened. "Why?" His head cocked and eyes narrowed. "Ma, even if I were the most selfish bastard on earth, the only motivation I'd need is to avoid going down with the sinking ship."

"That's what you'd have me believe? You're doing this to save your own skin?"

He took another small puff from the joint. "No," he answered, "but that's exactly why you're going to do it."

Emily tilted her head forward. "I'll do what?"

"In around an hour, my boss and your old boss will arrive here to offer each and every one of you the exact same deal—"

"Of course," someone butted in.

Ignoring them, Rob continued holding up his index finger. "One: join a labor battalion" his middle finger came up. "Two: join the Red Army," the ring finger rose. "And three: join the dead."

Emily sighed, her shoulders feeling heavier with each listed choice. She scoffed. "And I assume there's nothing you can do?"

Rob answered with a grim smile. "Actually, the existence of both choices preceding number three, is in fact the best I can do."

"They're not really going to kill all of us," Scott insisted.

Emily's face fell. "Rob, when this is over, do you have any clue what they'll do to you and your insane friends?"

He nodded. "Yeah, they'll torture and kill us. Assuming they manage to take us alive. Which is going to be a bit of a challenge."

"Your 'boss' can't do this, he'd be signing his own death warrant, and everyone else's!" Emily hissed.

"Oh, but you see, Ma, that's exactly why he **is** going to do it. Think of it like a mass blood pact. No point in giving up, cause you'll just be killed anyway. 'Course, it was always going to be like that." The two shared eye contact in silence for a moment before Rob went on. "Look, I didn't come in here to debate moralities, I came to stop you from getting yourself killed… again. Please listen this time."

"What do you care? Your friends almost killed me once already," Emily pointed out.

Rob sighed. "Yeah, they weren't supposed to do that." He took off his hat, scratching the freshly-shaved stubble on his head before putting the cap back on. "The idea was to capture as many of you guys as possible, obviously though many had other ideas."

"Like mass murder?" she growled.

"Something like that. It turns out that mass uprisings and bloody purges are not the most precise of tools. But, when all peaceful avenues have been closed off, what's a freedom fighter to do?"

"Is that what you are, freedom fighters?" Emily demanded in disbelief.

"Yeah," Rob stated. "Trouble is, you guys are kinda the polar opposite of freedom fighters. Oil and water and all the that."

"We don't just annihilate anyone who doesn't like us, Rob! We don't destroy whole families!" Emily pressed.

Rob's eyes became dark, he leaned forward, almost to where their noses touched. Emily felt Scott shift beside her, until a guard beyond the bars pivoted his Uzi over.

Rob searched Emily's expression for a moment, before smirking. "Yeah ma, you do." The certainty, the conviction behind those words, cut far deeper than any insult ever could have. "The only difference, is that you cover it in this veil of legality so it looks all clean and just and *right*. We don't really need to do that though, so everything is a lot messier."

Emily became silent.

"Look, how we feel about each other's life decisions is kind of irrelevant right now," Rob said, "Neither of us are dead so nothing's set in stone yet, and as long as you make the right choice, it'll stay that way."

"You mean join your 'army'?" Emily asked, holding back tears as best she could.

"Yes," Rob insisted. "The alternatives will get you shanked and shot respectively."

"If you hate me so much, then why do you care?" Emily questioned.

Rob stood back up. "I don't hate **you**. And besides, if you actually do get killed, what becomes of Zechariah and Chris? No one to care for them, no one to raise them, but yours truly."

Emily leaned back all the way against the frigid concrete as Rob turned back toward the cell door and started walking. "Just think it over, you've got a little time still." The second he passed the doorway, the cell slammed shut. He turned back around to face Emily. "Your head will eventually be fine by the way, the bullet 'just' grazed it."

"Uh, hey, Rob, what about the rest of us?" Scott asked in a concerned tone.

"Like I said, you've all got the same choice, but I don't really care what the rest you do," Rob replied with a dismissive wave of his hand. He started to walk back off to the right down the hall, then stopped. "Oh, and by the way, any one of you lays a hand on her, and you'll all be crucified." His pointing finger passing over each of Emily's cellmates in turn, before leaving with most of the extra guards in tow.

"So… I guess that explains how we got caught." Scott managed.

Emily buried her face in her hands, her soul shredded by an undirected, illogical rage on one side, and a crushing, debilitating sense of confusion, despair, and guilt on the other.

"How could you not know that your own son was one of them?" the other woman in the cell asked.

Emily had no answer.

#

The rattle and clank of engines resonated off mud walls, down roads of sand and dirt. Open doors, open windows, open gates. No vehicles, chunks of litter tumbling across the ground. A soundtrack of explosions off in the distance kept everyone hyper-focused. Somehow, abandoned places whose inhabitants fled, leaving their lives scattered around in mid motion, felt far more unsettling than long empty ruins. Then again, Alexander still preferred the desolation to worrying about the accidental (and otherwise) killing of civilians. Even though they intended to leave and never come back, turning the locals against them any more than they already had still carried huge risk. *Empty is way creepier though.*

Everyone kept any eye to the sky, watching for the inescapable UAVs that seemed to spy on them from afar in shifts. When one disappeared, another would soon take its place. Then the sudden clamor of something blundering around inside a looted store prompted dozens small arms and mounted weapons to lock onto every window and door the place had. A ragged mutt shoved its way past a loose-hanging door and took off down the road. A burst of gunfire kicked up the dust around the poor dog, causing it to flee in manic terror.

"Stand down, just a fuckin' dog!" The weapons lowered, a few tight breaths released. The advance continued.

Another Apache shot down earlier, crashed not far off. Pilots fled, blew the wreck to pieces. Still, not a good idea to stick around any longer than need dictated. Whole place considered Jihadist territory. The rhythm of artillery continuing in the background made it clear the area wouldn't remain that way for much longer. A burst of gunfire a few blocks ahead sent everyone at the ready once again.

"Contact! Apartment block 3rd floor, heavy MG!" the vanguard called over the radio.

"Try to get around it," Alexander responded, poking his head above the cupola, "we don't need any fights we can avoid."

"Understood!" came the reply.

"Sir?" Escobedo asked from the seat behind him.

"We need the ammo and we can't waste any time. We're not trying to take the place over, just pass through it," Alexander explained. "If things get too bad, we'll hit them with our main gun."

Escobedo nodded, still not too happy, but understanding nonetheless.

"Hey Alexander, you as happy as I am that this'll be one of the last dusty mud villages that we'll ever have to

42

crawl through, sir?" Derrick asked over the radio.

Alexander smiled a bit. "Right now I just want to make sure it isn't **the** last village we sneak through, Lieutenant."

"Funny you mention that, because the resident spook just reported in. Says the Iranians are about 13 clicks northeast, and closing. Saudis apparently ain't doing so well," Derrick said.

Alexander groaned. "Shocking." He rubbed the sweat from his brow. "Any drones in sight yet?"

"Negative, captain. This is Raven One, skies are clear over," Lieutenant Roscoe answered from the Apache passing above the convoy's head.

"Good, keep your eyes peeled." Another outburst of gunfire, this time from a different direction, still ahead, but much further off.

"What's that green thing down there in that courtyard?" Roscoe asked no one in particular. Before anyone could answer, a stream of tracers surrounded the helicopter, spanking off its sides in showers of sparks. *"Oh, it's a Shilka, okay!"* The chopper peeled away and backed off to the west. No need to rush an AA platform by themselves.

"Fuck!" Alexander snatched the radio back up. "Keep your distance! Can anyone put a shell in that thing?"

"Negative! Got no visual on target over," Captain Joyce answered from the leading Abrams.

"Heads up! Possible RPG, same apartment block. We found a way around it though," the vanguard reported.

"Then let's take it. Move out!" Alexander commanded. "And somebody fire something at that apartment block."

Seconds later a trio of cannon blasts smashed into the building's face, tearing out huge holes and creating a shower of dust and smoke. No more gunfire. No way to tell if they'd bought it or just ran off. The Shilka, in a frustrating display of wisdom, stayed put. *Shit. That's not ideal.*

A faint glimmer in the sky pulled Alexander's attention upward. An Osprey, painted in all black, hovering a long way off to the north above yet another small desert hamlet. Under normal circumstances, Alexander wouldn't have batted an eye at the sight of one of the unique tilt-rotors, but none of those he'd ever seen before were black, or so far inland away from a carrier. *The fuck is that thing doin' here?* He knew no marines were deployed anywhere near this region, and he wondered if the U.S. military controlled it at all. Alexander brought the radio up to his mouth again.

"Do we have an Osprey in the air above town?" he asked, hoping in desperation that someone did.

"Negative, it is not ours. I can see it though," Derrick replied.

"Yeah, that ain't ours, boss," Roscoe confirmed.

Alexander switched to an open radio channel. "Unidentified aircraft, state your designation or you'll be considered hostile."

With that, the black Osprey swiveled around and took off, flying low and disappearing behind a range of hills.

"The hell was that!?" Derrick inquired via radio.

"Whoever they are, we can't catch them going at full tilt," Roscoe grumbled from his Apache. *"Want us to chase 'em off anyway?"*

"Negative, lets pick up the pace, people. The hornets've be stirred up now." Alexander knew sometimes it could prove dangerous to worry too much about losing lives in war. But he also knew he couldn't afford to risk anyone. And besides that, who in their right mind would call this a war anymore?

This was survival.

#

Judith knocked on the faded blue door four times, stepped back a couple of feet, and waited. The sun had just started to drag itself over the horizon, and she hoped Zoey would be awake by now. No telling for sure, though. *Hope she's not still on a depressed bender.* Her childhood friend hadn't taken the news of the world's unraveling well. Not that Judith could blame her, Zoey's big heart had room in it for everyone.

"Agh, I'm coming… Jus' hold on."

"Sure, take yer time," Judith taunted with a playful grin.

"Judi!? What…" the door swung open revealing Zoey's freckled face. Obviously having just awoken, she rubbed her baggy blue eyes, and fluffed her disheveled auburn hair. She'd shuffled to the door in an exhausted stance that left her even shorter than Judith remembered. Her eyes only made it up to Judith's collarbone. "What're you doin' here so early? Birds ain't even up yet…" She yawned, craning her neck upward, assuming a more normal posture.

"I'm doin' it, Zoey," Judith smiled.

"Doin' what? Wait… yer not…"

"Yes I am," Judith insisted.

"B-but—" Zoey blubbered, collecting her sluggish thoughts. "I thought yer folks had said no?"

"They did. And I'm still doin' it. Want to come with?" Judith hefted the bag strapped over her shoulder.

"Judi, I… I just don't know. What if one of us gets killed? What if we both get killed?"

Judith brushed it aside. "These days we're almost as likely to get targeted for stayin' out of it as gettin' into it. C'mon, what have we really got to lose? You've heard 'bout all the crazy nonsense goin' on everywhere. It'll all migrate here 'ventually, unless we're there to stop it," Judith declared in her most confident tone.

"Well… I guess that's true, innit?" Zoey conceded.

"Besides, are you really gonna let me go off with no one to watch my back but Thomas and Will?" Judith pressed with a knowing grin.

"Nah… I wouldn't." Zoey ran a hand trough her long, fiery mane. "I dunno, Judi. I gotta talk to ma folks first."

"You mean you ain't even talked to 'em yet?" Judith questioned with a raised eyebrow.

"No…" Zoey admitted. "I thought for sure you'd get talked out of it, or at least that your folks wouldn't let ya."

"Well they did. Sorta," Judith corrected, releasing a heavy sigh. "So get thinkin', and figure out what matters to ya. I'll be at the recruitin' office fillin' out forms." She turned back to the road.

"Judi wait!" Zoey's drowsiness dissipated in an instant as she latched onto Judith's backpack, spinning her friend back around. "I won't let you go off alone! Jus' wait till I talk with my parents, I'll get 'em to understand. I promise!"

Judith beamed and gave her oldest friend a bear hug. "I know ya will, Zo! Everybody always listens to you."

"For sure—" Zoey croaked before Judith released her. "We gotta stick together, right? Especially now, with everybody gunnin' for everyone else."

Zoey, always the silver tongued negotiator, could talk her way out of a mugging. Judith on the other hand was the tomboy who feared nothing and no one. Together, they'd always managed to get by, and Judith dreaded both the thought of not having Zoey around as well as what might happen to her if she stayed behind.

"Yeah," Judith agreed. "Definitely now…"

CHAPTER 6:
FALLING DOMINOES

Anyone who has ever looked into the glazed eyes of a soldier dying on the battlefield will think hard before starting a war.

— Otto von Bismarck

Harper's eyes bored into her self-declared boss's skull. He remained an enigma in her eyes, having already obliterated any expectations she held prior to meeting him. The one thing she remained certain of though, she would never lower herself for anyone ever again. She might have to follow his orders, for now, but the second his instructions veered from business, or his hands wandered anywhere near her: the end. No more crazy white boy. Harper spent most of the van ride to the indoor basketball stadium the assembly chose to gather in imagining all the excruciating ways she could go about ending his life. Bashing his skull in, driving her thumbs into his eyes, throwing him off a bridge perhaps.

She'd put up with enough self-important "superiors" in her life. No way in hell would Harper let this kid step into that place. Especially just after escaping the last holder of said title, even if it had required her to lead a full-blown mutiny.

"You okay? Feels like I've got a target on the back of my head," Singh stated out of the blue, stirring Harper from her musings. "Have I offended you in some way?" he asked, lighting a blunt while looking her dead in the eyes, smiling a bit.

Harper's own eyes sharpened. "Everything about you offends me."

One of Singh's eyebrows came up, making it clear he didn't buy the explanation. "Really?"

"You don't believe me? Fine, whatever," she dismissed, turning to the window to distract herself with the insanity continuing outside.

Singh went on. "I believe that someone knew you would require an... 'altered' version of the situation in order to join the fold, yes?"

Harper's gaze whipped back around. The intense look in his eyes told her everything. *Shit, it is him. This punk really is the one behind all of this.* She felt a mild twitch in her left eye.

"Oh yeah? Just what sort of, 'altered version of the situation,' did I need to hear?" she growled.

"One where you would end up in charge of everything. In which the people were looking to **you** specifically to deliver them," he replied before taking another draw from his wrap, eyes still locked with Harper's.

This annoyed the general, used to her subordinates avoiding giving her any direct look in the eyes. But this guy couldn't seem to stop, as though he intended to scour her inner being. Never a woman to back down, Harper leaned across the narrow gap between the opposing seats.

"And what if I were given this 'altered' impression?" she asked with fake sweetness.

"Then I would want to make sure you were aware that said impression wasn't *total* bullshit," he explained with a nonchalant tone. "You're just not the supreme head of everything..."

A hand shot out and grabbed Singh by the throat, fingertips positioned with expertise around his windpipe. Singh became rendered immobile, only moving his lips to unleash a breath of smoke, then gulped. A hint of a dark smile crept up Harper's lips. Feeling his confidence melt away in her grip felt glorious, almost good enough to distract her from the fact that her man and Singh's had guns held on one another.

"You mean it wasn't total bullshit when one of the people I thought was mine told me the fate of all our people depended on me?" Harper spat.

"No it wasn't," Singh insisted. "If you hadn't joined us, imagine how many more would be dead."

"That matters to you, does it?" she challenged.

"Well, I care about **my** people getting killed," he answered with honesty.

"And why should I believe that you, the fucker who's behind all of this, would ever view me and my people as 'yours?' You've left a trail of death and destruction across the whole coast!" Her grip grew tighter. "Why should we want anything to do with you?"

"Why should **we** want anything to do with **you**?" Singh reversed. "A bunch of imperial mercenaries, happy to murder anyone you're told for money, grind whole nations under your heels without a thought, and blow innocents to pieces for fun?" he asked with a soul-piercing gaze. "You really think this is somehow worse than the kind of shit you *people* do all the time?"

Harper wanted nothing more than to pull this man's head right off his shoulders. "So, we're both evil," she ground out. "I'm still not sure why the hell I should work with you."

"Because whether or not you like it— or even understand it, we want the same things," Singh squeaked. "We are the only ones who will help you realize them. By any means necessary."

That last bit gave Harper pause. *By any means necessary. Malcolm.* She scanned his eyes for any indication of treachery, but found none. Harper saw Singh was no fool. Just determined to win. More importantly, he didn't seem scared so much of dying, but that everything would stop here, and he could push no further.

This might prove problematic. Harper already knew she couldn't kill this man, though it pained her, but she'd hoped to at least cow him into a level of submission. Clearly not happening. The only choice now, pray. And keep an eye on this kid.

Harper released Singh's throat, leaning back into her chair and crossing her arms. Singh rubbed his windpipe before looking back at Harper in a way that made it clear his mind now busied itself deciding whether or not he should destroy her. *Time to help him make up his mind.*

"Prove it," she demanded. Singh's dire eyes blinked. "Put me in charge of the army."

Singh chuckled a bit. "Are you kidding?"

"You said by any means necessary. Me being placed in charge of the fighting is a necessity," Harper explained with smug look.

Singh took a deep breath. "I can't do that without the Assembly's approval."

Harper's face hardened again. "Can't or won't?"

"Both," Singh answered at once. "I really am trying to at least pretend like I can tolerate those fetchers, and they expect to be part of the process," he explained with a stoney face. "Besides, I see no reason to put all our fates in your hands just yet."

Can't argue with that. The van came to an abrupt stop before she could respond. "Comrade Singh, we've arrived sir!" the driver called back, prompting Singh to surge out the rear doors and into the stadium plaza. As the recently promoted general climbed out after him, she managed to catch a red blur that came flying at her chest. Harper looked down at the soft wad, a simple band of red cloth.

"Put that around your arm. Wouldn't want you to scare anyone," Singh prompted with just a sliver of irony.

Harper looked around the plaza at the dozens of uniformed and suit-clad bodies swaying from lampposts, then to the back of the man in the black coat and cap walking toward the stadium. Taking a deep breath, she marched after him, tying the crude band around her left arm.

The second the guards opened the doors, a wave of sound washed over the pair. The unmistakable bedlam of unrestrained and furious debate. The whole place swarmed with rebels, both armed and not. The power seemed active, lights on, and AC flowing. Everything buried under an atmosphere of vocalized disagreement.

Harper sighed, turning to look down at Singh with a smug grin. "These your 'true people' then?"

"Bah!" Singh said with a hand wave. "Politicians are the same everywhere." He headed in, Harper staying at his side. "So long as they aren't openly murdering one another, they serve a useful purpose."

46

"And if they do start openly murdering each other?" Harper questioned.

"Then the assembly as it stands will cease to serve said purpose," Singh answered.

Harper frowned. "But don't you fancy yourself some kinda politician too, boy?"

Singh jeered, climbing the stairs leading into the seating area. "Not any kind you know of." Again, the guards opened the doors, unleashing the full vitriol of the ongoing "debate."

In a moment, Harper knew the lay of the land. On one side sat a wide assortment of characters, all wearing either red or black armbands on their upper left arms. A smaller but still considerable group occupied the other side. They wore a mix of green, gold, and orange armbands with a meager handful of blues. Harper didn't need to understand the nuances at play, only that this revolution consisted of two broad groups, and by walking into this room wearing a red band, she'd already chosen a side. Harper growled. She'd find some way to get into this insane game, come what might.

Singh walked right up to the guardrails, leaned on them, and looked all around. No main argument dominated the room, just thousands of individual shouting matches and discussions. Across the stadium, a makeshift speaking platform looked over the abandoned basketball field, which itself seemed to have become a giant trash bin. Behind said platform, looking exhausted and resigned, sat a tall dark-haired woman flanked by a pair of uniformed guards.

Singh groaned. "Of all the poor schmoes I've unintentionally gotten killed over the last few days, why couldn't **she** be one of them?" he asked no one, before glaring up at a flickering light on the stadium's scoreboard.

Harper knew that woman, or at least knew **of** her. Lauren Galloway, one of the senior leaders in the Red Movement, and one of the only originals left. A veteran and declared American patriot until recent months, Lauren stood out and Harper never understood her involvement in such a far left movement until now. *They may not all be extremists, but the driving forces are…*

Before she could push Singh for answers, a Hispanic Red walked up and handed him a clip microphone. "Ah, thank you." Singh nodded and took it. As the soldier turned to move away, Singh put a hand on his shoulder, stopping him mid-motion. He guided the soldier over to the guardrail, pointing up at the flickering light on the overhead scoreboard. *"Podrias disparar esa luz por favor?"* Singh asked in Spanish. Harper felt her eyes widen a bit. *So he's multilingual? Great, better keep that in mind…*

The soldier looked from Singh to the malfunctioning light before adopting a mischievous grin. *"Si, camarada."*

Singh gave the man a couple pats on the shoulder. *"Muchas gracias, hermano."* Then he took a few steps back, and the soldier cocked his Kalashnikov.

A single gunshot reverberated around the packed stadium, snuffing out the chaos before the sound even dissipated. It became so quiet in so short a span of time that the tinkling and shattering of falling bits and chunks of glass as they impacted the wooden floor formed the only audible noise. Across the court, the woman at the speaking platform looked first surprised, then dumbfounded upon realizing the identity of the new arrival Singh stepped back up to the railing, clearing his throat with the mic covered.

"Friends, revolutionaries, the opportune moment for us to finally liberate ourselves from the shackles of greed and lies has arrived at long last! All loyalist forces within not just this city but San Fransisco as well, have either locked arms with us, surrendered, or been utterly annihilated!" His proclamation evoked a wave a cheers and applause, primarily coming from the black and red side, but with plenty from the other as well. "We must now seize this opportunity that the people have created through their sacrifice, or all will be undone once the hated Profligates have a chance to organize themselves!" This evoked a chorus of loud and insistent *"Yeah"s*, along with a symphony of stomps and pounds.

Lauren stood up opposite Singh, taking up her own place at the guardrails. *"You,"* she began in a dark and accusatory tone, "have singlehandedly destroyed any chance we might've had of negotiating with Washington." Cries, boos, but also some forceful assent. "And you've turned this city into a hellish bloodbath!"

"I believe what you mean to say, comrade, is that *the people* have lain waste to the sick, despicable lie that has been used to deceive and destroy us for three hundred years." A chorus of agreement. "And that we have ensured the very same cancer that continues to poison and leech off the rest of the empire as we speak, would never have a chance to grow back and spread its rot either within this assembly or amongst the masses." Singh glanced around the expansive room as pumped fists, calls of support, and accusations of treachery and corruption exploded from behind him, directed across to the opposition.

Harper couldn't see Lauren well from so far away, but the woman made her dismay apparent nonetheless. She turned back to Singh. "You radicals have derailed the original goals of this entire movement! This was never supposed to be about separatism and war!"

Someone else behind Lauren, another woman, stood up and shouted, "You're monsters! Your hands are covered in blood!"

This ruffled more than a few feathers, but Singh just raised up his hands in a surrendering gesture. "I accept my responsibility in everything that has taken place," The stadium fell silent. "We have taken up arms in defense of the lives, freedoms, and very humanity, of not just ourselves, but our children and grandchildren. Against a machine, that will not rest until our very ability to exist snuffed out forever."

Harper felt the tone of the whole room shift without a sound.

Singh continued. "There are those victims of passion and petty vengeance who have been unjustly cut down, and I freely admit to that. But this is the nature of the beast!" He pounded his fist on the rail. "A revolution is not a thing of logic and reason, it is a thing of the deepest passion and the most unshakable of conviction. In the grip of such things, we all can take leave of our senses. As one of our less fortunate forbears once asked his compatriots: do you want a revolution without a revolution?" Not a sound. "If one of us must be seen as a monster, so that the rest of us might have a chance to live, then I say— so be it! For against us stand a whole legion of monsters preparing to wipe us all out as we speak!" Again, cheers and calls for immediate action and reproaches rang out everywhere.

"You can talk all you want about monsters and war, Singh, but you understand nothing about the real nature of war, do you?" Lauren demanded.

"On the contrary, Comrade Lauren, we understand full well what it is that we ask for," Singh declared in a far more quiet voice, before looking around the whole stadium. "We ask for the blessing of this assembly to speak with the Owners, in the only language they have the mental capacity to understand!" More *"Yeahs"* and cheers.

A spiteful grin appeared at the edge of Lauren's mouth. "Very well, it seems we have no choice but to formalize a command structure," she stated. Singh released a pent up breath, but Lauren went on. "I nominate Comrade Singh as Marshal of the new Red Army."

Harper's eyes exploded open and pivoted over to Singh, who had frozen in place. "What?"

"Well, clearly if you know exactly what you're doing, there's no better man to see us through these tragic days ahead," Lauren explained.

Harper could tell even from behind that Singh felt no enthusiasm for the idea, but the whole stadium behind him did. Already a chant of *"Singh, Singh, Singh!"* had started up. Harper saw how quick the demagogue thought on his feet, and felt every muscle in her body tighten. He cleared his throat.

"Very well, if the people demand that I lead them to victory, I exist to do as they instruct!" A roar of cheers and cries.

Once out of the main stadium, Harper closed with a somewhat dazed Singh, grabbing the back of his coat and intending, in her own semi-delirium, to slam him against something. Instead, Singh whirled around to face her.

"I don't need anymore shit from **you**," he snapped. "You're not the one who just got saddled with a job you're completely unqualified for, in a deliberate bid to sabotage you." He rubbed his forehead and paced in a slow circle. "This, was not how things were supposed to go."

"You mean, you really were going to give me the gig?" Harper asked with an elevated brow.

"Yes," Singh groaned. "I was going to send you and Bennigsen off to run the war, while I managed, well, everything else. Everything going on here at home."

Harper folded her arms. "So what will I do now? Go off and lead some siege of some city?" she asked through clenched teeth, preparing to lash out against getting sidelined yet again.

Singh straightened. He turned to her, in epiphany. "No," he answered with a conviction that shook Harper from her anger. "You will do exactly what you would've done had everything gone as I wanted. I'll make you quartermaster general, or something, and you'll run the battlefield side of things," he explained, "I might not be trained in any of that, but managing logistics? Keeping morale up? Running an insurgency? Those things I can do just fine."

Harper considered her options, and realized she didn't have much choice at the moment. But Singh might not know she understood that. *Time to get something more substantial out of this "deal."*

"If anything like that is going to happen, my say has to be final, and the credit has to go to whoever deserves it. I'll promote people who can do what I need them to do, not just people you find 'acceptable.' Oh, and one last thing…" she took a step toward Singh. "If I'm going to be in on this crazy ride, then I want **in**. Nothin' held back."

If Harper's demands surprised Singh at all, he gave no sign until the very end. "Well, first off, you and I will make final decisions **together** unless there's no other choice. And like I said, I have full faith in your expertise." Harper frowned a bit but allowed him to go on. "As for the credit and meritocracy, I would've hoped those were a given. The commissars will be around, sure. But their purpose is to maintain morale and root out treachery, not interfere with the orders of commanders. Unless, again, they're trying to do something unfathomably stupid."

"Really?" Harper questioned with folded arms.

Singh rolled his eyes. "**Yes**. I may not be a professional, but I know enough to understand what an atrocious idea it would be to allow that. And the commissars themselves also understand this. It shouldn't be an issue, but if it becomes one, do let me know." Harper nodded, satisfied, and Singh moved on. "But as for that final condition of yours, what exactly do you mean by *in*? I mean you **are** in." Harper's eyes must've caught fire or something, because the look of mild panic in Singh's, made it clear he realized his mistake. "I mean, uh," he sighed, "Look, do you even know what it is you're asking for?"

"Yeah, you're some kinda cabal within this 'Red Movement' and you're more violent and crazy than anyone else," Harper quipped.

Singh's face became blank. "Not exactly 'wrong' from your point of view, but far from the whole truth." He rubbed the stubble on his chin for a moment, thinking. "You'd more or less become a sort of…" he searched for the right words, "communist monk, is the best shorthand I can give you."

Harper's eyes opened up. "What?"

"Yeah," he nodded, "you'd have to give up any personal wealth and valuables, you'd have to read a book, you'd have to swear an oath, and of course the only way out is… um… death."

"You're kidding. You done all that?" she asked with a piercing stare.

"Yep," Singh answered without a moment's pause. "If you need time to consider, I completely understand. It's a big decision after all." He closed his eyes and shrugged, leaning all the way back against the wall with crossed arms.

Upon opening his eyes, Singh found Harper standing right in front of him, just inches away. "You don't want me to join your little club, do you?" she asked without emotion.

"I don't care if you join our 'little club' so long as you know what the hell it is," Singh answered with more than a hint of annoyance.

"Good," she stated, leaning forward to Singh's growing skittishness. "Now, where's this book I have to read?"

His jaw locked in place, yet his eyes remained fixed with hers. "Here." He produced a small, rather thin red book from his coat and held it out to her.

Harper snatched it up and looked it over. Fake leather bound, blank cover. Flipping through it with her fingers, she knew it couldn't be longer than a hundred pages.

"Let me know once you finish. Now come on, we've got work to do." Singh headed back towards the exit.

Harper grumbled, cramming the book into her own coat pocket as she followed after him, wondering just what kind of cult she had gotten herself into.

#

Paul couldn't believe he ever agreed to take part in something this insane. Of all the military installations in the U.S. empire, few had the history and reputation of Norfolk Naval Base. And they planned to take it. The last great war between Americans had begun with the attack on Fort Sumter, South Carolina, a minor skirmish in which no one got killed. Not in this war though. Already this new conflict had seen dozens if not hundreds of such battles with scores of deaths, but nothing of this scale had occurred yet. At least, not so far as Paul knew... In any case, this would prove a daunting undertaking, and one that few held much enthusiasm for. Nobody had attempted something like this in almost two centuries. No telling how it might play out.

The "plan" involved pushing up against the militarized city, and seeing what happened. If they faced resistance, they would apply pressure. If they faced no resistance, they would keep advancing. The gunfire already emanating from the darkened cityscape told Paul that the campaign might prove a bit more complicated than expected. But maybe not as brutal. Advancing from the south, they would take the airfield, then move on to Military Sealift Command HQ SP47, aka the local headshed.

The columns of Saints infantry hugged the fronts of stores and industrial buildings on either side of the street as they advanced. Just behind the vanguard, a trio of Abrams tanks plowed through and crawled over the burning wrecks of cars that clogged the road. Behind them followed technicals and big army trucks carrying more troops and machine guns in the back. Paul always preferred having the vics as opposed to not, but he cursed the racket their engines made, which drowned out everything else. Without thermals— or anything really— they didn't have any way of seeing any potential hostiles either. Not until they walked into view, or opened fire.

Mason followed behind a few soldiers, clutching onto his M4 and peering into the storefronts and windows they passed. A looted Dollar Tree, a trashed KFC, a burned out Micky D's. All dark. Still. Empty. A few scattered plumes of smoke cropped up from between the buildings like black monoliths into the darkened sky. Everyone spoke in whispers and dashed between openings in unpracticed imitations of proper tactical movement.

The Military Circle topped the list, but they'd found it abandoned. None of the civilians they'd encountered thus far had any interest in fighting them. The meager handful of sailors, police, and even marines who they stumbled across surrendered without resistance. They all appeared devoid of hope, in a state of utter confusion. No way they would stay so lucky, though. Somebody had set all those fires— and the ongoing firefights started long before they arrived. The Saints avoided I-264 and I-64, so as to not get easily detected. This, at least, was "the plan."

The man up on point poked his head around the corner of the last building on the block, an Auto-Zone, and ducked back around at once. He clenched his fist and held it up above his head, signaling the driver of the lead tank to stop, which he did. As the Abrams clanked to a halt, Paul rushed up to the pointman, stopping beside him.

"What is it?" he asked the ragged fellow.

"A whole buncha navy guys up ahead with three MRAPs," the fighter replied.

"How ya know they're navy?"

"Cause a bunch of 'em are wearin' that blue camo. And look at those three idiots out there in their Cracker-Jacks."

Paul grinned, nodding, and headed over to the lead tank. The MRAPs' engines would have the same effect of masking their presence from the navy boys. With any luck, they could push the violence-free streak just an itty-bitty bit further. If the Rebs rushed in and got enough guns pointed at these squids quick enough, they might just throw in the towel. Then again, they might not. Only one way to find out.

The tanks led the way, careening into the the street. Infantry swarmed around the corpses and vehicles. The poor navy guys didn't even notice at first. Only when one of them happened to look up and see the pain train approaching, did they at last spring into action. Too little, too late.

Once the sailors scrambled to cover, and the the MRAPs started to gear up, the tanks decided fighting time had

50

arrived. The first shell fired by the lead Abrams buried itself into the engine block of the closest MRAP, a fraction of a second before blowing the whole thing to pieces and knocking anyone nearby to the tarmac. *Well fuck.*

"Open fire!" Paul ordered.

Despite his voice getting drowned out by the Abrams' 50 cal, a ragged volley erupted from the chaotic rebel line. The gun battle didn't last all that long.

Another Abrams shell blasted apart the rear of the second MRAP. A third shot missed, destroying the face of an insurance building. After around half a minute of rampant gunfire tearing up the crossroads, and several rebels and sailors getting cut down, all the muzzle flashes from up ahead stopped. Paul ducked back behind the street corner, grabbing the radio clipped to his jacket epaulet.

"Cease fire goddamn it! Cease fire!" he barked out over the airwaves. After a few seconds, his troops' assault petered off, replaced once more by the background ambiance of distant gunfire.

A chorus of shouts came in unison. "Don't shoot!" Several pleaded. "We surrender!" They called. "For God's sake, hold your fire!" They prayed.

"Drop your fuckin' weapons, assholes!" Came the bitter response.

The telltale clatter of metal and plastic emanated from the smoke, as scores of stunned and bloodied men and women stumbled out into view. The crew of the surviving MRAP abandoned the thing like a curse, throwing up their hands.

"Alright people, move up!" Paul commanded. "Check the wounded, search the prisoners for weapons. Take all their shit, and secure that last MRAP." His words rang through the streets and over the airwaves. The Saints emerged from every corner and surged forward without any more instruction.

Paul contained a sigh, standing amazed that they'd gotten this far despite the lack of any real training. *This might be funny, if it weren't so damned dangerous.* The handful of wounded produced by the brief battle groaned and cried over the tank's engines. Only eight of his own people had gotten hit this time. Two deaths. *Eight casualties.* **Only** *two dead...* Back in Iraq or Afghanistan, the idea of encountering a force of far inferior strength, and still suffering eight losses in the course of taking them out... absurd. Here, just a matter of course.

The squids hadn't done as well. Not a surprise, considering they'd gotten ambushed by a goddamn tank at point-blank range. Nobody riding in the two obliterated MRAPs survived. Five K.I.A.s, so far as Paul could tell from what remained. Four others killed in the bullet storm outside. A total of nine wounded to one extent or another. *18. Jesus.*

Paul approached the final navy MRAP to inspect it more closely. He noticed something on the ground near the first destroyed vehicle. As he approached, he realized that the strange tube splayed across the battered street in fact, led to up a human torso. Before Paul could think to look away, his eyes met the fading brown irises of an auburn-haired young woman wearing a blue camo jacket. All that remained of her lower body, a red mess of flesh and torn bone. Blood leaked from her gaping mouth, her whole expression frozen in one of surprise and confusion. *19.*

Paul tore himself away and moved on. *Great, yet another nightmare for the rotation.* He forced his train of thought back to the vehicles. Each of them featured the seal of the U.S. Navy on its doors over a gray paint job. Paul declared, after giving it a once over, the sole surviving MRAP serviceable. Not in the way the Navy'd seen fit to use it though. *I guess they're just handing those damn things out to everybody. What else'r they gonna do with 'em?* He turned back to the surviving prisoners. Some gave off an aura of defiance, but most looked quite subdued.

"Why you guys wearing those old school blueberry uniforms?" Paul asked.

"Th-they put them back in circulation..." one of the shivering sailors answered.

"Alright, I need the five of ya to hand over your yer jackets, hats, pants, and helmets," he commanded.

The sailors looked around at each other, until a number of saints closed around them.

"Come on now, get strippin'. Don't worry, we'll trade ya clothes," Paul assured them as he removed his camouflaged coat.

Mason approached him from behind. "Whoa man, are we really gonna...?"

"Yep."

Mason didn't believe Paul could do something this insane. Worse than that, he couldn't believe Paul would rope him into it. On the inside, Mason got plenty of practice at pretending "nothin's up" whenever the guards came by. This felt something like that.

The eyes of the one actual sailor in the MRAP darted from person to person. As the runt of the lot, he seemed the logical choice. Mason drummed his fingers against the front handgrip of the M4 lying across his lap, betraying his anxiety. He kept his head facing forward as they cruised in casual fashion through the base. His eyes scanned everything and everyone as they passed. Lots of guards, but not as many as he expected. Defenses broke the base into segments, but all the gates sat open. All kinds of vehicles drove through at high speed. Hummers, GSA sedans, civilian pick-up trucks, deuce-and-a-halfs.

Mason watched in amazement as a group of sailors came stumbling out of an old brick building. Inebriated beyond reason, one of them lost his balance and collapsed into a pile of uncollected garbage bags. Others smoked and loitered around burning oil drums, looking quite sullen and without direction. *No surprises there, the scavenging party we nabbed this MRAP from sure didn't seem too "with it." This whole attack should've gone on a hell of a lot longer, and cost us way more blood. But if nobody wants to fight, well, I ain't gonna complain.*

"Its just up here, yeah that blocky one with the columns," Paul told the driver. "See it over there?" He turned back to everyone else. "Everybody just act tired and like you don't give a fuck."

Mason smiled a bit. *'Least he's no fool.*

As the MRAP began to slow down, Mason's eyes zeroed in on a rapid movement as the HQ's doors swung open and a trio of suspicious characters strode out into the dark night. Two of them wore the stereotypical all black spec ops gear that Mason had become all too familiar with. But the guy in the middle... everything about him screamed G-man, even from almost half a block away. Gelled blond hair with black square shades and a long overcoat. Hell, the guy even had a steel briefcase which glimmered in the cones of illumination cast down by the base's floodlights as he and his apparent bodyguards made their way down the steps.

When this small group turned down the road past the MRAP full of disguised Saints, the blond guy in shades did a sudden turn of his head, making direct eye contact with Mason. After looking away back towards the HQ by instinct and waiting for a handful of heartbeats, Mason cautiously checked back to find the G-man had continued on towards a cluster of helipads, ignoring him. *Whew.*

"Who was that guy?" Mason asked aloud.

"No one we need to deal with for right now," Paul replied. "Let's just focus on securing the headshed."

Yeah, right.

The MRAP at last lurched to a stop in front of the base headquarters, guarded by four guys behind some haphazard sandbags. The vehicle's doors had swung open, and six men piled out. Paul led the way, with Mason and the one unlucky "volunteer" from the scavenging party close behind him. Mason shoved an unloaded M4 into the sailor's hands.

"Take this, bitch. It ain't loaded, so jus' act natural," Mason instructed.

The guy just accepted the useless weapon and nodded in meek silence.

Their "squad" just walked right up the stairs, barely paying mind to the card-playing guards outside. They didn't even look up from their game. *Poor bastards.* Mason hoped—for all their sakes—that the explosive charges in the locked MRAP would go unneeded.

An electromechanical whine caught Mason's attention, drawing his gaze back towards the helipads. He watched the G-man and his guards step aboard a helicopter-looking aircraft with dual rotors, one off to either side, and a ramp raised closed behind them. Seconds later, following the escalating chops of a spinning up aircraft engine, the weird helicopter ascended and headed off to the south with a whirling grind that sounded both similar to and different from other helicopters Mason had been around before. Mason watched the jet-black aircraft depart in the direction they themselves had just come from. He'd seen those things in movies, but didn't know their actual names. Mason checked over his shoulder to find the doors being opened and Paul beckoning him to follow. The ex-con turned infiltrator released a tired sigh. *Cool, more spooky government bullshit.*

Inside the HQ, things looked somehow worse than the rest of the base. Maybe because it came as an even greater surprise. People rushed around, going through files, looking over folders overflowing with paper. *Lookin' for somethin'. Guess it's been a while since they needed papers.* Paul led everyone straight up the stairs like he owned the place, and just like that, they waltzed right through all the madness. Only one guy paid their band any mind at all, a very young marine who marched up to Paul with a questioning glare.

"What do you guys need?"

"Where's the C.O.'s office?" Paul asked in a strict-business tone.

"Up there, 3rd floor," the marine answered, pointing behind him up the staircase. He then slung his rifle over his shoulder and wandered off. Without any words, the "guide" led them up to the C.O.'s office. Guarded by two guys who didn't stand a chance. Walking right up to the pair, Paul and Mason just snatched their rifles away and their compatriots took the two confused fellows prisoner. The door swung open and everybody flooded inside, a decisive clang ringing behind them.

The man behind the desk, face down on its wooden surface, held an open scotch bottle in his right hand. His grizzled hair matched his dress uniform, a complete mess. He remained motionless as the rebels piled in, gazing up only when Paul, Mason, and their volunteer walked right up to his desk. His face looked as though it had lain on that desk for days. *Shit, what the hell?* Mason couldn't hide his bewilderment anymore.

"Admiral Winters?" Paul asked him.

The man looked between the three. "Mhrm. WHAT?" he demanded.

"Sir, I'm afraid that we're gonna have to commandeer your base," Paul answered in an apologetic manner. Mason snatched the bottle from the admiral's hand and looked it over with a whistle. The label read "*Bowmore Isle, aged 25 years.*"

"Damn y'all, this here is the good shit!" he peered into the amber glass. "He dun drank most of it though…"

Winters rubbed his eyes, grumbling. He belched, unleashing a blast of scotch fumes upon everyone in the room. "On w-whose authority?" he slurred.

"By the authority of God himself," Paul joked, rubbing his eyes against the stench as he raised the muzzle of his M4 to the admiral's head.

The old man stared back up at him, his eyes lighting up with exhausted hope. "O-okay."

CHAPTER 7:
CROSSROADS

In the midst of chaos, there is also opportunity.

— Sun-Tzu

Yujing found herself heading back to D.C., but saw the city in a far more quiet state this time. Not peaceful, mind you. Just quiet. An awful tension gripped the air. The stench of bodies that still lay scattered among the burned-out cars and heaps of rubble and trash infected the breeze flowing through the area.

Sporadic bursts of gunfire still pulsed through the streets like echoes of the previous days' carnage. Yujing thanked God it wasn't the sweltering spring or early summer, which would've amplified the putrid miasma a hundred fold. The "Brotherhood of Patriots" and their new government had driven the Popular Front out of the capital, but that did not equate to peace. The P.F. still occupied many of the major coastal cities. New York, Boston, parts of Baltimore, and even as deep inland as Philadelphia. Not to mention the regular people literally killing each other in the streets over random shit.

Before getting back to the heart of the capital though, Yujing had to pass through Alexandria, a suburb just south of D.C. proper. But she found herself sidetracked by the ramshackle tent city surrounding the entire wharf area, and the mass of humanity writhing around the docks themselves. She made her way to the head of an amorphous "line" to discover that only one seagoing vessel of any kind sat tied to the dock. A British light cargo ship. A cadre of sailors vetted people, ushering them up a rope and wood gangplank, or sending them away. Those who got rejected gathered, stewing in the shantytown. Lots of weapons— baseball bats, pipes, boards with nails, various pistols and shotguns— but nothing too serious.

Yujing made her way to the front of the group. The sailors stopped her, but almost on impulse she reached for her BBC press pass. They lightened up, and one of them said. "Oh, you're with the Beeb!"

After a brief chat with the sailors, they allowed her aboard to speak with their captain before the ship departed. The *Birmingham Maiden* out of… get this… Birmingham… looked aged, yet sturdy. Faint traces of rust here and there. A petty officer met Yujing at the top of the stairs and escorted her through the corridors and crowds of passengers to the bridge, where the captain and quartermaster busied themselves with manifests of supplies.

The captain, a tall and bulky fellow with a full beard of amber hair, and gray-blue eyes like storm clouds, looked up from his books. He examined Yujing for a moment.

"Good morning, mam. My yeoman said you were a reporter with the BBC?"

"That's right." She held out her credentials, which the captain accepted. "I wish to ask you some questions about the situation, if you'd be so kind as to answer."

The captain's eyes widened a bit upon hearing her posh accent. "You wouldn't happen to be from Hong Kong would you?"

Yujing smiled. "I am, but my family fled to London… after the siege."

A look of real sympathy and regret flashed across the captain's eyes. "I do so miss the Pearl of the Orient." He stumbled. "No offense, mam. Perhaps you'll get the chance to see it again someday."

Yujing smiled a bit and shrugged. "I hope so."

The captain thought for a moment, but soon decided, nodding his head. "I see no harm in answering some questions. What do you say we step outside, I need some fresh air."

Yujing followed the captain as he strode out onto a catwalk overlooking Alexandria's wharf. A loud argument had broken out at the foot of the stairs. An American man demanding he and his family be allowed aboard. An armed sailor became annoyed, telling him to "Fok off!" This started a brawl. Before things could escalate though, another sailor fired his pistol into the air, sending everyone scattering. Somehow about 70% of the crowd stayed in place. British subjects, no doubt. Or maybe just people **that** desperate to escape these shores.

The captain shook his head and turned to Yujing. "I'm terribly sorry you had to witness all that. The name is Hammond by the way." He produced a package of cigarettes, offering one to Yujing, which she politely declined. "Do you mind?" he took one between his teeth, lighting it when Yujing shook her head.

"Yujing Huang," she answered.

"A pleasure, Yujing. So, what kind of questions do you have? I'll answer what I can, but I'm afraid I don't know too much."

"No worries. I'm more interested in your perspective on all this," she assured him with a smile. "Are you are limiting the refugees to British subjects only?"

He nodded with a grim face. "We can't save everyone, of course Australians and Canadians are welcome. But the Yanks can be such menace. We picked up a crew of Portuguese sailors who had their fishing trawler stolen from them by an armed mob."

Yujing nodded along, scribbling, recording everything on her notepad as the captain spoke. All the while, wishing that her phone hadn't gotten fried. "So what's your overall view of this situation? What do you think about what's happening?"

The captain rubbed his brow. "Well, I think it's an unmitigated bloody disaster." He waved a hand across the D.C. skyline. "I served in the Royal Navy for nearly 30 years, I've never seen anything like this. And I thought things in Europe looked bad."

"How many of those trying to escape from the violence would you say are Americans?"

The captain sighed, thinking. "Most of them. Couldn't put a number on it though."

"Have you seen any U.S. military forces so far?"

"Not yet, thank God. Apparently they're just as nasty as the rebels. Robbing and murdering, we've heard plenty of horror stories. This ship has more-or-less been turned into a looney bin until we get back home. Poor buggers." As Yujing jotted down her notes, a smile formed on Hammond's face. "You know, I have an old digital camera taking up space in my office drawer. Why don't you take it to replace whatever the EMP destroyed."

Yujing felt her shoulders lift a bit. "Oh, thank you. That would be marvelous!" After a moment though, the last part of the captain's sentence caught up with her. "Wait... the EMP? Is that what's taken out all the power?"

Hammond nodded with closed eyes. "Just about every un-shielded piece of tech more complicated than an old radio was destroyed. People were arguing for a while wether it was the Russians or the Chinese, turns out it was both. So I've heard."

Yujing processed this information. "Are they going to invade?" she asked, her throat tightening.

Hammond gave a grim smirk, shaking his head. "Doesn't look like it, mam. They'll probably back some factions, but aside from that they'll just sit back and watch it all burn."

"Do you think the violence will spread into Canada? And if so, do you think the British government will become involved in this civil war?"

"Oh, frankly I don't see how it won't spread if it hasn't already. Not based on what I've seen. And no, I don't think there's a bloody politician in the whole U.K. that wants a thing to do with this bin fire. Nobody does. We'll just have to help out however we are able without getting dragged in."

"And do you feel this way as well?" Yujing asked.

"I do." Hammond nodded. "In these sorts of dreadful situations if you support the wrong side, you can end up with a lot of blood on your hands. And you can make an enemy of whichever bloke wins at the end of it. I know that sounds cold, but frankly its not like they did us any favors after the whole Brexit fiasco."

"Is it this bad everywhere you've been?" she asked.

"Or worse. The insanity's broken out all along the Eastern Seaboard. Between the Brotherhood, the P.F., the

Loyalists, and now the Saints, there's no shortage of terror to run away from."

Yujing knew with the southerners now moving north from Virginia, and the Brotherhood determined to impose its will on everyone, things would only get worse.

"Do you know what's going on west of the Rocky Mountains?"

"No… not much's come out of the West so far. Just rumors really." His response sounded almost dismissive, as if any potential answer he had to offer couldn't possibly be true. *Not a good sign…*

A massive burst of gunfire emanated from the streets of Alexandria, provoking a wave of outcries and screams that washed through the refugee camp, followed by a few pot shots from the ship's crew guarding the deck.

"Cease fire! Cease fire!" Hammond bellowed, tossing his cigarette off the side of the boat, "Fuck…"

Yujing peered over the edge of the guardrail to try and see… something… anything. A trio of pickup trucks loaded with armed people rolled trough the camp, right up to the docks. As the occupants piled out, a man wearing a leather jacket and a gray marine field cap marched right up to the British sailors and began making demands. It didn't take a genius to deduce that he wanted to come aboard, moreover he wanted to look for something specific. "You need to turn over any American traitors to us! Any politicians, libs, Wall Street scum, any of 'em!"

A mob of all white men stood at his back. The Brotherhood of Patriots. Almost all white men. A hodgepodge mix of militaria spanning the last several generations along with assorted outdoorsman's wear. A chaotic variety of weapons, some with far too many attachments for practicality. Lasers, suppressors, and night optics would perhaps prove useful, for a few weeks.

Captain Hammond, who'd also taken immediate notice of the commotion, put a hand on Yujing's shoulder to get her attention. "Go back inside, tell my first mate Olson that I gave you my old camera. He'll know what you mean, and he'll see you off as well." He extended his hand, which Yujing shook. "A pleasure speakin' with you, mam. I hope you find whatever it is you're looking for in this godforsaken country."

"Good luck getting back home, captain," Yujing said.

Hammond looked over his shoulder at the escalating argument taking place down on the pier, and sighed. "Thank you, I believe we'll need it." With that, he headed down the stairs to the main deck, over to the gangplank, as Yujing ducked inside the bridge of the *Birmingham Maiden*.

#

Alexander wondered from time to time what Rommel must've felt, charging across the deserts of North Africa, chasing down the British to conquer the Suez Canal. Alexander believed he understood Rommel now. Of course, the Desert Fox had hoped to save a fascist empire by taking the oil of the Middle East, thus achieving everlasting glory for himself. Alexander, by contrast, wanted only to get his army the hell away from this goddamned desert and its accursed oil. He didn't care how history remembered him. Not for now, not so long as they escaped.

The greatest threat at the moment: an army of angry Persians sweeping aside the hopeless Saudis and overrunning Iraq. Alexander didn't have any intention of trying to stop them. But the Iranians might try to exact a bit of revenge for the whole "getting invaded" thing, so vigilance remained a must. The locals had split between the two sides, the Sunnis either sitting it out or joining the Saudis, and the Shias going all in with the Iranians. It didn't matter to the Americans, of course. Everyone involved hated the Yankees and wanted them gone. Alexander knew a fair number of the troops saw his combat-averse strategy as chicken-shit, but he didn't care. So long as they didn't mutiny and continued to tackle the occasional skirmish, the plan rolled on.

They'd managed to avoid most of the action, since it seemed the Iranians had invaded Iraq through the south. Once they'd finished tossing the Saudis around, he figured they'd seek to take over everything else. He didn't have any idea if— or for how long— they would ignore Israel.

"*Jefé! We got trouble up ahead,*" the voice of the lead Bradley commander, Lopez, crackled through his headset.

"Whatcha got?" he asked.

"*BTRs and BMPs. They got the whole place locked down, man.*"

"Shit." Alexander wracked his brain. They needed to cross the Euphrates to make it into Syria. And they **needed** to control the town to use the bridge without getting killed. No choice. "Alright boys, we gotta push all the hostiles outta that town. Form up."

A chorus of affirmations came over the radio. None of the bravado or rejoicing of the past, though. Just grim acceptance. The marines' armor led the charge, knocking out two BTRs before the first AT missile came sailing out of the town. The unfortunate Bradley deployed countermeasures, which failed. After the missile buried itself into the front plate of the IFV, huge tongues of flame erupted from its turret hatches. After that, a volley of shells ripped and blasted the edge of town apart. More missiles and rounds flew back in reply.

"Keep us just behind everyone," Alexander instructed his driver.

"Doin' my best, sir!" he replied with a look of deep concentration.

Alexander ducked down as a shell from something struck the Abrams in front of his Humvee on its turret cheek. Big flash and a shower of sparks. The tank's turret wheeled around 45-ish degrees and fired another round, before something landed and exploded just 15 feet in front of it. Great plumes of sand and dirt rose up with each blast, and it didn't take long before a veil of searing dust blanketed the whole battlefield. Over the maelstrom, Alexander could hear Warwick calling down an airstrike on an unknown model of Russian tank. He saw a pair of Apaches carry out a strafing run on the center of town, creating a trail of explosions and knocking down a few buildings. Then he watched as a surface-to-air-missile rose from the nebula of dust like a vengeful spirit, and smashed one of the choppers into flaming bits.

Something bigger hit the Abrams in the hull this time, making a loud *PUNG* sound as if the tank had just gotten whacked by a giant metal pipe. Alexander could hear someone vomit over the radio as the whole vehicle vibrated from the impact.

"Goddamn it, what the fuck is doing that!?" the commander demanded.

As Alexander started to realize his plan needed some adjustment, an Abrams off his right had its turret blown off by a jet of fire that rose in a miniature mushroom cloud.

"Fuck!" he fumbled with his headset, "All callsigns, all callsigns! Advance and close the distance, now! If you're on the flanks, try to spread out and surround them! We've got to get out of the fucking open!" Before he'd even finished, the whole line started rolling forward again. A brief string of rounds spanked off the lead tank's turret in a series of shrapnel-spewing detonations. Laser-like glowing streaks of green tracer rounds streamed overhead and pattered on the outer armor of Alexander's Humvee.

"Spread out, Spread out!"

"How many tanks!? How many fuckin' tanks!?"

"MEDIC! I need a medic!"

The chaos began to resonate. Things started to fracture.

"We've lost another tank! Another tank is down!"

"Somebody take out that Karrar!"

"Blue Eagle One to command, over!"

Alexander focused his attention, ignoring the tank round whistling overhead. He hit the transmit button. "Command reads you, Blue Eagle One. Go ahead, over."

"Command, we have Iranian armor and vics retreating from the town, heading north-northeast. Should we break and engage, over?"

"Negative, Eagle One! We want these guys to cut and run, not fight to the fucking death. Focus on the dumb bastards who aren't running away, over."

"Copy that command, Eagle One out!"

Alexander returned his attention to the immediate surroundings, and realized the quantity of bullets and missiles launched at his advancing forces had petered off. By the time they **finally** reached the edge of town, only the occasional burst of gunfire and offhand explosions billowed out from the settling dust storm. As his command Humvee rolled passed the first bombed-out structures, the sharp sounds died out, save the occasional distant echo.

"Blue Eagle One to command, they're all pulling back, sir. Looks like we're clear for now, over."

Alexander released a tight breath from his exhausted lungs. "Alright people, we have to move our asses before they can round up some more friends. Jar-heads take point."

"You got it Jefé. Hey, anybody got a towel or some shit? Fuck, man...."

A few laughs and jeers came through the speaker before Alexander cut them off. "Okay, who did we lose?"

The channel went dead for a moment before Lopez answered. *"We're down four Bradleys and three tanks. No head count yet."*

"Alright, have somebody check. Move fast, people. Command out." Alexander closed his eyes and rubbed his forehead, remembering the days when he'd thanked God for not getting sent to die on Taiwan. Instead, he found himself leading his people across one of the world's oldest and most storied rivers. Reduced to a stagnant, tepid, decaying mess. His gaze became drawn to the furious blaze of a destroyed T-72. An old design upgraded to relevancy, fighting against other old designs upgraded to relevancy. As his Humvee came to a halt on the southern side of the bridge, Alexander watched the sprawling convoy of mismatched vehicles roll across. Old deuce and a halfs loaded with troops and supplies, cars and sedans packed with civilians, Toyota 4x4s turned into technicals for recon. All of them going about as fast as they could without ramming into each other too much.

Alexander had no idea where or when the Iranians would strike back, he could only hope they wouldn't need to find out. He grabbed his radio. "Maxwell, keep your guys on the northern bank until we get everyone across, be ready to book it on the double."

"You got it," Derrick answered. *"3rd platoon, form up and lock down the streets!"*

Now, they would wait. And keep watch.

#

Judith stood outside the Texas National Guard recruiting office of Fort Stockton. She watched as a black painted dual-rotor helicopter of some kind took off from behind the building, sending out a flood of wind that washed away anything not nailed down as it hurtled off into the distance. Despite the invisibility of the wind, Judith had to shield her eyes from the dust and trash flying all around, but she wondered why such an odd looking vehicle had appeared in such remote place as this. She recognized the thing a some aircraft that the U.S. military used, but had no clue what to call it. Her only point of reference was the giant Chinook helicopters she'd seen—but those looked like flying shipping containers in comparison to this sci-fi thing. It looked awful weird.

The Lone Star flag rippled in the agitated, scorching wind. Once the state emblem flew beneath the Star-Spangled Banner, but now streamed proud and alone. The sign that previously said "U.S. Army Reserve and National Guard Career Center" had received a slapdash facelift which left the now asymmetrical sign just reading "National Guard Career Center" with a big redacted space in front of it. Judith could feel a shift in the air all around her, could see it on people's faces. The inescapable despair and simmering anger that once poisoned all interactions no matter how unnoticed, had given way to a cautious optimism and relief, although the overall uncertainty still remained. No one openly doubted the course taken by their current leaders, yet the very real possibility of the Fed bringing the hammer down upon their infant nation loomed large.

None of this dimmed Judith's determination, though. She might not know for sure what would come of the new Texas Republic, but she knew for sure what would happen if they stayed chained to the rest of the U.S. More wasted lifetimes of slow agonizing decay and abuse. Judith refused to grow brow-beaten and resigned like her parents and so many of the older folks around her.

Feddies didn't scare her.

Marauders didn't scare her.

Fanatics didn't scare her.

Commies didn't scare her.

She would either grow old in a free land that she could truly call home, or she would die trying to create it. Straightening her rancher hat, she opened the heavy steel and glass door, stepping through a wall of relieving cool air. Judith took in a deep breath, thankful that they'd already gotten the state's power grid up and running again. *Texas, the only state with it's own power grid. At least we have that going for us to start off...* To her shock, Judith nearly walked into the broad back of a tall man in a green canvas jacket. She peeked around his well-built form and discovered a line that stretched back ten people, almost to the door. Looking over to her left, every Spartan chair sat occupied and three guys stood leaning against the wall. A rough 50/50 mix of men and women, most of them either dozed off or buried in a book or magazine, but a few nodded her way or tipped their hats.

"Howdy," she greeted, fingering the brim her own cap. Sighing, Judith leaned back in her boots and got ready to wait.

"You, there." A man behind one of the desks pointed at Judith. "What're you doin' here?"

Judith, taken a bit off guard, cleared her throat. "I- uh... I came here to join the cavalry."

The man at the desk gave Judith a quick up and down. "You want to join... *the cavalry?*" he asked, raising an eyebrow.

"Ye-yeah. I Wanna join the the cavalry corps."

The man blinked several times. "Have you ridden a horse before?" he asked with skepticism.

Now Judith was angry. "I grew up on a farm, I been ridin' horses all my life!" she proclaimed, doing her best not to get flustered.

"Well now, it just so happens that we have a few horses tied up out back." A stocky guardswoman approached behind the recruiter. "Care to give us a small demonstration?"

"Don't mind if I do."

Judith followed the woman out back in a huff, finding herself in a large dusty backlot occupied by a couple old cars and three bored horses tied to a two-by-four on the back of the recruiting office. A few guys in camo uniforms seemed hard at work loading a big stack of cases onto a pair of box trucks, a shallow blast-like impression visible in the soil nearby where Judith guessed the helicopter she saw earlier had take off from.

The woman gestured to the smallest of the horses with a smirk on her face. "Well lil' miss, get on up there."

Judith straightened her cowgirl hat before more-or-less jumping up the stirrups and onto the brown mare's back. She did so a little too quick though, causing the horse to rear up and whinny, but Judith just managed to regain control and kept herself from getting thrown. Ignoring this hiccup, she brought her new steed around and took off down the lot.

"Wait— what the hell?" the guardswoman spluttered, swatting away the dust left behind in a turbulent cloud.

Judith flew down the road, around the recruitment building, back into the lot. She rode the horse in a figure eight around the whole thing before arriving back in front of the stocky guardswoman, where the found several recruiters from inside who'd joined after seeing her sail past the front window. The entire trip had taken less than half a minute. The guardswoman just blinked in stunned silence.

Judith could feel a proud smile bloom across her face. "Proof enough for ya?"

After a moment of glancing between Judith and the horse, the guardswoman's smirk returned. This time with a much less demeaning air. "Yeah, proof enough."

After another half an hour of reading every last poster on the walls about half a dozen times, and absorbing all the information thereon, Judith watched the big man with a deep voice thank the woman at the desk, and head over to the now half empty waiting area. *Finally, my turn.* Judith slid right into his place. Perhaps a bit too quick, though the woman at the desk didn't appear to notice. She looked up from her work after jotting something down on a form.

"Your name please?" the recruiter asked with a tired voice.

"Judith Travis." She fished out her wallet and handed over her almost expired driver's license. "I'm here to enlist, two of my brothers are already in."

"Oh, good." The woman, who couldn't have been much older than Judith, gave another smile as she accepted the plastic card. "The more the merrier. Have to say, I was a bit nervous before folks started signing up left'n right. We need everyone we can get to help now." The woman only gave Judith's ID a quick examination before she handed it back. After a few rapid scribbles on a brand new form, she looked up at Judith. "You wouldn't happen to have your birth certificate with you? We normally need to see that for you to enlist."

Judith became a bit concerned, rubbing the back of her neck. "Ah, I'm not sure... I don't even know where to find those."

Before she'd even finished, the recruiter waved it off with an unconcerned smile. "Don't worry about it, we can get you in no problem, hun. So what are you thinkin'?" The sergeant asked. "Infantry? Armor? Air? Cavalry?"

"YES!" Judith blurted out, catching herself with some embarrassment. "I mean, uh... Yeah, I'll join the cavalry. Please."

The exhausted woman laughed. "I take it you work with horses, hun?"

"Yessir, all my life. Just rode one 'round this place to prove myself." Judith answered with no small hint of pride.

"Well, alright then, that simplifies things." She bundled Judith's new form together with a couple others and handed them to her. "Just fill these out and wait your turn to get called in, miss. We're going through folks as fast as we can."

"Thank ya, ma'am." Judith took her papers, and slid out of the way quick as she could.

Taking a newly vacant seat, Judith turned at the sound of the metal door swinging open and watched a quite nervous Zoey slink inside. The freckle-faced redhead would've looked out of place in a recruiting station on any other day, a day where half the locals hadn't decided to enlist. Zoey looked over at the waiting area to find a smirking Judith waiting for her with crossed arms.

"I knew you wouldn't leave me hangin,'"Judith said.

Zoey huffed. "Of course not!" she asserted in mock offense. "I would never string you along after all that."

Judith leaned back, marking away on the papers arrayed across her leg, her earlier exhaustion now dissipated.

"Psst, Jude! What branch did you sign up for?" Zoey whispered. Judith's satisfied smirk became a full blown grin, causing Zoey's eyes to widen. "You're kiddin'..."

"Get ready to saddle up, Zo. Cause we're gonna ride into battle!"

CHAPTER 8:
MARIPOSA

Whoever fights monsters should see to it that in the process he does not become a monster.
—Friedrich Nietzsche

Never in a thousand years did Emily expect she would face this. Marched along with Scott and a column of their fellow cops into a fenced-in parking lot outside the county jail. Only five ways in, three walking paths and two vehicle entrances. The Reds had four of them blocked off by large trucks, all heavily guarded. Reds with riot sticks and billie clubs corralled the group through the sole remaining access point, prodding everyone to keep moving at any hint of hesitation. Emily felt a crushing weight dragging down on her shoulders. Meanwhile her heart, her soul, and her mind warred against one another. She knew in mere minutes she would have to confront the most difficult choice in her life. Most of her colleagues, however, knew nothing.

Someone a few paces ahead of Emily broke away and made a run for one of the vehicle gates that led to the streets. She recognized him almost immediately as Officer Jack Pike, famous as one of the best sprinters on the whole force. She remembered working a car chase with him last year. The perp's Taurus hit a median, and he took off toward a suburban neighborhood. Out of eight cops, only Pike managed to get anywhere near they guy, eventually tackling him to the ground. If anyone could escape from these motherfuckers, it was him.

"Hey, what the hell!?" a Red officer uttered as the rogue cop gained distance from the group. Everyone came to a shambling halt and watched. He might've made it almost halfway to the gate before no less than four AKs and two handguns spat metallic death into his back. For just a second it looked like the poor man might've only tripped, before he crumpled into a shuddering heap on the pavement. Still, he tried to get up. But the bullets didn't stop. They chewed up and shredded both his body and the blacktop all around him. A red mist of blood and pulverized asphalt danced into the air with each impact. Only the bellowing of the Red officers halted the shooting.

"Cease fire! Cease fire, damn it!"

"Conserve your ammunition!"

Emily stared at the broken corpse in disbelief. *That happened. This is still happening. How long will this keep happening?*

"Get moving, pigs!" one of the Reds commanded, menacing anyone who didn't move with the bayonetted muzzle of his AK.

As she got walking again, Emily kept staring at the body, not knowing why he would try something so impetuous. She watched as the pockmarked lot became a miniature swamp of blood surrounding the shattered corpse.

"Christ, guys. You think he's dead enough?" one of the Reds chided.

"Fuck you, man! These bitches used to do that shit to us all the time," one of the shooters retorted.

"Well, that one won't no more," a Red officer pointed out. A snicker rippled through the horde of insurgents.

"Bastards! You won't get away with this!" someone shouted from within the column.

Emily felt the collective tension within the mass of her fellow officers. Looking with apprehension at the Reds surrounding them everywhere. She noticed the eyes of a scrawny-looking officer snap to the mob, open wide, and check the expressions of every cop in the crowd. He'd dressed in a black leather coat and cap with a red star sewn on the front, a colorful tattoo of a serpent dragon wrapped around his neck. Really, he looked like some demented reflection of the cops he now tyrannized. Pistol in hand, scanning the group for any hint of the one who'd spoken, never even bothering to demand they step forward. Eventually, he found his mark.

"That one," he called to his troops, pointing to a brown-haired cop. Without another word, two of the Reds swooped in, grabbing the sputtering guy and carrying him over to one of the waiting trucks, shoving him inside.

Although Emily tried to avoid any eye contact or bring attention to herself, she still ended up catching a dark glance from the same tattooed officer by mistake.

Everyone not crazy enough to make a break for it got herded into lines, one behind another, arrayed in front of a large steel cargo container. Once they all had formed up, the Reds instructed them to sit. Scott nudged Emily's shoulder once they'd settled.

"Hey, are we really going to do this?" he asked.

"Don't think I have any choice. There's no way in hell I'm leaving my babies to… whatever it is these lunatics are planning," Emily answered.

"And Rob?" Scott pushed with some hesitation.

"Heh, Rob…" Emily's throat clenched up for a moment. "He and I… are going to have a little chat soon. Once I can talk to him without getting… shot… again."

Scott took a deep breath. "Well, good luck. He didn't seem too keen on listening to you before."

Emily's focus shifted to the shipping container, where a familiar figure struggled for a moment to climb on top.

"Is that… who I think it is?" she asked everyone around her.

"No fucking way…" Scott sighed.

"It can't be, that can't be him!"

"The chief? They got the chief!"

Right before all their eyes, Chief Samuels clambered up to the front of the crate. For a long while he just stood there, straightening a blue uniform jacket stripped of its badge and patches. The shocked murmurs died away.

Clearing his throat, Samuels addressed the crowd of prisoners. "Alright people, we are officially through the looking glass. As of right now, all of our beliefs about the world, and the people in it, are meaningless."

A near complete silence enveloped the whole lot, disturbed only by the cracking of embers, and the footsteps of patrolling Reds.

The chief continued. "Governor Bannockburn is dead. General Manahan is dead. And if it weren't for a few of these 'bleeding heart commies'"— the chief made air quotes above his head— "seeing us as more than evil robots, we'd all be dead too."

The cops' eyes drifted to the dozens and dozens of Reds prowling about the place, watching the assembled mass like a pack of jackals waiting for any excuse to lash out.

"But they have given us a chance… to survive the destruction of the old world, and build a place for ourselves in the new one."

This provoked an uproar.

"What are you, joking? Join with them!?"

"Come on, chief! Don't do this!"

"He can't be serious. Is he serious?"

"They can't just kill us all, that's insane!"

"All this shit is insane, man…"

Emily stayed quiet, looking over the Reds' faces, trying to find Rob. She could tell that her compatriots sitting around her—those who she'd shared a cell with, and heard Rob's "deal" beforehand—all remained quiet. Their faces making it clear they remained trapped in a similar existential debate to the one Emily endured.

A man in a simple gray uniform and worker's cap ascended the ladder to the top of the container. Straightening his featureless coat, the man approached the distressed chief's side. As he strode into the illumination of the burning garbage cans, Emily realized that she'd found her eldest child.

In the flames, she could make out details that she hadn't recognized in the twilight of the jail cell. The upper corner of his left glasses lens had cracked. A set of fresh scars ran down the left side of his face. A bruise marred his chin. But what got to her the most— his eyes. The way they shimmered in the fire. The depths of hatred and anger in those eyes scared Emily.

After giving the rabbling crowd a quick examination, Rob whispered something into Samuels' ear. The expression on the chief's face melted even further, exacerbated in the strange light.

"Look, you don't understand!" he blurted to the crowd. "To them, we're a bunch of worthless scum! Whatever you think of them, they think a thousand times less of you!"

That got everybody's attention. Emily kept her gaze on Rob, whose expression remained unchanged, searching the crowd, until their eyes met.

"They all know that if they fail they'll either be killed or…" he hesitated, only for Rob to jab him hard in the ribs with his elbow. "…enslaved, for the rest of their lives. They don't care anymore." Samuels paused, looking exhausted. "We rise or fall with them, or we just fall. That's all there is to it now."

"What about our families? What happens to them?" someone demanded from behind Emily.

Rob stepped forward before Samuels could speak. "If you join us, nothing," he answered. "If you refuse, they will be placed under the oh-so benevolent care of the revolutionary state. Whereupon, they will be… **re-educated**." Rob let the answer sink into the once again murmuring crowd.

Another voice sprang up. "Hey buddy, you know sooner or later Washington is going to come after you for this, right?"

"Yes they will," Rob answered, still unfazed. "And we will be waiting for them with all the firepower they've stashed away in the mountains and deserts. But you don't have to be."

Emily swore she felt shards of ice tearing through her veins. Her attention got yanked away from her son to one of the trucks, which had moved to allow a new group of Reds to enter. One of them, a young white man dressed in all dark gray and black, strolled right over to the container. At his side walked a African American woman in a California National Guard uniform with a red band around her left sleeve. The striking, tall woman seized the attention of all the prisoners, causing another buzz of chatter as everyone tried to figure out what her presence meant.

"What the hell is going on? Why hasn't this been wrapped up yet?" the man in black demanded of Rob in a tone more irritated than angry.

"Trouble with the lists, Comrade Singh. It took longer than expected to recover all the necessary files," Rob answered.

Singh. Emily had never heard that name. She would've remembered. Not that it mattered now. *So, he's Rob's "boss." Got it.*

Singh examined the mass of helpless cops with a shrewd squint, until his eyes popped open in recognition. A man a few rows ahead of Emily started to stand up, his hands held out in front of him in a begging gesture.

"No! No! No! Wait, please! I-"

The crack of a pistol silenced him in a jarring instant. Emily blinked at least four times as the man fell backwards onto the pavement, twitching for a few awful moments. Vital red fluid pulsed out from a his spasms expired. His last choking and guttering seconds hung in the air for a solid minute. Emily could feel and hear everyone's hearts beating in aggregate over the crackling flames.

Eventually, Singh appeared to realize what he'd done, as a somewhat embarrassed expression creeped across his taut face. For a moment he just stood there, revolver in hand, before at last lowering the weapon. "Well… shit." Singh rubbed the back of his neck with his free hand. "This, wasn't part of the plan."

"What the fuck did you do that for?" someone from the crowd demanded.

"Well, back when our roles were reversed, he killed one of my men in front of me, before then laughing and joking about it. Far before any of *this* started," Singh explained, gesturing all around at the flames and chaos. "No one is beyond the reach of vengeance, children."

The tall national guard commander cleared her throat, punching Singh in his shoulder, causing him to pivot into her icy glare. He winced and turned back to face the crowd.

"Yes yes, very well," Singh continued with a raised hand. "Listen here you pawns of a dying empire, if you don't want to join this cretin, then you must make a choice between military conscription or forced labor. At least, until the end of this conflict. After that, we don't care what you do. You can stay here, you can go somewhere else, whatever you choose,"

It baffled Emily that he seemed... honest? But she couldn't find any hint of deception in his words or face. Only indifference.

"You're saying, that you'll let us go?" someone asked.

"Yes," he reassured in resignation.

A moment passed before another spoke up. "Seriously?"

Singh groaned. "Yes!" he insisted in growing aggravation. "It's far more convenient for us if we don't have to destroy every one of you we come across. Such benevolence won't always be practical, but... you don't need to worry about that. So as long as you don't do anything stupid like... betray us perhaps?" he hinted with narrowed eyes. "We *really will* just let you go... No strings attached. Besides, we could use some people in this army who have at least the *vaguest* notion of actual discipline, and won't do things like create a pyramid of severed heads without any instruction to do so." Singh glared around at all his armed troops, who now looked far more sheepish and less capricious than before.

"What about the lists?" Emily shocked herself even as the words pass between her own lips.

"Ah, yes!" Singh remembered with a maniac gaze, raising a finger into the air. "The lists." He pointed to everyone in the crowd. "Have you ever killed anyone for no legitimate reason over the course of your career? If the answer is yes, then we've got something very special planned just for you," Singh explained, his face a mask of dire, but hidden hatred. "If you haven't, then congratulations, you have a dramatically higher chance of actually surviving the course of this war." An oppressive silence hung over the lot for a moment. "So, why not just do the reasonable thing? You have a chance to live on and join the new world... or you can be forgotten, having died for a bunch of worthless capitalists and corrupt politicians, who don't care about you anyway."

"Alright. Everyone who wants to be included in 'the people,' line up by the gates," Rob instructed. He turned to Emily with an expression that said *"**please** just do this. Don't be a stubborn idiot and get yourself killed."* She knew it's meaning because she'd seen it just days ago, on the morning of the farmhouse raid, when it all began. He'd pleaded with her to stay, to call in sick, and she'd refused. She couldn't afford to ignore him again.

Emily released a shuddering sigh. *Compliance... or death. Perfect.*

#

Paul felt like a man trapped in limbo. Part of his brain still sat locked up in that damned prison. Yet the world continued to turn. Conroy, aka "Maniac Jesus", had somehow appropriated all the most dynamic aspects of the fire and brimstone preaching style, while avoiding the more ritualistic droning that dragged down some other congregations. Harnessing the uncertainty and confusion of the masses. This represented, in the truest sense, a spirit of revival. Paul felt himself being drawn into the fervor, the triumph of the "congregation" all around him. He'd never lived through an out-of-body experience, until now. Something about Conroy's spirit had shaken his long-held cynicism. The speaker's words felt dynamic... iconic... yet human. Dressed in ragged, stained outdoorsman's hunting gear—which had seen extensive use— he looked like a woodland preacher. An American John the Baptist. A prophet for this mad new world. The long shaggy beard, his filthy grease-ridden hair and manic eyes dispelled any doubt of his purpose.

"The end of the age is upon us, children! The heathens and heretics must be cast out of our promised land! Their poisoning of the water and air shall be avenged, their spreading of vile plagues among us shall be undone, and their countless other sins shall be judged!" A wave of cheers washed over the massed crowd of troops and citizens. Conroy spread his camouflage cloak like a set of angel's of wings before wrapping it around himself. "This mighty fortress fell to us faster than Jericho to the Israelites, the Lord shines upon us! We cannot stand by while the Godless continue to plunder all life from this world and spread their unholy plagues!" He cast off his robe, grabbing his gnarled wooden staff from the stage and making a wide sweeping motion. "Revelations 19 verse 11, 'And I saw heaven open and behold a white horse, and he who sat upon it is called faithful and true, and in righteousness he judges and wages war!'" He made another swoop over them with his staff. "We must stand as the righteous hand of God, my apostles, we must trust in the Lord! For he has shown us the way, and vested us with the power to overturn the nations!" More cheers of adulation. "Praise the Lord Jesus!"

"Praise the Lord!" the mob roared in reply.

Paul knew well his own parents would embrace this movement with open arms once it spread to their small Mississippi town. Assuming it hadn't already. Tens of millions of Americans would flock to Conroy's colors, yet tens of millions would not. Paul still held a grudge against his folks for their hand in getting him thrown in the slammer, yet he still hoped they would make it out of all this. Whatever they may or may not have done, they didn't deserve to die.

"Man, can you believe dis? Shit, maybe the world really is endin'." Mason's voice grabbed Paul's attention.

"Oh it be endin', brother. Question is..." Paul lowered his voice to whisper, prompting Mason to lean in a bit. "Is it the 'rapture' kind of end, or just a dead end?"

"Damn. Thanks for the lost hours of sleep, bro."

"The prosperity and power of America has been hoarded! Stolen!" Conroy surged on with his speech a roar of fury and outrage from the crowd. "The elites of Washington have bled us all dry, they've bled the nation dry! Out there, children, lies all the treasure and power of God's earth, sealed away in the vaults of the evil and corrupt! Go forth and reclaim it, for it is yours!"

The mob howled in exuberance, flowing out of the square. Prayers and rejoicing fluctuated like the roiling sea. Then, as Conroy stepped back to take a break, Paul caught a glimpse of a familiar face. The same blond haired man dressed in black and wearing shades whom they'd seen leaving the Norfolk base in an Osprey, now appeared at Conroy's side.

"Holy shit," Mason half whispered into Paul's ear. "That who I think it is?"

"If you think its the guy from the naval base then, yeah," Paul replied.

"That's sketch as hell," Mason stated.

"They did give the place up right after he left, remember?" Paul pointed out.

"True. What you think he's doing here?"

Paul gave a nervous chuckle. "Hopefully the opposite of whatever he... did... last time..."

Paul trailed off as he noticed the shadows all around him start shifting as though time had begun to pass faster than it should. The sun faded away, twilight shrouding the city. The two crusaders looked up. The sky had darkened to night. The sun became veiled by an encroaching disc of shadow and the temperature dropped several degrees as baleful wind washed over the crowd. Everyone stood in place shivering in the gloom, looking to one another in trepidation.

"What the hell is going on?" came a concerned murmur.

"Eclipse?" someone suggested.

"Whatever it is, it's a sign!"

A familiar messianic voice rose up from behind them. " You see! You all see the sign! 'Then the LORD said to Moses, "Stretch out your hand toward the sky so that darkness spreads over Egypt, that darkness can be felt."'" The pair turned to find a transfixed Conroy gazing up at the now smothered star dominating the heavens. Just an eclipse. But it still felt like peering into the abyss of eternity. As though the the eye of the universe itself stared down upon them. "My brothers, we have before us an ordeal of the most dire kind. I hope you are all prepared."

#

Yujing paused, at first suspecting a storm front moving in, as the daylight dimmed and a chilly breeze picked up. Curiosity gave way to bewilderment as she gazed into the clear sky, which continued to darken.

An eclipse.

That answered all questions in an instant. A terrible omen. Both the intelligent and the superstitious could see the celestial phenomenon's portents as self-evident today. No one out on the street wanted to stay there any longer than necessary, certainly not Yujing, who arrived within sight of her goal. The local branch of ABC, where she had hoped to meet up with someone who could tell her more about the situation. But fate didn't seem on her side. Faint white smoke rose in whips from the crumpled roof, every window shattered, every door smashed in, furniture and office supplies strewn everywhere outside. Yujing had seen houses and businesses gutted by looters countless times, but she understood at first sight that this place had just been destroyed.

With more than a little trepidation, Yujing made her way through the battered down entrance, covering her nose as she did. Things were no better inside, everything trashed and singed to varying extents. Burned and soaked papers draped across every surface like mortuary sheets. She found blood splotches on the cracked tile but no bodies. As she made her way to the studio as quietly as she could, Yujing thought she heard someone else blundering around without a care up ahead. Thinking fast, she grabbed a section of piping which had somehow ended up discarded on the floor. The clatter became more loud and random as Yujing approached, giving her a faint hope that it might be a dog or some other animal.

With great care, clutching the pipe to her chest, Yujing took a peek trough the cracked double door into the studio... only to find about the last thing she expected. A middle-aged man with thin red hair, wearing a beyond ruined suit and holding a quarter-full bottle of liquor in his hand, rummaged around through desks with abandon, tossing the contents all around. Yujing blinked several times in surprise, peering in with gradual ease to make sure that no other armed men stood waiting in any of the corners. Confident that she wouldn't be ambushed, and with the suited man still blissfully unaware of her presence, Yujing approached, remaining about 30 feet away, still gripping the heavy pipe.

She spoke up, "Excuse me?"

The man didn't so much flinch as he did flail with a loud, "WOAH!" as he both dove and rolled across the clutter-covered desk he'd been searching, all while still holding his bottle. After landing in a heap on the floor, the man drunkenly staggered to his feet, propping himself up against the wall with his spine. He looked Yujing over with a befuddled mix of suspicion, surprise, and confusion.

Yujing didn't feel quite as worried now, but couldn't quite decide what to say. "Um... are you... okay?"

"Duh... who are you? What do you want?" the man slurred.

"My name is Yujing Huang, I'm a reporter for the BBC."

The man straightened up just a bit, leaning away from the wall. "You're... press?"

"Y-yes?" Yujing answered after a hesitant pause.

"Oh, well... hi Yujing. I'm Don." He placed a hand on his tattered suit jacket, before using it to unscrew his bottle's cap and take a long drink.

"Hello, Don." She looked around in another quick sweep. "Are you alone? What are you doing here?"

"I used to work here, damn it! But due to..." he gestured around at the devastation while taking another drink, "unusual circumstances, I didn't get a chance to pack my things first."

"Where is everyone else?" Yujing asked.

Don emptied his bottle, looked down in disappointment, and chucked it away before looking back up at Yujing. "They're dead."

Though the revelation didn't surprise Yujing at all, it hit her hard in the gut. "Dead?"

"Those Brotherhood bastards descended on the place when it all started and scooped them up," Don explained. "They're either dead or... worse."

"How did you get away?" Yujing asked.

"I hid like a coward," Don admitted, collapsing into a chair and causing it to roll a good five feet away. "A few others tried, but they didn't find me for some reason."

Yujing was at a loss. She'd hoped to get information, or maybe even find some like-minded people to work with. Instead, she found a ruined building... and a broken man.

"Well, what will you do now?" she asked.

"Get the hell outta this country!" Don raised a finger to punctuate his inebriated declaration. "My parents and sister left yesterday, and I'll be gone just as soon as I find some good evidence… or something valuable in this place."

"Why here?"

"I helped make this local station what it was! I got more right to anything here than the bastards who took it all. Besides, my apartment's been ransacked too…"

Yujing sighed, this hadn't turned out like she'd hoped at all. "I suppose I'll leave you to it. Good luck finding a ship, Don."

As she turned to leave, Don's head lurched up. "Wait, have you seen the other guy who came through here? Was he still outside?"

Yujing whirled back around. "Who?"

"Tall Puerto-Rican guy, short hair. He was lookin' for other people too, said he was a combat reporter or some such. Fresh back from Taiwan."

Yujing perked up further. "I didn't see anyone outside. Do you by any chance know where he might've gone?"

Don cleared his throat. "Yeah, I might. Asked me where he might get a drink, after I told him what I just told you. I'll mark the place on a map if you got one, it's near the edge of town…"

#

After a hair-raising sneak through desolate streets and echoing alleys, Yujing at last arrived at her ultimate destination. A seedy bar with an ambiguous name: the Hatch. Yujing didn't know what was going on anymore, but she did know she needed a drink.

She opened the groaning door, casting a beam of piercing light into the smoky gloom of the candle-lit bar. Yujing felt dozens of eyes glide over to the entrance and hone in on her silhouette. The reporter ducked inside and out of the suppressed daylight with haste, making her way over to the bar. A cast of bedraggled characters clung to, slept on, and leaned against the bar, each consumed by his own unique and dire reality. The short, balding bartender with a soul-patch and a trident tattoo on his left shoulder addressed Yujing in a thick Brooklyn accent before she even arrived in front of him.

"Can I help ya', miss?"

"Oh, of course… um… whiskey?" Yujing asked, digging a fan of various bills out of her pocket.

"Ooo… Well, miss… you've certainly been around." He fingered through the assortment held before him, discovering the few Taiwanese dollars within. "Heh, ya even got money from a country that don't exist no more," he noted with a hint of lamentation, before picking out a few Euros. Yujing felt her heart stall out for a few beats and her eyes well up at the mention of her adopted home. "Anythin' else I can do?" Throwing a glass of whiskey in front of her.

"You know, actually…" Yujing decided to take a gamble. "I'm looking for someone who came in here recently. Hispanic fellow, short hair, tall. Military bearing maybe?"

"Hmm…" As the hairy man leaned on the bar, he glanced down at her press pass, which she'd thought it wise to hold out. He then scanned the patrons of his zombie-like business. "Look, miss," he began in a quieter tone. "I could make an introduction, s'not like they're goin' anywhere, but what's in it for me?"

"What do you want?" Yujing asked with thinly veiled suspicion.

"I've been stuck here since this whole mess started! I ain't got a clue what's goin' on out there in the world," the bartender explained. "You take some time right now to have a seat'n tell me what you know, I'll show ya where he is. Like I said, he ain't goin' nowhere."

Yujing relaxed a bit, having a seat on the most stable looking barstool in sight and taking a sip of her genuine American whiskey. "Alright, where to begin…"

For the next couple hours—and it was hours— Yujing unloaded upon the man with everything she'd gathered over the last month of pure chaos. Right-wing militias had seized the capitol alongside mutinous soldiers and placed a

67

puppet regime in charge, religious fanatics had risen up in the south and pried it away from central authority, and Texas had declared its independence. The fate of the West still remained unknown. Everyone seemed either excited or terrified, and no one knew how it would all end up. The bartender poured Yujing more whiskey and some scotch for himself as she spoke.

"Goddamn, those bastards. They did it. They really did it. Most of us didn't think they could, but they found a way. They ran it all into the ground!"

"Who?" Yujing asked, curious as to who's feet this man laid the blame at. "Who ran it into the ground?"

"All of 'em!" he declared in exasperation. "The brass, the fat cats, the politicians! They all did it! God, **we** all did it…" the man rubbed his face with his free hand before downing what remained of his scotch.

"I'm sorry. I know what it's like to have your whole world crumble around you," Yujing said.

The bartender gave a sympathetic chuckle. "Yeah. I guess you do, don't cha?" he sighed. "Well, thanks anyways, miss. I'd rather know everything's burning down than sit here without a damn clue. Now as for our deal, I'm thinkin' that the gentleman over there is the man you're lookin' for." He pointed over to a corner booth with a lone occupant.

Yujing could see the hunched over man wore a U.S. army battle dress uniform like several others in the place, though he looked a good deal more sober than the rest.

"Is he a deserter?" she asked.

The bartender shook his head. "Nah. Came back from Taiwan a few weeks ago, he said. Didn't even get a chance to land on his feet before it all went to hell. He's been here ever since. Used to run around taking videos and pictures, he said. Sounds like he's right up your alley. Seems a solid guy, doesn't like alcohol enough, though. Just gets a couple beers a day and sips on em for hours. Do me a favor, and get him outta 'ere, eh? He needs something to do."

Yujing found her interest piqued. The U.S may have failed Taiwan, but she didn't blame the regular troops for that. The prospect of sharing experiences with someone else who witnessed the fall of the island appealed to her a great deal, though she knew any extended discussion on the subject would have to wait for now.

"Alright, I'll talk to him. Thanks." Yujing nodded and turned to the lonely booth.

She found the man spinning a rifle bullet of some sort on the table with his index finger, the gentle rattling just audible over the bar's commotion. A green-eyed man with a clean-shaven face, black hair, and olive skin. He rested his cheek upon his idle left hand, gazing intently at the brass shine of the bullet casing as it rotated under the glow of the candle flame.

"Um, excuse me? Could I trouble you for a moment, please?" Yujing asked in a polite voice.

After the man's brow furrowed, he looked up with a bloodshot stare. "Sure, miss…" he powered through a slur, rubbing his eyes. "Whatcha need?"

"The man at the bar told me you came from Taiwan?" She chose not to mention the TV station yet.

He grumbled. "Yeah."

"Well, I lived in Taiwan for a long time. I covered the war there… from beginning to end."

The man perked up at that. "Oh, damn. I'm sorry, miss. You have any family there?"

"No, fortunately. In fact, I hadn't been back for some time, I'm a reporter with the BBC. I'm here now because I've been charged with covering the unrest in the U.S. capital," she explained, handing her credentials to the ex-soldier who adjusted his glasses as he inspected the press pass. "Except, of course, now the unrest in the capital has evolved into a nationwide civil war, and I need a local who can guide me…" she trailed off as she noticed that the man was staring up at her with huge, unbelieving eyes.

"You're a reporter?"

"Y-yes?" Yujing answered with more than a little hesitation.

"And you need someone who can show you around, help with your stuff, keep you not dead?" he posited.

"Yes! I've already been between a few cities on the East Coast, but if I want to discover what's really going on out there I need to travel much farther—"

"Where do I sign up?" he blurted.

Yujing shook her head, blinking. "Uh, well… nowhere. I just—"

"Great! There's no time to waste!" he gathered up the rucksack next to him in the booth and slid out. "Let's get going!"

Before Yujing could utter another word, he'd flown out the door at a speed that should've been impossible. The mystified reporter chased after him, the laughter of the bartender following her as she did.

"Wait! You haven't even told me your…" Yujing emerged from the dark bar to find him standing in the middle of the empty street, in front of a stripped and looted SUV.

"What the hell? I didn't think it was dark out?"

"Eclipse!" Yujing told him as she arrived at his side.

"Eclipse? Then it's a sign, girl! It's a sign!"

"A sign of what?"

"I'm a reporter, you're a reporter, we were meant to meet here! In this place, in this time! We can shine a light on the darkness for the whole world to see! Don't you understand!? It's perfect!"

Well, I did have to track you down…

Once again the spellbound man gazed up into the sky at the fleeting moments of the eclipse that Yujing had almost forgotten about. The far off shooting and explosions that Yujing wished she could forget hung over everything. After a few more moments, he turned to face Yujing with an already sobered face.

"Jose, Jose Everett," he at last introduced himself with a firm handshake, "I was a 25 victor, combat photographer for the army. I recorded everything for the higher ups from the ground. But I did my share of fighting too."

"The man at the bar said you came from Taiwan…"

"Yeah. Bad times." He nodded. "And your name is…?"

She straightened up a bit. "Yujing Huang, from Hong Kong originally."

Jose nodded, an empathetic glint in his eyes. "Well, Yujing, where is it you wanted to head first?"

She thought for a second, "Well… the word around the campfire is that the Saints are going to make some big declaration in Atlanta after taking Richmond and Norfolk. I think that sounds like something worth recording for the world to see."

"Sounds good enough for me." He shrugged, heading off toward a dilapidated garage to the left down the block, slinging the bulging rucksack over his shoulder. "You know, Ms. Huang, you might've just saved me from disappearing into the mire for good," Jose told her with an almost whimsical smile, staring off down the street.

"Oh. Well. wonderful!" Yujing tried to keep the nervousness out of her voice, wondering what she'd just gotten herself into.

#

As a waft of sand assaulted the cracked glass of the Humvee's window, Alexander recoiled from the opening. Even the land itself wanted them to suffer and perish.

Alexander watched his ever expanding de-facto unit crawl through the dust, his mind wandering to something he'd tried to keep at bay. His girlfriend, Samantha. *Sam.* What could have become of her? *Anything.* He knew it wouldn't help to delve into the rabbit hole of possibilities, but he couldn't help it. He missed her. He worried about her. He thought about how she looked in that red lingerie she loved so much. Did she worry about him too? Was she already dead? Had she looked to some other man for safety and comfort?

Before he got too distracted, his savior appeared in the form of Derrick. "Hey man, we've got trouble. You okay?"

Alexander's brain switched gears back to the present. "Yeah, I'm fine. What do we got? Locals?"

"Yes an' no. The Syrians have linked up with the Iranians, and word on the street is that they're gonna move to cut us off from Israel."

Alexander sighed. "No shocks there. Any chance we're going to beat them to the border?"

Derrick rubbed the back of his neck and shrugged. "It's gonna be close..."

"Damn. The Israelis?"

Derrick shrugged. "We've made radio contact with one of their border patrols, so they know our situation. But who knows when they'll get here in force?"

"Can our air run interference?" Alexander asked, climbing out of his vehicle.

"Not if we still want to have anything left for later, sir."

Alexander surveyed the ground of these Lebanese borderlands, having in hand the only two maps of the area they possessed. The Israelis had occupied Lebanon, and this sparsely populated region north of Damascus provided the easiest rout into Israel proper. A long ridgeline of scorched rock ran more-or-less from northwest to southeast, a deep ravine below its northern face. Just over a klick to the west, a dried out riverbed surrounded by steep banks. A few scattered hills and dunes. Aside from that, sand, sand, and yet more sand.

Better than nothing. "We'll post two companies up on the ridge and hold them off from there until everyone can get across the border. Or until the Israelis arrive."

"What if they don't give a shit?" Derrick wondered aloud.

"Oh they'll care. At the very least least they'll care about the Iranians entering their territory," Alexander assured. "We just need to hold out until they show up, or the last of our people slip away."

Derrick leaned up against the command Humvee. "You think they'll help us get home? They'll want at least some of us to stay."

Alexander held back another sigh. "We'll work out something. Haven't we talked about fighting one battle at a time?"

"We may not have a choice for much longer, man." Derrick walked up to Alexander, "Once we leave Israel and get to Europe, what then? What if we can't get back home, or if there really is no home to go back to?"

"Have to take it as we go, I'm afraid. We just don't have enough information yet," Alexander conceded. He hated flying by the seat of his pants, but what choice did he have? Since leaving Kuwait, it felt like they hadn't gotten a chance to breathe. Endless raids, endless skirmishes, endless foraging for fuel and basic supplies. Getting into Israel lingered just beyond their reach, taunting Alexander as his troops faced a grim future if the depravations went on.

Big bullets for the armor running low, aircraft munitions almost exhausted, small arms ammo sufficient... for now. Food rations growing scarce. But, the greatest concern of all: water. Without water, nothing else mattered. Alexander chuckled under his breath, the most powerful war machine in history, and they couldn't escape the all-humbling power of the life giving liquid. Despite having followed a river for much of this time, it hadn't mattered since the water had long become tepid and undrinkable without extensive purification.

They could still delay the Iranians though, at least for a little while longer.

#

The illumination of the thermal goggles turned the desert into an alien wasteland of blues and scattered greens. One by one, a series of glowing red blobs appeared on the waving horizon of dunes. Heat signatures. The Iranians had arrived.

"Contacts at 600 meters," an even voice reported over the radio.

"All callsigns hold fire until targets close to 400 meters. We need to conserve ammo."

Moments passed, the red splotches grew larger. Alexander pulled himself away from the display and peeked over the humvee's hatch, out into the abyss of night.

Nothing. Darkness. Wind. Metal treads clanking, rattle of engines, footsteps.

Alexander took a deep breath. *Just breathe... wait...*

Something flared up just beyond the dunes. Then another...

"500 Meters..."

"Choose your targets—"

70

Flashes. More flashes.

Alexander's eyes shot open. He ducked back into the Humvee and grabbed onto the radio with desperate hands. "Now! Fire **now**, damn it!"

The second the command left his lips, Alexander could hear the whistling of rockets and shells for just a moment, before every weapon around him roared into the ether. A few heartbeats passed before the first Iranian shell detonated along the ridge. Looking back into the thermal, Alexander watched as multiple red heat signatures bloomed into flame, and the others began to advance even faster.

A tank to Alexander's right erupted in sparks and torn steel. SAMs ascended into the night sky, accompanied by tracers of auto cannon shells.

"Keep back from the edge, shoot and move boys!" Alexander commanded over the radio.

The disciplined M1 commanders started "poking" their turrets just above the ridgeline to fire, before backing away and maneuvering to their alternate positions. This caused some confusion in the chaos of darkness and combat as vehicles bashed into each other. Still, they'd planned for it. The idea: to present as mobile a target as possible, for as little time as possible.

Alexander's Humvee lurched as it reversed away from the ridge, just in time for them to get slapped by the shockwave of an Iranian ballistic missile. The warhead had landed around 50 meters away from the ridgeline itself, blasting a huge chunk out of it in the form of a crater so blatant it could clearly be seen even on the NOD. Sand and dust flooded in though every last opening of the Humvee.

Looking back into his sight, Alexander watched as yet more red shapes appeared, flashing as they hurled ordinance at the American positions. Looking up, he could see the zooming flashes of aircraft on both sides as they struggled to support their comrades, as well as engage in de-facto dogfights with each other.

"Contact to the southeast! They're trying to flank us!" Eagle one informed him from the night sky.

Alexander whirled the scope around in response. Sure enough, more heat signatures. Lots more. Helicopters too. *Shit!*

"Withdraw! Right flank, redeploy southeast!" Alexander barked into the radio before turning to his driver. "Get us out of here!"

"Yes, sir!"

The Humvee peeled away from the ridge just in time to avoid getting flattened by a retreating Abrams that came flying over just behind them.

"Better make that withdrawal fast, Captain! Things are starting to get tricky up here!" Lieutenant Ford called in from his Apache.

"Dump all the AA you have on the choppers! The choppers!" Alexander ordered.

More SAMs twisted up into the sky, prompting countermeasures to rain down in response. Scattered flashes as the American missiles found either their target or a flare. A few flaming wrecks spiraled into the barren ground. Rockets streamed out of the sky, blasting apart in the midst of Alexander's men as they scrambled to face the new oncoming threat. The night disappeared across the battlefield as dozens of strewn metallic skeletons blazed uncontrollably. Chaotic pyres repelled the darkness, crackling and roaring as all their remaining ammunition cooked off. Each pulse of every inferno cast dancing shadows of men and their machines across sand and stone.

Alexander had hoped the plan would hold up longer, now he needed a new one. One that got them the hell away from here ASAP. The only cover they could hope to get behind came in the form of an old dry riverbed, or as the Arabs called them a wadi.

"We got more drones coming from the west!"

"Move it to the riverbed! Cover fire!"

The ordered movement became more of a scramble as men rushed to escape the open desert while strafing runs tossed up the sand in sporadic rows. Another SCUD came crashing down just a few dozen meters away from a tank, a

Bradley, and a Stryker, obliterating them all in a mushroom of high explosive force. More missiles streamed overhead from the west, passing the Americans by and causing havoc among their pursuers. The Iranians rushed to the now abandoned ridge just as the first American tanks and IFVs charged down the wadi's slopes to escape.

"New drones are friendly! I think the Israelis have finally noticed us!" Ford reported.

"Great, just hold on for a little longer boys!"

Alexander ducked down, covering his head as chunks of shrapnel punched through one of the Humvee's armored sides and out the other.

"ARGH! Shit!" The driver cried out, grabbing at his right arm and bending over. Alexander grabbed onto the wheel with both hands, trying to hold it steady.

"The gas! Keep your foot on the gas!" he screamed at his driver. Some kind of round came through the roof and pierced right back out through the floor, just inches from his right foot.

"I got it! I got it!" The driver promised though his teeth, clutching his arm with closed eyes.

The Humvee rocked and bucked as its speed increased and the wadi became closer. A shell launched a cone of sand into the air just ahead of them causing Alexander to jerk the wheel, careening the humvee out of the way. Alexander's world narrowed down to the banks of the withered riverbed, all the tracers flying past and the explosions tearing up everything around him. It all melded into a singularity of blurred chaos. A few more .50 caliber rounds pierced the Humvee's body, one of them destroying the headrest of Alexander's chair, a shot that would've killed him had he not been leaning over holding the wheel for dear life.

After what felt like an eon, Alexander and his unfortunate driver plowed the battered Humvee through the sand embankment and down into the wadi. They slid between a pair of Abrams tanks and numerous dismounted infantry trying to re-establish themselves as the rockets and shells continued to rain down. Now that Alexander could process the radio chatter again, he realized at once that things had deteriorated to a dangerous extent during the ad hoc relocation. Frantic orders and desperate demands for orders monopolized the airwaves. When the hummer got stuck in the bottom of the wadi, Alexander managed to get hold of the microphone again.

"Everyone dig in as best you can, we've got no more cover to fall back to!" Without waiting for a response, he tossed the mic aside and turned to his driver. "Let's go! If we stay here we're dead!"

"No arguments here, sir!" the young man replied as he climbed out the passenger side, still nursing his bloody arm.

Alexander tore into the makeshift medical area that the medics and camp followers had set up hours ago in preparation for the fight. Humvee ambulances parked spread out from one another, surrounded by layered tents. His driver, without a word, headed inside one of the ambulances as Alexander made his way to the mobile command post aboard a modified Bradley, the BCP. His new steed.

The scream of Mirage jet fighters passing low overhead toward the east sent Alexander running right back outside to watch as a whole squadron unleashed their loads of ordinance on the enemy's advancing armor. *The Israelis really are here then, took them long enough.* Squads of infantry lying and crouching along the edge of the wadi cheered as napalm and high-ex lit up the desert like daylight for a moment.

Alexander watched through his goggles as the enemy forces that had flanked their position on the ridge were now themselves outmaneuvered by a fresh force of new arrivals. It could only be…

"The Israelis?" he asked the first man he saw, the de-facto intelligence manager of the caravan.

"Yeah, the IDF has finally arrived," Agent Price answered.

"Iranians and Syrians are pulling back, sir!"

Without warning, another row of bullets rained down from above, tearing across the wadi and puncturing the armored hulls of several vehicles, including ambulances. The flaming debris that remained of one of the drones responsible smashed down into the sand beyond the burm. Alexander turned back over to the makeshift medical ward, to the ambulance he'd just left behind, and saw it in flames. Nothing emerged from the wide-open back doors.

Turning away, he returned his attention to the BCP's command display. He'd have to mourn later.

"Goddamn. This is lookin' bad… they're still turning back though. I hope we're not chasing after them?" Captain Warwick asked.

Alexander closed his eyes, holding back a deep sigh. "No."

A moment passed where the crackling of flames and snaps of cooking off bullets dominated Alexander's mind.

"Gather all the wounded in whatever vehicles have room, and let us know where they are." The voice of Dr. Bowman commanded over the radio.

As suddenly as it began, the exchange of fire died away as the hostile army melted back into the night, the remaining American air cover sticking close to the wadi and the Israelis not venturing much further.

"Looks like we managed to survive yet again, jefe. I hope we aren't using up all our good luck."

Alexander almost chuckled at Escobedo's attempt to ease the heavy feeling in the air, but he couldn't allow to laugh even a little right now.

#

A squad of Merkava tanks emerged from the churning dust, the lead vehicle approaching the parked BCP as the others came to a halt. Alexander, Price, Nakamura, and Warwick stood outside their command vehicle, waiting as the column of troops and refugees flowed westward off to their right. As the lead Israeli tank stopped in front of them, the commander's hatch popped open and a thick hairy muscular arm shoved it aside. A blast-scarred face peered out over the Merkava's cupola, scanning Alexander up and down, before its owner lifted himself out and onto the tank's upper glacis. For a long moment, he stood there and looked everyone over, then he took a decisive leap onto the sandy ground.

His eyes never leaving those of his counterpart, Alexander stepped forward. The two met between their respective clusters of machinery, each alongside a gang of subordinates. Alexander took off his helmet and braced it at his side, noticing the rank insignia on the other commander's epaulets.

"Captain Harris, U.S. Army. In command of elements of 7th Cav, 8th ID, some ash-and-trash, and far too many civilians. We appreciate the help, Colonel." Alexander extended his right hand with the best smile he could manage. "I'd have a lot fewer men left alive live without it."

At first the colonel looked between Alexander's face and open palm, before at last the suspicion melted just a bit and he accepted the handshake.

"Colonel Daskal. It was my pleasure. I'm just glad you are able to see reason."

Alexander felt his eyebrow incline. "What do you mean?"

The colonel waved it off, as if dismissing a heap of foul-smelling garbage. "There have been some small contingents of Americans raiding along our borders, shouting over radios, blaming us for everything. Agh! Ridiculous!"

"Well, we don't want any trouble with your people. You have my word."

"Hmph. Good. One less crisis bearing down on our heads!" Daskal chuckled, peeking behind Alexander. "I hope you are ready to get on the road to Israel, they will come back eventually and getting all of you through Lebanon will take at least a day."

Alexander cleared the dust from his throat. "Of course," he turned to Nakamura. "Are we ready to move out yet?"

"Yeah, Bowman's had the casualties rounded up and we've grabbed all the vehicles that are still working," his fellow captain answered with a heavy voice.

"We will return later for anything that can't be moved." One of the Israelis standing behind Daskal piped in, a bookish young fellow with thick glasses and a thin mustache.

Alexander regarded him with curiosity before turning back to Colonel Daskal. "We'll follow your lead to wherever it is that you want us to work things out."

Daskal nodded in approval. "We are to escort you to Haifa. I imagine most of you want passage to Europa, yes?" he turned back toward his waiting Merkava, "As for what the 'brass' and politicians will want in exchange for said passage…" the colonel shrugged.

In his natural habitat, Daskal bounded right back up onto the tank, rallying his forces with a pointed finger spiraling overhead. His fellow Israelis flowed back into their respective vehicles as they broke away, heading off the the south and west.

Alexander turned back to his BCP just as a Bradley marked by blackened shell impacts crawled up to the assembled leadership. Escobedo jumped out the back of the battered IFV and rushed over to Alexander. "Hey, we managed to catch something after the shooting stopped— the Hadjis left 'im behind..."

The captain watched as two of his soldiers hauled a wounded man in a black Iranian Revolutionary Guard Corps uniform with an OD sandbag tied over his head out of the Bradley. He belonged to the IRGC, an elite military unit, intelligence force, and a bunch of other things all packaged together. Not a surprise to see them involved here... taking one of them alive, though?

Alexander removed the bag from the soldier's head and looked over his bloodied face. The bearded man's sharp eyes betrayed the same hatred and fear that Alexander had seen dozens of times. But, some kind of confidence and control lurked beneath the surface. It would some time to get **anything** out of this man.

"IRGC, you're sure a long way from home, aren't ya?"

"Not as far as you, Yankee," the Iranian pointed out with an impassive smile.

"You're now a prisoner of war. I'd advise against trying to escape. A lot of my people had friends in Kuwait City," Alexander told him with narrowed eyes.

The prisoner nodded in silence, his escorts leading him back to the Bradley. After he'd watched their prized catch leave, Alexander sighed and turned to Nakamura.

"How bad did we get hit?" he asked.

Nakamura said nothing. Alexander turned to see the man rubbing the back of his neck, trying to find the words.

"Come on, now. How bad?" he pressed.

"We're still trying to work it out, but at this moment it looks like... around... 10%," Nakamura managed with sunken eyes.

Only the sounds of whirring engines and helicopter blades filled the air. At length Alexander found his voice.

"One... in ten?"

"Yeah."

More silence.

"Let's... let's just get out of here," Alexander said at last.

"Yeah, there's nothin' here for us now," Nakamura added.

Damn, ain't that the truth.

CHAPTER 9:
GATHERING STORMS

"Those who make peaceful revolution impossible will make violent revolution inevitable."
— John F. Kennedy

The flame-wreathed disc of pure twilight transfixed Emily's soul, even as her torso lurched back and forth with the rhythm of the old army truck's suspension. As the deuce-and-a-half negotiated the brutal terrain, its 24 passengers swayed into each other like wasted choir members, with their collective gaze locked on the heavens. Dusk gripped the whole land despite the midday hour, the air now cool like the onset of a hurricane. Her new "comrades" remained fascinated by the celestial occasion, chattering and whispering with tones conveying both fear and excitement. The ex-cop took off her cap and ran a hand through her dirty, sweat-mopped hair before wiping it off on her new "uniform." A sandy brown workman's jumpsuit that looked, felt, and smelled a century old. Each shoulder featured a crude red star made by cutting the shape out of some felt and then gluing it into place. Emily grumbled, at least they hadn't taken her favorite hat, or her boots. Though they had removed the S.P.D. S.W.A.T. team badge from the front, and had replaced it with... nothing. *Guess I'm not even worth another fucking star.*

The only other piece of gear she had received so far: a beige and red Arab-style scarf, so dingy that it looked more like yellow and pink. One of the guardsmen had called it a *shemagh*, but to Emily it looked like a dishrag her grandmother would've used. She couldn't decide if the scarf or the coveralls smelled worse. For now, Emily had it wrapped around her neck, ready to defend her nose and mouth against the swirling dust she knew would pose a serious problem. Getting her hands on some sort of eye protection, one way or another, sat at the top of her priority list. Of course, she still didn't have a weapon. Neither did many of the others riding in the truck with her.

Emily and her fellow conscripts had good reason to feel anxious. She'd expected to have at least some of her old equipment—and weapons—returned upon accepting the Reds' deal. No dice. Instead, the commies told them such equipment had to go to more "reliable" forces, and that they would have to make do with what the state could manage for now. In California nobody could easily go house-to-house and collect guns, because most of them were owned illegally. For now, the quality weapon taken from of the "imperial state" needed careful deployment, and these guys had to round up and use every last one they could make functional. And so, Emily sat there, dreading what the "revolution" might ask her to do, but knowing that she couldn't fight anyone without a firearm.

And of course, there was the guilt.

Emily hated herself. She felt disgusting.

Not a single thing had gone the way she'd hoped. Their great operation to take down the insurgents and end their reign of terror over the state had ground down, even before the botched raid that ended in her own botched execution. By the time she woke up, "law and order" as she knew it had become an distant memory, and she found herself greeted with a fait accompli.

After chasing her family across the overrun city, dodging the angry rabble, she'd managed to reunite with her children against the odds... only to have them ripped from her arms. By Rob, her own son. Now they could be anywhere. Her only comfort lay in the knowledge that they still lived. Emily couldn't do anything to about it.

The universe had stripped her of her identity, her freedom, her home, her dignity... everything. She had existed as a strand of the thin blue line, the barrier between order and chaos. And chaos had won in a matter of days. With Emily powerless to stop any of it.

She'd sold out every one of her friends and colleagues who'd gotten killed by these crazed savages, for nothing more than a chance at survival. The fact that thousands of others had done the same gave her no sense of consolation. She embraced anger—deep anger— as the only way to keep herself from choking up. Taking on the Reds had transformed into an impossible task in the span of three days, instead she would just have take it out on anyone who they happened to set her against.

Three days. Scott told her it had taken just three days for everything to fall apart. It still sounded impossible. Even as she sat surrounded and confined by its consequences. Although **it** remained an amorphous entity in her mind. Emily had never followed politics, to her it always felt like a disingenuous circus of corruption and horse-trading. One side stamping the other down to prop itself up. Since the the war though, everything had become much more complicated. So much more visceral. Extremists pushing in so many directions, and they had all received the same treatment by the police.

But now... Emily had no choice but to learn, and fast. Unless something drastic changed yet again, her fate and that of her whole family seemed tied to the success of this movement. Yet she had no idea what success meant to these people, or what they would demand of her. She'd heard bits and pieces of information of course, most from her own colleagues, that the commies wanted to make everyone's pay the same, that they wanted to turn America into an economic basket case, that they wanted to throw everyone into Gulag work camps for political incorrectness and other such nonsense. But this Red revolution had used sheer overwhelming force and brutality in their seizure of power, not package bombs or protest signs. The ruthless efficiency with which they had executed the takeover led Emily to believe those "facts"—accepted as gospel—represented nothing more than right-wing punditry. Emily didn't know any leftists... apart from Rob. But he'd told her so little that she really didn't understand her son's connection to this movement, or why he and so many others seemed so ready to kill and die for it.

Rob...

Now Emily had become one of them too, whether she liked it or not, and she believed it in her best interest to at least find out what they actually wanted, and why. Then, maybe she could bring some vestige of sanity to this shit show.

Got to get him alone, somehow...

The geriatric squeaking of the truck's airbrakes announced their arrival as the hulking slab of Cold War steel came to a lurching halt.

"Everyone, up! Pile out!" a voice commanded from the back of the flatbed.

Emily groaned and rose with everyone else as two dozen people blundered out onto the dusty ground. She could see as she stood up that their truck had pulled in along with ten others outside a gutted fuel station that the Reds had turned into some kind of apocalyptic workshop, with even more trucks parked in dispersed groups. Piles of guns of every caliber and variety, magazines, loose bullets, grenades, and all manner of melee weapons covered a set of tables which waited under the gas station roof, surrounded by gas-masked guards. There Rob stood, dressed in a grey army coat with black trousers and a visored cap with a blue crown and red band, busily conversing with the man Emily assumed ran this place. The fellow in question, a burly Hispanic man, wore a tattered wife-beater with brown cargo pants, his face dominated by a dense handlebar mustache.

Her son and the presumed gunsmith conversed in a broken mixture of their two languages, somehow appearing to more-or-less understand one another, as the mob of hundreds of unarmed conscripts thronged around the heaps of weapons. The handful of Reds already standing there, very much armed, blocked them from just walking right up and taking their pick of the goods, causing Rob to finish up his conversation just as two desert camo Humvees skidded into the lot.

Emily watched as the same African American woman she'd seen earlier at the jail parking lot glided out of the armored vehicle and strode across the fractured, blistering asphalt towards the tables of assorted arms. This woman bewildered Emily more than anything else so far. How could she so completely turn her back on everything they'd stood for? On the oath she and her fellow guardsmen had sworn? As the general approached, Emily could see that if this woman held any reservations about her choice, she hid them well.

"Alright! Everybody line up into rows of ten!" the tall woman bellowed.

For a moment the crowd just looked around at each other in reluctant confusion. Rob groaned and rubbed his forehead. For her part, the ex-guardswoman looked none too pleased.

"Uh… who the fuck are you exactly?" someone questioned from deep within the mob.

With a mild twitch in her brow, she stepped to within a few feet of the horde. "Who the fuck am I!? I am General Jasmin Harper— of the Red Army! **Singh** has put me in charge of you ragbags! And the first step of turning you from a rabble into an army, is to get organized. So I repeat, everybody get into groups of ten, and LINE THE FUCK UP!"

No hesitation this time. After a chaotic scramble, Emily found herself in a row between a towering white dude on her left, and a young Latina who stood a few inches shorter than herself to the right. The blue-eyed man sported a five o'clock shadow and tattoos of barbed wire veins running down his neck, his broad muscular frame raked with various scars. A crudely dyed brown prison jumpsuit with the number patch torn off revealed his identity as an ex-con. Emily appreciated the oppressive heat for the first time, as the sweat it created served to mask her own nervousness. The girl seemed less intimidating, black hair tied behind her head with a red bandanna, an oil-stained green mechanic's jumpsuit serving as her makeshift uniform. A hood rat. Emily took in a deep breath.

Okay, so… what comes next?

As the last of the rows blundered into form, yet another pair of ancient deuce-and-a-halfs rolled up on the opposite side of the station's overhang. The trucks deposited around fifty men and women, wearing the same blue and red cap as Rob, who craned his head in the direction of the lined up recruits as the new arrivals passed him by. Armed with riot batons, billie clubs, and two-by-fours they flowed through and among the rows, shuffling people around between groups, breaking them up, and reforming them anew.

It took Emily a couple minutes of covert observation to realize what these soldiers connected to Rob intended: they wanted to break up any groups of similar people, rearranging them with others who looked nothing like them.

"Listen up!" Rob shouted in a voice like gravel. "I am Comrade Bennigsen, your friendly neighborhood Commissar." Somehow, the crushing weight on Emily's soul became even heavier. "In a moment you will approach the tables by platoons, and you will receive your weapons! Your platoon is the line that your ass ends up standing in!" He paced up and down the front of the arranged ranks, speaking above everyone's head so all could hear. "The man or woman that rode in here in one of those trucks is dead! From here on, none of you are white, black, brown, yellow, blue, or green you are all RED! In the eyes of our enemies you are the scum of the earth, the lowest of the low! Vermin, deserving only of extermination! They brand you as such for the heinous crime of lashing out against those who would starve and enslave you!"

Emily blinked, hearing such a screed from Rob's own mouth somehow managed to throw her for a loop, despite everything.

Rob went on. "They will underestimate us! They will seek to demoralize, divide, and destroy us! They will stop at nothing to achieve their goal of domination over the whole world for all time, and use us as their pawns to keep it!" He paused. "But… we are going to prove them wrong! We will outlast their arsenal of tyranny, and their campaigns of lies and terror! We will turn their own weapons against them, and forge new ones from whatever we can! We will crush their wicked systems of exploitation, and haunt the nightmares of their minions! Either we will be free, or they will be ruined!"

A gradual wave of cheers erupted from the haggard rows of misfits, themselves surprised at the enthusiasm that Rob had created from thin air.

"First platoon! Step forward!" Harper commanded once the noise had died down. The beckoned troops approached, got weapons and bags shoved into their arms, and were then shunted along towards the back of the loose block of lines.

It didn't take long for Emily's unit to get called forth.

"Ninth platoon, forward!"

Her line snaked over to the far end of the tables, and the process began. The large man beside her went first, and got handed what Emily could tell counted as a light machine gun. An archaic looking design soldered and welded together from all manner of non-firearm components, including corrugated metal which made up the barrel shroud, and a shovel's handle, which had taken the place of a stock. The man gave his hulking new weapon a brief look-over, grinning in bemusement as he gave the thing a solid whack, and it *didn't* fall to pieces, much to Emily's surprise. Satisfied, the man grabbed his two bags of magazines and moved along, allowing Emily to take his place.

Without even standing there for three whole seconds, the joint-smoking, dreadlock-wearing Black man in front of the tables tossed a rifle and a burlap sack into her hands. Emily looked down at the weapon she now held, and felt her heart sink. An M1 Garand. The semi-auto, full-bore rifle that had served as the standard main infantry weapon of the U.S. Army… in the Second World War. Almost ninety years ago. The only modification? An ACOG scope jury-rigged to the top.

"Are you… are you kidding—?" Before she could say another word, the "armorer" shoved her along, and handed an RPG with a bag of rockets and a Mac-10 to the Latina behind her.

"Remember, anything you find in the field is yours to use. For now, we just have to make do," Rob told everyone, though Emily felt like he'd spoken to her directly. "You will all have to play to each other's strengths, and cover each other's weaknesses. Now, our first objective as part of the Revolution is the liberate the southern valley from a Christian cult," he went on to explain with a frightening grin. Emily looked down at her ancient rifle and gulped as Rob continued. "You see, these cretins believe that the whole world is ending, rather than just the empire. So they've taken the logical, well-reasoned course of ritually sacrificing any outsider that their leader claims to be the Antichrist— in the name of their false god."

As Rob explained, a wave of murmurs washed over the horde. Some angry, others confused. A good many sounded worried. Emily found herself blinking at the overt backhanded slap against Christianity, and her stomach churned at the prospect of getting sent to fight a doomsday cult with the most obsolete weapon she'd ever imagined using in a live-fire scenario.

Shit.

"It falls upon us to save those trapped under their insane rule, and protect ourselves from whatever horrors they might unleash upon us… *unbelievers,*" Rob declared. "And once they have been dealt with, we will move on to Los Angeles, then San Diego, then Vegas, until every one of our cities is free from the hated Profligates!"

Another cheer arose, and a new set of characters filed out to take charge of each "platoon." The man to assume command of Emily's unit turned out to be a Black man in his early forties with a Fu Manchu mustache, wearing an older digicam army cap and a green surplus coat from a passed era. A veteran. *Odd…*

"Alright people, I'm Sergeant Coleman. Now let's back onto the truck, we'll get to know each other on the way."

#

Harper watched as the final platoon of her latest "Banner" filed past the tables, getting dealt the anarchic mess that made up her available armory. Heaps of scrap-built guns, every kind of Russian arm imaginable, a grab-bag of U.S. military weapons from across modern history, alongside piles and piles of type-95s, the dirt-cheap Chinese assault rifle that Harper had become all too familiar with. She sighed. *I guess I should be happy they have **something**.* Harper knew that units of well equipped and experienced Reds existed, wearing gas masks and heavy armor often times. She'd been chasing them up and down the coast during the insurgency, but Singh had chosen to keep those troops close to his chest and out of her hands. *No surprises there.*

The arrival of yet another tattered jalopy roused Harper's curiosity, then shock as none other than Singh himself appearing through the arid wind, his eyes now hidden behind a pair of mirrored aviators. Harper groaned, straightening her cap as she headed over to his entourage.

She aimed a withering glare at Singh, then demanded in a ragged whisper, "Is this really the best we can do?"

Singh groaned, not so much at Harper as the universe itself. He cast aside the filter of a roll and shook his head. "Unfortunately, yes. Most of the stockpiles we've gotten control of so far had already been cleared out to equip the forces in Taiwan. We've taken a few further inland along with much more supplies, but we haven't been able to link up with them just yet."

"And we're working on that, right?" Harper hinted with crossed arms.

"Already being taken care of." Singh assured with a hand wave as he watched the jumbled columns of rebels pile back into their various transports. "Trains can only be put back in order so fast you though," the revolutionary sighed, no more satisfied with the state of things than Harper herself. *Good, one less thing I have to twist his arm over.* Singh turned back to her with an expression of resignation. "Well, at least the cultists haven't got any artillery, armor, or anything that flies. Still, you should be careful. Crazy is its own kind of dangerous."

"You would know, huh?" Harper prodded.

Singh scoffed. "Nonsense, I just puppeteer the crazy ones. At least it won't make too much difference for now. Who knows? Maybe we'll even manage to preserve the craziness while imposing just a tiny bit more control over them. Enough to manage their impetuosity, anyway."

"Oh, I don't think it'll be too hard, given enough time…" Bennigsen offered with just the vaguest tinge of optimism.

"Between the three of us and the overhanging threat of extermination, I'm sure we'll manage," Singh declared with returning confidence.

A man in a long ragged coat with the disfigured features of a plague survivor, stumbled after his platoon, carrying bags and boxes of ammo. The haggard fellow tripped and fell to the ground with a pained grunt. He lay stuck there for but a moment before one of his comrades following behind yanked him up to his feet.

"Yep…" Singh continued, "I think we're gonna get along just fine."

"So, what *exactly* do you want us to do?" Harper asked, watching the carrier scuttle off.

"Eliminate the hostile presence by any means necessary," he answered on reflex, igniting a wrap. "Most of the young women and children should make suitable candidates for reeducation, so take as many of them prisoner as possible." Singh took a long draw and released a huge plume of smoke followed by a slight cough.

"And… the men?" Harper inquired with a raised eyebrow and rising concern.

"The men are totally expendable," Singh responded, waving it off. "Kill any of them who don't surrender immediately."

Harper stood blinking for a moment as it dawned on her that Singh based his objections to the killings in the city on pragmatism, not any altruistic or universal concern for human life. *What was all that about women being easier to brainwash!?* Harper felt a snarl crawl up her face.

"Why do you think the men will be so much harder to 'convert,' or whatever," she prodded.

"For the same reason that my kinsmen stood idly by for centuries while yours languished in repressed poverty," Singh answered as he took out a Cartier Diabolo pen and a notebook bound in leather. "Until now."

The eyes of the various assembled commanders and commissars grew wide, glancing between their two leaders with obvious unease. Harper spoke in a tone that could've ground stone, her face molded into a stoic mask.

"That being?"

"It's immeasurably easier to convince someone who is oppressed by a structure of power to turn against it, than it is to convince someone who is isn't **actively** being oppressed or perhaps even benefits from said structure, to do so. Whether or not said benefit is actually real." he explained, while going through his book without bothering to turn around. "These guys essentially believe that women exist to serve as breeding stock, and treat them as such. With enough time and… *perseverance*, I have confidence that most of them can be made to see the way."

"These motherfuckers think that they're living the way that God meant them to. They don't even know how fuckin' evil they are," Harper admitted.

"I did say capture any that had the sense to give up, didn't I? And to kill anyone who didn't regardless of gender. There are *always* exceptions after all," Singh agreed.

Harper noticed for the first time the absurd quality of the pen Singh used, "That's a nice fuckin' pen. Where'd you steal it from?"

"Well the governor is dead, so technically I 'looted' it from his office," Singh responded without looking up.

The incredulous Harper didn't get a chance to respond, a distinctive whirring sound began to rise over the marching of boots and the rumblings of vehicles. She turned to the sky with a jolt as two squadrons of three Guardian drones tore overhead. The other Reds became nervous as the guardians hummed over the hills, all except Singh of course.

"As you can see, the drones have been restored to full functionality."

"So, your eggheads got all the drones working again?" Harper groaned. "And what's to stop the Feds from using those damn things to pull the same shit on us that you did to them?"

"Something that you…" Singh said, pointing to her with his luxurious pen, "don't need to worry about for now. Just know that if such a breach of control occurs, they will immediately self-destruct. No muss, no fuss, boom." He made an explosion with his right hand, still holding the pen.

Before Harper could dig further into why this dude was so ready to use a weapon system that had been terrorizing him mere months ago—and how he even could—a wild racket assailed her ears that she hadn't heard in what felt like eons now. The chopping rotors of an approaching Osprey. Harper didn't even get a chance to look around as three of the aircraft appeared above them, having come in low and fast over the hills and mountains. As they hovered in to land, throwing up an appalling wave of dust, both Singh and Bennigsen shielded their faces with their coats. At first Harper thought to poke them for being pansies, until she realized the two were in fact protecting their glasses from getting sandblasted.

"Worthless," Singh grumbled aloud as the rotors spun down and the artificial hurricane died away. "I want to know how he knew where I was," he said, turning to Bennigsen.

"I'll see what I can do." The commissar answered with an uneasy voice.

"Who's this?" Harper inquired. "More of your friends?"

Singh sneered as he straightened his coat. "Certainly not."

Harper watched as the rear door of the center Osprey lowered to reveal a pair of well equipped soldiers in all black who disembarked in short order. But as they took up positions on either side of the door, a third man stepped out from the shadows of the Osprey's unlit interior. He stood over six feet tall, wearing a black overcoat longer than Singh's, black fatigues, and of course… the shades. A pair of Sunglasses so dark that Harper could see almost nothing through them at all. His gravel-like voice felt like a perfect match to Harper.

"I don't know how you plan on defeating anything with an army that still looks like an angry mob, Singh," The Man in Black said.

"You say that as though I have some other choice available to me," Singh retorted. "Besides, it isn't a state of affairs that will last any longer than it has to."

"That may be too long, especially since you refuse to organize them into a real fighting force."

"I already explained…" Singh took a joint out of his coat. "The military's organization scheme is incomprehensible to anyone who isn't 'in the club' as it were. More importantly, it's a scheme that our enemies *already know*."

Harper realized for the first time that dozens of armed Red Army fighters had "decided" to just loiter around the area, watching the new arrivals like fixated addicts.

The Man in Black gave a dissatisfied grunt, before pivoting in Harper's direction. "You must be the general I've heard so much about."

Harper shot Singh a glare, only to receive a look in reply that made it clear the Man in Black had heard nothing from him. She gave the obvious g-man a sideways glance. "Funny, I haven't heard anything about you."

"I wouldn't figure. Singh here isn't too proud of associating with us. Even though he understands it's for the best."

"And why is that?" Harper asked with narrowed eyes.

"Because we've provided immeasurable assistance to you and others like you," The Man in Black explained. "And when people refuse to see reason, they don't tend to remain around for long."

"The hell's that supposed to mean?"

"It means that all of you have a role to play in the great transformation this country is undergoing right now," he gestured back towards the trio of Ospreys where his men had begun unloading a series of steel crates, "provided you remember who your friends are."

"Yes, and what is it that our... *friends* want this time?" Singh inquired.

"We want you to remember, Singh. We want to at least try and follow the plan a little better?"

"Your plan?"

"**The** plan," The Man in Black ground out. "The plan where you bring the more dangerous tendencies of your movement under control." He turned back to Harper. "This is the best we could do for now, but I will try to get more to you soon."

Before Harper could ask anything, a pair of black-clad soldiers dropped a huge steel crate in front of her and flung it open to reveal shoulder fired missile launchers of both the anti-aircraft and anti-tank variety. Harper felt her jaw almost fall open at the sight of such cutting edge weaponry, then her eyes narrowed with suspicion.

"Why?"

The Man in Black gave a bitter sigh. "The United States is dying, General Harper. There's nothing anyone can do to stop that now. Our goal is to try and facilitate the transition from the world we know to... something else."

"What else?"

"We don't know yet," The Man admitted without shame. "But you're going to be a part of it, whether we like that or not. And that means you all get a seat at the table." He turned back towards the Ospreys. "Soon as there's a table to sit at anyway."

"Was there anything else?" Singh prompted.

"As a matter of fact, there is," The Man in Black stated. "The Brotherhood has taken power in D.C."

"How shocking," Singh replied in mock surprise.

"Yeah, I know..." The Man groaned. "Look, the point is, they've ordered everyone back to the Eastern Seaboard to deal with the Saints and the Popular Front. So almost everyone east of the Sierra Nevadas has cleared out."

"Almost?" Singh queried with an arched eyebrow.

"There are a couple mountain divisions who've decided to sit tight in Utah and Arizona. They're tough customers, you may want to try reasoning with them."

"Well of course we'll try," Singh mused, "but it's up to them to actually be reasonable."

The Man in Black grunted, heading back toward one of the now emptied Ospreys. "Just remember to get things more under control."

Before anyone could question it, all of the figures dressed in black had filed aboard their aircraft, which spooled back up and took off towards the desert faster than Harper had ever witnessed. Harper, Singh, and Bennigsen just stood there and watched the three Ospreys disappear over the dust-coated mountains, a sense of dread even more palpable in the air than normal.

"So, if those guys aren't our friends, who are they?" Harper asked after a long moment.

"What they are is *useful*," Singh clarified in a bitter tone. "Which, by the way, is exactly how they perceive us."

"Fuckin' fantastic."

"They're just one more obstacle we've had to put up with until now. Don't worry about Shades Man and his Illuminati wannabes," Singh assured with an icy voice.

"Oh I don't need to worry about the people who just gave us this like it was no big deal?"

"No. Because our greatest advantage over them is something they don't even know exists," Singh asserted, moving on before Harper could question further. "Now then, I'm off to deal with that supply issue I mentioned. Shouldn't take more than a few days to sort out. Have fun!" He waved, turning back to his ragged car followed by just three others, the rest remaining behind and heading off to assume their respective positions in the horde. Bennigsen remained by Harper's side. An odd sensation.

"You sure its a good idea to deal with that alone?" Harper asked. "We've got a lot of self-propelled guns…"

"Already bringing them," Singh told her as she followed. "Only three, don't worry. And I'll be bringing a few of your friends along as well. Just in case."

Harper frowned at how Singh could both give a reassurance and make a threat in the same sentence. "Boy… you're lucky I'm so damned jaded."

Singh grumbled. "Yes, yes. You can't stand me and all that. I'll be back soon with some better toys. Then we can decide how to deal with the marines in Camp Pendleton, yes?"

Harper felt her skin go cold. "Right… the marines…"

"Relax, General!" Singh told her as he climbed back into his jalopy, "So long as **I** leave the soldier-talking and overt ass-kicking to you, and **you** leave the backstage work and… less battle-related murder to me, none can stand before us!"

#

Yujing missed home. The clatter and sway of the ancient Amtrak Crescent served as a sharp contrast to the smooth and punctual locomotives of Asia. The Japanese systems in particular put these American rail carriers to shame. Yujing had spent almost three years in Tokyo after first getting her job with the BBC, and she personally considered the Shinkansen Line to be one of the island's greatest contributions to the progress of humankind. Although Japan existed as a vassal state to America for nearly a hundred years, so much of Japan's infrastructure seemed eons ahead of the empire's own capital. It served to illustrate a truth which had just started to become realized in Yujing's mind.

The U.S. was dying.

Ever since she had arrived, Yujing had scrambled from one story to the next, fighting just to learn **what** was happening. She'd never gotten a chance to ask **why**. This war, terrible as it appeared and would no-doubt become, seemed more the end of a process than a spontaneous disaster. Despite the enormous political and religious differences between the various factions, they'd all been motivated by a common set of factors that dominated every aspect of life within the nation. The totalitarianism manifested in the form of poverty, the absence of opportunity, and a corrupted parody of justice. This had led Americans to abandon any real desire for national unity, even if many didn't appear to realize it. Of course, everyone hated the state… but they hated each other almost as much.

"Hey, Yuj," said Jose, rousing her from a daydream.

"*Yuj*?" she asked with incredulity. "You know my name. Why do you call me *Yuj*?"

Jose shrugged in surprise. "Uh, you know. Short for Yujing?"

Yujing bristled.

"What if I called you *Ho*?" she poked with a raised eyebrow. "Short for Jose?"

"Yeah, yeah fine. No nickname," Jose conceded.

Yujing straightened in her chair a bit, satisfied. A long pause followed.

"What about *hermana*?" he posited.

Yujing took a deep breath with closed eyes before turning back to Jose. "*Hermana*?"

"Spanish for sister," he explained with evident embarrassment.

She decided to meet him halfway. At least he didn't seem motivated by arrogance. Softening a bit, Yujing answered. "That is acceptable, sometimes."

"Sometimes. Got it… hermana," Jose smiled. "I'll get better."

Yujing looked back out the window, rolling her eyes.

"We'll be at Peachtree Station soon. It's a ways away from the Mercedes Stadium, so we gotta find some bus or

82

truck or something to get there," Jose explained from the seat next to her. Another tremor resonated through the train, putting Yujing on edge. "Take it easy. We got a long day ahead of us, si?" Jose encouraged with a grin.

"How do you know Atlanta so well?" she asked.

"I was stationed at Fort Benning for a couple a years, we used to come down here and kick it all the time. Its a party town!"

"Of course," Yujing glanced down at his intertwined yet empty hands. "Shouldn't you have your gun ready? For when we arrive?"

Jose looked at his overstuffed rucksack in the corner as it wobbled with the rhythm of the train, then back to Yujing, his eyes wide with realization. "Ah, well see... I... Don't have a weapon right now..."

For the first time since meeting the ex-soldier, Yujing's face became stone-cold serious. "You don't have anything?"

"Well, I got my KBAR. But no firearm."

"No gun?"

"Nah, I had to turn mine in to the armory when I got back to Cali," Jose told her.

"But don't all you Americans have your own guns?" Yujing demanded.

"I didn't have any money before I joined up, and what I made ain't worth shit now," Jose admitted.

Yujing pouted in frustration. "Marvelous, so I'm being protected by the one American without a gun in the middle of an American civil war."

"Hey, hey no worries! We'll find some weapons in the city. Rednecks always have guns fallin' out of everything," Jose promised. "Besides, I've got a camera, you've got a camera, people won't have any problem with us!" he assured her.

"I thought Americans are supposed to have fairly negative views on the media?" Yujing asked. "Yet, while plenty of the people I've met since this all began have been suspicious of me, the open hostility has been less than I expected."

"Yeah, well... people hate the 'mainstream' media for all kinds of reasons," he explained. "They don't hate the concept of news or media, just the version that they been stuck with." He grabbed a canteen from one of the countless pouches on the outside of his pack. "So! What's the plan?" Jose asked in an attempt to change the subject. "What is your mission here in the 'land of the free'?" A chuckle escaped his lips before he took a long drink.

Yujing became lost in deep thought, she hadn't gotten much time to consider her ultimate goal. It didn't take long to recognize the historic opportunity that lay before her. "People across America, all across the world will be desperate for any information about what's happening here. Speculation will be rampant, everyone will twist whatever information is available to their own ends. If we can create a broad picture of who is fighting, where, and why, then *we* can fill the void with the unveiled reality. It might even convince some people to help."

Jose's eyes grew wide. "What, you think you can change the world? You think the news can still do that?" he asked. "And I guess the fact that we'll both become crazy fucking famous? Well... that'd be a happy coincidence, huh?"

Yujing became flustered. "I didn't think about it that way, you..." she struggled for an appropriate derogatory term. "...you, **yank**."

"Yank? You might as well call me a goddamn Aryan!" he laughed, "I'm half brother and half Puerto Rican. I ain't no damn colonizer. But, whatever." Jose waved her off.

A lurching jolt informed them both of the train's deceleration.

"Are we there, or has this relic just broken down?"

"C'mon," Jose grabbed his rucksack and stepped out into the aisle. "Let's go talk to some loonies."

Yujing came out behind in a quiet huff, following him to the end of the packed train car. She knew little of this Conroy man, save that he'd been in and out of jail multiple times. And in a collapsing authoritarian state, what better savior could America's faithful ask for.

You know, that train doesn't seem so primitive anymore... Yujing mused as she clutched for dear life onto an improvised cargo rail welded to the roof of the decrepit school bus. Cruising through the teeming and fog-blanketed streets, drinking from her water bottle, blinking the moisture from her eyes. They passed ruined building after ruined building, a few even covered in plastic tarps, having been condemned due to viral contamination before the war even began.

"You alright?" Jose asked, sitting opposite her. He leaned against his rucksack, hands behind his head with a smug expression, until a pothole erased it.

"Just fine..." Yujing grumbled, wiping away the sweat from her brow.

"Pretty good weather for Georgia, wouldn't want to be here in August," Jose added, looking around at the throngs of religious zealots, militia, and common citizens streaming around the old bus as he chewed on a piece of stale beef jerky. The roof had a tarp wrapped across so that riding on it could at least be tolerable, but the steel's heat still seeped through. Some of the people on the street dressed like pilgrims of old and carried great crosses over everyone's heads, made of everything from glittering gold to pairs of two-by-fours nailed together. An apocalyptic Mardi Gras, with candles, torches. Street preachers sang the praises of those responsible for the *glorious* victories across the region, declaring that angels walked with them and of course, that God was on their side. A general hum of enthusiasm radiated through the masses, varied as they were. The roof of the bus had become seating for over a dozen other people in their shared desperation to reach the stadium.

As she scanned the shopfronts, office buildings, and apartments, she saw all kinds of flags featuring the Christian cross which festooned countless windows and streetlamps, drifting in the rainy breeze. A massive example of THE Christian ecumenical flag draped down the front of the Bank of America Plaza like the sail of an old ship. Heaps of papers and computer towers burned in bonfires with biker-looking characters piling more fuel upon them. *Not a bank anymore, or ever again by the looks of it.* The sickening toxic smell of burning plastic, paper, and gasoline wafted over the bus as the pitiful breeze shifted direction, prompting Yujing to look away and cover her face. Jose didn't notice in time.

"Ah, damn!" he coughed. "That's nasty as hell!"

Every imaginable variant of flag hung from... well, everywhere, even the bare walls and billboards had gotten covered in graffiti of Christian icons. No way to mistake what ultimately dragged these people together, despite their numerous and fascinating differences.

Yujing took in the surreal atmosphere of this city embracing its perceived past in an effort to face and withstand the terrible future that hung over everything. She perceived herself more than ever as an outsider, and felt relieved that no one else seemed to notice or care about her presence. The transcendent experience of apocalyptic societal rebirth consumed all their attention. In Yujing's eyes, she might as well have gotten dropped into a new dark age Europe, but with far superior firepower.

"Has this been happening at all before now?" Yujing shouted to Jose over the chaotic ambiance.

"Not really..." Jose answered after some thought. "I mean they held protests and rallies and whatnot, but this shit is somethin' else!" His equal astonishment at the scene playing out around them somehow both reassured and concerned Yujing.

"You really think they're going to go after the government in Washington?"

"Who knows? Let's see what Redneck Jesus has to say." He pointed down the street, toward an silver dome peering from between the buildings. Atlanta possessed very few skyscrapers outside the immediate downtown area, so nothing could distract from the bizarre and imposing hexagonal shape which sat almost alone like some grand altar. Searchlights ringed the whole perimeter of the stadium, projecting their beams through the morning fog and into the heavens to form columns of light encompassing the whole premises. Among them, stood tanks, armored cars, and gun-toting rebels with weary faces, the sheer number of acolytes putting them on edge as they knew full well the potential for catastrophe should anything go awry.

"Have you ever been to this stadium before?" Yujing asked Jose, drawing his attention away from the "columns" of light.

"Y-yeah, couple times," he answered. "I watched a couple football games there 'fore I got deployed. Hell of a thing, huge, never envisioned the place as a church though…" he trailed off.

Yujing watched in anxiety as the river of humanity flowed into the building's entrance, pulling a pair of latex gloves and face mask from her coat pocket.

#

Whatever Yujing had mentally prepared herself for paled in comparison to what awaited them inside the huge arena. Some hopeful occupied every conceivable place where one could stand or sit, with a square platform that sat at the center of the field as the only open area in sight. Now Yujing could remember what this all reminded her of. Over a year ago, the BBC had sent her to Saudi Arabia to cover Murmim al Ealam—the latest in a line of recent claimants to the long-defunct Caliphate—on his Hajj to Mecca. During his spiritual pilgrimage, he had called for all Muslims to stand together against corruption and tyranny, both bywords for American influence in the Middle East. To Yujing, the ocean of people who had flocked from across the Islamic world to hear him speak before they circled the Kaaba appeared all but identical to these desperate Christians. If what had followed al Ealam's Hajj across the Middle East served as an indicator, the madness had yet to begin.

Yujing gripped Jose's rucksack with her left hand to avoid losing him, raising her handheld camera up with her right. For the first time she had an opportunity to use the gift given to her by the Captain of the *Birmingham Maiden*. She panned across the whole stadium, capturing the electrifying scene for later. *Don't see any other cameras…*

"Hey!" someone shouted from behind her. "You with the camera! You press?"

Yujing's head spun around to find a bearded man with an AR-15 looking her over. *Too late to lie now.*

"Eh, yes? We're from the BBC," she answered with all the confidence she could rally.

"Aw good!" A battered smile exploded across his face. "There ain't that many of ya. C'mon this way, we'll take ya up to tha fancy club suites. Ya'll can see everything from up there."

Without any real choice, the duo of reporters followed the the gun-toting hillbilly up multiple packed staircases, through overcrowded lobbies, and into an enclosed box seating area. Maybe the only part of the whole arena not filled beyond capacity, yet still quite crowded. Yujing took a seat in one of the few unoccupied chairs near the window with Jose following close behind. Frayed wires snaked down from the ceiling in place of the massive TVs which had hung there, probably now in some looter's hoard. The bar, ransacked with tipped over glasses scattered everywhere, crushed beer cans of almost every brand, and countless cigarette butts mashed onto every flat surface. Someone had passed out in a corner, slouched against the wall, a bottle of top shelf whiskey in hand. The raucous bedlam of the stadium billowed in through a shattered window, which still had a stool hanging halfway out of it.

Of all the people in the suites, most looked like they had once sat near the upper-lower strata of society. The former "middle class." Of the few other reporters Yujing saw all came from America, most of them from East Coast and Midwest.

Yujing melted into the most comfortable chair she'd gotten to sit on in weeks, letting go a deep breath, allowing the noise wash over her. Looking up, she noticed Jose still stood. He contemplated the empty chair without moving, then Yujing saw the steak knife buried in the cushion. After a moment he pulled it out and tossed it aside, then took his seat.

"Well, looks like these guys have had some fun," Jose noted.

"You could say that…" a drawling voice drew their attention off to the right, where a man in a black t-shirt with a plate carrier stood with a somewhat embarrassed expression on his bearded face. "Sorry 'bout the mess. Most'a these boys've never sniffed a place like this in their whole lives 'fore now."

Before Yujing could respond, the sound outside had begun to die away. She aimed her camera down at the one spot she knew would be the central focus of all attention. A bearded man in a rough beige robe carrying a walking stick ascended onto the small platform, helped by two others. Taking slow deliberate steps, he entered the center of the de facto stage, resting his hands upon his walking stick and taking in the sea of followers who surrounded him.

"My brothers, I cannot tell you how overjoyed I am, that so many would hear the voice of God and rally together in these tragic times. For only together can we survive!"

His voice cascaded though the massive bowl of a structure, assisted by the speaker system which the Saints had somehow gotten working again. A ripple of cheering affirmation spread across the stadium, until Conroy raised his hand, causing the near absolute silence to return.

"We all know that Jesus once said 'a house divided against itself cannot stand' right? Abraham Lincoln knew that. He reminded his countrymen of that the last time they had cause to turn on each other. But what no one ever brings up because it does not suit them, is that Jesus told us not just that a house divided against itself could not stand, but that *every* kingdom divided against itself is brought to **desolation**." He allowed the more complete proverb to sink into the collective mind, a wave of concerned murmurs confirming his success. "**Every** kingdom, **will**, be brought to *desolation*." Another pause, more whispering. "Now, there is much debate and discussion on how to intemperate this or that part of the good book, as there *should be*! If God intended us to all read it the exact same way he would've had the Bible written like this throughout. Because if you ask me, there ain't a whole lot to interpret there. Pretty direct, isn't he?"

The crowd vocalized their universal agreement.

"But we have fallen into the same dream the Romans did, and the Greeks before them, and the Egyptians before them even, we all know the story of Pharaoh and Moses. What we have in common with them, and every other empire after those, is that we fell victim to the imperial dream. That we were the greatest there's ever been, that we knew all there was to know, that our way would go on and on forever and that we would never have to change. Ignoring our sins instead of repenting for them. Pushing away those in need instead of guarding them. And here we are." His voice became quiet at the end, remorseful even. "Here we are standing at the end of our world, huddled together for safety. Scared for the future, for our children. Staring down the barrel of a gun held by an unspeakable evil. But we are not lost, children! For we do not just stand at the end of the world we knew, we stand at the dawn of a new one."

Surprised muttering flared up around the arena.

"Just as our ancient forbearers did when they spread the word of Jesus through an empire crumbling under the weight of its own sin and corruption, we have the chance to shape that new world. To light the way for those who come after us, that they might fare better than we did."

The crowd voiced its approval. They seemed to like the idea that the whole world wouldn't end after all.

CHAPTER 10:
HOSTIS HUMANI GENERIS

Feelings of superiority always stem from an illusion.
— Marty Rubin

The road through Lebanon felt like it went on forever. Alexander had spent most of this journey gazing out a tiny window slit at the abandoned devastation passing him by, simultaneously keeping an ear open to the radio. Colonel Daskal had only called in once to warn him about Hezbollah making a SNAFU of things along the road at one point. They passed some burned-out buildings and the aftermath of a checkpoint ambush, but no one came after the convoy as it drove through. Not a soul around. Just more empty streets and ruins. Even after crossing into Israel itself the emptiness remained, save for the occasional IDF patrol or checkpoint—friendlies. *Finally in allied territory again, at least in theory.*

For their part, the Israelis seemed in the midst of preparing to withdraw. Troops with crates running back and forth between buildings and vehicles, trucks loaded up with cargo lumbering in a general southwest direction, helicopters lurking over the city amid the gloom of a pre-dawn sky. Daskal hadn't told him anything more, and Alexander didn't need to ask. Defending friendly territory under siege from several directions? Hard enough. Holding enemy land at the same time? The worst.

"Hey, Harris." Price grabbed Alexander's attention. "I'd like a chance to talk to our Iranian guest before we hand him over to the Israelis."

"Who said we were going to hand him over?" Alexander shot back.

"Well, I mean they're going to more-or-less demand we do that as soon as they find out we have him," Price explained with an almost embarrassed face.

"Hmm, yeah. That'll be fun, I'm sure," the Captain mused with bitterness. "Take as much time as you need once we get bivouacked, but I get first crack. We need to figure out who the hell he even is. Lucky we managed to capture anyone."

Price nodded. "I'm hoping he knows something about Kuwait. Not counting on it, but we'll see."

Derrick then entered the main cabin from the driver's compartment and gave Alexander a head-to-toe. His eyes bore the distinct strain of concern as he raised an MRE in each hand.

"'Chicken and noodles' or 'Spaghetti with Beef'?"

Alexander's own tired eyes narrowed, his lips curled. "What desserts do ya have?"

"Carrot pound cake and a cinnamon bun."

"Ah, gimme the spaghetti. I guess I'll take a cinnamon butt plug."

Derrick chuckled. "A what?"

"The damned desserts in these MRE's are so dry they make me constipated."

Derrick tossed Alexander the two packets as his laughter subsided. "How ya holdin' up, sir?" he asked.

Alexander dragged his hands across his own face, wiping away sand and crust. "Well enough," he answered while tearing into the MRE bag with a sneer. "You?"

"'Bout the same," the Lieutenant sighed, taking a seat across from Alexander as Price went back to work on his briefcase laptop. "I might be Jewish, but I don't trust the Israelis. You ask me, at least half of this shit is their fault."

Alexander nodded, taking a swig from his canteen, "Been thinking about what the Israelis will demand before they send us home," he said, rubbing his eyes. "No avoiding it, really."

Derrick nodded. "I'd figure they'd want some of our heavy equipment, gear maybe." He scratched his head. "They're not in a position to be generous, so I don't blame them. But, depending on what we find back home, **we** might need that stuff."

Alexander nodded, forcing himself to swallow the revolting spaghetti ration. " And as our spook pointed out just before you walked in, they'll also want us to hand over the prisoner."

"And... you don't wanna do that?" Derrick presumed.

"Not yet," Alexander clarified. "If there's even a chance he knows anything about Kuwait or anything else, I ain't givin' that up to anyone."

"Fair enough," Derrick conceded. "Just make sure the Israelis don't find out, sir."

The captain groaned. "Yeah, I'll do my best. For whatever it's worth." *Wouldn't be surprised if they already know about him.*

The exhausted squeal of the BCP's breaks announced their arrival in Haifa. All three men had stood and collected themselves by the time the ramp dropped.

Alexander had nothing comparable in his memory to the scene awaiting them. A Scramble to pitch tents and unload wounded—in just the narrow area available between warehouses and dockyards—played out all around them. Most vehicles had at least a few blast marks from shells or missiles, some had whole chunks blown off and had lost their battle-worthiness.

The calibrated American death machine that had inflicted appalling devastation upon its enemies while receiving minimal losses itself—had disappeared. The psychological effect created by this huge loss of advantage had Alexander worried. *Last thing we need right now is some sort of mutiny, or even more deserters making things complicated.* He didn't think them cowards or anything, but such volatile circumstances could affect anyone in drastic ways.

The Merkava with the blue scorpion came to a stop in front of them, Colonel Daskal sitting in its open hatch.

"Get your people tended to, American. We will talk shop in the morning," Daskal said.

Alexander hid his surprise. "You don't want to talk now?"

"Agh," the Colonel shrugged. "The head monkeys are still making up their minds. Don't worry, American, you won't get stuck here." And with that ominous reassurance, he rode off.

It didn't take long before a humvee rolled up right next to the newly raised command tent. Alexander hoped no one noticed as a hooded and bound man got dragged from the vehicle and ushered inside. The captain took a deep breath as he started making his way over, Price following close behind.

The inside of the tent had almost nothing except a steel folding chair, bought from a Kuwait Sports Club employee while on RR a while back, one of them occupied by their unknown prisoner. A guard stood on either side of him, his hands tied around the chair's backrest and a black bag covering his head. *Just like Abu Ghraib. Perfect. Wonder how long it is 'till they call me a war criminal.* A single electric lantern illuminated the tent. Alexander just stood for a moment, watching as the man sat in silence, barely moving except to breathe.

In a single motion Alexander took another step forward and pulled the bag from the prisoner's head. Again the shrewd, piercing, impassive eyes stared up at him, green and gray like a shrouded marshland.

"We meet again, American," he said, smiling through his sand-flecked beard.

Alexander took a seat on the empty camp stool across from the Revolutionary Guardsman. "Take those off of him, please." The soldier to his right, one Private Flores, took out his K-Bar, pointed down it at the prisoner, and cut off the plastic handcuffs after the slightest moment of hesitation. The prisoner remained impassive as he watched the knife move around him. Focusing his attention back to the Iranian, Alexander responded. "So, you're happy to see me again?"

The prisoner rubbed his raw wrists. "I figured you'd hand me over to the Jews by now," he answered flatly.

"I haven't decided yet. Depends on whether or not you cooperate." Alexander scanned for a reaction, but saw none. He continued. "Let's start with your name. You got a name?"

The response came in an instant. "Bahram. Bahram Farzan."

Alexander cracked a quick grin. "Okay, Bahram. I'm Captain Alexander Harris. You took off your insignia before you were captured. Care to tell us your rank, General?"

Farzan smirked. "No General. Nevertheless, I followed standard procedure. Surely you don't expect me to believe you would've done any different?"

"Nah," Alexander admitted. "In your shoes, I would've done the same."

A short pause. Alexander could almost see the calculations going on behind his eyes. Then Farzan spoke. "Lt. Colonel, I.R.G.C. intel division."

That made Alexander's eyes flash open. "Intel, huh? Didn't mention that earlier."

"Of course not," Farzan said.

"What were you doing so close to the front lines?"

A slight twitch. Not much, but Alexander caught it nonetheless. Farzan answered after a moment. "I don't like being too far from the action. Too easy to become detached and... soft."

Alexander nodded. Not a lie, but not the whole truth either. "Well then, if you're an intelligence officer, that means that you might actually be worth keeping around." He leaned back on his stool with a smirk.

"I know about Kuwait City," Farzan declared out of the blue.

Alexander's expression morphed into one of stunned incredulity. "Well shit," he leaned forward again. "That was awfully forthcoming of you... do go on," he urged with a heavy air of skepticism.

"You get nothing more than that, until we reach an agreement," Farzan stated.

Alexander scoffed in response. "And why should we believe that you know anything about Kuwait other than that it happened? Why the hell should I stick my neck out for you instead of just handing you over to the Israelis!?" he demanded.

Farzan gave a small, but supremely confident grin in reply, then revealed, "Because that is hardly the only thing I am aware of. There are a great many forces moving against you and your Jewish friends, American."

Alexander's eyes narrowed. "Such as?"

"Such as the drone and LPV attack intended to strike Israel's supply lines in their most vital point..." Farzan's grin became a full blown smile. "The attack that will strike here, in Haifa."

Alexander's eyelids flew back open. "How the hell do you even know—"

"Please," Farzan shook his head. "The air is thick with the smell of the sea, and we arrived here in less than a day. Even the Jews aren't crazy enough to dump you in Bahrain, so this must be Haifa."

"And you say that your people are going to attack the port to shut it down?" Price asked for clarification.

"And the Syrians, of course," Farzan answered.

"Of course..." Price scratched the chaotic stubble on his chin.

Alexander decided to just challenge the Persian's story. "Bullshit."

Farzan leaned back, shrugging as his grin dissolved. "Makes little difference to me I suppose. Shot by you, tortured to death by the Jews, or destroyed by the bombs of my own people."

Silence loomed in the empty tent.

"You ain't tellin' us anymore without a deal then?" Alexander asked.

Farzan's smile returned. "No."

More silence.

The blare of a ship's horn washed over the tent.

After a long wait of contemplation, Alexander stood up from his stool. "Well, we'll have to check out your story and mull this over. Do stay put would you?"

"Oh perish the thought, American. Where would I go anyway?" Farzan assured.

Alexander nodded to the guard to place a new pair of zip-ties on, then headed back outside with Price once again in tow.

"Okay, what the hell!?" Alexander hissed, trying his best to keep quite. Not a hard thing with the ongoing bedlam.

"Is that how these things normally go, Price?"

"No, Captain," Price stated with certainty. "It is not."

"Well, how the fuck are we supposed to find out if he's full of shit or not?" Alexander prompted, already knowing he wouldn't like the answer.

Price sighed with a resigned expression. "I'm afraid we only have one way of doing that, sir."

"Perfect." Alexander rubbed his forehead, thinking. "Alright, we gotta find Daskal. We'll tell him that we recovered the data from a *dead* Iranian officer that we found after the border fight."

After another moment, Price nodded in agreement. "We have to play this very carefully, sir. Who knows what the Israelis'll do if they realize where we really got the tip."

Alexander groaned. "Let's do our best to never find out."

As the odd duo headed for the BCP to use its powerful radio, Alexander spared one backward glance at the command tent. *This guy had better not be feeding us a line just to save his skin, or he'll become Daskal's problem. But if he's not, this could be the break we need in figuring out just what the hell is going on.*

#

Paul hated feeling out of his depth. The only comfort he had for now lay in the knowledge that nobody else understood how they had gotten dumped into this situation either. Another rocket crashed down to earth, launching a column of dirt and debris which rained upon everything and everyone. Another suburban home—empty, thank God—blasted into oblivion. A stream of tracer rounds shredded through the roofs of several other homes, killing an unfortunate pair of snipers who had posted up on them.

"Stay down! Stay the fuck down!" Paul commanded, diving behind the engine block of a wrecked SUV.

A shout came from the right, down the street. "Baker!"

Paul turned to find Mason sprinting towards him, M4 in hand. He slid into the irrigation ditch just behind Paul's SUV. A mortar shell blasted a crater into someone's front yard, compelling everyone to hug the dirt as five more fell like giant sledgehammers up and down the street. Paul abandoned the SUV and joined Mason in the ditch.

"Captain, there's Feddie tanks and MRAPs tryn'a cross the river to the west!" Mason practically screamed into Paul's ear. "Command wants us to push them back!"

Paul tried to gather his thoughts. He knew the devastating cost to his troops if they counterattacked U.S. forces. The troops themselves harbored no illusions about the horrors they faced going forward, and it fell to him to make sure their sacrifices mattered. Managing this hell lay in his hands. His troops' lives were his responsibility.

"Let's move west, people! C'mon, them Feddies are tryin' to flank us! Couriers, gather 'round!" A group of five young and lean characters, three men and two women, huddled around the recently promoted Captain. Close enough to hear what Paul said, but not so close as to get turned into fertilizer should a shell land on his head. "Okay, we'll do this real careful-like." He stood up, turned west and broke into a run. All the couriers looked on in surprise, then began to follow him. He slowed to a jog to let all the wandering unit members catch up to him. As they converged around, Paul reverted to a fast walk and began speaking, "The company will divide into three, we'll surround their bridgehead and pressure it from every direction," he explained using his hands and arms to identity the various locations he referred to. "Our first job is **not** to wipe out the Feddies already on our side, but to keep them engaged while preventing any reinforcements or resupply from reaching them." He noticed one courier taking mental notes. "You, kid! Get your notebook out, all this shit is important!" The embarrassed youth rushed to whip out a notepad as instructed.

"Any more details, sir?" one of the Couriers asked in expectation.

"We'll rally up in the high school down the road and go over the details," Paul explained. "Now, go gather the officers up." With that, they took off towards their respective commanders.

The breakneck pace left many of the inexperienced recruits sweating under the weight of their gear and packs. Confusion remaining only just held at bay while the amorphous force lurched towards the edge of town. Gaggles of refugees staggered past them toward the south, some marred by burns or bloody wounds, some hauling a meager collection of belongings, all with faces of shock, agony, terror, or despair.

Paul took a swig of water from his canteen before turning back to Mason. "You ever done anything like this before, man?"

"Naw." Mason grinned, drawing in heavy breaths as he wiped sweat from his brow. He kept his eyes forward down the street as they all advanced. "I threw a glass bottle fulla glue an' glitter at the windows of one of them police MRAPs one time, but bein' able to **actually** fight back? That'll be new."

Paul nodded, his gaze also locked ahead. "Keep calm and stay low. No one quite knows yet how this is all gonna work."

"What!?" Mason demanded, quiet as he could manage.

"Armies like ours haven't fought since World War Two," Paul explained between his teeth. "It's anyone's guess what will happen."

"Well that's great. Even the vets have no clue what'll happen," Mason grumbled.

After about a mile of scuttling along and making sure everyone else had in fact started moving as Paul instructed, the scratch militia unit assembled around the abandoned James Monroe High School. Overlooking the northernmost vestiges of Fredericksburg, the building served as the closest thing to a vantage point in the whole area. Better yet, it sat right beside THE main road, U.S. Route 1 itself, that the Loyalists would have to take into the city since all the others just branched out into suburbia where the Saints could stalk and ambush them with impunity.

Paul wasted no time sending several of his machine-guns and AT missiles to join the scouts already occupying the school and take up the best available firing positions. A few snipers clambered onto the roof, along with the crew of an M40 recoilless rifle who hoisted their weapon to the top with the aid some rusted chains. Once he met up with his five lieutenants in the main entrance hall of the school, he wasted no time and had them send some of their troops to occupy the surrounding points of interest including two strip malls, an auto garage and a shuttered jewelry store. He also dispatched Mason with a courier and a few scouts to recon the bridge and find out just the Feddies had planted themselves for the moment.

Paul examined the faces of his five subordinate officers. Hill, a sharp-looking cadet turned rebel. Romero, an iron-jawed descendant of Cuban exiles. King, a scholarly young Black man in thick glasses. Skeet, a stereotypical redneck-looking character with a dangerous restlessness in him. And Miller, a brown haired woman with green eyes and the demeanor of a raccoon.

Within their eyes he saw certainty. A sort of grim determination, and a deep fear. Fear of death, fear of the enemy, fear of defeat. Yet not the kind of fear that compelled men to flee, but to fight like cornered beasts. They all knew the price of failure. Torture, slavery, submission… death. No options left but to fight.

Lieutenant Skeet decided to speak up: "You sure we shouldn't just rush 'em? Push 'em out 'fore they get a chance to dig in?" he asked, mopping away the sweat between his cap and brow with a pale yellow scarf wrapped around his neck. Skeet's red beard came down almost to his chest.

"I'm sure," Paul affirmed with a nod. "We might push 'em back, or we might charge headlong into a disaster. We can't afford risks right now."

"He's right, man, we gotta take this kinda easy," Romero added, a scar-faced veteran of the Iranian war.

Skeet shrugged. "Good enough for the vets, good enough for me. I just don't wanna give 'em time to get ready is all."

"We won't," Paul decreed with a face like a statue as he pulled a map of the city from his jacket pocket, isolating the grid in which they found themselves. He clicked on his helmet lamp, providing just enough light for the five men and lone woman to see the folded paper despite the total darkness of the school's interior. The clouded sky outside provided little illumination despite their group standing just a couple dozen feet from the smashed facade, barraging them with thunder instead, sending jolts down every spine. "Alright, here's the plan—" Paul pointed to the street that ran parallel to the river, then traced his finger to a road four blocks away from the bridge. "First platoon will hold

Bridgewater Street as far as Charles…" Skeet nodded as Paul indicated the roads. "Second and third platoons will occupy Charles as far as Bridgewater." He glanced up to confirm the understanding of Miller and King, receiving both in the form of concise nods. "Platoon four will and five will form a skirmish line to keep the Feddies busy until reinforcements arrive. Our ancestors beat these guys before in the name of a flawed cause, we'll do it again for a righteous one."

"*Baker this is Ryan, do you read?*" the radio cracked, almost making Paul jump.

Colonel Ryan. "Speak of the devil." Paul grabbed the radio. "I read you, sir. Go ahead, over."

"Baker, we've sent a few fast movers to even the odds for you, so don't get too close to the bridge."

"Understood, Colonel. Baker, out." Paul's mind raced as he switched channels with the click of a knob. "Overwatch, roll the flag out! We're about to have angels pay us a visit."

"*Got it, sir!*" came the reply.

Paul turned back to his subordinates. "Everyone ready?"

#

Mason flinched as a cool drop of rain splashed down on the visor of his cap. Thunder rolled over the deserted city as more droplets began to fall. Mason gave a silent thanks to the heavens as he led his small detachment of three forward along the southwestern wall of a plundered electronics store. The precipitation made his team's job more difficult, but it also gave them a veil of sound and motion to hide behind as it gathered in intensity, a tsunami of wind rolling in from the east. They arrived at the building's corner, and the resident scout, a lanky blonde girl named Stuart, stuck just the lens of her Starlight scope around the corner, taking care to keep her head behind the wall. Mason took a deep breath as the wind and water built up into a deluge, blinding and silencing all of them. Even over the drumming of the rain, the mechanical hum of dozens of engines still channeled down the road like a crushing blanket.

After a few moments, Stuart motioned everyone back as she pulled away from the corner, fumbling to reattach the scope to her AR as the group shuffled away. She turned back to Mason.

"Damn, this shit moved in fast. But I did see they're all over the damn bridge," Stuart yelled in an almost ragged voice. "They've rallied on the gas station to the west, and I think I saw some others in a building on the east side. Gotta be hundreds of 'em."

"I'll take your word for it." Mason handed her the squad radio.

An IPV rumbled down the road and turned in front of a KFC. A couple of empty deuce-and-a-halfs sat parked beside the gas station as a new column of Humvees began to arrive at the southern mouth of the dual bridge. Hundreds of red splotches indicating human beings bobbed to and fro within the perimeter surrounding the bridgehead. Mason both cursed and appreciated the many trees between them and the enemy. A distant swirl of jet engines reached his ears from high above the storm clouds. A hand landed on Mason's shoulder prompting him to whirl around.

"Captain Baker says we have air on the way," Stuart told him. "We have to stay put until the front moves through!"

Before Mason could answer, the sun broke through the clouds and the rain eased. They all stood there soaked from head to foot as the wail of engines became a scream. Mason snatched up his binoculars and poked his head around the corner back to the bridgehead to find the Feddies now in the midst of scrambling confusion, trying to skitter across the bridge and clear out as four fast movers came in low. *KA-THOOM!* A massive blast erupted from the ground just a dozen feet from the southern end of the bridge, tossing a pair of armored vehicles rolling into the air and onto their roofs and sides like plastic toys. *KRA-KOOM!* Another warhead obliterated an entire section of the western bridge causing the structure to collapse, forcing scores of vehicles and uncounted Loyalists down into the swollen river with it.

Two more bombs hammered down simultaneously, one on the gas station and the other to the right of the bridge where tanks and IFVs idled. The reaction of the underground fuel storage buffeted the high explosive, shaking the ground and churning into a column of fire piercing upwards in defiance of the storm. Several tanks just disappeared. The IFVs lay strewn around on their sides. The reverberating gunfire fractured the air all around them.

And the screams.

"Alright, everybody move, back to the school. Let's go!" Mason shouted.

Without another word the detachment started running back the way they'd come. Echoes of jet engines following behind. A roar of motors told Mason that at least some of the remaining vehicles had charged down the main road toward their destination. *Not good.* Mason called everyone to a halt once they reached the edge of a convenience store, not a place they wanted to linger. "Frazier, get up here!" Mason shouted, motioning with his arm. A man with icy blue eyes, his face covered in hunting camo, unslung an M72 LAW from his shoulder and hung back. "Stuart!" Mason called, taking a small bag off Frazier's pack. "Satchel charge. Put it in one of them trashcans by the pumps."

Stuart complied. Taking the explosives, she rushed around the corner, staying as low as she could, using a huge line of bushes along the lot as cover. She dumped the bag in the nearest trash can and darted back around, rejoining her comrades.

A massive MRAP rolled towards their position, right down Route One. Then Mason motioned for Stuart to move back as Frazier took a crouching position next to the back corner. They both got down on the muddy ground.

An agonizing series of heartbeats measured the time as they waited, the grumble of engines growing louder. Mason looked up in time to see the engine block lumbering past the building. Frazier stiffened as Mason gripped the satchel's detonator in his hand.

Frazier fired. The back-blast stripped a shrub behind of almost all of its leaves, and blew Mason's cap from his head. Before the deafening whoosh of the LAW rocket had passed, the cry of shredding and twisting metal filled the drenched air.

"I got it! I got it!" Frazier celebrated as he tossed the now useless LAW aside and grabbed his M4 back from Stuart.

Mason listened. Amid the growing din of gunshots he picked out gruff voices shouting to move and return fire.

He hit the detonator.

Another massive explosion slung debris in every direction, forcing the three rebels to hug the convenience store's wall. Screams. Frantic orders shouted. A wave of heat washed past. Plumes of black smoke hurtled into the sky.

"Move! Down the street, move!" Mason commanded.

Sprinting as fast as they could the trio slipped behind a looted bank, Mason glancing over his shoulder.

Flames consumed the store and station, obliterating their ambush spot. An MRAP with the bold white letters ATF on the side rested at a strange angle caused by the loss of its right front wheel. Gouts of fire surged from a great hole torn out of its right side.

Corpses and bits of corpses littered the concrete. A man with half his face tried to drag himself away from the blazing pump station, one of his legs reduced to a mangled wreck and the other little more than a stump. Patches of fire clung to his skin and clothes. Mason turned and kept running, regretting his choice to look back at all.

The trio arrived at the far edge of yet another bank and skidded to a halt to catch their breath. Mason took a wide look around. If they kept going the way they had, it would mean running in a near straight line across an empty parking lot. If they went straight for the high school, it would mean running right across the main road that the Feddies intended to use. He watched the flaring of muzzle flashes from broken windows and shrapnel holes in the school. Then he saw a crater torn in the outer metal fence by some manner of shell. Mason made his choice.

"When I say go, we go! Make for the gap in the fence!" he shouted over the ongoing bedlam of gunpowder. Stuart and Frazier gave frantic nods of their heads in response. The drone of jets pierced the sky once more, and Mason knew their best chance had arrived. "**GO!**"

He charged onto the gleaming wet asphalt, torrents of rain washing over him, shells and rockets shrieking far over his head. Checking over his shoulder for a second to confirm his companions had indeed followed him. Mason darted past the obliterated carcass of an old minivan, lightning jolting up his bones as the distinctive sound of bullets striking steel rang out behind him. He looked down the road towards the bridge to see another huge cone of dirt and shattered concrete launch into the air as yet another bomb landed, and lines of tracer streaking in his direction.

Mason leapt across the crater in the fence and onto the grassy campus of the school. Again he looked back, and still his desperate comrades continued to follow him. Rushing past a puny tree far too small to provide any cover, Mason saw an explosive shell blast apart the school's wall, just missing a window where a machine gun crew nested. Preparing to duck inside the building at last, he heard a voice behind him cry out.

Mason whirled around to find Frazier on the ground, dirt kicking up around him.

"Shit!" Mason spun on his heels and turned around. Stuart also heard and started to turn to assist Frazier, only to have Mason smack her shoulder as he ran passed and shouted, "Cover us!"

Mason yanked the struggling Frazier off the ground and supported his left shoulder before lurching as fast as he could toward the blast hole. Stuart backed towards the makeshift entrance as she fired away with her M16 at the encroaching Loyalists, supported by the machine gunners in the window. As the three scouts tripped over themselves to get inside, the distinctive sharp and ringing boom of the recoilless rifle on the roof echoed across the city, shocking Mason's heart into skipping a beat.

Mason came to an exhausted, panting stop after pushing his way into the gym. For a moment he struggled to regain his bearings, only to notice a pair of other Saints with red square crosses on their arms take Frazier away. He offered no resistance, looking down at the blood streaming from his squadmate's leg. Mason dragged himself away, gradually accelerating to a brisk pace, headed for the entrance, following the signs on the walls. Turning one last time, he confirmed Stuart had both survived and continued following him. She nodded with a shell-shocked expression on her mud-spattered face. He needed to find Paul. *So far so good.*

#

A callous jab from the truck's backrest shoved Emily awake as she continued to cling onto her ancient weapon out of reflex. She looked around to find herself still trapped with a truckload of equally annoyed Reds, trying in futility to get some sleep in defiance of their grueling conditions. Not much complaining though, just groans and murmurs. Emily sighed, hunching over in her narrow spot on the bench. She didn't know where this road ended by name, only that her death could very well be waiting for her there. Her knowledge of Communism had severe limits, but what she had gave her little cause for optimism. If she survived the battlefield, they could just have her killed anyway once it all came to a fiery end. And the thought of getting disposed of like garbage, and her children at the utter mercy of those who did it, turned her soul into an inferno.

*No. I'm not going to let those bastards enjoy the satisfaction of getting me killed. They will **not** take my children from me. If I have to fight with these lunatics just to stay alive then so be it, but I will make them pay. I **will** find the ones who made this happen, and I will make them pay.*

Emily took deep breaths through her scarf, closing her eyes and grasping her rifle hard enough to make the veins on her hands and arms pop out. She needed to keep calm, relax, and submerge her rage as much as she could. She'd go insane otherwise. Besides, none of the rebels in the truck had orchestrated anything, they just wanted to lash out at the boot on their necks. Emily couldn't decide if she should hunt down politicians or rebel warlords first. Both held blame.

A voice in Emily's right ear grabbed her attention. "You okay?" She turned to find the short Latina from earlier poking around with the optics of her RPG, a warily curious grin on her lips.

Emily grumbled. "Yeah, sure," she lied, hoping the girl would let it go.

"You're a blue-blood aren't you?" The ex-cop whipped her head around, fixing the smirking Latina with wide open eyes. The girl scoffed. "Relax, I won't say nothin.' Not that I have to. The whole "Terminator" bod and endless glare. Kinda dead giveaways."

Emily leaned back on the truck bench, exhausted. "I just want to live, understand? I just want to get back to my kids. You can all have whatever you want, I don't even care anymore," she said with a bitter voice.

The Latina chuckled. "Well that's good, cause my house got blown to hell and I wanna loot me some Beverly Hills mansions!" she half-joked, putting her arm around Emily and leaning a smidge closer. "I'm Sophie by the way, Sophie Huerta. You?"

Emily sighed. *If I have to do this, might as well keep the number of people who want me dead to a minimum.* "Emily... Dawes. Nice to meet you."

"Yeah right," Sophie rolled her eyes. "You looked ready to squash some fool's head a second ago. Who ya got it in for? Singh?"

Emily's eyes opened up again, she remembered that name. *Rob's boss.* "I don't know, who's he?"

"Oh just the white boy who masterminded all this shit. And our boss, if you wanna be technical," Sophie replied.

Emily blinked several times. *That guy.* The one she'd watched shoot one of her colleagues in the head right in front of her. *That guy's in charge.* She picked up an emotion that she couldn't quite place in Sophie's voice. "What do you think of him?" she asked.

Sophie shrugged. "Eh. Instead of an old, greedy white guy in charge, we've got a young, crazy white guy in charge," she admitted. "Wouldn't go after him if I were you though, that doesn't end well from what I heard."

"You heard right," a voice rumbled from across the tuck bed.

Both women's gazes locked ahead on the burly ex-con Emily had seen in line before, cleaning out the barrel of his improvised machine gun. Sophie gave Emily a raise of brow telling her she didn't know this man.

Emily turned back to the bench across from them. "And who are you?" she asked.

The shaved-headed man looked up with a narrow steel grin. "Kniva."

Sophie stifled a laugh. "You give yourself that name?"

"Yes," he answered without hostile tone, making Sophie visibly awkward as she pulled out a wrapped Twinkie to snack on. The unfazed Kniva went back to tinkering with his weapon.

"So, what do you know about this Singh guy?" Emily intervened.

"My brother's been in this since before the power died, he told me Singh's some kinda psychic. Always like five steps ahead of everyone else. He's outlived or out back-stabbed anyone who had the juice to replace him. So like him or not, you'd best keep clear of that one."

Before Emily could question him any further, she heard the distinctive chaos of an explosion up ahead. Not a full second later the truck ground to a stop along with those behind it, a great cloud of dust shrouding the column.

"Everybody out!" Sergeant Coleman's voice ordered from behind the truck cab.

The entire platoon filed out and lined up along the left side of the truck, Coleman emerged last with his finger over the radio set over his ear. They found themselves in some kind of gorge or valley created for the highway running through it, its walls neither steep nor high. Emily tried without success to see what had happened down the road, but she could hear scattered gunfire and explosions. "Alright people, we got Feddies on the road and command wants us to help surround and destroy them," Coleman explained. "We advance to the left. Let's move out, c'mon!"

Emily followed the lead of Kniva, sticking close to the relative safety of his machine gun. Sophie followed along too, RPG resting on her shoulder. Glancing back, Emily watched as the units riding in trucks behind theirs also began skittering off to either the right or left side of the road. Dozens of platoons flowed together like a swarm, its members keeping far enough apart to avoid anything explosive taking out multiple people. Their brown and khaki "uniforms" moving beneath a veil of dirt and sand made it look as though the ground had begun to flow like a river.

Climbing over the gorge walls and into the rocky hill surrounding it, Emily and the others halted to allow a technical to fly past towards the head of the column. A massive Ford F150 with a pair of .50 caliber machine guns mounted on the back in a single pedestal, the truck rumbled over or smashed through any minor obstacles in its way. Emily watched as the big red star on its tailgate disappeared into the mire of dust.

"Keep moving, stay behind that thing as best you can!" Coleman instructed from just over Emily's shoulder.

Emily grumbled under her breath, safe amidst the chaos of shouts, guns, and engines. Pulling her scarf back up as high as she could Emily lowered her cap's visor to protect her eyes from the oncoming waves of grime, even if she could only see Kniva's feet. At least this made it easy to keep her legs on the rugged terrain. Before long Emily heard the iconic zip and snap of bullets overhead, the revving of the F150's engine and chugging blasts of two 50 cals answered.

As the resulting dust cloud dispersed, Emily tilted her head up to find their group had arrived at the destination. She found herself atop a ridge overlooking a three-way intersection of highways with several vans, SUVs, and MRAPs parked around it. Some manner of checkpoint she assumed. Emily hunkered down and did her best to determine how many people she could see dashing between the vehicles. Before she could focus, the familiar voice of her eldest son jumped between the crackling of gunshots and roar of engines.

"Ninth Platoon! Spread out along the ridge and let them have it! Fire at will!"

The second that his orders ended, Emily found him. *Bennigsen. Why that name?* There he stood, pistol in hand, mid-sweeping motion with his index finger in the direction of the Loyalists while speaking with some NCO type in a riot helmet. He glanced up at her and motioned toward the ridge line with wide eyes as if to say, *"Get on with it!"*

A surge of rattling gunfire drew Emily's head around 180 degrees to Kniva as he unleashed another burst from his scrap Maxim gun upon the circled vehicles. Emily turned back around to find Sophie loading an anti-tank rocket into her RPG. Once Sophie had gotten the rocket secured, she looked up at the unsure Emily and smiled a bit.

"Relax, Blue! They're Feddies, not your friends!" With that, she poked the unwieldy weapon over the crest and raised her head just enough to look through the side-mounted scope. "Clear!"

Emily turned away and covered her ears as the back blast erupted behind her, kicking up yet another huge cloud of dirt. She checked back over her shoulder to find Sophie sliding back down their side of the ridge and heading right, closer to the road. The other seven members of her platoon maintained an endless torrent of fire on the Federal forces, backing down from the crest and repositioning every so often. Emily would've sat dumbstruck at this revelation for some time, were it not for her many previous experiences on the opposing side of this situation. Disasters, many of them, and when not disasters then empty victories than achieved nothing. While the Red's basic competence improved Emily's chances of survival, it also spelled doom for the Loyalists in the valley below.

With no options left, Emily clicked the safety off her Garand and took aim. The ACOG scope's crosshair drifted over the assembled vehicles, now peppered with bullet holes. Federal agents in black and green military gear popped up and down from behind sparse cover, firing in what seemed like every direction and crumpling under streams of lead. At last Emily settled her crosshair over the helmet of an agent firing a .30 caliber machine gun from an MRAP turret.

She took a deep breath, exhaled… and fired.

A crack. A poof of red. The agent's skull rocked back as he slumped down into the armored vehicle. Emily slid down from the crest and moved a few paces left before climbing back up, hearing another launch from Sophie's RPG as she did. She watched as the rocket arched into the air on a slight upward curve, then plummeted down into a parked MRAP. The smoke and dirt cleared to reveal fire cropping up from its hatches. Emily's gunsight landed upon an agent crouched beside the vehicle carrying a pair of binoculars. She pulled the trigger again.

Another crack and the man slumped down to the earth.

Emily turned away from her victim, watching as an old Taurus station wagon blundered its way across the rock-and-crag-ridden soil. The whole back roof of the station wagon was gone, replaced by an open deck occupied by a helicopter rocket pod. As Emily watched in something like confused horror, the station wagon technical stopped behind a collection of boulders, turned its weapon 90 degrees, and began launching an entire volley of rockets at the Federal checkpoint. With each round, the station wagon tilted sideways in almost comical fashion, but it did not tip over.

Like a drumbeat of annihilation one rocket after another detonated amid the assembled vehicles. Emily could only look on as armored trucks got torn apart and people disappeared amid cones of dust and fire. Once the explosive onslaught ceased, a far reduced number of muzzle flashed flared out from the checkpoint. The snap of bullets impacting the ridge near her sent Emily scrambling away from the peak. A high-pitched mechanical whine dragged her attention to the sky as a trio of Guardian drones buzzed over the crest firing a cascade of missiles in the enemy's direction.

Emily heard the explosions as she clambered back up to a spot much closer to the road and found herself between Kniva and a Hispanic man who she didn't know in a dark green baseball cap and brandishing an AK. Kniva's eyes stayed on target, still dumping rounds from his machine gun, while the man with the Kalashnikov regarded her with a brisk nod before firing again. Emily settled back into place, gritted her teeth, and peered back into the scope.

She caught a detachment of six agents sprinting for a rocky outcropping and tagged the last one in the side, right in the gap of his vest. The man stumbled to the ground, clutching his stomach as he curled into a ball and Emily tore herself away. As the other five rushed behind cover, Emily watched another platoon of Reds appear over the ridge **behind** the Loyalist position and began shredding any exposed Feddies with a variety of automatic weapons. The agents behind the rocks scrambled to escape back the way they'd run only to get inundated with bullets. Down on the road, an Abrams tank with a red flag hanging from its barrel fired a high explosive shell into a Federal MRAP, blasting it into hunks of charred scrap metal. Emily did her best to ignore the sinking sensation in her guts as she pivoted her Garand back to the checkpoint, scanning for any targets through the fog of war. Then… she spotted something.

A white undershirt, waving at the end of a stick.

Emily's eyes widened.

"Cease fire! Cease fire!" Coleman bellowed.

The orchestra of gunfire petered out as half a dozen other voices echoed Coleman's order. A pitiful collection of dazed survivors floundered away from the circle of devastated vehicles.

"Keep them in your sights!" Rob shouted from further down the slope. "It could always be a trick!"

Emily did as instructed without thinking, observing as the haggard agents became enveloped by numerous technicals and, of all things, horsemen with rifles. Soon enough, a black MRAP with a red star painted on each side rumbled down the highway from the opposite side, with several more technicals and armored trucks behind it. Yet another tank also crawled onto the battlefield, half a dozen Red soldiers hanging on for the ride.

As Coleman arrived at the crest beside Kniva, Emily could overhear voices crackle through his radio headset as the sergeant listened.

"Is it over?" a voice sounding like Rob asked.

"Yeah they've had it. It's over." answered a Spanish-accented voice.

"Good, we need to get moving again," decreed a voice that Emily thought she recognized and General Harper, their direct superior. *"Get the infantry back in the trucks and start the column back up. Everyone who isn't apprehending or salvaging mount back up."*

"Roger that," Rob answered.

Now Coleman addressed Ninth Platoon. "Alright people, back to the trucks! Move!"

The trudging slide back to their transport felt like a whole odyssey in Emily's conflicted head. She had just fought against the United States Government. She'd taken part in a hostile act and killed two, possibly three Federal Agents. No denying it now, no arguing it anymore.

She was a traitor.

Emily removed her cap, wiping the sweat off her forehead, breathing deep to try and not get dizzy under the ruthless sun.

"Well, that wasn't so bad." Sophie slid down the last stretch of ridge and ended up right beside the same deuce-and-a-half they'd rode in on.

"My ass," brawled a lanky, bearded Black man with a bayonetted M16. "We got lucky."

"Aww c'mon… none of our platoon got killed!" Sophie pointed out in a pouty voice.

"Back on the truck, people, no time to waste!" Coleman interrupted, prompting everyone to embark upon the venerable truck once more. This time Coleman climbed aboard last, pounding the stock of his rifle into the truck bed twice as he did. A few seconds later, the truck lurched forward and began to roll on ahead. Emily sat just one seat away from the back of the truck, her gaze fixed out the back at the passing world. She waited with dread to see the aftermath of their assault.

Hordes of mechanics and scrappers covered every vehicle that hadn't gotten obliterated. Those that had sat as blazing wrecks surrounded only by bodies. Rebels in hazmat suits picked over the dead, gathering any pieces of armor or equipment that could still be used. A crackle of rifle shots almost made Emily jump in her seat. Turning to the right, she watched as a group of Reds on horses and motorcycles wandered away from a line of fresh corpses lying scattered in front of a ruined MRAP.

Emily felt a sharp pain her forehead, compelling her to nurse her now scabbed-over wound.

"Damn, ain't that a little harsh?" the lanky Black man asked no one in particular.

"Nah, fuck 'em! They're a bunch'a soulless bootlickers," Retorted a balding white man in wrapped shades with a goatee.

"Not like they'd do much different to us," Sophie added with a cool stare.

"Just add torture and slavery to the process," Kniva said as he unloaded his Maxim gun.

Emily watched the defeated roadblock vanish behind clouds of dust and valley walls, listening to the words of anger, hatred, and fear bounce back and forth. The U.S. government didn't tolerate **real** opposition or dissent, they quashed it without mercy, whether through overt force or infiltration. Everything these people said was true, and she knew it. *But these people are Reds, traitors! Destroyers of their own country! They deserve such treatment…*

…Don't they?

"You have all done well, comrades."

Rob's voice intruded into Emily's thoughts. Her head whipped around to the speaker on the back of the truck cab.

"Thanks to you, our path remains unimpeded. However… we must not allow ourselves to become complacent, comrades. This time we had every advantage on our side, including the incompetence of our foes. But things will not always be so easy. Check your equipment and rest, if you can manage it, our objective isn't far off now."

Emily felt dizzy again…

No. Not going to faint like before.

Deep breaths…

Smell's not so bad anymore.

Emily's posture steadied, she jostled her head, blinking fast.

Robb, you'd better keep giving me nothing but the ruthless truth.

CHAPTER 11:
THE ABYSS

Pride is born as a mountaintop on a valley, but dies as an abyss in which it is too deep and too dark to see the better.

— Criss Jami

Grass. An endless sea of grass.

Whispers on the flowing wind.

Foul smoke in the air. Burning her eyes and nose.

Screams. Screams of terror and panicked shouts.

Judith turned around in slow motion, straining to move faster. Shapes rushed around her, people, running, yelling. Judith looked down at her hands, they clasped some manner of rifle, but she couldn't see… the smoke…

More screams. Not of fear… but rage.

Judith's head shifted toward an encroaching red glow at the edge of her vision.

Fire.

Fire everywhere.

Trees. Houses. Grass. All enveloped in fire.

And figures.

Huge, dark figures. Riders. An endless horde of riders and vehicles emerging from a wall of jagged stone, like ants.

Judith watched in paralysis as fleeing person after person fell under guns, axes, swords, and lances. She tried to lift her weapon and fight back as those few around her with their own arms got hacked down, but her body felt like a useless mass. The sky filled with dark shapes, swooping down like birds of prey before peeling away and leaving new blooms of flame behind.

The stamping of hooves on the dirt brought Judith's struggling head around to find a screaming, hooded rider bearing down upon her. Judith twisted her stricken body in desperation, only to face an oncoming lance.

She watched in helpless dismay as the sharpened steel plunged right into her eyes.

Judith awoke with deep, stuttering breaths. Looking to either side, relief washed over her. Neither of her tent mates had awakened, and the night still reigned. Dreams did not come to Judith often. Most times they arrived on the eve of some much anticipated or loathed event, about which she would imagine an unending stream of possible outcomes. Appropriate then, that she should dream in the midst of this "journey of enlightenment" as the sergeant called it.

Two weeks of riding and training had left Zoey at the end of her rope, but Judith had faith that she'd pull through. Zoey had always needed time to adapt when new expectations or conditions appeared. As for herself, Judith could get used to this. Sure it beat the hell out of ranching, but not by that much. So far planks of wood and old cars made up the only enemies they'd faced, but Judith knew that couldn't last.

As Judith lay in her bedroll the world outside the tent grew ever brighter and she realized that dawn had arrived. Judith groaned. *So much for getting some more sleep.* She rested with her eyes closed as best she could until at last their commanding officer unzipped the tent and poked her head inside.

"Rise and shine, boys and girls!" First Sergeant Taylor announced as she poked each of the three sleeping figures in the side with her walking stick. Once the iron-jawed woman had woken them to her satisfaction she moved on, leaving the tent flap unzipped.

"Aw God, I was dreamin' about the most awful things…" Zoey slurred as she rose, rubbing the sleep from her eyes.

"Same here," Judith replied.

"I don't remember much, but it wasn't any fun," Zoey elaborated as she wormed her way out of her bag. "What happened in yours, Judy?"

Judith hesitated for a moment. "Fire... death. Some kinda... horde of horsemen. I don't really know either, just that it was terrible."

"Ugh... Never thought I'd feel lucky to dream about home," Camila spoke up, still wrapped in her bedroll.

"What's wrong with home?" Judith asked, not only curious but also not wanting to intrude.

"Nothin'. Just that it's an empty fuckin' wasteland. Left to rot by D.C.," Camila answered as she too began to emerge with groggy brown eyes and frazzled black hair.

"C'mon, lets packed up 'fore the valkyrie chews our heads off," Zoey whispered with a mischievous grin.

The 28th Cavalry Battalion of the 3rd Cavalry Brigade consisted of roughly 1,000 riders and around 250 vehicle crewmen along an unknown number of medics, scouts, cooks, mechanics, and others. Like most cavalry units, their current task amounted to patrolling the borders of their new Nation. Texas had been the second largest state in the union, behind only Alaska, but now for the first time the entirety of its history those huge borders faced threats from almost every direction. Not even including the dangers of the other major factions, rumors of bandits and marauders raiding small towns and camping in the wild had become rampant, and the cavalry formed the most adept force to respond.

Once Judith had finished helping Zoey and Camila pack up their camping gear onto their respective horses, they lined up along with the rest of their unit and waited for orders. Judith ran her hand through the thick mane of her brown mare, for whom she hadn't thought of a name yet. She had a brand on her left hind leg of a "W" with an arrow rising out from the center, a ranch Judith didn't recognize. Just like their riders, these humble creatures had come from across the vast expanse of Texas. Judith gave her steed's neck a good scratch.

"Ya ready for a day of runnin' girl?" The grumbling snort she got in reply brought a smile to Judith's face.

As the sun rose over the northern plains of Texas, Judith felt beads of sweat slide down her face and neck. At last their CO, Major Hayden, appeared atop his white-faced bay, rifle over his shoulder. With wrapped shades beneath his brown cowboy hat, a handlebar mustache drooping down his jowls, and a fat cigar hanging out of his mouth, he looked every bit the part he played.

"28th Cavalry!" Hayden bellowed, "It has come to my attention, that a bunch a killers an' thieves have decided to turn part of our country into their own lil' playground." His head cocked as he took large puffs from his cigar, "Are ya'll okay with that?"

"**Sir, no, sir!**" came the united answer.

Hayden nodded. "Well alright, should probably do somethin' about 'em then. We ride north to Durant! We'll hold up in Calera and get the lay of the land, find out how many we're dealin' with and what they've got."

"Sir, ain't both a those places in Oklahoma?" someone asked from among the ranks.

The Major smiled. "Not anymore it isn't. Effective at twelve hundred hours, Oklahoma's appeal to join our great republic has been ratified by the senate and the president. As of now, keepin' the Okies safe is part of our mandate. That understood?"

Another chorus of "yes, sirs."

"Alright, good. Now move 'em out!" Hayden ordered, chomping back down on his cigar.

The battalion deployed in squadrons just as they always did, groups of between 30 and 50 riders with a handful of technicals and MRAPs as support. Judith and Zoey stuck as close as they could with Camila tagging along behind. Camila came from Odessa, a smaller city that Judith had never seen but which Camila described as bland. Her eagerness to join came from a desire to escape the mediocrity as much as the desire to secure her country's freedom.

Zoey sighed. "Well, I guess that's all good? Except for the bandits I mean..."

"Yeah, I guess the Okies aren't all that useless. Certainly can use all the help we can get," Camila answered.

"Rather have 'em with us than against us," Judith said as a technical with a .50 cal on the back bumbled past through the dry grassland.

"Sure!" Camila laughed, "We just gotta save 'em from a buncha goons first!"

As Camila rode on ahead, Judith came up alongside a wary Zoey. "You sure yer up for this?" she asked.

Zoey looked almost indignant. "Of course ah am!" she declared, hand on her heart. "I just can't believe we're gonna be huntin' outlaws like in the old wild west!"

Judith laughed from head to toe. "That's right! Zoey Earp and Judith Holiday."

"You don' wanna be Wyatt Earp?" Zoey asked in surprise.

"Nah you're the noble one. 'Sides, I'd make better Doc Holiday. Minus the disease an all." After doing a quick look around to find Taylor nowhere in sight, Judith drew the .357 magnum revolver from her hip and spun it around back and forth real fast before holstering it again. She then repeated the process but with greater speed and flare. "I'll be your huckleberry."

"Not bad!" Mordecai, one of the squadron's snipers, spoke up from alongside them. "Where'd you learn that?"

"Old movies," Judith answered as she drew and spun the revolver around once more without looking. She wore a smirk on her lips.

"Quit foolin' around, Private!" Taylor's voice battered Judith from behind, prompting her to holster the gun again and adopt a more rigid stance.

"Sorry, Sarge!" Judith blurted.

"Save the showin' off for when we're not movin'! What if that discharged and hit somebody, or gave away our position to some evil varmints?" Tylor demanded, somehow leaning her narrowed eyes right up to Judith's despite them both riding horses.

"Sorry, Sarge!" Judith repeated. "Won't happen again, Sarge!"

Taylor nodded, satisfied, before whirling on Zoey and Mordecai. "Don't you two be snickerin', I know you were eggin' her on! Let's go, we've got helpless villagers to save!"

#

Riding across the Red River made all of this feel more real in Judith's mind. To have other people join them in their bid for independence gave it more "legitimacy" as Major Hayden put it. Still, if an entire town had gotten captured by lawless gunmen it might as well be enemy territory. The Southwest had always existed as a kind of eye in the storm, yet everyone already felt the side effects of the chaos raging all around them. Judith felt a sense of both relief and unease as the battalion rode into Calera.

Most of the couple thousand inhabitants of the small town had barricaded themselves in their houses or the few large buildings near the center of town. Other townsfolk, armed with a plethora of guns, patrolled the streets which they had barricaded with cars and piles of junk and debris. These ad hoc militia made no secret of their relief after letting the Texans in, they might've had reservations still, but they all seemed to prefer joining the republic to getting run over by marauders. Another group of people drew Judith's notice upon entering the center of town: the refugees.

Men, women, and children, huddled around tents and battered cars, scooping food from cans and Tupperware bowls, and gazing off into space for minutes on end. Only a few of them looked up at Judith as she rode past, vacant eyes staring right through her. Others sat shaking in a state of disbelief. Judith wondered how she and her fellow riders must look to these poor souls. Like some army of noble knights come to rescue them from the nightmare their lives had become? Judith had to look away eventually, she hoped they could be the heroes these people needed.

Before long, they reached their designated campsite outside a community building on the northern edge of town known as the Jack Stockton Building. Plenty of open space, enough for several squadrons, though Judith couldn't tell how many got assigned to the spot.

"Everybody dismount and set up camp!" Taylor barked out. "Travis, Mordecai, Kitchener, Sanchez! You're all on first watch! Take up post over there in that house waaaay across the field, there." She pointed to a large suburban house with a separate garage building. "Command says it's been abandoned."

"You got it, Sarge!" Judith answered, doing her best not to clench her teeth as she did.

"Yeah, nothin'll get past us!" Zoey added in her usual bubbly tone, trotting ahead of the group after giving Judith a discreet pat on the back.

"Ah, I wasn't sleepy anyways…" Camila grumbled under her breath.

Mordecai said nothing, though he did take the opportunity to light a homemade cigarette while still far off from their post.

Judith waited until they'd made it halfway across the field before speaking again. "I swear that woman has it in for me," she muttered.

"She has it in for everyone." Camila smirked, "You just poke her buttons more than anybody else."

"Yeah, well that don't make this suck any less." Judith scanned the horizon in the fading daylight. "We get to keep an eye out for any raiders or whoever these guys are."

"Eh, it could be worse," Zoey said. "I feel kinda antsy about this anyways, bein' camped out so close to the… *enemy.*"

Judith chuckled. Zoey said the word with such trepidation, and a hint of excitement. "They might not even know we're here yet, Zo."

"Yeah? Well, let's do ourselves a favor an' act like they do," Zoey replied, eyes darting around.

The four tied their horses up behind the two story house and entered through the open back door. After sweeping the place and finding it empty, Camila and Mordecai occupied the second floor master bedroom, giving their rifles overwatch of the open pasture opposite the Texan camp. Judith and Zoey set up their machine gun behind the main living room window on the first floor, which offered a similar field of view as the upper story. Judith aimed and fired while Zoey fed ammo and kept a shotgun at her side in case anyone managed to get a bit too close. The old Browning .30 cal looked as though it'd sat in a crate since the 1960s, faint traces of rust visible here and there, but still functional.

Judith blew her bangs out of her face as she rested her chin on the box that made up the machine gun's receiver. Zoey went to lock up all the doors as Judith stared out the window of a darkened house into a darkening field. A couple of trees and bushes, but mostly just grass. *Nowhere to hide.* And yet… it felt wrong somehow. She tried to shake the feeling as Zoey returned and took a seat on the floor to her left, open canteen in hand. The expression on Zoey's made it clear to Judith she'd failed to hide her unease.

"What is it?" her friend urged.

"I dunno," Judith answered with honesty. "Somethin' just feels off. Maybe I'm just paranoid."

Zoey took a swig of water as she scanned the outside. "Not many places to sneak through."

"Yeah." A sudden flash of light compelled Judith to pivot the gun towards a dried-out bush about a hundred yards from the house.

"What!? What'd you see!?" Zoey prodded, ducking down a bit.

"A light! I saw a light!" Judith answered.

"Where?"

"By that damn bush." Judith gave a brief jerk, pointing with her left thumb, keeping her right index finger on the trigger.

The two young women held their breath for several heartbeats before another flash appeared just below the bush.

Then another above it.

Judith realized she'd spotted a firefly. She took a deep breath and leaned back away from the gun. Zoey did the same, wiping some sweat from her eyes as she chuckled.

"Okay, maybe we're paranoid. But that don't mean nothin's out there," Zoey said.

"Nah, it don't," Judith agreed, placing her chin back on the receiver.

"You heard anything about your brothers?" Zoey asked.

Judith sighed. She'd tried not to worry about it. "Nope. Not yet."

"I'm sure they're both fine," Zoey assured as best she could.

Judith gave Zoey a tired grin. "Yeah, those two screw-ups can handle themselves," she joked.

More than an hour went by, the noise pollution from the camp died away, the moon cast an ethereal glow over the landscape. Judith lost herself in the view. The swaying of grass. The reflections in puddles. The figures rising from the waving sea of blades.

"What—?"

The crack of a rifle over their heads left Judith and Zoey stupefied until a storm of bullets punctured and shattered the front window. Judith used the brim of her hat to protect her eyes from a shower of broken glass as Zoey covered her face with a raised arm. The second the shards landed and Judith could see again, she took aim at the still firing and now charging figures. Without thinking, Judith gripped the trigger of her machine gun, holding her left arm down over the receiver to try to control the recoil like First Sergeant Taylor had shown her.

The old gun chugged out a stream of lead, tearing away the remaining wooden frame and glass. The muzzle flash blinded Judith, forcing her to strain her eyes between each burst to re-focus on the attackers again. Everything became an insane whirlpool of chaos. Bullets crashed through the walls sending splinters flying across the room. Shelves and furniture got obliterated. A shotgun blast shattered the front door's center.

Judith pointed the weapon's smoking nozzle at the new hole and fired three long bursts through it. Amid the pause, she heard the sharp cracks of her squad-mates' rifles upstairs, before aiming back out the now open window and unleashing another torrent of fire.

"Rot in hell ya damn psychos!" Judith screamed over the crunching of glass and the blare of the machine gun. She felt a hand on her shoulder, and turned to find Zoey with her other hand on the radio.

"It's over, Judy! We won!" Judith stopped firing and allowed her eyes to adjust again.

The gunfire had ceased. She saw a few figures approaching with their hands raised. This made Judith uneasy, until figures on horses began to fill the scene, coming into view from behind the house. Zoey jumped up and ran for the back door, unlocking it as Judith picked up the Browning and folded the bipod back under the glowing barrel.

"What in the Lord's sacred name happened here, Travis!?" Taylor demanded as she and several other National Guardsmen entered the devastated home.

Judith spun her head around to address the furious and bewildered first sergeant. "The bastards jumped outta the grass and just started shootin' the place up." A pause hung in the air as Judith looked back and forth between Zoey and Taylor. "You're all caught up, Sarge," she said at last with a shrug.

Mordecai and Camila chose this moment to descend the near-ruined staircase as several other riders headed up to replace them. Taylor rubbed her forehead and groaned.

"Alright, I guess you're all relieved. Head back to camp and get sum shuteye," the NCO commanded.

#

The setting sun crept further over the horizon, dragging the vanishing light away with it. Alexander preferred the freezing night to the searing day, even while waiting on a battle. The Mediterranean gave a sense of calm the open oceans lacked, like an oversized lake. He watched as the waves rolled in and withdrew over and over, seagulls crying and circling overhead. The cool wind of the sea billowed through the streets of Haifa, between the buildings and over the BCP, across Alexander's greasy, sand-covered head.

He might be lying, but he might not. If he is bullshitting us he's dead. Which he has to know. Unless he doesn't care... but he didn't strike me as the type to blow himself up. Alexander shook his head, taking a drink from his half-empty canteen.

"You think the Persian's full of shit?" Derrick asked from his seat within the BCP.

Alexander shrugged. "Was just thinking about that myself. I wouldn't be surprised either way."

"Too bad Israel doesn't have much of a navy," Derrick lamented, cleaning his Beretta.

*Too bad **our** navy is nowhere to be found.* Alexander thought to himself.

A high-pitched whine began to drill it's way into his head. *That sound...*

"Contact!" came an Israeli voice over the radio. *"We've got multiple radar contacts closing fast from the north and east!"*

"Fuck!" Derrick scrambled to shut his canteen and put his helmet on as he ducked out the back of the BCP.

Alexander searched the visible horizon with his binoculars, and sure enough, a set of vague shapes approached in a beeline.

"There, drones coming in at three o'clock! Hit 'em with whatever you've got!" Alexander commanded.

An orchestra of anti-air weapons, both American and Israeli, flung their glowing munitions into the late evening sky. The whining grew ever louder between streams of fire as the formations of crude suicide drones descended on the port like locusts. Most of the polymer and foam aircraft got blown to pieces by the array of weapons blazing away at them, but several others made it through. Explosions of varying sizes rocked the waterfront area, a huge mushroom of fire ascended from the smashed-open roof of a warehouse as a squadron of Israeli Mirage jets appeared and engaged the drones.

Just as the number of drones decreased, another powerful blast emanated from beyond the port itself, from the sea. Seconds later, a message came in over the radio.

"Uh... we've got some kinda hostile aquatic assets approaching the dockyard. They just vaporized an Israeli Coast Guard boat," an American voice informed everyone.

"Everybody who isn't on an AA weapon, get to the docks!" Alexander ordered as he ducked into the hull of the BCP, grabbing his M4 and helmet.

The whir of a drone's propeller sent Alexander jumping back inside as the small machine went straight over him and crashed into a building, blasting the wall apart. Alexander shook his head and tried to ignore the ringing in his ears as he sprinted over toward the waterfront. Derrick appeared alongside at the head of a few soldiers with missile launchers, all of them scanning the darkened sky.

Upon reaching the docks through an open storehouse, Alexander and his men found a scene of anarchy. Soldiers, Israeli and American, fired their heaviest weapons at boats which sat so low in the water that at first Alexander thought they might be submarines. The craft had ravaged the entire area with machine guns and rocket launchers. They knew these things were more than refitted patrol boats. One of the craft fired a battery of rockets that obliterated a pair of soldiers, others got machined gunned by strafing drones.

Everything fired back with a desperate vengeance. Alexander watched as a wake created by what looked like a steel oval approached a docked freighter on the opposite pier. Before he could even call it out, the small vessel detonated, tearing the ship and surrounding docklands apart. Burning debris and pieces of shattered steel rained down everywhere. *Kamikaze boats. Perfect.*

"Get those launchers set up, move!" Derrick ordered his squad before firing a burst from his assault rifle at one of the craft as it strafed the docks.

"Don't let anymore of those things get close! Shoot anything in the water you don't trust!" Alexander shouted into the radio. With little else to do for the moment, he joined Derrick in taking pot-shots at the boats as they flew past.

As Alexander took in the complexity of the situation, he saw yet another narrow and ultra-low craft racing toward... him. The thing weaved between bullets and rockets, dodging splashes and trails of splashes. As Alexander started to get nervous, the boat hit a piece of steel wreckage from a ship, creating a shower of sparks as it launched itself into the air. The slender form of the boat sailed toward him like a cruise missile. The diabolical thing reached its zenith, then dove straight for the spot on which Alexander stood.

"Move!" he shouted over the bedlam.

Just as the stunned Americans started to take off in every direction, an IDF soldier manning a grenade launcher at last scored a direct hit on the flying boat. The resulting cataclysmic explosion sent everyone nearby, including Alexander and Derrick, to the deck. A wall of heat washed over them as bits of metal and fiberglass pelted their armor and helmets. Once back on his feet, Alexander took in the extent of the damage to the docks. A great half-circle hole now existed where the boat had reached closest to the pier, twisted bars of steel jutting out over the flotsam-covered water.

"Too fucking close!" Derrick proclaimed, firing at another vessel.

The swarm started to break up, dumping all the rockets and missiles they had before turning away and disappearing. Alexander watched two of his men get cut down by Dushkas, taking cover himself as explosives sent debris and water flying all around him. Alexander's senses returned as the chaos of gunfire began to die away. One of the sub-like boats exploded in the wake of a white contrail. A Mirage roared overhead as the other craft slipped away beneath the waves. The whine of drone engines no longer buzzed around within Alexander's mind.

"Congratulations, ladies and gentlemen!" Daskal's voice cracked over the radio. *"It appears we have survived another day. See to the wounded and regroup."*

"Okay let's gather up everybody who's hurt and get them back over to the tent, let's go!" the voice of Dr. Bowman drew Alexander's attention to where the woman stood carrying an unconscious man with no lower legs. The captain yanked himself away before he got lost.

Alexander turned back to Derrick and found his friend returning a gaze that conveyed everything he himself felt as well. A terrible and ominous realization.

The Iranian had not lied.

If he knew about this, he may well know about Kuwait. He may well know about a lot of things.

"Can you rally everyone up here, Lieutenant?" Alexander asked.

"Yes, sir! We'll have this cleaned up in no time," Derrick answered with a salute, well aware of what business needed attending.

"Good, see to it. I'll be at command." As Alexander turned away, he heard the stamping of boots on the steel deck.

"Captain, sir!" A private skidded to a halt beside Alexander. "One of those things crashed on the shore over there." He pointed to a section beach beyond the docklands where a long and slender boat had indeed ended up trapped at the end of the sand trench it had created. A sporadic cordon of army troops, IDF, and marines had materialized around the thing, though far enough away to avoid getting vaporized should it blow.

Alexander made his way over to the edge of the docks, looking over the disaster scene. Smoke billowed from the small viewing window of the conning tower. Too small for anything more than two men. A hatch near the craft's bow flung open and the barrel of an AK poked out through the black smoke. Gunfire echoed across the waterfront as bullets shredded the stricken craft. Alexander shook his head, turning away.

His journey back to the tent in which Farzan waited felt like walking through the set of some disaster movie. Alexander thanked God that the bloodshed had been minimal, six dead and 18 wounded. The fact that they'd known what to expect made the difference. Now he wanted to know why the Persian told him about it. Alexander found Farzan sitting in the same spot he'd left the man, his gray-green eyes having already locked on the "door" of the temporary structure.

"I take it everything went well?" he asked with a neutral expression.

Alexander stepped inside, walking to within a few feet of his prisoner. "You betrayed your own people."

Farzan smiled, chuckled at this. "I have inconvenienced my people. If anything, I've betrayed the Syrians. And seeing as they will remain our friends for just as long as it takes to get rid of Israel, I can live with that."

Alexander scratched his chin with narrowed eyes. "You said before that the nuke wasn't part of your master plan. Can you elaborate on that?"

Farzan scoffed, shaking his head. "We want you gone, Yankee. But we're not stupid."

"So who did it?"

"Who else? Everyone's favorite Wahhabist fanatics," Farzan said with a hint of bitter irritation.

Alexander sighed, handing a plastic water bottle to the Iranian. "Which ones? I.S., or the Saudis?"

"Both," Farzan answered between long drinks. "Your old friends have learned to make good use of their wild

105

dogs."

Alexander became too wrapped up in implications to care about Farzan's diss. He thought carefully, gazing into the exhausted and wary eyes of the prisoner. If the Israelis discovered his presence, it could all unravel, but they might never have another chance to get answers.

"We'll get you away from the Israelis, then you tell us everything?"

Farzan gave a light shrug. "That is the deal, American."

Alexander took a deep breath with closed eyes. "Alright," he said at last. "You've got a deal."

Farzan gave a slow, almost bow of a nod. "Out of curiosity, how is it you plan to extract yourselves from this… abyss you've been abandoned to?"

Alexander scoffed. "I'll let you know when I get a chance to find out."

With that, Alexander just turned and walked out as his mind echoed with doubt. He'd hoped to find some friendly force in Israel to attach himself to. Instead, more stragglers arrived by the day and attached themselves to him and his.

As he left the tent again to find Derrick, one thing kept gnawing at the back of his mind. They still had received no news from home, and the Israelis knew nothing more than they did. Still no orders from the Pentagon. Still no word from their families, no one to even send death notices to. Still nothing from Samantha.

Hang on Sam, I'm coming.

#

Yujing had become accustomed to less than welcoming receptions from angry governments. In Hong Kong she'd once spent over a month in jail for covering an anti-mainland protest-turned-riot. In Turkey she'd nearly gotten arrested just for speaking to Kurdish hill fighters. Almost a dozen times she'd danced this dance, and yet for the first time in quite a while she felt worried that this might end worse than previous incidents. Jose's sleeping form shifted in restless motion across the cell from her. The flickering light giving Yujing a surreal and uneasy gut feeling as she waited, stewing in her thoughts.

She and Jose had only asked for a one-on-one interview with Conroy, the leader of the Saints. That resulted in the duo getting tossed in here while the rebels figured out what they wanted to do with them. Yujing found herself flabbergasted by their paranoia, but she hoped that once they did some investigation the Christians would deem them not a threat. At this point she had discarded the idea of an interview. She could only focus on her own labored breaths in the sweltering, humid, stagnant air.

This is it. I'm going to die here. Forgotten in this awful place or shot to death by some American hillbillies for whatever reason they dream up. Will I ever see home again? Will I ever even see London again? Yujing imagined herself and Jose in orange jumpsuits kneeling in front of a camera as fanatics with knives ranted away before slicing their throats open.

Yujing forced her focus away from the despair to other concerns, if only as a coping mechanism. The most mundane thing she could dream up in that moment: money. She only had a few hundred American dollars left, she couldn't remember how many, and couldn't check since her captors' had "confiscated" it. That left her with the 24 euros hidden in her sock. If they were let out, how would she make her way around? If the levels of violence that she'd witnessed escalated to their logical conclusion, movement would become extremely dangerous and difficult.

The unmistakable plodding of footsteps outside roused Yujing from a half-sleeping stupor. She lurched up from the steel bench and shook Jose awake as the stamping footfalls came to a stop outside their door. The battered lock slammed and the ancient door it held in place creaked open to reveal a pair of bearded and armed men. One wore combat sunglasses and a drab green headband, while the other had a ball cap and an earpiece with nothing to shield his piercing blue eyes.

"Get up," the guard with sunglasses commanded.

Yujing rose to her feet. "Where are you taking us?"

"Yeah, where we goin', man?" Jose asked with a good deal of drowsiness as he stood up.

"Ya'll gonna clean yourselves up? Then you gonna go talk to Conroy," the guard with blue eyes replied, no hint of deceit in his voice.

"Well, shit. The hell took so long?" Jose gave a half-hearted grin.

"Did you think we were spies?" Yujing asked with caution.

The man with shades gave a shrug in response. "Sumthin' like that, I guess."

"They had to clear ya upstairs. Nobody's ever done an interview with him before, ya see. Can't be too careful, people been assassinated by folks claimin' to be reporters and such," Blue Eyes explained.

Yujing only nodded and followed them out of the cell, Jose trailing her. The guards didn't seem to harbor any personal hatred or suspicion of them, just doing as instructed by their superiors, whose jobs consisted of being suspicious.

After a quick wash-up and change of clothes in the stadium's locker rooms, the pair followed their guides to a car in the parking lot. After a journey of just a few blocks through the still reforming city, they arrived at the golden-domed State Capitol Building. Every approach to the huge structure sat occupied by some manner of improvised barricade, junk vehicles dragged into place alongside hunks of rubble. Guards prowled the grounds in small groups or kept watch from fixed positions.

"C'mon."

Blue Eyes led them from their ride, across the main plaza, up the stairs, and through the concourse, which now bustled with all sorts of religious and militant types, a few politicians and business-looking characters mixed in. Then up more stairs, and finally to the Office of the Governor of the State of Georgia. But upon reaching the outside of the huge polished doors, Yujing could hear a conversation taking place inside.

"Wait up here."

The pair stopped and listened. Yujing could only catch the gist of the discussion between what sounded like just two men.

"...even worse than you've been told. Whatever you may think of the military, not all of its members are willing to obey an openly fascistic regime."

"If only half of them have, it might be enough to crush us."

"You can reduce that ratio a little more. The Garrison of Fort Polk is ready to abandon their orders if you are willing to open a dialogue with them."

"I'll do what I can. Even if they just give up and go home, everyone not trying to kill us is a victory. For those who come against us all the same though, I can promise nothing."

A deep sigh. "I understand. I'll get you whatever aid I'm able. Both to convince those who can be, and to destroy those who can't."

Heavy footsteps approaching prompted Yujing to feign disinterest. Thankful for the first time that her press badge had yet to be returned. The massive doors swung open, revealing a huge blond haired man in sunglasses, dressed in all black and built like a rock face. He gave Yujing and Jose a suspicious once-over, before barging past them and heading off down the hall, two well equipped soldiers, also in black, following close behind him. Yujing knew better than to ask who the man was, but filed the information in her brain to be noted down as soon as she got the chance.

"Go on now," Blue Eyes beckoned.

Yujing nodded, and passed through the now opened doorway alongside Jose. The guards closed the door behind them. Waiting on the inside sat a bearded man in simple brown robes, a figure neither of them could mistake for any other.

"Father Conroy?" Yujing stepped into the dim illumination of torches at the center of the room.

"The infamous," he answered with a jolly smile. "And you must be the reporter who gave us some cause for concern?"

"I am," she answered.

"I hope you understand. It isn't exactly unheard of for assassins to pose as reporters."

"I understand,"

"Wonderful. Now, what is it I can help you with?"

Yujing cleared her throat, "I just wanted to hear your perspective on this war. Your reasons for doing what you've done."

Conroy stroked his chin. "And how do I know you won't spin this against me? Make me look like some kinda crazed cult leader?"

"I don't have to spin anything," Yujing answered with conviction. "In the BBC we only report the facts. I won't make you look like anything."

"I guess we'll see about that…" Conroy sighed, leaning back in his chair. "So, where should we begin?"

CHAPTER 12:
DEVILS AND ZEALOTS

"Men and women believed and proclaimed God was firmly on their side – an easy and shallow assertion that reduced God to a sort of house deity."
— Gustav Niebuhr

Harper growled under her breath. She watched alongside her recently assigned subordinates as a black 1959 Cadillac Sedan DeVille cruised its way down the dusty backroad towards the assembled command staff. The harsh wind swept across the road from the west, driving waves of sand and dirt over its surface like a searing river. The venerable car came to a gradual stop about 20 feet away from the nine officers. Four ramshackle technicals serving as an escort formed a half-circle behind it. Harper began to approach the vehicle as the doors opened, and out of the back stepped Singh who looked more... charred... than before. His charcoal overcoat and cap now pockmarked by scorched patches, the buttons open to reveal a simple light gray Mao suit beneath.

Harper had half expected him to be wearing an old Che t-shirt, or maybe something about 'Rage Against the Machine.' But as unexpected as the Mao suit was, it tracked.

Singh's face betrayed nothing, the expression beneath his aviators one of... boredom. Harper had something on her mind, though. To hell with her boss's fatigue.

"Okay, who had to die for you to end up with that car?" she demanded with crossed arms.

Instead of becoming furious at getting so openly accused by his de facto second-in-command, Singh took it in stride. "I'll have you know, good madame!" he declared in feigned offense, "I not only didn't kill anybody to end up with this car, but I got it by preventing people from being murdered!" he finished with a grand gesture.

"How so?" Harper asked in disbelief with an arched brow.

"I talked an angry mob out of looting a classic car shop and killing the dudes who ran it. More of a road stop on the way to the actual objective if I'm honest," Singh elaborated in his normal voice as he resumed walking towards the ridgeline opposite the parked sedan.

Harper and the others followed along, the general examining Singh's now tattered coat as they did. "And how'd that objective go?" she asked with a forced smile, expecting to get brushed off.

"It was a total success!" he proclaimed with a sudden upraised fist. "We're now connected to our comrades in Nevada, which means endless manpower for them and endless military hardware for us." As the group arrived near the precipice of the ridge, Singh appeared to just notice all the conspicuous damage to his clothing. "Though, uh, it did end up involving a lot more napalm than I originally anticipated."

Harper's eyes widened. "Napalm!? How the hell did it involve napalm!?"

As the group came to a stop, just able to see over the ridge, Singh groaned and rubbed his brow. "Harper, can I just deal with the image of dozens of people getting melted alive in front of me in my fucking nightmares, please?" he asked in an annoyed voice, not turning around to face her.

Shit. Now I'm the asshole. What an asshole.

Before Harper could think of a way to respond, Bennigsen intervened verbally, all but throwing himself between the two. "We have the whole town surrounded, Comrade Singh. About a dozen deserters have come out since we arrived, and our forces are ready to begin the attack."

"Good," Singh responded, just as happy to move on. "What have these deserters said?" he asked, peering through a set of binoculars. Harper took out her own pair and did the same, studying the unusual town of their interest. Lebec, a small hamlet of less than 2,000 people. It wrapped around the mountains like a splayed crescent, almost separated in two, but connected by a string of crude houses. What made it so important to the Reds, apart from the presence of religious crazies, boiled down to its location. The town sat right on one of three ways to travel south by land, meaning they had to take it if they wanted to move on to LA and San Diego. So the conquest of this little nothing, represented a necessity to them.

"Apparently all the women and children are being kept in the churches and schools. Most of the people not willing to go along with all this are either dead, or left when everything started. North to us or south to L.A.," Bennigsen explained. "And the general number we've gotten from them is around 200…"

Harper scanned over the backwater town until her eyes landed upon a simple church typical of American Protestantism. The immaculate bricks and wood, the near spotless white paint of the steeple, in a town where most of the structures could easily be mistaken as derelict.

"Hmm…" Singh kept the binoculars glued to his eyes. "Shake things up for them a bit first, see what happens."

"How?" asked a tall Hispanic officer with a full black mustache. "Sir," he added in a hurry.

"Just use some mortars to start off, nothing too absurd," Singh replied, pretending not to notice as he brought his binoculars down. "Let's see if we can't make this… a bit too **real** for them." His face morphed into a wicked grin that only Harper could see from right beside him.

A shiver wormed down Harper's soul, as she wished for a desperate moment that something, anything would show her the way. *Is this it? Is this how this terrible, insane story ends? With terrible insanity? There is no way back from this, for any of us… or them.*

"Harper!" The general's eyes shot over to where Singh stood pointing directly at her. "Gather some of your more competent forces. We're going to try and grab the only thing on this Earth that these people at least pretend to care about."

"Their families?" Harper asked with narrowed eyes.

"Bingo," Singh answered before taking a draw from his pipe. "And the people who are just plain old hostages to these fools."

"Right, cause we're the good guys," Harper muttered.

"Remember, General, in a world overflowing with horrific brutality it would be a huge detriment for us to *not* use it," Singh all but chided. "The difference between us and them is that we are using horrific brutality to create a new civilization, not to extract as much wealth as possible. Besides, we could just glass the whole place if we really wanted them *all* dead."

Harper sighed. *True.* "What if they refuse to leave?"

"Well, if they're that insane, then we can't really do much, can we?" Singh answered with a tired voice.

Harper closed her eyes for a moment as she steeled herself. *Well, at least he isn't excited about this or some shit.* "I guess not."

"Seriously though, lets get the people who aren't up for this out before we level the place. Speed is key, don't give them a chance to respond," Singh emphasized, turning to face Harper and the others.

"Of course," Harper answered, her face a mask of stone. She felt both irritated at the obviousness of this, and unable to blame Singh for stating it openly, given the circumstances.

Singh grunted. "Let's get this over with."

#

Emily stood under the blazing sun. Sweating, breathing, trying not to shake at the hollow echo of mortars firing in clusters all around. Her platoon waited alongside eight others, spaced out like a checkerboard and hidden behind yet another mountain ridge. She had no clue how their superiors intended to deploy them against this small rural town. Or even why. They had plenty of units in this new "army" so why did she get lucky? Anyone could take out a bunch of religious crazies. She might've held suspicion that this Singh character intended to use her and other ex-cops as cannon fodder, but this force consisted of a wide mix of people.

And of course… the tanks. Six of them. Abrams tanks with all manner of bells and whistles attached. Not things to

110

just throw away. The sheer amount of weaponry at the Reds' disposal made Emily feel conflicted in a strange way, as it both increased her chances of surviving this engagement and made her feel more trapped than ever.

The chopping of Guardian drones overhead deepened Emily's unease. Once they represented in her mind the all powerful reach of the technology at her back. Now, they represented only how the things Emily thought would never change could in fact disappear in a moment. Maybe the Reds would disappear too? But Emily couldn't afford to hang her hopes on that. At least, not yet…

"Comrades!" A Red Officer's voice resonated amid the symphony of war. "Beyond these hills is a church. Within that church is half a town's worth of hostages. Our mission is to rescue them." He walked between the rows of troops, arms behind his back. A pair of Reds trailed him with submachine guns. "If anyone refuses to surrender immediately or fires upon us, they will be destroyed." The officer went on, "Trust nothing, because our enemy here is capable of anything."

The crackle and boom of explosives cascaded over the rocks, plumes of soil and debris following close behind as Emily checked the receiver of her Garand, blinking away sweat… and fear.

"Headsets on! Move out!"

Everyone put in earplugs and fell in behind sergeants, who guided the units around the ridge. The tanks led the way, blasting shells into any building that gunfire burst from. Those walking right behind the armored hulks fired whatever weapon they had into the buildings with reckless abandon, ignoring only the church. Emily stayed well behind one of the tanks alongside the rest of her platoon, ducking her head down as sparks flared up anytime the tank took fire. The vehicles powered through the madness without getting destroyed, and only one man got injured by shrapnel as the Red conscripts closed the open space. Emily looked over her shoulder to find machine gunners and snipers lined all along the ridges and hills around them, dumping rounds into the settlement.

This is no battleground, it's a slaughterhouse. The tank rumbled to a stop before turning its turret five degrees and obliterating someone's house with a high explosive shell. Emily ducked, covering her head as a volley of automatic fire spanked off the Abrams' engine deck. Looking back up from a more crouched stance, she could see the silhouette of someone up in the church steeple, the only place high enough for the shots to have come from. Lining up her rifle, Emily decided to just fire a whole clip up there after calling it out.

"Up in the steeple!" Once the words had left her lips, Emily sent eight rounds of 30 ought six into the wooden tower's openings. She heard the iconic ping of her spent clip getting ejected from the Garand's receiver and hunkered behind the tank to reload. As she did, Kniva propped his machine gun onto the tank's engine deck and fired his own stream of rounds into the church tower, shredding it apart as chunks of wood and brickwork rained down. Eventually, a Bradley noticed the attention directed against the church and annihilated the steeple with a handful of shells from its auto cannon. The tank jerked onwards once again, and the advance continued.

"Section 1, clear that long-ass buildin' by the church!" Coleman ordered alongside a hand signal.

Shit, that's us! Emily realized.

"Aight, Sec 1, let's go!" a voice ushered from behind her. Turning around, Emily saw the corporal she now knew as Guzo, moving off to the right with Andres, a rifleman carrying an old M16, tailing right behind him. Emily followed them alongside Sophie and Kniva as the tank continued on towards the church itself. She noticed for the first time a home covered in part by a tattered clear plastic tarp featuring black and yellow biohazard signs. As Emily and her squad moved along the structure while doing their best not to touch it, she wished for the days when the plague represented the greatest threat.

The five of them hugged the wall of the long community building, glancing with primal suspicion between windows, clutching their weapons at the ready. A stray round from… something… tore a hole through the wooden wall, forcing all of them to halt. They continued, stacking up around the door while evading the windows. Once everyone had shuffled into their poorly trained but adequate stance, Guzo gave a brisk nod. To Emily's surprise, Kniva then used his MG stock like a battering ram, smashing the door over before diving away as the section's other four guns poked through the frame.

A pair of low-caliber gunshots rang out, bullets snapped past Emily's shielded ears. All four of them fired back. A moment later, nothing. With great caution, Andres led the way, flipping on the flashlight attachment of his weapon. The dim room contained destroyed furniture and walls, but no hostiles. No living ones anyway. A young man lay crumpled in the main hallway, a 9mm pistol at his side. Andres proceeded through the doorway alongside a wary Guzo, while Emily and Sophie remained propped up in the door on overwatch. Kniva stayed just outside, watching everyone's backs.

The illumination of the doorway and their weapon lights revealed only whips of dust and grime kicked up by bullet impacts. No one said a word, the interior of the building remained silent… until a door on the far end of the room flung open with a cacophonous slam.

"Die ya god—!" *BLAM!* "HUK!" A middle-aged white man collapsed to the filthy carpet, grasping his chest with his left had as his right tried in futility to cling onto an M4.

The entire section pivoted their heads over to Emily, who sat panting, leaned against the doorframe with her smoking rifle in hand. She looked between them, not quite sure what to say, having reacted on instinct. "Uh… hostile down?"

Guzo looked over to the panicked man, now choking and gasping as he lay on the floor, his weapon out of his immediate reach. Guzo listened for a moment, as did the rest of them, channeling out the chaos of outside while trying to discern if anyone else remained in the building. Satisfied, Guzo rose and walked over to the writhing man before drawing a pistol and ending his suffering with a single shot.

That done, he turned back to Emily with his narrow, shrewd eyes. "Nice shot, thanks."

"Don't mention it," Emily replied, not sure how else to respond.

"C'mon, everybody inside." Guzo motioned them in with his sidearm before holstering it again and switching back to his AK.

Sophie leapt inside with Emily and Kniva right behind her. Emily kept her rifle pointed ahead, making her way over to the man she had shot. Doing her best to not linger on the corpse, Emily slung the Garand over her shoulder and picked the M4 off the ground. Lasers, optics, foregrip, taped magazines. *Hmm, hillbillies.*

"C'mon, girl. We ain't got time to wait," Sophie hissed over the din of battle as everyone else moved ahead through the building. Making a swift removal of the dead man's ammo belt, Emily did her best not to linger on the looting of a body, instead turning to find Kniva sliding the first man's pistol into the back of his pants. The ex-con looked down at Emily's new rifle with an approving nod as he moved to follow the others.

"Let's go. You can show your new toy to the crazies." Sophie gave her a hard smack on the backpack, following Kniva. Emily suppressed a groan as she returned to her feet. *Apparently I'm the only one here who still has any reservations about this.*

The eastern room windows, which had already gotten shattered by mortar rounds, revealed the Abrams tank, along with the rest of 9th platoon hiding around a corner. Emily wondered what they waited on as they sat out of the church's view. She didn't have to wait long.

Emily ducked back into the shadows as the dirge of chopping helicopter blades rippled through the air. Peeking out around the window sill, she watched in something like amazed horror as an Apache with red stars on each of its sides peeled into view then hovered over the church for just a moment, before delivering a volley of missiles into one of the town's few two story structures. The building, whatever it had served as, turned into a blazing tower of debris and soil, the shockwave tearing through the town. Emily raised her head again with caution to find an assortment of unarmed people staggering out of the church with their hands raised, begging not to be killed. With a couple of orders, the Reds barged past them into the church, leaving them for others to bind and pull out of the way. The gunfire began to die off with remarkable speed as the Apache assumed a higher position above the town.

"*Section 1, get all yer asses outside the damn church. Help us watch these hicks,*" Coleman's voice crackled through the radio.

"Got it, Sarge," Guzo answered. "Let's go, guys."

"What are we going to do with these dirtbags?" Emily asked Sophie in a whisper.

"Nothin', just send em back to the city. Unless they do somethin' crazy…" Sophie replied while scanning the windows.

Emily followed without another word.

Once outside, she watched as a growing line of terrified civilians emerged from the church, ushered along by armed Reds. Several men in various stages of dishevelment appeared from ruined buildings and threw down their weapons. Tanks, APCs, and trucks started advancing over the flattened town, rumbling over the chunks of buildings and scattered bits of rubble. Emily couldn't believe a violent battle like this could end with such abruptness. But as Emily witnessed the devastation, she started to understand why. The Reds' combination of overwhelming firepower and ruthlessness meant these poor dupes never stood a chance. Echoes of explosions to the south boomed like thunderstorms, and gave Emily chills.

"Hey, guys!" The voice of Andres grabbed the attention of everyone nearby. "You'll wanna see this."

Emily headed over to where Andres stood: a corrugated metal shack with scorch marks around every little crack and hole as if it had burned from the inside out. Sophie hunkered just behind Emily's shoulder as they both watched Guzo stick his head into the hut… before yanking it back out and gagging and with his hand covering his mouth.

"Fuck! *HACK! COUGH!* Son of a bitch!" Guzo staggered away, waving his hand.

Emily turned to see Andres' lifeless thousand-yard stare, and knew what he must've found. But she had to know, had to see for herself. Could it possibly be true? Could they have really done what the Reds accused them of?

Emily approached the broken shack door with great apprehension, standing far away from the entrance but moving to an angle where she could peer inside. A heap of melted, blackened shapes greeted her, accompanied by the sickening odor that Emily knew all too well. She turned away, fighting to hold down the ramen noodles she'd eaten for lunch… and to keep the tears away. *What the fuck has become of this place?*

#

Harper watched the smoke rise into the blackened sky as columns of vehicles flowed through the blazing ruins of what just hours ago had been the town of Lebec. She felt ripples of heat wave across her face with the wind, carrying the wretched stench of old wood, drywall, fuel… and human flesh… as each burned. Harper's eyes glazed over as her whole body went numb. She knew fighting against her countrymen came with the territory. The choices she'd made. But she never expected it to come with such ferocity—or such pitiless regularity.

Harper once read about the collapse of an eastern European nation called Yugoslavia, though so much time had passed that she couldn't remember the book's title. She did remember how unreal the tale sounded. That families, neighbors, coworkers, people who had lived together all their lives could turn against each other so completely and in so short a time seemed like a work of dark magic. Had Harper read it from a novel, she'd consider it lazy writing. She still didn't understand it, even as she watched it unfold around her.

A stifled cough drew Harper's gaze to a gray-clad figure, Singh, rifling through a stack of papers. Dispatches from unit commanders and God knew who else, brought in by courier multiple times an hour. Harper did her best to track them as they came and went, but soon found it impossible. Singh had switched his mirrored sunglasses for the cheap, round spectacles he usually wore. He looked more like a bored accountant than a military commander, even as an entire community disintegrated to ashes around them. Harper felt her jaw tighten, then relax. She still couldn't decide if she hated his unrepentant demeanor more than she hated the idea of him *pretending* to care, but either way it made her not worry too much about giving him a hard time.

"So… what's the plan for L.A.?" Harper prodded with a southward gesture.

"To swarm in," he announced in a distracted voice, "support our forces besieging the LAPD, consolidate our control, then keep moving south." Singh never even looked up from his array of papers.

"Any idea what to do about all the looting and murdering that's still goin' on? Or about whatever everyone in LA is up to?" Harper questioned.

Singh looked up at her with deadpan eyes. "No." His attention fell back down to the papers. "We focus on the big picture, no point wasting time trying to contain something uncontainable."

Harper turned around at the sound of frantic shouting just in time to watch a man in a sheriff's deputy's uniform get his head blasted open by a Red soldier with an ancient pump shotgun. Her gaze whipped back around to find Singh had not even noticed.

"So, we're just going to let all this shit go? Without even tryin' to stop it!?" Harper snapped.

"Stop it? No. Contain it? Yes," Singh answered in monotone.

"*Contain* it?" Harper asked.

Singh released a sigh, folding his papers up and shoving them into his coat pocket. "As long as we can guide their vengeance-driven rage in the direction of the people who don't like us, and away from the people who can at least tolerate us, I will consider our efforts in that regard to be a success." He made his way past Harper and out of the now vacant church as a pair of Reds with jerrycans started dousing everything in fuel. Harper followed, still trying to process what she'd just heard.

"You mean, we're not even going to try and get more people on our side?" she pressed.

"Don't be absurd, of course we are," Singh responded in mounting irritation. "We have to choose our battles carefully. The rurals are stupid enough to loathe us unconditionally without even understanding what the words they deride us with mean. And they've also been brainwashed for generations to believe they can defeat any 'evil invader' with a guerrilla war. Again, without any understanding of what such a thing would entail. To try and win 'hearts and minds' while also fighting against the many armed forces trying to destroy us would not just be a waste of time, it would be a fatal error."

"So we just destroy them? What the hell's wrong with you?" Harper demanded in a dry voice.

Singh stopped, turning around with an expression not of anger or suspicion but… curiosity. As though he couldn't understand why this bothered her so much. "Listen, Harper, I've already thought very carefully over the desperation, the cause, the consequences of defeat, and the possibilities for victory. What is wrong with me is that I have accepted the unfortunate reality in front of my eyes. Either we reign supreme in our corner and push out those who hate us, or they reign over **us** and push **us** out. I'm sure you think I'm insane or something, but once news starts arriving of what has gone on in the east…" Singh paused for a moment and Harper thought she saw a faint shudder emanate from him. "Everything will get so much worse, and our job of even focusing the outpour of fury will test the limits of our capacities."

I'm in hell. "What is it you're trying to prove anyway?"

"Its not about proving anything," Singh answered with an even voice. "Its about victory."

"And that's worth it to you? Victory at any cost? Even if it leaves everyone hating and fearing us?"

"They already hate and fear us," Singh stated, lighting his ceramic pipe.

"But you think a victory built on a pile of corpses is going to lead to the world you want?"

"All victories are built on heaps of corpses. It is what it is," Singh answered, taking a long drag from his pipe before exhaling a cloud of smoke. "Without victory, we will never have a chance to build any kind of world, flawed or utopian." He coughed once, covering his mouth and groaning, "Despite its horrors, our present course offers the possibility of improvement, evolution, *change*. Leaving things as they are—and continuing to waste time trying to save that which cannot, and *should* not, be saved—offers nothing but the certainty of perpetual suffering, exploitation, and decay." Singh at last turned back around from the flowing torrent of their advancing army to face Harper, his bright jade eyes reflecting the inferno that now consumed the church. "You may value the lives of those who see you as subhuman vermin and seek only to rule over you as kings… but *I* do **not**."

Harper watched in speechless despair as Singh headed off towards his waiting black sedan, a pair of gas-masked bodyguards following close behind. *I am in hell. And I've made a deal with the devil.* She headed for her own adopted command vehicle with heavy steps. Singh truly, genuinely, to the core of his deadened heart neither believed in nor cared about the America she knew.

She couldn't call him crazy since he at least appeared to live by his own ethos, but his code bore little resemblance to either her own, or to anyone else's she'd ever heard of. Harper might have turned against a command structure that had betrayed its own nation, but she still viewed the American people as her people. Even if they did not all reciprocate this feeling. Subutai Singh, though… really, *really*, **didn't**. He'd chosen a side for his own reasons, and everyone who couldn't be wrangled onto that side: they could all just rot in hell.

A wicked part of Harper's brain, a part she loathed, had always pushed the inevitable idea that such a tribalistic breakdown would occur. But she'd always imagined an unconscious stumbling into sectarian conflict… that people would divide further as a natural consequence. Singh, though? This man seemed to have made it his mission in life to lead everyone not just off the reservation, but so far away that they'd never find their way back, even if they wanted to. Harper had done terrible things when deployed, things she could never forgive herself for. But to this kid, it all amounted to some kind of mathematical problem that he could solve by just reshaping everything in the way he preferred.

After all, as Singh had said, the conservatives would've done the same to them had they won. Right? The exact same rationale she had heard from the lips of countless army personnel, and which she'd told herself more than once. Funny, now it felt more like a justification.

Harper had long clung to the hope that somehow she could remake things, that she could at last undo and repair the old injustices. That she could welcome the alienated into society. That the promise of America could truly be realized. A foolish hope that now lay in ashes. As disturbed as Harper felt about all of this, she knew Singh had the right idea. The madness in the east would without doubt match or exceed what Harper had witnessed, and Singh knew it. She hated him for that. Hated him for diving into the snake pit of sectarianism without hesitation. Despite hating him, Harper still needed to understand him and his fellow revolutionaries—at least if she had any hope for survival.

Getting rid of Singh still didn't seem like an option. Based on all she knew about these people, Harper felt more than certain anyone who replaced Singh would have to be just as bad. Maybe worse. And she knew it could be **so** much worse. That, and trying to take on a merciless psychotic with an army at his command seemed like a bad idea. She had to own her decision, whether she killed it or not.

Harper shook her head. The General would have to figure out how to deal with Singh later. For now, she needed to focus on corralling her unruly horde into LA and bring the place under revolutionary control. Harper drew in a deep breath, pushing the inescapable dread permeating everything to the back of her mind. For now, making the most of the terrible situation seemed like the best option available. She felt her lips twist into a dark grin. If any group of people existed on this planet who she wouldn't feel bad about eradicating, that group was the LAPD. *Maybe this doesn't have to be so bad after all.*

#

Paul gave his ex-cellmate a concerned look as he stared at the fresh scar across Mason's chin. He drank like a man who had just walked out of the desert from the canteen Mason offered him, then handed it back with a look of gratitude. The water cleansed the haze from his mind, as he felt a hand come to rest on his shoulder.

"You okay?" Mason asked.

"No. But I'll survive." Paul wiped the sweat and grime from his forehead. "What is it?"

"We got a ton o' people tryin' to cross the river from the north," Mason answered with a surprising lack of panic in his voice.

Paul couldn't help but groan. "More Feddies?" he asked in irritation.

"Nah, all civvies. They say they're headed west, but they wanna pass through our land to get around the Brotherhood," Mason explained.

115

"Libs?" Paul queried with an arched brow.

"Looks like it," Mason replied with a shrug. "Whole lot of 'em look pretty raggedy, and they been tellin' sum nasty stories 'bout what's goin' on up there. They say the Brotherhood's roundin' up all the Libs, Lefties, and anyone who don't agree with 'em. Nobody knows what happens to 'em, but s'not like it takes a genius…" he trailed off, scratching the back of his neck.

Paul wiped the mud and grit from his short beard, rising to his feet with a creaking of exhausted joints and bones. "Well, hell, sounds like I better have a look at 'em."

With Mason at his side, Paul made his way through the battered ruins of the high school, past lines of wounded men and women awaiting medical attention, and out into the rain-soaked misery of northern Virginia.

A column of disheveled, terrified, and crestfallen people staggered down the main road, heading to the south and west. Some armed with a chaotic mess of weapons, but most lugging bags or cases full of everyday possessions. Others carried nothing as they shuffled on towards an unknown destination, their eyes clouded with incomprehension and sorrow. The group presented no uniformity whatsoever. Workers and homeless, young and old, cops and prisoners, soldiers and rebels, the weakened and the resolute. All worn and ragged, clutching to what few possessions and supplies they still had.

Paul just stood for a moment watching the refugees as they plodded on—unable to escape the feeling that he had gazed into an old photograph of some terrible war long past. He approached the river of humanity with Mason and two other Saints at his side. None of them would give the Saints a straight look, preferring to move on without engaging at all. The Rebel Captain came to a stop with some hesitation, not wanting to make the mass of people nervous.

"Where are y'all headed?" Paul asked no particular person.

For a while everyone marched on without anyone saying anything.

"West," came a lone voice from among the otherwise silent marchers.

Paul's gaze fixed on a dark faced man in a military cap and brown canvas jacket who strayed from the edge of the column. "Sure you don't want to stay, brother?"

The bronze-skinned refugee gave a forced smile. "Yeah. We're sure."

Paul shrugged. "Well, alright. What is it y'all hope to find out west?"

"Can't say for certain. Everyone says it's the only place that the rightwing militias or the Feds don't control. We don't know what the fuck's out there… but it's the only chance we got."

"Won't cause any trouble passin' through will ya?" Paul asked.

"Not unless trouble comes to us," the man answered.

"You the head honcho?" Paul wondered aloud.

"People listen to me, so I guess I'm close as it gets."

"Name's Paul. You got one?" he asked.

"Roberto," came the answer.

Paul nodded. "Well, Roberto, I wish you good luck. We won't hold ya up."

Roberto tipped his field cap. "Much obliged. Good luck fighting off those Feddies and Nazis."

Paul gave an exhausted smile in reply before a familiar voice came from over his shoulder.

"Excuse me, sir?" came a familiar feminine voice. Both men's gazes shifted over to the Asian BBC reporter from earlier heading toward them, her much taller companion of mixed-race trailing just behind. "Did you say your people are making their way west?"

Paul grumbled a bit under his breath but managed a smile of recognition. So far as reporters went, this girl had behaved well… but still.

Roberto stopped, scratched the back of his head. "Uh, yeah, the hope is to at least reach the Rockies. Why do you ask?"

"Well, as it happens, I need some way of reaching the west, and since all of my other options have disappeared thanks to the war, we were hoping to eh… 'tag along?'" Yujing asked with a nervous smile.

"We won't slow y'all down or cause you no trouble," Jose assured.

The tired refugee looked the pair over for a thorough moment, before releasing a heavy sigh and making a broad gesture. "Sure, why not. Isn't like I could do much to stop you anyway. But who are you guys?"

"We're reporters with the BBC." The young woman extended her hand, which Roberto shook with some care. "Yujing Huang, nice to meet you. This is my… colleague, Jose Everett. We won't bother anyone who doesn't want to speak with us."

"Sure, sure. Let's just get out of here." Roberto waved the pair of reporters over as he made his way back to the column. Paul watched them go, kept watching as they melted away into the human river flowing westward.

Almost as if on cue, a column of deuce-and-a-halfs came roaring down the road into the high school parking lot. This caught Paul's attention, and that of the two reporters he'd just seen off.

Paul groaned, wiping his brow. "I guess it's never enough."

Paul jumped into a jeep with a huge machine gun in back with Mason riding shotgun and they drove back across the grassy medians to find yet another scene of impromptu chaos. Half a dozen of the large trucks had lined up outside the entrance, a myriad of saints and soldiers dressed in all black gear busied themselves unloading a series of long, narrow wooden crates. As Paul approached the bizarre display to demand an explanation, he got intercepted by a young man in a black coat with sandy brown hair and dark sunglasses. The young man handed him a folder.

"What is this?" Paul asked in confusion.

"This contains your new orders," the man explained. "These," he gestured to the wooden crates still being unloaded, "are explosives for destroying all of the bridges into town, as well as a series of other vital infrastructure sites."

"The hell? We're going to go scorched earth on the whole place? Says who?"

"Conroy." The Man in Shades gestured to the file, which Paul at last opened.

Sure enough, right there on top sat a signed order from Conroy to do as he had just been instructed.

Paul glared back up at the Man in Shades. "Who are you?"

The man's face didn't budge a micron. "A group of people who want to see you succeed."

Paul looked back down at the folder, rifling through the maps and plans, finally releasing a resigned sigh. "Alright then, I guess we'll do it."

"I'm only here to facilitate your leader's will." With that, the man turned and left.

Paul watched as he climbed into and armored SUV, refusing a request for a comment or identification from the female reporter who, together with her partner, had followed Paul and Mason to the school on foot. With a screech of tires, the mystery man vanished back down the same road he arrived on, followed shortly thereafter by the now emptied trucks.

"Guess this ain't a bed 'o roses for anybody, huh?" Mason floated before taking a drag from his e-cigarette.

Thunder rumbled, Paul gazed up into the still pouring heavens. "Nah, It ain't."

CHAPTER 13:
ODYSSEY OF OUTCASTS

"Faithless is he who says farewell when the road darkens."
— J R. R. Tolkien

Alexander's mind reverberated with the same mechanical sounds and indistinct voices that had surrounded him all day. The random-yet-monotonous swoosh of the tent rippling in the harsh desert wind, the groans of the injured. The Israelis had given the Americans a case of Golan Heights Yarden Rosé Brút as thanks for their tip and assistance. Israeli champagne. Alexander drank straight from his bottle as if it were water, immediately feeling bubbly and buzzed. He tried to dismiss the feeling, he needed answers and ships, not booze. But for now, he had to make do. *Waiting on the Israelis.* Alexander hadn't gotten much firsthand experience with the IDF until now, and so far he couldn't tell if that had helped or hurt him.

"Sir?" Sergeant Major Escobedo beckoned.

Alexander's head cocked toward the stark voice in the tent entrance behind him. "What's up Sar'major?"

"The IDF colonel wants to talk, jefe. Says it's important," Escobedo replied.

Alexander gave a grunt and a nod. "It better be."

The commandeered shipping office they arrived at moments later sat almost empty, aside from Daskal, Derek, Captains Nakamura and Warwick, Price, and an IDF officer who Alexander didn't recognize. The weary and slightly drunk captain wasted no time.

"Any news from home?" he prompted.

Daskal's face morphed from a look of surprise at his directness, to one of uncertainty.

"Come on, just let us have it. What the hell's going on?" Alexander pressed.

"We don't know for certain, but it's nothing good. The Russians and Chinese did take out your satellites, and everyone else's with them. But they also hit your homeland with an EMP attack, fried all of your electronics—more or less."

Alexander's eyes widened a bit more with each word. The fact that his country hadn't gotten reduced to an ocean of slag was good… but the implications of what Daskal said made his veins run cold. *No power…*

"**All** of the power is dead?" Derek asked, vocalizing Alexander's thoughts.

"Everything with a microchip in it," Daskal answered.

"What about the government? The Pentagon? What are they doing about this?" Alexander reached in desperation.

"Getting torn apart, from what we can tell," Daskal replied in a grim voice that Alexander hadn't heard him use before.

"You mean…?" Alexander asked, his face going numb.

"Some kind of civil war," Colonel Daskal confirmed. "We don't know the details, unfortunately."

"*A civil war?* Between who? Over what!?" Derek demanded.

"As I said, we know very little," Daskal repeated. "Several groups are fighting to control the government in Washington, others are fighting to escape its control. All the specifics remain hazy for now, though."

Alexander struggled to process the massive and terrible revelation dumped in front of him. *Civil war. What must've happened since this whole disaster started?*

"But… there haven't been any nukes?" Alexander managed to ask.

Daskal shook his head, causing a small but welcome wave of relief to wash over the room. "No. It seems your enemies just want to neutralize your nation as a threat, not invite total destruction upon themselves."

"Unbelievable…" Price muttered as he fumbled with a cigarette.

"Well, what the hell do we do then? Who do we even get our orders from?" Escobedo demanded in mounting frustration.

Daskal shrugged. "So far we've heard about no less that four regional commands trying to assume control over all your deployed forces, though none seem to have had any success so far."

"We still need to reach Europe," Alexander stated, trying to get everyone focused on the present.

"Yes… we can help you with that, but we must ask you for two more favors before we do."

"Are you fuckin' kidding me!? Haven't we done more than enough already?" Derek demanded.

Alexander started to intervene. "At ease, Lieutenant."

"It's alright, Captain," Daskal assured him. "I understand this must feel unreasonable, but these are most desperate times… and sadly it isn't my choice to make."

Silence hung over the room for a moment as everyone mulled over the complex situation facing them in their own heads.

"What favors do you want from us?" Alexander managed.

"Well to start, another army is knocking at our door to the southeast," Daskal said.

"More Iranians?" Escobedo asked.

"No, they seem to have gotten the message. It's the Saudis this time," the IDF colonel answered.

"Of course…" Nakamura groaned with bitterness. The Japanese-American had spent time training Saudi forces in the past, an experience about which he grumbled often.

Now we get to fight against our own shit? Awesome. Alexander sighed. "What else?"

"The second is less a favor and more of a concession. We need some of your vehicles and heavy equipment when you eventually go."

Alexander's eyes narrowed. "How many is some?"

"Half," Daskal uttered, obviously aware of the contentiousness of the request.

"No way!" Warwick blurted. "If there is some kinda civil war goin' on, we're gonna need all that stuff, man!"

"And how do you plan to get it there… without our help?" Colonel Daskal queried in a calm voice.

Another silence permeated the room, far more tense this time around. Alexander rubbed his brow with his right hand, thinking. "Colonel, would you give me a few minutes to discuss with my compatriots?"

"Of course," Daskal replied in an instant, opening a steel door and stepping deeper into the building with his fellow IDF officer just behind.

As soon as the door clicked shut, Derrick spun on Alexander with desperate eyes. "Come on, sir. There has to be some way out of this…"

"If there is, I don't see it," Alexander admitted.

"If we show up in Europe with just half of our shit, that's a whole lot of clout right down the drain," Warwick pointed out.

Alexander grumbled in his head. Despite his characteristic bluntness, Warwick had a point. It would prove far easier to get others to listen to them if they had a bunch of tanks, choppers, and other vehicles. Who knew how necessary that might prove? Not to mention the optics of just handing over a bunch of U.S. government property without even trying to consult the higher ups.

"We have already helped them out twice, this other 'favor' they want will make three," Nakamura added. "Is it really that unreasonable to demand they just let us go with all of our stuff?"

"No, it isn't," Warwick assured.

Alexander's eyes shifted over to Derrick, who could only offer a brow raise and a shrug. *Fuck.* He didn't want to antagonize the Israelis, since they represented his people's best and only chance to get home. On the other hand, his comrades were right. They had to at least **try** to push back.

Alexander thought it over and a long silence ensued. Everyone in the room stared in trepidation until their undisputed leader spoke.

"When we leave here, none of you breathe a word of this to the troops," Alexander told them.

"Wait, what!?" came the flabbergasted reaction from Derek's mouth. Nakamura crossed his arms and looked away, shaking his head.

"Look!" Alexander stated. "We still don't really know anything. This 'civil war' could be a complete disaster, or it could be another failed coup that will fizzle out into nothing by the time we get back. There's no point sowing seeds of chaos among our own when we've got nothing to go on. Alright?"

The American officers exchanged uneasy glances, but Alexander knew they could see his point. A collective nod of affirmation followed, and Alexander gestured for Derek to go ahead. With a deep breath, the lieutenant opened the door and waved the two Israelis back in.

Daskal looked over the strained faces throughout the room, his own betraying no joy at having put such a pressure on them. "So, have you decided?"

"Yes, we have," Alexander answered in a determined voice. "And I'm afraid that despite the dire circumstances, you have asked for more than we can comfortably offer you under our own authority."

Daskal arched an eyebrow, but showed no outward sign of displeasure. "Oh?"

"We can offer you assistance in dealing with the Saudis, or we can give you half of our heavy equipment, but we can't give you both," Alexander explained, the faintest hints of a grin appearing at the edges of his lips.

Daskal stroked his stubbled chin in deep thought for a long moment. "I think... I can talk my superiors into accepting this. They will not be happy... But I believe they will settle for taking what they can get."

"Which option do you think they might pick?" Alexander posited.

"Probably helping with the Saudis," Daskal replied.

"Figures..." Warwick muttered.

"We truly appreciate your willingness to aid our cause, and we of course respect your abilities. But we must wait until we hear back before I can give a definite answer." Daskal added.

"So... you're okay with this deal?" Derrick clarified.

"I serve my country just as you do, but the truth... I am as you say, the middle-man here. You go talk to your people, I will get on phone with Jerusalem." Daskal stood as if to walk back out of the room, but stopped and turned suddenly, "But if the Saudis attack before then, you will have no choice but to fight with us. And that would almost make all of your equipment ours," he smiled.

With those last ominous words, the colonel and his man left the room again. The small collection of American leaders exchanged a few more words of encouragement before parting ways and heading for their respective commands. As Alexander tried to come up with what to ask Farzan next, a voice that he hadn't heard in what felt like years blasted him from the direction of the camp.

"Harris! What in the high hell is goin' on!?"

The bewildered captain turned to find his superior officer, Colonel Baxter, approaching with a near manic expression, a very nervous Dr. Bowman at his side.

"How the hell did we end up here? What the fuck is goin' on, Harris!?" he demanded.

"You've been catatonic for almost a month, sir," Alexander responded. "Myself and the other Captains led everyone here to Israel. We agreed it was the best option available to us."

"What about regional command!? What about *the States*!?" Baxter barreled on without pause, looking more frantic. Alexander sighed, rubbing his forehead.

Bowman placed her hand on Baxter's shoulder while giving Alexander a cautionary look, before turning her attention back to the colonel. "Sir, I think we should head back to the tent and discuss it there. You really need to take this slowly or you could relapse."

Alexander met the mystified gaze of his former superior. "Yeah, that will take a while to explain. Go get some rest,

120

sir."

#

Judith deflated her lungs, pushing out all the air and focusing in on her rifle sights. ***CRACK!*** The already broken bottle exploded into shards.

"Goddamn it, Travis!" Sergeant Taylor griped. "Quit wasting ammo when it ain't time for target practice!"

"Sorry, Sarge…" Judith replied, slinging her rifle over her shoulder. *Soooooo… boring…*

"Relax, Judy. We're headin' out soon," Zoey reassured her.

"Yeah, well… can't be soon enough," Judith grumbled.

She took the reigns back in both hands and ushered her steed forward and away from the bullet-riddled house they'd gotten jumped in the night before. Sullen prisoners sat in a line along the structure's southern wall, dressed in an assortment of regular civilian clothes, most looking like hell. The men and a couple of women all kept their heads and eyes down, well away from the Texas National Guardsmen surrounding them with guns and batons in hand.

One of them stole a glance at Judith up on her horse, but quickly looked away once she noticed him. Judith sneered down at the tied up man, feeling a little triumphant at having survived her first brush with death. A bunch of outlaws trying to rob a family of all they owned and probably worse. *Bastards deserve whatever's comin' to 'em.* She spit on the ground beside the prisoner's feet, and led her horse over to where the rest of the 28th Cavalry had prepared to leave Calera behind. Zoey, Mordecai, and Camila had clustered around Sergeant Taylor. Judith joined them.

"**Company, move out!**" Major Hayden's voice echoed across the flatlands, amplified by a crude megaphone.

In a stuttering jumble of motion, the mass of horses and light vehicles began moving north like a migrating herd. Judith's attention got caught by the chopping of blades above. She craned her head upward to find a pair of Chinook helicopters coming in for a landing near the center of Calera.

"Hey, Sarge, what do you think's on those?" Judith inquired, "Backup?"

"Nah. Bullets and bandages, I'd bet," Taylor replied. "Come on, it's a lil' ways to Durant and we might run into more of their friends on the way." The sergeant jerked her head toward the line of prisoners as the squadron passed them.

Looking down at her brown mare, Judith smiled and ran a hand through her mane. "Think I'll call you… Savannah. Feels like you were meant to be out here, not cooped up in some stable." Judith followed along with her unit, watching the ensemble of military power roll out, enthusiasm and terror warring within her mind.

#

Durant lay motionless, hidden behind a thin veil of forest that separated it from the open prairies and fields. Only a scattered array of trees and shrubs provided any concealment for the national guardsmen lying in wait, with hundreds of feet of open ground between them. From the south side, all Judith and her comrades could see consisted of low-density housing, a tiny apartment complex, and a cluster of large warehouses. With fewer than 20,000 people it barely qualified as a city. Of course, the only people the guardsmen could see represented the greatest threat at hand. Handfuls of men roamed the streets on foot and in vehicles, all heavily armed and looking on-edge. Judith couldn't see any regular citizens.

"Where you think everybody's at?" Zoey asked from Judith's left, her own pair of binoculars in hand.

"Dunno," Judith answered with a taut voice. "Maybe hidin'."

"I kinda wish we were part of the group going to 'liberate' the Choctaw Casino and Big Lots instead of dealing with these guys again," Mordecai said, carving up a stick into a point with his knife.

"They did try to kill us without even knowin' who we were. Probably some nasty stuff going on in there," Camila added.

"Hmm…" Judith pondered in agreement as she watched a technical armed with something that looked like a bazooka onto its flatbed. "Hey, Sarge, what are they fixin' to back of that truck?"

"Looks like an ATGM launcher," Taylor responded.

121

"AT…GM?" Judith asked, trying not to sound like a moron.

"Anti-tank-guided-missile. Does what's on the tin," Taylor explained without condescension.

"What do we do, Sarge?" Zoey half-whispered.

"Nothin' for now. Jus' keep an eye on 'em," Taylor replied, chewing on a strip of beef jerky.

"Wonder how many of 'em are lurkin' 'round in there…" Judith wondered aloud, trying to peer into the darkened windows for any signs of movement.

"Hey, cowgirl, how many of 'em did you take out last night?" Camila prompted before getting an elbow jab in the ribs from Zoey.

Judith felt a kind of gnawing in the back of her head. She'd watched human forms crumple in the flashes of light under her desperate torrent of gunfire. Keeping score couldn't have been further from her mind. Instead, she'd focused on enduring shattered glass, wiping away dust from drywall, and periodically making sure that Zoey hadn't gotten hit. She'd also made a deliberate effort to avoid the aftermath of the attack out in the field as they departed.

Without answering, Judith moved on to the larger of of the two warehouses, where a .50 cal machine gun sat deployed behind a ramshackle barricade. Five armed men defended the position with two more manning the MG.

"Four," said Camila, sounding out of breath.

"Four? Four what?" Judith asked.

"That's how many I got," Camila replied sheepishly.

"Aren't we supposed to be good guys? Should we really be keeping score of all the people who force us to murder 'em?" Zoey asked no one in particular while trying her best not to sound *too* accusatory.

"Yeah… that is kinda fucked up," Mordecai concurred in an even tone, before adding. "I think I got seven."

"Okay chill y'all, chill!" Camila conceded with a nervous laugh, holding up her hands in a defensive gesture. "It's not like I'm gonna to start carving tally marks on my—"

A familiar sound just tickled the edge of Judith's senses, drawing her eyes to the sky just in time to see something streak right overhead and toward the front of the big warehouse. Everyone shrank a bit by instinct as a pair of Cobras hurtled over them. What felt like a small tornado plowed though the group, thrashing the trees and sending leaves and bits of branches everywhere. The bedlam of whirling blades canceled out all other sound for a moment before dying off into the more usual rhythmic chopping.

"Damn!" Judith cursed as she covered her eyes with a hand just in time to deflect a careening branch.

The orange bloom of an explosion filled Judith's vision. Two more blasts followed soon after. Judith stood blinded by the flashes, waiting for her night vision to re-adjust. In the early morning gloom, they could only hear the series of deep blasts echo across the plains. It took what felt like a couple minutes for Judith to see clearly again, and once she finally could, the view left her stunned yet again. Everything that Judith looked over with her binoculars not a minute prior had vanished from the face of the earth. The Cobras barreled away from the town as streams of tracer rounds reached up into the air just behind them. The southern winds carried the columns of smoke from the aftermath of their run over their heads in slow motion.

Hundreds of infantry and dismounted cavalry gathered at the tree line to watch as an Apache approached from the west and unleashed its own barrage of rockets upon Durant. Tracers rose from all over the town.

"Alright, boys and girls," Taylor announced, radio in hand, "leave the horses, its time to get moving."

Their approach to the town, which would've otherwise posed a huge risk, went off without incident as the outlaws scrambled for cover or wasted their ammo trying to shoot at the helicopters. Judith's squadron advanced across the dry pastures, hunkering down behind the boxy form of a Bradley IFV as a choir of guns chanted their dirge across the prairies, drowning out even the cacophony of engines. Judith scrambled to keep up. She stepped in a gopher hole, almost tripped over a flattened barbwire fence, and nearly twisted her ankle in what looked like a rusted-out car door. As the sweat evolved from a constant dribble to a pouring stream, Judith's training with her high-school track team re-emerged as she worked to regulate her breathing.

Judith turned to the sound of Mordecai's voice through the mayhem as he stumbled just within Judith's peripheral vision.

"Aww… shit, man!" he yelled into the ether.

Judith gave him a quick glance to make sure he hadn't gotten hit. He looked fine. Judith turned back around and shouted to him over her shoulder. "What is it, Mordi?"

"I stepped in a fuckin' cow pie, man!" he griped with a bitter voice. "A fresh one too!"

Judith shot him another quick look, easily spotting in the orange dawn his leather boot engulfed in a fibrous green-brown mess. Judith couldn't help but snicker as a round of brief, but therapeutic laughter arose from everyone around.

Once they reached the outer edge and slipped into a run-down neighborhood that constituted the suburbs of Durant, the officers and NCOs directed their troops to hug the buildings. Judith and Zoey watched as an M1A1 Abrams tank led a pair of M60 Pattons deeper into the array of pitiful buildings.

"Listen up," Sergeant Taylor commanded, "we're headed for an abandoned grain elevator by the railroad tracks not too far from here. It's the tallest spot on this patch of flatland, and from up there we can get a bead on just 'bout everything in town. Third squad's comin' with us, now keep your eyes peeled and *stay out of the open*!" she hissed. "Got it?"

The whole squadron, Judith included, gave vigorous nods in reply. Without another word, Taylor waved them around the into back yard of someone's house. The blast waves of explosions thumped against Judith's chest as she kept right behind Mordecai, with Taylor and Camila in front of him. Zoey brought up the rear, with third squad trailing. They all slipped from behind vine-covered fences into a row of trees, then sprinted across the double railroad tracks and into the opposite woods. Sliding down an embankment between trees and dense shrubs, the ad hoc unit found itself within a dry riverbed surrounded by forest.

"We can get all the way to the elevator through these woods. Lets move!" Taylor ordered in a hushed tone.

Judith kept her "new" Winchester scanning the trees for any movement. Sweat streamed down her face and back, the sounds of crunching leaves and her own breathing filling her mind. Judith nearly opened fire on a small flock of crows that emerged from the trees and took to the skies with a cacophony of squawks.

"Fuck!" Camila bit out, making it clear Judith wasn't alone in almost making a dire mistake.

"Keep movin', a bit slower now. We're gettin' close." Taylor led the way again, with Judith and Zoey behind her this time.

For an interval, the din of battle lessened to a creeping pace and the ambiance of cicadas, birds, and all manner of woodland critters returned, bringing a short-lived air of calm to Judith's mind. The unmistakable zip of bullets passing close by brought everyone to a stop, either taking a knee or going prone. They waited for what felt like a minute before Taylor gave a silent hand wave as a signal to move on.

The chatter of gunfire and drumbeats of explosions resumed, ripping through the air at intervals, causing the group to stop and take cover. Each time they returned to their feet, they would make a sprint of movement, crunching through a swamp of dried leaves. At last, Taylor signaled for everyone to halt.

"Travis, get up here," the sergeant whispered over her shoulder.

Judith leapt to her side, rifle in hand, heart rate off the scale.

Taylor pointed up the embankment to the forest's edge just ahead of them. "Find a spot you can see through, and tell me what we've got."

"'Kay, got it…" Judith crept ahead to a short, fat oak with splayed branches. Peeking around the edge of the weathered trunk with her Winchester, Judith found a huge but dilapidated industrial structure surrounded by bushes and saplings. A collection of armed men encircled the building. A group of three patrolling the outside, while six gathered next to the only visible entrance. Judith noted at least one up in the elevator's main tower. It looked like they'd ripped the door off to get inside, leaving it in a smashed heap next to the breach. Two vehicles sat parked along the outer wall, an old pickup truck and a bullet-riddled sedan.

Having mapped out everything visible from her position, Judith snuck back down to where the others waited. She relayed everything she'd seen back to Taylor, and paused as the Sergeant wracked her brain. Silence gripped the air for a handful of heartbeats, then Taylor emerged from her deep thought and looked back to Judith.

"You get the one in the tower, then we'll get the others," the sergeant ordered.

Judith nodded in silence before turning and slinking back up the embankment, this time followed by the careful footsteps of her compatriots. Judith didn't hunker down behind the tree, instead opting to use a thicket of bushes as concealment for the shot. This gave her a more direct view of her target. Kneeling, Judith placed her right elbow on her knee for support and leveled her sights at the open tower. A man in a camo hunting jacket and cap held a rifle of some kind, peering through his scope into the town. Facing 120 degrees in the wrong direction, he had no chance of spotting the threat.

Judith cast a glance over her right shoulder, making sure everyone else stood ready. They waited with their own sights locked on the ground level hostiles. Craning back around to her own target, Judith took in a deep but shaky breath. *Easy, girl. You've already done this before. People are counting on you.* Judith shuffled her grip on the old lever-action, trying to ignore the droplet of sweat gathering on her eyebrow. A muted flash emanated from the tower, followed by a sharp *SNAP!* The bandit had fired into the town, and killed any remaining trepidation Judith felt. Zeroed in on his back, she took in one last deep breath, compressed her lungs, and squeezed.

The crack of her own rifle spat out a far louder report than the one from the sniper's weapon, followed not a second later by an eruption of gunshots off to her right as everyone else opened up. Judith watched just long enough to see the sniper lurch forward and out of her view, then she leapt to her feet and took cover behind a huge log. Not a moment too soon, because just behind her, a torrent of lead chewed up the shrubs she'd fired from, before then pivoting to the fallen tree and tearing into it.

Judith worked the lever action to cycle a new round, then peeked past the left side of the tree to try and get eyes on her attacker. A dark open window on the second story of the elevator's main building. She couldn't see inside at all, but didn't have to, as a stuttering muzzle flash bloomed out from the window, forcing her to duck back behind the log. Judith sank ever lower into the dirt and covered her face as the chattering machine gun whittled away at her only cover, dousing her with splinters and wood shavings.

Clambering in desperation to think of what to do, she realized that the gunshots not directed against her had started to die down. Just as Judith had psyched herself up to take another look and try to get a shot off at the gunner, an explosion like the biggest firecracker she'd ever heard brought an end to all the shooting. Staying down as debris rained all around her, Judith cautiously poked her eye around the right side of the trunk. The window, used as an MG nest just seconds previous, had transformed into a smoldering, blacked hole.

"C'mon, Travis! Let's move!" Taylor shouted. Judith followed the voice to find her sergeant standing at the base of the elevator's main building just below and to the right of the obliterated emplacement. Taylor waved her over, before peeking around the right corner of the building with her M16. As Judith warily rose to her feet, Zoey appeared beside her.

"Hey, you alright? He didn't get you, did he?" her friend asked with a concerned voice. Judith looked down at the pulverized log, realizing how close she'd come to ending up much the same.

"Nah, he didn't get me," Judith answered, giving Zoey a quick nod and an unsettled look. "Let's roll."

Judith felt the next minute or so pass as a blur. Rushing inside, checking around at a frantic pace, flying up the rust-coated ladder of the grain elevator's main tower. Once she'd lifted herself into the tower, Judith surveyed the rest of her unit as they rounded up the handful of marauders who'd had the sense to give up. A tap on the shoulder brought her attention back to Zoey as her friend extended a scoped bolt-action rifle toward her.

"Take this! The guy down there must've dropped it," Zoey insisted.

Judith hefted the massive weapon in her grasp, taking a glance back down the ladder. There, splattered across the ground floor lay the bandit she'd killed to open the attack. Eyes open, a cavernous hole in the upper center of his back.

Judith looked up and away, back towards Durant, bringing the scope up to get a look at what.

#

Under any other circumstances, Yujing would've enjoyed lingering in this place for as long as she liked. As she looked upon the forests and hills of western Kentucky, she could almost forget the tragedy unfolding on the coast. During the long train ride there, she had witnessed yet more caravans of refugees heading for the Kentucky border town of Wickliffe. The many ragged groups of exiles from urban centers across the east and south had begun to converge within the lush, green hills of Ballard County, all of them intending to flee as far west as they could go, and bearing grave rumors of Brotherhood forces advancing south through Illinois. A pair of still standing bridges represented their only route forward. The first crossed the Ohio River just before it joined the Mississippi, leading into the Illinois town of Cairo. The second bridge went south into Missouri.

Yujing's heart palpitated as she contemplated the narrow country road overflowing with desperate people hemmed in by a thin veil of trees. Beyond the woods lay a vast swamp on the right, and the roiling Mississippi River to the left.

A tap on her shoulder. Yujing whirled to find Jose toting an American-made assault rifle of some kind, a satisfied grin on his sweat-varnished face.

"Where did you get that?" Yujing prompted with an arched brow.

"I was talkin' to some of the cops—well, I guess **ex**-cops now, and they said if I help 'em fight off anymore trouble I can just keep this beautiful thing here afterward," Jose answered, stroking the railing of his new weapon.

"It's about time you found a gun," Yujing deadpanned.

Jose nodded as he drank from a half-empty water bottle. "Yeah, the problem is they only gave me one clip, thirty rounds, so it's up to me to find more bullets." He gave the rifle a concerned tap and continued. "Apparently not a whole lot of law or military guys here. Sounds like they need all the help they can scrounge up."

Yujing scanned the nearby crowd, noting several armed people, but only one in a tattered military uniform. "So… the army and police have just left these people on their own?"

"Yeah, not a surprise, really. Most of 'em are just right-wingers. And the rest desperately try to present themselves as 'a-political', whatever the fuck that even means anymore."

Another voice, somehow familiar, spoke up from behind them. "It means they've decided to ignore the sickness of this country, and pretend like they can force everyone into just going back to normal."

Yujing and Jose rounded to find Roberto walking behind them with an heavy World War II rifle slung over his shoulder, a sad smile on his face.

"That doesn't seem very likely to work…" Yujing retorted.

"No, it won't," Roberto laughed, "But they're still gonna try. I'm not sure they can think of anything else to do."

"The Feddies seem more than willing to burn every bridge they can get their hands on," Jose added, looking around at the few gutted buildings as they passed.

"Don't have to tell me," Roberto sighed.

Both parties decided to drop the subject.

They continued on, crossing the first bridge over the very end of the Ohio River, keeping their paranoid eyes to the sky, hoping and praying that no flying death machines would appear. Attacking fleeing refugees didn't make much military sense, but that had never stopped the Americans or anyone else before. The mass of humanity shuffled in near silence as they crossed the bridge. Once Yujing and her partner had reached roughly two-thirds of the way across, the puttering whine of a aircraft's prop engine crept into their ears. Searching the skies in silent panic for the source, eyes scanned the horizon. The aircraft's engine hummed closer.

"Look! A plane!" someone shouted from up ahead, pointing to the northern sky.

Yujing pivoted her gaze upward to find a single-engine Cessna flying parallel with the bridge, heading west over Cairo. The entire column surged forward as a wave of dire concern rippled through the crowd.

"Keep moving, don't stop! Just keep moving!" a gruff male voice shouted over the panicked masses.

"We need to get the fuck off this bridge!" Jose urged, grabbing onto Yujing's forearm and guiding her through the horde of people.

Having never seen Jose act or speak to her in such a way, Yujing decided to just comply. The Cessna's engine overtaking all of Yujing's senses.

The small aircraft had come around, now flying on an eastward parallel course, much closer to the bridge this time. As it buzzed past, a muzzle flash burst from the plane's rear window. With nowhere to run, every person carrying a firearm—Jose and Roberto included—returned fire, sparks flying off the sides of the Cessna as it veered away. Yujing watched as the plane dove right into the Ohio river, smoke billowing from its lone engine.

Before the gunfire even ended, the terrified rush began. Yujing turned to Jose, who had her right arm in his strong grip. She slipped free of his grasp before latching onto his forearm, clinging in desperation as she allowed him to drag her onward. As Yujing struggled to keep up, she nearly tripped over two casualties from the strafing run. An old man lay collapsed on the road, arms locked with an old woman who sat slumped against the northern guardrail, blood pooling between them. Their faces stared unblinking into the oblivion of the river below. Yujing wrenched up her meager breakfast across the asphalt. Jose pulled her close and carried her forward.

For a brief moment, Yujing breathed relief. They had at last reached the peninsula. Then, she heard more gunfire, a hectic scattering of shots piercing the air from every direction.

"Left! Left! Everyone who isn't armed head left and get across the other bridge!" Roberto shouted to those who had slowed and huddled in confusion.

"Get the the fuck across that second bridge! Move!" Jose amplified, following Roberto's lead as the mob continued its headlong charge. Jose grabbed Yujing by the shoulder and smiled. "Come on. You wanted to see action, right?"

Yujing pulled the camera out of her bag as if conceding Jose's point. She didn't want to get separated from the only guide she had, but she hoped he wouldn't get himself killed. As the gaggle of armed refugees sprinted north, up the peninsula and away from the main group, the terrible bedlam of a gun battle grew ever more defined. Bursting through a line of trees, they stumbled into a spongey, fetid drainage ditch. Hundreds of armed refugees hunkered down around them, ducking to avoid bullets, some crying and cradling their weapons. At the insistent shouting of their de facto officers, the ad hoc formation of exiles began pouring rounds into the outskirts of Cairo, visible just beyond a stretch of open field.

A number of vans and pickup trucks formed an impromptu roadblock on the two-lane asphalt highway, all of them riddled with bullets, a number of bodies splayed out behind them. At the edge of the town, more ramshackle barricades gave cover to numerous hostiles exchanging fire with the ever growing number of refugees.

Jose took up position and released three short bursts of fire on the distant barricades, causing one of the defenders to stagger backward and collapse out of sight. Two others ducked to avoid the lead death.

"Fuck! The hell are these asshole even shooting at us for!?" Jose demanded of the heavens.

"Don't know!" a woman in a ragged police uniform shouted as she scrambled to load a fresh magazine into her assault rife. "Soon as we crossed over, the bastards just started shooting from the road!"

"Heh heh, not their best choice!" a tall Black man in tattered jeans added before firing a shotgun with a thunderous blast.

Yujing watched as a shower of sparks erupted from a narrow point on the roof of an overturned car, and the redneck standing behind it got flung backwards into the ground.

"Yeah, motherfuckers! Get some!" a young blond guy in a shredded undershirt and sweatpants shouted as he unloaded a stream of lead from his AK.

The monstrous rumbling of an engine drew Yujing's attention behind them as an armored truck squealed to a halt before driving into the makeshift trench. Yujing fixed her camera onto the word "police"—marred by a crude yellow "X" emblazoned on the side. She caught several frames, then panned up to the vehicle's .50 caliber machine gun as it chugged away into the outskirts of Cairo. As the number of shooters on the refugees' side continued to grow and those of the enemy continued to dwindle, more and more locals began to break off and flee back into their town. Windows shattered, walls torn apart by bullets, bodies crumpled. Yujing captured everything she could on film, even as the gunfire died away and the last hostile gunmen retreated from view.

"Now what? Do we go after 'em?" someone asked in an cracking voice.

"Hell no!" the police woman to Yujing's right asserted. "We need to get the fuck outta here, the caravan is defenseless without us!"

"She"s right, no telling what they've got waiting for us in there," Roberto confirmed before lighting and taking a drag from a cigarette. *Where did that come from?* "Everybody who has a rifle, stay behind for a second and cover everybody else, then follow. Let's fall back to the bridge!"

No arguments came from the armed bunch of misfits as those without long-range weapons beat a hasty retreat back into the trees.

Jose lowered himself out of sight before turning to Yujing. "You okay?"

Yujing could only give an uncertain nod as she caught a glimpse of a mortally wounded refugee getting lifted out of the ditch by two of his shell-shocked comrades.

"Yeah," she answered without breath. "I'm fine."

CHAPTER 14:
IRA POPULI

"Boasting about wealth is an open invitation for others to divest you of it."
— Stewart Stafford

Emily could only gaze out over the sprawling megalopolis, gusts of wind blasting her from behind every so often, enthralled by the spectacle playing out before her. From her perch in the Hollywood Hills, she watched as a forest of smoke columns rose from the second largest city in America, one of the largest in the world, as an orchestra of detonations and gunfire echoed all around. Behind her, the studios that produced most of the movies she'd ever watched now sat occupied by the zealots in blue caps. The city Emily had remembered as a "beehive of cars," now lay silent of all but the sounds of war. Mountains, canyons, and valleys resonated with the clattering dirge of machines and the stamping from thousands of boots. The northern ring of lesser towns and cities had already fallen to the Red Army. And Emily knew that it now was an army. The materiel might've been crude, but their organization couldn't be denied. The visible deficiencies they started with had either disappeared or improved before Emily's eyes. Each day, as units re-equipped themselves with weapons, vehicles, and gear taken from dead "loyalists," as the Reds called them. The soldiers and the command had become more and more efficient in their operational capabilities.

Now they stood ready to conquer, for the first time in history, the City of Angels—and every other community from the Pacific to the mountains. Emily had already witnessed this once before, but she couldn't help becoming nauseous seeing an identical fate dealt out to an even more prominent place than Sacramento. Her optimism made her hope that this would've all ended by now. That the Reds would've gotten bogged down fighting their enemies, or that their leaders would devolve into pointless squabbling. Yet here they stood. From her mountaintop perch, Emily could already tell the city was overrun. She watched at least three helicopters ascend in desperate bids to escape the burning skyline, only to get obliterated by missiles and heavy weapons fired from the ground. Drones of at least three varieties, all U.S. government designs, circled the metropolis in wide rings, diving every-so-often to strafe or drop bombs. Helicopters prowled, riders shoving oil drums out the sides that blasted apart buildings and barricades.

Emily's brain had turned to jelly. Nothing made sense anymore. Without warning, a voice Emily could never mistake for any other spoke up from behind.

"Hey, you want to talk now?"

Emily whipped her head around to find Rob waiting in trepidation. Blunt in hand, looking exhausted. His coat had a fresh bullet scar cross the shoulder, less than an inch from the skin. Emily slid down from the rock outcropping, coming to within arm's reach of Rob, who stood motionless. For what felt like an hour, Emily just gazed into her son's eyes. A small weight lifted off her soul as she realized that for the first time in years, he did not even try to hide his emotions from her. His pain, his fatigue, his uncertainty, his resentment, his distrust… his fear. Emily tried to summon anger against him, but couldn't. Instead, she ignored the shock on his face and pulled Rob in for the tightest hug she'd ever given anyone. She felt Rob tense up at first, but his lanky form loosened as he returned the embrace with some hesitation. Emily felt herself melt into him. She fought tears but failed. As much as she'd wanted to punch him in the face not an hour ago, now nothing mattered. And she didn't care who saw them.

Rob sighed. "I never wanted any of this to happen, you know? It just crammed into my life before I could blink."

Emily held him tighter for a moment. "I know."

"Do you hate me?" Rob asked, "I don't blame you if you do."

Emily squeezed her eyelids tight, as she felt tears escape and slide down her grime-coated cheek. "No. I don't." She stepped back, her arms clasped on his shoulders. "I can't."

Rob gave a weak smile before looking down into his coat as he dug something out of his pocket. "Here, Christi and

Zechariah want you to have this." He held out a small golden pin in the likeness of a blazing torch. Emily recognized it in an instant: the Girl Scout Ambassador's Award Christina had won a few years ago. Emily knew how much it meant to Christi, and remembered the sense of pride the family had in her for earning it.

"I— She wants me to—?" Emily stammered.

"Just take it," Rob insisted, extending his arm further before dropping the pin into Emily's cupped hands. "They thought it might bring you good luck. And between you and me, we can use every last drop of that we can find. Don't worry, we'll see them again after we liberate California."

Emily just stared down at the small metal badge for a long moment then fumbled as she pinned it on the inside of her jumpsuit's chest pocket. Taking a deep breath and closing her eyes, Emily decided to prod at her son once more, still desperate for so many answers.

"How did this happen, Rob?"

Rob released a heavy sigh, scratching the back of his head. "Honestly, I could spend hours answering that," he admitted, "the gist of it is that as things deteriorated, and you guys kept cracking down, the number of people who violently hated your guts kept growing and growing,"

Emily flinched. "Just—! Just call them the cops from now on, please?"

Rob gave a neurotic nod and continued, "The only reason we ended up here was because of Singh deliberately provoking— *the cops*, and *the cops* provoking everyone else. An army of peons desperate for survival and... purpose. Yeah that's us."

Emily felt an icy grip on her soul once again. *That name*... "You said Singh did this? All of it?"

Rob rolled his eyes. "Not exactly, but he's certainly guided us down this path. He considered it inevitable, and he never pretended otherwise. I always hoped he was wrong but... well..." he held his arms out to the world around them. "Guess I was just naive."

Emily gave a sad chuckle. "You and me both." She gazed back up to meet Rob's eyes. "But he is your leader? Or... *our* leader, I guess?"

Emily felt sick at that.

"Yep," Rob answered. "If there is a mastermind in this story, it's him. Crazy bastard has improvised his way through most of this madness."

"And you're okay with following this guy?" Emily challenged in a hushed tone, hoping no one overheard.

Rob took a deep breath. "Lets just say, I'd sure as hell rather be on his side than not. You've seen how well that tends to work out."

Emily groaned in a mix of weariness and frustration. "Yeah, no kidding."

"Don't worry," Rob said, placing his hand on her shoulder, "He listens to me, hell if I know why, but I'll make sure you don't get burned. Alright?"

Emily gave a reluctant nod. She found it hard to trust her own son at this point, still he'd never straight up lied to her... he just never told her anything about his "social life." And of course, she knew full well that he felt the same. This caused to Emily chuckle a bit. "Yeah, alright. But you owe me more answers." Rob nodded as Emily's gaze drifted back to the burning city in the valleys below them. "What are we supposed to do here?"

"Help the locals take the place over, then move on to San Diego," Rob answered matter-of-factly as he lit up his joint, shielding it against the dust-infused wind.

"Of course..." Emily turned her attention to the valley below her, an abyss of chaos in incomprehensible motion. The violence tore through one of America's most famous cities. "What did I expect?"

"We'll get through this, I know it," Rob reassured her. "Just... just don't do anything stupid, Ma. Please?"

Emily felt her muscles tighten, knowing exactly what he meant. "Yeah, I'll do my best..."

Footsteps from behind heralded the arrival of Emily's platoon sergeant, Coleman, who didn't look at all phased by seeing them together. He grasped the shoulder of Rob's coat and pulled him in close. "Sir, General Harper wants to speak with you. Says it's urgent."

"Of course she does…" Rob grumbled under his breath. "Let's not keep her waiting then. C'mon, Ma."

Emily's eyes darted between her son and Coleman as they began their casual walk back down the mountain slope to the command post. She caught up to Coleman in a few bounds.

"So, uh… I'm guessing he told you everything… Sergeant?" Emily asked the middle-aged rock of a man, prompting a grunt from behind his grizzled mustache.

"Yep. Wanted to make sure I wouldn't just execute ya at the slightest offense. Lotta officers and such ain't forgiven anything that ya'll did. Sendin' you folk on suicide missions as revenge," Coleman replied.

Emily's mind turned, not for the first time, to Scott and what might have become of him. Shaking the thought from her mind for now, she turned back to Coleman. "You don't want that, though?" she asked.

"Nah. I'm of a mind with him," he nodded to Rob as he lit up a cigar. "I think most folks deserve a second chance. But, to be real honest… I can't blame the others for wantin' vengeance."

Emily sighed as they passed a row of M163 Vulcans and reached a camouflaged tent which Rob disappeared into. Inside, the shelter bustled with anxiety. Couriers and adjutants rushed back and forth, commanders shouted into radios, and one voice broke over all the others.

"I don't care who the hell you've been listening to before now!" General Harper hissed between gritted teeth. "You take orders from **me** now, just like everybody else! And if you've got a problem, you can take it up with Singh on your own goddamned time!" As she finished, the commander glared at the radio handset before slamming it against the ancient PRC-77 squad radio with a metallic clang. No equipment got broken, but the entire scene made Emily shudder.

Harper glared at the tent's occupants from behind her semi-circle of radios and scanners, but she narrowed her eyes when they lit on Emily. She turned her head away, sending droplets of sweat flying from her cap visor. Harper's gaze then pivoted to Rob. Her face flushed with anger as she pulled a folded paper out of her pocket and shoved it into his hands.

"Read this," she commanded.

Rob took the paper without a word and began looking it over, but stopped after just a couple lines, looking back up at Harper.

"How did you end up with this?" Rob asked.

"It doesn't matter how I got it, Bennigsen!" Harper bit out, slamming her fist on the table, grabbing everyone's attention as she did. "Your boss has laid out a plan to sack this whole damn city, wipe out the whole legal system, and he didn't think it necessary to inform me!?"

Rob took a long drag from his blunt before answering. "Seeing as it doesn't affect any of your forces, he didn't think it necessary." A tap of ash from the joint into a can full of pens. "That, and he figured this was more-or-less how you would react once you found out. Obviously he didn't try that hard to hide it from you. And for the record, the ritziest parts of town hardly counts as 'the whole damn city.'"

Emily looked between her son and the irate general with growing nervousness. Most of the armed troops in the building wore national guard uniforms, Harper's men. But Rob didn't seem to mind much.

Harper buried her face in her hands and let out an exhausted, bitter groan. "Would it kill you guys to try being benevolent and generous to everybody? Just once? Instead of appeasing certain sections of the population while writing everyone else off!?" A vein throbbed in her neck.

"Yes, it would most likely result in our eventual destruction," Rob answered without a pause. "That's kind of why we haven't been terribly… lenient?"

"Lenient, huh? That's what you'd call this?" She laughed.

"Yeah it's basically a war of annihilation. But they were already waging a war of annihilation against us so… what did you expect, man?"

"Weren't you the one who pushed Singh into sparing the cops who survived the uprising in Sacramento?" Harper pressed. "What's changed?"

"Nothing," Rob stated. "I know, and believe in, several people who were part of the SPD. I don't know anyone in the LAPD, and none of our people who do have made any such request."

"So what, we're just disposing of everyone who won't join us at the first suggestion!?"

"Only if they insist on posing a threat. Which the former leaders and enforcers of our society definitively do," Rob answered.

"You can't expect me to just go along with this," Harper growled.

"You don't have to go along with anything. All you have to do is be the big hero while Singh, Julian, and the rest of us take care of all the *unfortunate necessities,*" Rob replied with a smirk.

For a while, only the rippling of the tent's windswept canvas filled the musty air.

Harper spoke with slow, deliberate words. "You say it won't affect my forces, but that can't be true. How many of my troops will you need for this... operation?"

"Ten," Rob answered in a second.

Harper's face became distorted in bewilderment. "You think you can do all of this with ten soldiers? Are you fuckin' kidding?"

"Ten of **your** soldiers, general. And really, I just need them for... security. My own forces will handle the actual dirty work," Rob assured her.

After another tense moment, Harper at last expelled an annoyed sigh as she turned back to the radios. "Fine! Just— Ugh! Just corral everyone to join with the rest of us in downtown once they've finished trashing the place."

"By your command," Rob responded before turning to leave.

Emily caught a glimpse over her shoulder of Harper shooting all three of them a scowl as they exited the tent and stepped back out into the stifling heat. Rob loosened his coat and took a deep breath.

"Well, that went better than I expected!" he declared with relief.

"So... are we going to pillage the estates of Hollywood or something?" Emily asked with evident dread.

"More like supervise the pillaging that's already going on," Rob told her. "And like I told Harper, you won't have to do much of anything. Hopefully."

A short truck ride later and Emily's platoon had arrived in Beverly Hills along with Rob and a handful of his blue-caps. They arrived at a palatial neighborhood already in the midst of getting stripped bare. Trucks and vans loaded with anything useful hurtled down the street, the windows and doors of every home smashed. Dead people lay in the streets and in yards, while others fled in blind panic, clinging to loved ones and prized possessions. Those with valuables had them ripped from their arms by rebel soldiers who then shoved them along without pity. Music blared from the sound systems of plundered luxury vehicles as armed men and women dressed in the finest of clothes used older residents as target practice.

Emily looked to Rob who wore a look of resignation as he gestured for the blue-caps to break up the random shootings. He checked the silver pocket watch in his coat, then turned to Coleman.

"Sergeant," he flicked the watch closed, "have your troops surround these trucks and guard them against being used for... that." Rob nodded toward a huge GMC pickup with a .50 cal attached to its flatbed. Piles of gilded finery overflowed from the vehicle.

"Can do, Sir," Coleman assured with an obvious sense of relief.

Rob turned to an approaching box van that had pulled up onto someone's front yard. More blue-caps unloaded from the van's back and fanned out through the area, but one of them approached Rob. A woman with gray-blue eyes, her red hair tied in a ponytail.

"Comrade Bennigsen, we're ready to begin gathering the orphans," she informed him.

"Good, let's get this over with." He gave a waving gesture, signaling the blue-caps to deploy.

Emily stood and watched the carnage up close now, saw as terrified children and teens got herded into the vans and trucks her platoon and nine others guarded. At last it hit her why this all felt so profound in its discomfort. She'd seen it before. This whole spectacle resembled a sort of bizarre parody of a police manhunt. People abused and killed, their lives upended and destroyed in the name of payback. But in this case, she knew of no specific target.

Once Emily saw Rob return at the head of a column of traumatized youths, she made her way over to him in near panic, her heart throbbing like it would spew from her mouth. Rob stepped to the side to meet her as the children got ushered aboard the assembled vehicles.

"This is insane!" Emily hissed into his ear once he came close enough.

"Should we just leave them to their own devices instead?" Rob queried.

"Are these kids all from here?" Emily managed in a dry hush.

"No, they come from all over," Rob answered with an even voice.

"So they're from you—our enemies? Or are they from our side?" Emily pressed.

"Both," Rob said. "We'll talk more about it later. Just, don't worry about it. They'll be fine… at least."

The crack of a pistol caught their attention. They saw down the road as a man trying to flee his home with an AR-15 got cut down by multiple Reds, who then proceeded to unceremoniously loot his body. Helicopter blades whirred above them as a Blackhawk sailed overhead toward downtown, someone getting dumped out the side door, falling through the air and crashing into the roof of a mansion.

"Did it always have to end this way?" Emily wondered aloud.

"Maybe not," Rob conceded. "But the last chance to avoid it passed us by a long time ago."

#

Harper surveyed yet another conquered city center, maybe the grandest she'd ever stood in. The huge white obelisk of Los Angeles City Hall loomed, battered and charred, but still standing. Reds had torn down the flags from every pole in the plaza. In their place, the city's previous leadership hanged by their necks. Apparently they'd done it prior to Harper's arrival. They had done it for her. Like cats bringing animals they'd killed to their masters. She noted that the mayor and chief of police didn't appear among them. Corpses of police and security lay scattered without care across the walkways and terraces, picked clean of all their weapons and equipment. Burning patrol cars, smashed armored vans, and even a few disabled main battle tanks surrounded the plaza. Red soldiers both professional and otherwise, milled all around like ants swarming up and down a mound.

Gunfire and distant explosions still echoed between the buildings as the battle for the city lurched toward its now inevitable end. Harper wanted with all her battered and withered heart to feel disgust and shame at what she'd done. Yet, she didn't. No joy or exaltation… just satisfaction. A deep pride in knowing that she achieved something impossible. An awareness that for better or worse, destiny had struck her. *Nothing can be certain now. If going back was ever an option, I just dumped it off a cliff.*

"Well, looks like things are well in hand down here," Bennigsen cut in from over her shoulder.

Glancing back, she found the Commissar approaching her at a stroll with a gaggle of troops around him. She sneered. "No thanks to you."

"You say that as if you want me around ever," Bennigsen replied with an eye-roll.

The now familiar chattering of Singh's Cadillac alerted Harper to his appearance. The old black sedan cruised up to the door of the city hall itself, bypassing the gangs of troops moving bodies and debris out of the roads. With a grimace, Harper made a beeline for the scorched white tower.

The entrance hall existed as a ravaged wreck. Torn U.S. flag banners hung from the ceiling, shattered glass of windows and lightbulbs covered the floor, bodies stacked to the side to clear a walking path, bullet damage perforated the blood spattered walls. The sound of an argument managed to draw Harper away from the screaming of her brain. On the far end of the lobby, Singh stood bickering with a lanky black-haired man holding an unusually thick laptop. Beside them waited a handcuffed middle-aged man in a police uniform. *The Chief.* As Harper strained to catch the gist of their conversation, she saw Singh draw the Python .357 he had used earlier. He centered its barrel on the chief's forehead, less than a foot away. Singh's lips twisted in measured movements, his words so quiet Harper couldn't make out a single one of them. The Chief said something to Singh.

"**Hey**! Don't you kill him!" Harper ordered, realizing only after the words escaped her lips that she had just made a mistake.

With a bemused smirk that made Harper's skin crawl, Singh pulled back the revolver's hammer... in a swift motion lowering the gun to point directly at the Chief's manhood. He fired. The cannon-like blast tore through the smoke-hazed air. The chief collapsed to the tile floor, howling like an animal.

Singh holstered his weapon as he turned to face Harper, wearing an expression of incredulity. "Hello, Harper. I take it things have more-or-less gone well?"

"I— You— Why the fuck did you have to do that!?" she demanded.

"What?" Singh asked in mock innocence. "He's still alive isn't he?"

Harper stared down at the bleeding man curled into a fetal position as two Red soldiers dragged him away by his arms. The general's eyes locked back with Singh's. "You are a sick fuck."

"Oh please. You have no idea what I've got planned for that guy." He waved his hand in the direction they'd taken the chief. "Come along, you two. We have a great deal to discuss."

"Damn," Bennigsen uttered as he passed, avoiding the oil slick of blood.

"Just what the hell did he say to you anyway?" Harper hissed as she lunged to catch up.

"He basically dared me to kill him," Singh groaned.

"So you blasted his junk off?"

"Yes."

"You're insane," Harper stated as the trio arrived in a windowless office overflowing with papers and boxes of discs.

Singh released an irritated sigh. "Harper, what do you think will go through people's minds when they hear about this?"

"That you're a fucking psycho?"

"Possibly," Singh conceded with a shrug, "But they're certainly not going to mistake us for people who level empty threats. Besides..." he went on, lighting a joint from his coat pocket. "The guy's screwed anyway. Every person in this city who I'm even remotely inclined to listen to has all but demanded his death. A smart leader listens when the people are angry, and people are very angry with the chief."

"You didn't have to torture him first," Harper pointed out. "And not every cop or government worker is irredeemably evil. No matter what you think."

Singh released a deep breath, running a hand beneath his cap, before turning to Harper with a look of decision. "How to put basically enough? I know that everyone else is trapped in this endless circle-jerk of whether or not they're all bad, or if more of them are bad or good, but personally... I don't care, because it doesn't matter. I want their institutions destroyed, because they threaten the new power structures that I'm building, and to make that happen, all of the heavily armed right-wing dipshits who run it have to go away. But I can't fire or imprison them, because then they'll just be this huge threat loitering around that any moron can weaponize against us. You know, the same thing that we're currently doing to them?" Singh's eyes widened in rising irritation, "And I can't just send them somewhere else like the hillbillies, because any one of our numerous enemies will finance them to overthrow and kill us all. All of which leaves me no choice but to be a *'psycho'* and weaponize the most heinous methods and tools we have available to us." Singh took a deep breath, regaining his calm, continuing. "Not that you need worry to about that, you have something much more dangerous to deal with."

"The United States Marine Corps?" Harper deadpanned in an exhausted tone.

"Yep," Singh confirmed with a dire look in his jade eyes. "The marines."

#

"Hey," prodded Mason, "didn't they used to give hurricanes names?"

Mason looked out the window at the driving rain. The storm had soaked the Eastern Seaboard for days on end, ripping apart buildings and infrastructure. Paul and Mason could only hunker down with the troops and wait out the maelstrom, listening as the deluge poured on.

Paul smiled and stood up, approaching the window beside Mason. "Well, maybe we could name it after my ex-wife, Hurricane Sarah." They shared a laugh.

Even the refugees had gone to ground, hiding within any building that remained standing. All the locals had already fled. Paul witnessed the sheets of rainfall as they overcame the river and town, tree limbs and shingles dragged skyward before crashing down to earth, even as the walls of the school vibrated under the onslaught.

"Damn. Can't believe we gotta jus' sit through dis," Mason said.

"Crazy, innit?" Paul agreed, musing, "fuck Hurricane Sarah."

The sustained assault by Mother Nature seemed to smooth over and wash away some of the scars from recent clashes. The storm's creeping devastation mirrored the ruined world beyond their shelter. Craters had became giant ponds, one of them now home to an alligator. Trees ripped down, power cables flailing in the torrent.

"How long you think this'll go on?" Mason asked.

"Well, much like the real Hurricane Sarah, she'll tear things up for a while before movin' on. I've never seen one of these storms last longer than a couple of days," Paul answered.

Mason laughed. "You've got a hell of a way of lookin' at things. Nah, man, I mean all the rest of this bullshit," Mason clarified.

Paul chuckled. "Oh, right. I almost forgot about the end of the world." He shrugged. "I dunno, can't see the future."

"C'mon, man, you gotta have some idea," Mason griped. "I don't wanna spend the rest o' my life dodgin' bullets and sloggin' through flooded warehouses."

"It goes on as long as it needs to go on."

"Fuck that. I want shit to go back to normal, man. Like how things were before everyone went crazy."

"I think this is the new normal."

"For how long, huh? Years?"

"Definitely."

A long pause.

"Decades?" Mason gambled.

"God… I hope not. But it'll probably last longer than my marriage."

"So, you got nobody to try an' find in this shit?" Mason probed.

Paul shook his head. "Nah. Not anymore. You got family in Miami though, right? Heard anything from them?"

"Nope." Mason continued gazing into the deluge.

Footsteps echoed through the crowded hall, the wet stamping audible over the apocalyptic monsoon. Paul watched a pair of figures approach him through the shadowed hallway, illuminated by brief flares of lightning. The man on the right he recognized as Frazier, one of Mason's troops. The woman on the left, wearing a tattered wool coat, he had not seen before.

"Sir, this is *Alice*. She's one of the refugees who arrived this morning. I think you'll want to hear what she has to say," Frazier explained.

Paul stepped away from the window, emerging from the gloom with a tired smile. "Well, all right, miss. What do I need to know about?"

"You aren't safe here. The Brotherhood has taken control of the army and they're moving south toward the river," Alice blurted out in near desperation.

"How do you know about it?" Paul asked.

"I overheard two of their officers talking about it back in Baltimore. They're gathering their forces in D.C. before going after Richmond," she explained. "And forces are on the move everywhere, I barely managed to make it down here at all."

"Sure…" Mason muttered under his breath.

Paul pretended not to hear him and went on. "Did they say how many?"

Alice hesitated for a moment, looking between Paul and Frazier several times before speaking. "They said two hundred thousand. I have no idea if that's true or not, though. That's just what they said… But we had to dodge a lot of militia and soldiers on the way here. Convoys of trucks and busses of troops and supplies headed this way."

"Why should we believe you?" Paul challenged.

"Yeah," Mason piped in, "you could just be talkin' mad shit."

"You don't have to," Alice huffed. "Ask anyone. The Feddies and Brotherhood are everywhere. The roads are death traps, they'll rob ya if you're lucky. Worse if you're not."

Paul and Mason shared a dire gaze for a moment before Paul turned to Frazier. "Thanks for tellin' us, this man here will take ya to safety." He then pointed to Frazier, "Get her back to command in Richmond, have them debrief her, and send a warning message ahead."

"Yes, sir!" Frazier answered before guiding Alice away by the arm through the marshy hallway. Paul and Mason watched them leave before locking eyes, goosebumps rising from their mud-caked skin.

"Well, that's about the 15th person to tell us that hell's on its way, but she is the first to give us a solid number," Paul said.

"Two hundred thousand?" Mason gawked. "Guess they're fixin' to take us seriously now, huh?"

"Ain't that just peachy?" Paul groaned. He knew the only choice would be retreat unless some serious reinforcements arrived within the next couple of days. And he had no clue if that would, or even could, happen. Even if it did, they could easily get caught with their pants down.

"We've already packed our shit and can move out whenever we want," Mason said.

"If we leave now, these people won't have a chance at escape," Paul pointed out. "And our guys further south will get caught flatfooted. The whole thing could come crashin' down, it would be a massacre."

"But stayin' here is suicide! We can't fight the **real** goddamn army."

"We can," Paul said with all the certainty he could muster. "At least long enough to give everyone else the time they need."

"Fuck. This is crazy," Mason declared, clawing at his bald head.

"Yeah. It is."

"Fine, bring 'em on. Better than waitin' around."

#

Alexander never wanted to see another desert as long as he lived. Yet again he had to fight "one last battle" before going home. This time for good. One way or the other. The ever vigilant sun continued to roast Alexander and his men alive as they waited. Behind boulders and dunes, in dry riverbeds and shell-holes older then the soldiers themselves.

As he sat around in his BCP, Alexander could see the burned out hulks of everything from T-62 tanks to Vulcan anti-air guns. A Centurion, an up-gunned Sherman, a Russian-made artillery piece. Epitaphs to the political maneuverings of previous eras scattered before the expansive ridge the Americans and Israelis had chosen to defend. He knew that the advanced weapons sold to the Saudis en masse for decades on end now sat arrayed against them across the trackless desert. Artillery, jets, helicopters, missiles, drones, and guided bombs. The greatest threats his troops faced. *Lord, please don't let a Raytheon missile blast me to shreds in this forsaken place. Give us a chance to save the land we've been led astray from.* The Israelis' woeful lack of information regarding the impending onslaught gave Alexander no cause for comfort.

"How many contractors did Daskal say have joined the Saudis?" Alexander asked Price.

"We don't know for certain, thousands maybe," the S2 answered from behind his laptop, sitting against the opposite side of the BCP. "Hundreds for sure."

Alexander let out a frustrated groan. "Figures. At least some things never change."

"The fickleness of mercenaries or the inescapable allure of cash?" Price asked with a grim smirk.

"Both."

"Don't the Israelis have a huge reserve program, where are those guys?"

"Still mobilizing, or dealing with other bullshit."

An alarm.

"Captain, we just lost a scout drone seven clicks to the southwest." Price's uncanny tone broke into Alexander's psyche, sending a chill down his spine. "Large armored force approaching fast."

"What!? How!?" Alexander shot up from his seat by the map and into the cupola of the BCP, scanning the shimmering horizon for the telltale silhouettes of armored vehicles. Straining his eyes through his binoculars, Alexander watched as sand-colored shapes materialized on the opposite end of the ridge.

Alexander's eyes went wide, his jaw slackened. With no time to waste, he grabbed at his radio, slamming the send button.

"Hostiles approaching to the southwest! Weapons free! Weapons free!"

Turrets rotated around one by one to face the approaching threat as the first shells crashed down among the defenders. Alexander's troops and the Israelis returned sporadic fire, explosions around them focusing everyone's sun-baked anxiety on the enemy. Alexander's whole world descended into chaos. He tried to follow the radio as everyone struggled in futility to remain composed in the face of the heavy attack from an unexpected direction. The allied anti-air weapons opened up on any unaccounted for contacts, as the sparse number of aircraft engaged their counterparts in the blinding sky.

Alexander's mind raced. *Have to make sure they won't flank us...* Again he grabbed the radio. "Bird-man, this is Big-shot come in, over!"

"Copy that. What can we do for you, Big-shot?" Derrick's voice answered, to Alexander's relief.

"Get to the plateau to the west and dig in, I think they might try and flank even further around us."

"Got it!"

Alexander watched Derrick's armor reposition itself as more fire continued to rain down on them. The whine of drones pierced through the sweltering air as the small flying machines darted around, unleashing their payloads while trying to avoid obliteration.

More silhouettes to the south grew ever larger and more distinct as the heartbeats thundered past. Eventually, the shapes became clear forms of Saudi vehicles, destroying and getting destroyed. He didn't need anyone to tell him they were now outnumbered. Alexander clutched the radio in his sweat-slick hands, trying to keep his voice calm and intelligible as he reoriented his entire force to keep them from getting flanked. The distinct mechanical whirl and strain of a crashing helicopter bearing down on him from behind sent Alexander curling into the BCP's turret just before a wave of fire washed across the cupola, knocking the hatch's handle out of his hands.

Alexander waited a long moment. He watched, ears ringing, as tracer rounds and missiles zipped past the open hatch. The rhythmic beat of his own heart caused Alexander's head to throb, as his ears rang from the battlefield's resonance. The Captain smacked himself on the helmet, shaking away the trance that paralyzed him. He dragged himself up to the cupola periscope. The Saudis and their mercenary friends had come to a halt about a thousand yards down the ridge from the allied positions, taking cover and laying down an intense blanket of fire.

"Mortars, shift fire, shift fire, three clicks to the west!" Alexander barked into the receiver.

As the seconds clocked by, shell after shell crashed into the enemy line, sowing all manner of confusion. Alexander saw an anti-tank missile launch from atop the turret of a Saudi Bradley and sail right into the side armor of an Abrams, annihilating the tank in a concussive blast. He ducked down further into his own turret's hatch as chunks of debris pinged off the BCP like hail.

"We need more air support here! They've got too many tanks!" Escobedo shouted across the airwaves.

Alexander held down the radio switch again. "Anyone in the air needs to be shitting all over the enemy's armor! Do not let more of them get onto the ridge!"

A faint whistle drew Alexander's eyes to the left as a Sidewinder missile smashed into the engine deck of a Bradley, blasting it into pieces and tossing the handful of U.S. and IDF soldiers around it into the sand. Following the the trajectory of the missile, Alexander felt his skin go clammy at what he saw. More of them. They charged out of a massive cloud of dust like steel demons, approaching now from the direction Alexander had first anticipated. *Damn. Well, at least we know where they all are now.*

"Back! Everyone pull back! We've got hostiles coming in from two directions!" Alexander bellowed over the radio before ducking into the hull of the BCP and shouting to Price in the driver's seat. "Get us the fuck out of here!"

"Don't have to tell me twice!" Price shouted, slamming the vehicle into reverse.

As Alexander clambered back into the turret and the BCP began to move, he heard the sound of drones low overhead. *Shit, probably not good. Should've shut it before.* As he returned to the cupola, Alexander heard bullets pinging all around him against the armored skin. Dirt and sand stung his face as a bomb detonated only a car length away from the BCP.

"Fuck!" He fumbled for the radio, switching to the vehicle's channel. "Get us moving right-goddamn-now, Price!"

Alexander reached his arm out as quick as he could and yanked the hatch closed with all his strength before switching back to the main channel. Everyone scrambled to get into some kind of workable defensive stance, the Saudis pushing ever closer.

"Captain Harris, I've called for support from IDF air assets. We just need to hold out for about ten minutes," the cool voice of Daskal informed him through the radio speaker.

"Sure, no problem…" Alexander said off the air as the hull of his vehicle shook from another near miss. He clicked the radio switch. "Copy that. Let's hope we can."

Alexander watched through his periscope as the battlefield became ever more obscured amid whirling dust propelled into the air by explosions and given flight by the rising wind. Visibility reduced to around a hundred feet, Alexander switched to the thermal setting. He wished he hadn't. What to Alexander's eyes looked like an ocean of American-made armor rolled towards them behind a veil of sand, lobbing shells into the allied ranks as they did. Alexander swore that if he got killed here on this ridge, he would curse General Dynamics with his dying breath.

Clusters of surface-to-air missiles erupted from the dust storm and ascended into the sky past the allied line. Alexander blinked the sweat from his eyes, breath held tight in his arid lungs. A handful of heartbeats later, a torrent of bombs thundered down into the mire of dust that veiled the enemy.

"Halt now!" Alexander ordered into the radio.

The BCP's brakes squealed as the rest of Alexander's force came to a gradual stop. Alexander released a shuddering breath as he watched Israeli Mirage and F-15 fighters swoop by, leaving blooms of fire behind that bored gaping holes in the dust storm. The bullets and shells continued flying toward the allies, but the Saudi advance still faltered.

"Big-shot, mercs trying to flank us from the west, lots of 'em." Derek's voice crackled in Alexander's headset. *"We could use some help down here!"*

"Dammit!" Alexander slammed his fist against the closed hatch. He climbed down from the cupola, wracking his brain about what to do next. They couldn't just sit back and try to absorb an attack of this scale, he had to do *something*. Then it hit him. He chose this ridge to defend because of its high steep southeastern face, but the opposite side had a much more gradual slope… exposed to fire.

"Bird-man this is Big-shot, hold on we're coming to back you up," Alexander responded at last. "First Battalion, Alpha Company, move platoons 4, 5, and 7 to reinforce 2nd platoon and hold your ground. Everyone else, pull back another click."

Alexander ducked his way into the cabin with Price. "Are you nuts? What's going on!?" the spook demanded.

"Get us into that depression! We're gonna hit them from their flank as they try to drive us off the ridge," the captain answered. "We' ain't finished yet."

Once more the allied line started shuffling backwards, the unrelenting momentum of the Saudis compelling them to follow. Alexander's BCP trailed behind the three formations of armored vehicles advancing down from the ridge to back Derek up. The situation remained serious, the massed exchange of fire continuing unhindered.

"This is Bird-man, we're getting messed up pretty bad, anyone else out there?" Derek ventured over the radio with unconcealed anxiety.

"We got you, Bird-man. Just hold on a little longer!" Alexander assured his friend as he watched his position grow larger through the scope as they rolled in closer. A volley of missiles and rockets tore up the desert all around their counterattack, dousing Alexander's troops in searing dust. Streams of tracers zipped past the BCP and spanked off its armor plating all around the one spot through which Alexander could see. Muzzle blasts from tank cannons created brief pockets of air amid the flowing sand that lasted for only a moment before the vehicles were swallowed up again. At long last, they arrived among the battered remains of Derek's unit, some vehicles coming within inches of crashing into each other, while plenty of others actually did.

"Everyone hold your positions, we need to stop their advance on the low ground so we can start flanking the bastards on the ridge! Pick your targets and keep your heads down," Alexander ordered. He had to find Derek and co-ordinate in person.

Stepping out of the BCP for the first time in what felt like an eon, Alexander thanked God for having not lost his goggles as a barrage of sand blasted into his face. The back-and-forth carnage had begun to take a massive toll on both sides as they tried to force each other out of the western depression. The fact that this low area featured countless boulders represented the only thing that the Americans really had going for them in this fight. The turret of an Abrams just behind the parked BCP popped right off its hull in a blinding flash, an inferno branching out into the already searing air behind it. Alexander dove behind a sun-soaked boulder, taking cover beside a pair of marines as bullets chipped away at the rock and the unending rain of shells doused the soldiers in grime.

"This is fuckin' suicide!" one of the marines declared before firing a burst from his M16, cutting down a pair of over-ambitious PMCs who had tried to rush their position. "Who's retard idea was this, anyway!?" he demanded of the universe.

"Hell if I know!" Alexander lied, searching for a way to advance to Derek's tank. He spotted the blazing wreck of an Abrams and lunged back out into the maelstrom. Alexander kept his head down as he bounded from cover to cover, the snap of bullets like sword swings narrowly missing his head. Through all the madness, Alexander at last found the command vehicle of Derek's platoon… burning, smashed, cut off from the main force along with a few others.

Alexander watched as a handful of men and women struggled to drag themselves and their friends away from the obliterated circle of vehicles, tracer rounds punching trough their bodies and explosions flinging them down.

"No!" Alexander blurted out as he brought his M4 up to his eyes and opened fire with a furious vengeance. As the mercs and Saudis tried to make their way past Derek's broken armor, dozens got cut down by a retaliatory storm of lead unleashed by the Allies. Alexander jumped behind a still-fighting Abrams as his magazine ran dry. Fumbling for his ammo pouch, his mind raced in a frenzy as he slammed down the radio button on his headset.

"Charlie Company, First Platoon, redeploy to the depression, all other units hold your ground! We have a Broken Arrow down here! Repeat, Broken Arrow!"

In response to Alexander's decree, the radio came alive with voices calling out coordinates to artillery and aircraft. The Saudi advance staggered and came to a disordered halt. The trade of ordinance blew armored vehicles and boulders alike to pieces, troops getting shredded by explosions and punctured by chunks of flechette. The streaking forms of burning jets, helicopters, and drones careening into the ground in distressing numbers— like some demented meteor shower— blasted columns of soil into the air. Alexander took occasional pot-shots with his now reloaded assault rifle, shrinking back into cover as rounds zipped and snapped all around him. He tried in desperation to find some way of helping Derek's group, but saw none. They couldn't move no matter how much cover fire the main line tried to lay down.

A massive cyclone of dust trapped Alexander, leaving him unable to see anything more than muzzle flashes, tracers, and of course… the flames. Alexander switched to his thermal scope to try and compensate, but found it malfunctioning. He lashed out in frenzied determination whenever he could see as his troops and their Israeli allies prosecuted a terrible vengeance upon the stupefied foe. But when it seemed that even still the enemy would overcome them, a monsoon of missiles atomized the whole occupied stretch of the ridgeline. Alexander watched as explosions illuminated—only for a moment—the silhouettes of men and vehicles before shattering them into dust. Alexander's gaze didn't move as a squadron of blacked-out F-35s swooped by, raking the remains of the enemy vanguard with their chain guns.

Like a fading mirage, the battered Saudi army and their mercenary allies melted away into the sand. They had fallen back. Looking to the left, Alexander saw that with the staggered line of his and Daskal's troops, the enemy forces on the ridge now stood exposed from the northwest. Alexander realized after a moment of soul-tearing uncertainty that the moment of opportunity had arrived at last.

"All units in the depression, sweep the ridge! Clear every motherfucker off that ridge!" Alexander croaked through his sand coated throat into the radio he hoped was still working.

He watched with tangible relief as tanks, IFVs, infantry, and the few surviving MRAPs pivoted their weapons around and began dumping munitions into the flank of the surprised and confused enemies still pressing their comrades on the higher ground. Before long they too started to buckle under the frantic assault of the resurgent allies. Now with momentum behind them and under their own initiative, they began pushing their way up onto the ridge as the Saudis reeled back.

Alexander could only now spare a glance at the writhing forms lying in the sand who made up most of the survivors from Derek's unit. Those few who could still stand did what they could to help as the medics rushed to their aid, Bowman at their head. Alexander wanted to lend a hand himself, and to look for his friend, but knew he could make a bigger difference by ensuring the Saudis did not return. He scanned his harness and realized that he'd ended up on his last magazine. Alexander hit the M4's release and removed the mag. One round left. His headset crackled to life as he heard an engine roll up right behind him.

"*There you are you mad bastard! Come back aboard, chief. Lets finish this.*"

After much chaotic exchange of deadly close-range fire, Alexander's forces arrived back on the ridge, now pouring fire into the last section of the Saudi army, having already rolled up the other two. With the assault deteriorating all around them and unable to change the situation, the final Enemy contingent began to withdraw under an ever more sporadic barrage of Allied fire.

As the gunshots and detonations came to a gradual and reluctant stop, the deep howl of the desert wind and the groans of the wounded immediately replaced them. Alexander took a long moment from his cupola to examine in the tattered state of his forces. Dead and wounded soldiers of every group present lay scattered amid smoldering and ravaged wrecks of numerous war machines from both the ground and the sky.

"*Hey, jefe. Tell me you ain't dead, man,*" Escobedo chimed in over the radio.

Alexander sighed, and as he watched the squadron of mysterious black F-35s circling overhead, he allowed the shadow of a smile to grace the edge of his lips for just a moment. "I'm alive, Sergeant. For now…"

CHAPTER 15:
TROUBLE ON THE FRONTIERS

"A great civilization is not conquered from without until it has destroyed itself from within."
— Ariel Durant

"TRAVIS!"

The shout launched Judith's consciousness back into the world to find a none-too-pleased Sergeant Taylor looming over her.

"Who in the hell told you that it was nap-time, Private!?" she demanded.

"Nobody, Sarge!" Judith lurched up from her seated position next to a half-destroyed silo on the edge of Durant. "Though now that I think of it, nobody told me not to neither. We've jus' been sittin' around here for hours…" A few laughs came from her tired comrades.

"Enough bellyachin'! You'll be happy to hear that we are movin' out. Buncha refugees showin' up tryin' to cross our land in one direction or the other, and command has assigned us to escort detail for now," Taylor explained to the whole squadron.

"Ah man, babysitting duty? And here I was starting to like trading rounds with a buncha batshit lunatics," Mordecai joked, getting plenty of chuckles.

"There may be more lunatics yet. Word is, things on the coasts just keep gettin' worse," Taylor added, a razor-serious edge to her voice. "They'll make it out here eventually. And when they do, you clowns are gonna be ready to kick their asses whether any o' you like it or not! Now then, boots and saddles, ya'll! Boots and saddles! Move it!"

Without a whimper of protest, the exhausted unit shuffled onto their horses' backs and fell in beside Taylor, who waited with a stern expression. Zoey pulled up next to Judith and leaned in to whisper.

"Sorry, Jude. I'll kick ya awake next time."

"Eh, don' worry about me, I can manage," Judith assured with a smirk.

"Sure…" Zoey rolled her eyes with a small grin.

"All right, now that you're all awake, let's move it out people!" Taylor ordered.

At her command, the entire line of riders plodded off to join the others headed east. Judith took a last look around at the traumatized Durant as they left, the covered bodies lining the sidewalks, the last few infernos smothered out by firefighters. Astonished civilians emerging from their hiding places to find their town free and their oppressors broken. Judith felt a smile grow across her face as they passed beyond the small urban zone. *Maybe this won't turn out so bad after all.*

#

The ad hoc posse of cavalry rode for almost two whole days away from the edge of the Great Plains and into the forests and rolling foothills of the Kiamichi Mountains. Just north of Lake Eufaula, and south of the Oklahoma town of Checotah. The winds came in sporadic gusts, providing brief moments of relief from the sweltering humidity. Judith had never travelled so far from home before, more from never getting a chance than lack of desire. She watched as a lone bald eagle soared high overhead, wondering what kind of advanced drones or aircraft might be lurking in the limbo between space and sky, far beyond the limits of her vision.

"Is that what I think it is?" Zoey wondered, marveling at the bird of prey.

"Yeah, I heard they like to roost around lake Eufaula in the winter," Judith said.

"Gosh, winter sounds nice right about now. Judy… how do you work in this all day?" Zoey moaned from just behind Judith's shoulder. She turned to find Zoey's freckled face covered in streaks of sweat.

"Yer such a city girl, Zo. You just gotta get used to it is all," Judith teased.

"Aw come on, ain't there some secret?" her friend pried in a quiet voice.

Judith chuckled as she thought up a checklist in her mind that she'd long committed to heart. "Keep your head under your hat, keep your breathin' even, and ration out your water. We should soak our bandanas in water if we find some. Ain't much more we can do'n that, I'm afraid."

Zoey sighed in frustration. "When in tarnation are we gonna find these refugees anyway? Why'd they come into our land so far north an' not down south where all the big cities are?"

"Cause they don't want to be here at all, an' they don't plan to stay." Sergeant Taylor's rough voice jolted the fatigued duo to attention.

"D-does that mean they might be hostile, sarge?" Zoey asked tentatively.

Judith shot Zoey a covert look, but Taylor just grunted in response. "Dunno, won't find out 'til we meet 'em. Here…" the sergeant dug out a pair of plastic water bottles from one of her saddle bags, tossing one to each of her subordinates. "Try to make these ones last a bit longer."

"Thanks, Sarge…"

"Will do, Sarge…"

Taylor rode ahead to the of front their small column. Numbering around a hundred riders and their horses, a herd of a hundred spare mounts followed along at the rear. The whole mass kicking up a cloud of dust that hovered behind them, clearing away for hurried moments by the southerly wind.

"Do you hate her?" Zoey asked with genuine curiosity.

"Who, the Sarge? Nah…" Judith waved it off. "She's a pain in my ass but I don' think she's a witch'r nothin'."

"Fast mover to the west, one of ours!" a voice called out from the lead of the column. A number of the troops' heads pivoted to the left. Everyone saw it before they heard it.

Judith craned her neck up as far as she could while keeping the brim of her hat between her eyes and the sun. Not without effort she picked out the silhouette of some kind of jet fighter. *An F-15 maybe?* Judith thought for a moment about how often military aircraft had flown overhead during the course of her life, realizing that she'd never really paid them any mind.

Not ten minutes later, a commotion at the head of their force rippled down the column like a line of dominos. Judith and Zoey exchanged concerned looks. The officers shouted for each squadron to separate and form into a wide line, which they did in rapid succession. Only when they had all assembled into this new formation, could Judith at last perceive the reason for her unit's change in posture.

Judith bore witness to the rolling hills of Eastern Oklahoma unfurled before her, and amid their valleys stretching from horizon to horizon a pair of uninterrupted human rivers flowed, one toward the west and the other to the east. The two vast caravans separated by no more than a football field's distance. Endless lines of disheveled people and trashed vehicles.

"What on Earth… where did they all come from?" Zoey wondered aloud.

"Everywhere," Taylor stated, not shifting her gaze from the endless hordes of refugees.

The Texans approached in a multitude of smaller groups instead of as a single mass in hopes of not inciting a panic. The exhausted and cautious unfortunates made no hostile moves against them, and the various squadrons settled alongside the west-bound column as their commanders tried to find someone with any authority. Judith could sense the tension between the two groups as she watched the bitter and suspicious glances they threw back and forth between each other. Many carried weapons.

"This… could be a bit of a problem…" Judith said.

"You're tellin' me? Looks like this mess's gonna catch fire any minute…"

"Hush now you two!" Taylor chided in a hiss, "Us bein' antsy ain't gonna make them any less riled."

The volatile anxiety remained amid the humid, stagnant air all the same. The large number of technicals employed by both sides didn't help anything, and Judith would've felt a lot more nervous were it not for the Texan aircraft she knew circled overhead. The longer Judith watched, however, the more she realized that most of these people wanted more than anything just to reach their respective destinations. Fighting against Judith and her fellow riders seemed the least of their worries.

Eventually the Texans' officers just gave up on trying to find someone in charge, and set the different squadrons on running patrols up and down the open space between the two columns. Natives from the town of Checotah came out and began doing the same. One of the Captains tried to talk them out of it, but they effectively refused so they got assigned the job of holding a few key high points along the road.

Judith and Zoey assumed a post next to a half blown-over road sign where Mordecai and Camila started setting up camp on Taylor's orders.

"How long you think we'll be here?" Zoey asked Judith in a hushed tone.

Judith gave a shrug. "Maybe until there ain't no more people tryin' to cross."

Zoey sighed. "An' that might not be until the wars on the coasts'r over, huh?"

"Yeah, they might find some better suited outfit to relieve us before too long though," Judith pointed out, trying to lift her friend's spirits.

"I hope so… Feels like my skin would jump off my back if somethin' happened. All these people, children…"

"Relax Zo," Judith soothed in a teasing voice. "We're the professionals now, 'member?"

For the next three hours, the Texan riders watched over the marching exiles, with only the occasional gap between their groups. After a while Judith became bored, no longer quite as worried about a sudden outburst of violence. Mutually assured destruction appeared to have kept them from slaughtering each other thus far. Mutual protection couldn't hurt anything either. Then something caught Judith's attention… a pair of refugees, an Asian woman and a Hispanic man, had tried to strike up a conversation with Sergeant Taylor, or so it seemed. *Ah hell…* a quick check over her shoulder and she saw that Zoey had noticed too.

"C'mon Zo, let's go see what the hubbub is," Judith urged, leading her horse over to the sergeant.

"Sure, what could go wrong?" Zoey sighed, following close behind.

As Judith approached the conversing trio, it became obvious that Taylor had become irritated with these two people.

"I can't tell ya nothin' about that. S'all confidential military information," Taylor stated in a tone that welcomed no argument.

"I'm not asking you for exact numbers or anything, just how much of your attention is being devoted to this," the Asian woman asked with just a hint of timidity in her voice.

"I ain't got a clue, Miss," Taylor grumbled.

Judith approached with some caution before clearing her throat. "Is, uh, there a problem here, Sarge?"

Taylor turned to Judith with a mild glower, but soon shifted to a look of realization. "Not anymore, Private. This here is miss, eh…"

"Yujing Huang, I'm a reporter with the BBC." The young woman extended her hand to Judith, who shook it after an awkward pause.

"Right, what she said," Taylor continued with a quick eye-roll. "I want you two to have chat with Miss Huang about… whatever it is she wants to talk about. So long as it ain't technical!" the sergeant emphasized through clenched teeth.

"Eh, you got it, Sarge," Judith accepted with an uncertain smile. "We'll take her off your hands."

"Much obliged, Private." With a smirk, Taylor turned her steed around and headed off west down the road to the command post, leaving a cloud of dust in her wake.

Judith let out a grumbling sigh. *Guess I did ask for it.* She turned to Yujing. "So, what'd ya'll want to know?"

The reporter cleared her throat. "Well, I was asking your sergeant how big of a priority it is to deal with the growing refugee crisis. We've been on the road for over a week, and not only is it getting worse but it all seems to be coalescing here in Texan territory."

Judith smiled, "We're in Oklahoma right now, not Texas."

"But hasn't Oklahoma joined the Republic of Texas?" Yujing asked.

Judith blinked a few times, "Well… yeah I guess it is." She gathered herself and contemplated her answer with great care. "Honestly, I couldn't tell ya, miss. I don't think anybody's attackin' us right now, but that could change in an hour. We don't really want these folks stickin' around too long—" she pointed a thumb over her shoulder at the two streams of people, "but we ain't gonna do 'em any harm neither. Don't wanna give their… 'friends' an excuse to come after us."

Yujing nodded as Judith noticed the reporter's companion for the first time, pointing a video camera at them.

"You filmin' us?" Zoey asked him.

"Uh… yeah. Do you not want to be filmed?" he asked in a tone devoid of confrontation.

"Yer fine. Innit he, Zo?"

"Yeah, yer fine," Zoey conceded, seeming more surprised at the prospect than anything else.

"It's okay if you don't want to be filmed," Yujing insisted.

"Nah, let 'em know who we are," Judith smirked.

#

Emily tried to keep herself awake as the orange sun just began to peer over the Sierra Nevadas. They'd sat outside Camp Pendleton for three days. After an initial exchange of artillery fire, followed by the drone bombing of the camp, very little had gone on. That only made Emily, and everyone else, more nervous and suspicious. None of the Reds had any interest in fighting against the United States Marine Corps, and that included the officers. Keeping the Marines boxed up, shelling them to pieces, and starving them out seemed like a much better idea. Not a glorious solution or one that made them look good of course, but the Reds couldn't have cared less about that.

Emily didn't care either, not anymore. So long as whatever they decided didn't involve her getting used as cannon fodder, she would be happy enough. Hunkered down in the trenches, Emily twisted the sweat out of her dark blue cap as Rob sat across from her, marking things out on a map.

"Please tell me that we're just going to sit here for the rest of the war," Emily prodded her son.

Rob gave a tired chuckle. "Not quite." He pulled out a joint, placing it between his teeth as he dug out a lighter. "Singh's gonna replace us with militia at some point. We'll head south to join up with your old unit and mop up San Diego while these jarheads starve to death."

"How is this even possible? Why would so many people join this 'Red Army' anyways? Is it all just about revenge?" Emily asked, taking advantage of this rare quiet moment for however long it lasted.

"For some it is, but most people are just desperate. It's obvious to all but the most delusional that the aristocrats don't care if we all live or die, so doing what they say anymore will just get us all killed. The conservatives couldn't run a decentralized insurgency to save themselves from literal crucifixion, and the liberals are too spineless to actually do anything, so that kinda leaves just us." Rob took a drink from his canteen and taping it with his finger. "That, along with the fact we control most of the food and water now. And our share of the shrinking pie is only going to increase."

"But can you win? Against everyone who will come after you?" Emily pressed.

"We don't have to win, we just have to not lose. With every month and year that passes, this region will become hotter and less hospitable without massive geo-engineering. All we have to do is whittle down the capitalists, until they can't afford to fight us over this ever more unprofitable region."

"They'll never hand anything over to you."

"We don't plan on giving them a choice." Rob's eyes became cold.

Emily looked away, turning back to the encircled military base. "You think they'll just sit in there while we overrun the whole West Coast?"

"Its about all they've done so far," Rob answered with a shrug. "Whatever they do, we won't be cutting them any

143

slack."

Emily gave a grunt and a nod at that. Anyone could see the whole Red line twitch with apprehension. Nothing that tried to escape from the base would go unnoticed. Emily's strained eyes caught a glimmer in the sky, drawing her gaze upward. All she could make out was a tiny blue shape hurtling over the nearby mountains.

"We've got about 50 drones patrolling the area and enough radars up to spotlight a B-2," Rob spoke up from under his cap.

Emily looked down and sighed before turning to her son. "Do you think 50 drones and some radars are all they have?"

Rob gave her a total deadpan in response. "It's more than what they have *in there*." He pointed to the lone, yet enormous, column of black smoke rising from deep within Camp Pendleton.

Emily remembered the massive explosion, distant from where she'd been watching at the time it happened. A huge mushroom of fire and a shockwave had torn through the base in the dead of night, giving a sense of confidence to the previously uncertain Reds.

"Yeah... how did you guys pull that off anyway?" Emily asked.

Rob lit his joint, careful to cover the lighter as he did. Taking a drag, he nodded his head to the nearby entrance of a trench dugout. Emily looked at him with questioning eyes and he repeated the motion. With some hesitance, Emily ducked inside. Rob followed, their eyes adjusting to the dim light of a lone oil can in the earthen room. Emily noticed a canvas folding chair in the corner, which Rob tossed his folder into. He started to say something, then stopped and waited until a squad of Red soldiers had slogged past.

"We had a man on the inside," Rob told her in a hushed voice.

"*Had?*" Emily questioned with a raised eyebrow.

"Well, considering he blew up their entire hangar row without orders, and that we haven't heard from him since, the working theory is that he's dead."

"Damn..." Emily pondered, "you guys even got a marine to turn to our side?"

"Several, actually," Rob smirked. "But only one in this base so far as I know. Spies aren't really my department."

Emily nodded in understanding, still a bit shaken up. "Did you do the same against us?"

Rob paused before releasing a breath of smoke. "Yes."

Before Emily could venture any further, a massive gunshot shattered the morning gloom. Everyone hunkered down, clung to the nearest trench wall, and readied their weapons as the crackle of gunfire multiplied. Mother and son crept from the small dugout as bullets snapped and impacted all around, covering them in burning dust. Rob fumbled with his headset for a moment before he managed to press the closed channel send button.

"Javier, talk to me, man! What's happening up there?" Rob demanded.

For a moment, no answer came. Then Emily just managed to overhear a voice through the earpiece. She resisted the urge to demand answers from Rob as he listened, surprise becoming evident on his face.

He turned back to Emily. "They're trying to break out south to the city!"

"Isn't that where we put all our most dangerous shit!?"

"The majority of it, yeah!" A cluster of mortar shells plastered the barren land around the Red trenches. "Seemed the most obvious place for them to attack!" Screams echoed from somewhere nearby, but Rob didn't seem too disturbed. "We need to get up to the heights, come on!"

Emily kept right behind Rob as he shuffled along the righthand side of the trench, the one facing the enemy, westward to the nearest hills surrounding Camp Pendleton. As the duo moved, they slid past dozens of Reds either moving in the opposite direction or taking potshots at the still distant enemy. So many drones filled the skies that they hummed like a swarm of mechanical bees. The resonance of detonating explosives battered Emily's eardrums every step of the way.

After climbing for what felt like an hour, they at last reached the heights. There the Hispanic man whom Emily had seen earlier in jail sat watching the Marine base from within a bunker of layered sandbags and corrugated steel. The mustachioed man turned to Rob as he approached and grinned.

"Glad you made it. Take a look at what our friends are doing."

Rob did just that, and reacted with shock at what he saw. He peered through the bunker's embrasure, scanning the position's fields of fire, but keeping a low profile so as to not become a casualty. "I can't believe it... They're retreating..."

Emily couldn't believe it either. She took a careful look for herself through a different opening. To her own equal surprise, the narrow pass between high hills that lead to San Diego just south, now lay strewn with destroyed vehicles and corpses. The Reds' own positions on the heights had taken a murderous beating, scarred by burning craters as it was. Yet the Red banner still flew over the hills in impudent defiance, even as the fighting continued.

"This is, good... right, Javier?" Rob wondered aloud.

"Maybe not." Javier pointed to a wild storm of movement within the base. "Looks like they're gonna try something else."

Emily watched with them as a mass of humanity and machines flowed northward, away from the rapidly dissipating battle in progress... and right toward them.

"Shit. Fuck!" Rob cursed as he tuned his headset. "Harper, come in, we have a problem!" He waited for a long moment, but no response came. He pressed the button again. "Harper?"

#

"GHRK—RAAAAAAAAH!!!" the marine bellowed at Harper with astonished rage in his eyes, sweat streaking down the dark brown skin of his agonized face. He clung to her bayonetted shotgun, the blade of which Harper had buried deep in his stomach. The general tried to wring her weapon from his desperate grasp, but when his strength didn't fade Harper forced the barrel upward and pulled the trigger, ending it.

Trapped in the spell of combat, Harper kicked the dead man off her shotgun and brought it around to smash its metal folding stock into the unprotected nose of another marine as they tried to dispatch a Red Guardsman who'd gotten battered to the dusty ground. The rebel then set upon the stricken marine at once with a combat knife, carving his throat out in one swift motion. In the same moment, Harper pumped her shotgun and fired a second shell into the face and upper torso of another marine just as he rose to the parapet, causing him to crumple back down the blood-soaked hillside.

Having loaded another round, Harper managed to somehow remember the voice in her ear, and pressed down on the radio. "I'm a little busy right now, kid—!" She stopped as a marine charged over the parapet and down into the trench. Harper blasted him in the side at point-blank-range before he even reached the ground. She watched the marine's body collapse like a rag doll, joining the several dozen of his comrades and Harper's own troops who lined the trench. "Just a **little** busy..." Harper finished in a rasping voice even though no one could hear her through the intensity of gunfire and explosions.

"General!"

Harper whirled around to find a Red militia soldier holding an M16 with a bloody bayonet. "What!? More of them!?" she barked.

"No, general! They've broken off and they're heading back into the base!" the shaking young man answered.

Before Harper had much chance to think, her radio headset crackled to life yet again.

"*Ooohhh, Harper! Are you dead!?*" Bennigsen's voice invaded her ears.

Harper growled before hitting the button. "Sorry to disappoint you, Bennigsen, but I'm still here. And yes, we won," she informed the commissar with no small hint pride.

"*I can see that, but now they're turning around to try and kill **us** instead!*" Harper's face melted at Bennigsen's words. She watched as the marine base started to empty of what seemed like everything the loyalists had. "*We need you to get the hell over here with whoever you can scrape up, or you'll be chasing the Marines all across the fucking hills!*"

Harper's face resumed its usual grim posture. "Hang in there kid, help is on the way."

#

Rob let out a frustrated groan before switching radio channels. "The enemy is attempting to break out to the north. All platoons hold position unless ordered otherwise. Retreat and surrender are useless! For the Western Revolution!"

A war-cry emanated from the winding lines of Red trenches as they unleashed a renewed torrent of bullets and shells into the already tattered perimeter of the base. Tanks and other vehicles charged out of the dust and smoke, clumps of infantry behind and around them. Emily watched as a trio of helicopters attempted to take off from the camp, only to get swatted down by missiles launched from a squadron of jet-powered drones as they buzzed past. The familiar din of war grew yet louder as the black shapes of enemies grew more distinct with each passing second.

Emily waited until the machine guns on their own hill opened up before she herself began firing at will, unable to believe she had found herself in this situation, and even less able to escape it. A series of bullets peppered the sandbags all around her opening, forcing Emily to duck down fully into cover behind them. Then she felt a sudden tug on her arm, and turned to find Rob with a determined look in his eyes.

"Come on, we've got to go find Harper!" he shouted at her over the sound of landing artillery shells.

The three of them—Emily, Rob, and Javier—ran out of the bunker and into the pandemonium that had taken shape outside. Swarms of drones cascaded through the sky like schools of piranha, careening down then racing back up. Dust and smoke chocked the air so that nobody on ground level could see anything. Yet the fight raged on. It grew in ferocity as the marines at last stormed up the bottom slope of the hill.

Thousands of Red guns spewed a desperate rain of lead into the equally desperate attackers, the Red Army fighters doing their best to both deal punishment and avoid getting killed themselves. Emily could see the fear in their eyes, but few of them seemed ready to turn and run. The advancing foe cut down any who attempted to flee, convincing everyone else to just stay put and continue firing. As the marines clambered up the hill, some crumpled up beneath the withering storm as others fired from whatever meagre cover they could find.

Emily picked out a target, a tall man with eyes shielded by wraparound goggles and a scarf covering his face. She fired a controlled burst of five rounds, and watched as the marine collapsed forward mid-sprint. Jumping back down and continuing on, Emily tried to focus on what she had to do. *Live, keep Rob alive.*

A mortar shell landed about two car lengths ahead of the trio as they made their way down the trench, killing several unfortunate Red soldiers. Emily brushed chunks of human flesh from the front of her jumpsuit in disgust, before noticing that a Red—killed by a huge chunk of shrapnel in his back—had fallen onto Rob and knocked him to the ground. Without a moment's pause, Emily hauled the corpse off her son with one arm then yanked him to his feet.

"Keep moving!" she yelled, giving him a push to jumpstart him. "Go!"

Rob required no further encouragement and took off with Emily at his side and Javier just behind him. They didn't make it far before a marine leapt into the trench from no-man's-land with a furious yell. He turned to Emily in his shaded goggles. She responded by driving the bayonet of her assault rifle into the man's throat without hesitation, but didn't have a chance to pull it back out before she took a hard blow in the back, knocking her against the trench wall. Emily pushed away from the wall and whirled around, bringing her bayonet across the face of a female marine. The woman fell backward, crying out as she clutched at her excruciating injury and one of her comrades slammed Emily into the wall yet again, trying to wrestle her weapon away. The frantic ex-cop managed to get the barrel of her weapon pointed at a marine on the parapet and held her trigger down, pelting him with rounds until he collapsed into the trench and the rifle, at last, got knocked from Emily's hands.

Now surrounded by enemies, her son held down by a bayonet at his throat, and no other Reds in sight, Emily flew into a savage frenzy. With a wild howl she drew the old 1911 .45 from her belt, flicked the safety off, and fired a round into the marine's knee point-blank. As she hoped, the man screamed in stunned anguish for the moment it took Emily to bring the pistol's barrel up under his jaw and fire again. Using her leg, Emily pushed the dead marine back with all the strength in her body, knocking two of his comrades to the ground before she blasted a third in the eye as he stared at her

146

in disbelief.

A tank drove over the trench at high speed and then barreled on, forcing Emily to dive out of the way to avoid getting squashed. The marine keeping Rob down turned to Emily, eyes hidden by tinted goggles, and started to bring his rifle up to her. No sooner had he started to move than Rob grabbed the end of the marine's weapon and pulled him down onto the knife that Rob held in his waiting hand. Javier had somehow gotten into a glorified fistfight with another marine after disarming him, and Emily couldn't see how to intervene without huge risk. Her eyes darted upward, sensing movement, to find six marines emerging from the wall of dust. Emily felt the life drain from her face as all the marines took aim at her, only to watch all of them disappear in an instant as a missile landed among the group and literally blew them to pieces. A drone hurtled low over the trench with a blaring whine, carving a short-lived gap in the cloud of soot.

A heavy blow to the stomach made Emily double over and almost knocked her off her feet, barely getting a chance to recover before another hit slammed into her face. Recovering herself as she coughed uncontrollably, Emily staggered to her feet and found the same female marine who's face she'd sliced open a second ago coming at her with a bayonet of her own. The woman's youthful face was contorted in hatred, streaked in her own blood, vengeful brown eyes raging beneath a layer of sweat and grime. At the last moment, Emily side-stepped the marine's bayonet and grabbed it with her left arm so the woman couldn't use it to stab at her again. The marine fired her weapon on full-auto, roasting Emily's side with the muzzle flash and sending dirt and dust from the trench wall behind her into the air. Emily brought her own pistol around to try to kill the marine, who dropped her M16 and grabbed Emily's right hand. In exasperation, Emily fired three rounds at her enemy's head, one hit the trench wall, another grazed the marine's helmet, the third took off part of her ear.

With a combination of pain and rage the marine head-butted Emily in the nose and twisted her arm, a surprise assault that knocked her gun away nearly ended it then and there. But Emily couldn't lose. She couldn't die. She couldn't let her son die. She couldn't let her family be left adrift, without protection. In a throbbing trance, all of Emily's pain numbed away from her smashed and brutalized body, and she drew the Ka-Bar from the sheath behind her back. Deafened to her own feral screams and barely able to perceive the world around her, Emily sunk the blade into someone's neck, then someone else's armpit, and then at last into the stomach of the female marine. Emily thrust over and over and over, pinning the woman against the trench walls as she did. An ocean of arms pulled at her, dragging her back and away, but Emily refused to stop. She kicked, stabbed, cut, punched, elbowed, and bit, until something hard crashed into the side of her head. Emily saw only darkness.

#

The chirps of bluejays blanketed the outskirts of Fredericksburg as Paul kept a weary vigil for the storm he knew would come. A crashing wave that he knew his forces couldn't stop, but hoped they could slow down. To Paul the idea of the old U.S. government taking back control of the South felt disgusting, but the prospect of living under whatever the hell they'd turned into horrified him. Did the libs annoy the hell out of him at times? Sure. Did that justify their systematic killing? Paul didn't think so. Weren't Americans supposed to be above that sort of thing? No one else seemed to agree. Either way, these wackos had no chance of taking over his adopted homeland. At least not without a hell of a fight.

Command had dispatched the few reinforcements that they could spare, but most of the Saints' army still needed assembling and organizing. They needed time they didn't have, Paul knew the only way to buy time: spend blood. Paul hated the idea, but no other options existed. Surrender? Not an option. Negotiation? Pointless. Retreat? Impossible. Paul still couldn't believe it had come to this.

"Hey, Paul. Got a minute?" Mason's voice asked from over his shoulder.

Paul waved his friend over without turning his head or uttering a word. "Sure, man. What troubles ya?"

"Same as you if I had to guess."

Paul chuckled, "Figures."

"We still not movin' till the Feddies make us?"

Paul nodded.

"Then this could be it, huh?"

"It very well could, yeah."

"Damn. Well then, I guess I wish you good luck." Mason extended his hand, which Paul readily shook.

"Good luck to you as well, Mr. Mason." Paul gave a tired but genuine smile. "I hope we meet again on the other side."

"Whatever side that may be," Mason said, nodding with an exhausted grin of his own.

As his friend departed, Paul couldn't help but wonder why God so often chose men of such low lot in life to change the world. He wanted his burdens to get taken up by another, but he knew that no other would come. They had fallen upon him, though he did not yet know why.

The rusted clattering of tank tracks began to emanate from the north river bank. Louder and louder became the mechanical cry as Paul took in a deep breath and held it. He could hear the blood rushing through his ears.

"*Prep for contact, here they come!*" The radio came alive with chaos as everyone steeled themselves.

Drones, helicopters, and jet fighters made the first move on each side, spraying each other down with bullets and missiles in an effort to rain hell upon their counterparts. They spun and danced like schools of fish in the ocean, one of them occasionally breaking from the group and plummeting to the ground consumed in smoke. Paul found the whole display so mesmerizing that he struggled to drag his vision back to ground level.

The metallic din only grew more intense until at last the first tank charged out of the tree line which concealed the suburban town of Falmouth. More and more vehicles emerged, skirting around the charred wrecks that remained of their predecessors. Not a moment later, the Saints on the ground opened fire. And the chaos ensued.

Paul used his binoculars to scan the whole northern river bank, watching as Federal forces emerged from the woods along almost its entire length. *Alright, here it goes…*

Paul grabbed his radio. "Now!" In a series of glaring flashes, the bridge across the Rappahannock River erupted in smoke and flames. Paul could see chunks of concrete and asphalt plummet into the river. "Don't get pinned down, fall back as soon as it gets too risky to hold!"

An F-15 wreathed in flames careened into a strip mall, tearing it apart in a blazing shockwave. From the high school's roof, Paul could see almost everything, which also left him exposed. He'd kneeled down behind a sandbag wall between a sniper and a machine gun team for cover, but the real threat at the moment came from the sky. An Apache made a beeline for the school, but instead ended up executing desperate maneuvers in a futile effort to avoid a volley of SAMs. Artillery from both sides plastered the river and the outskirts of town into oblivion as the devastating blanket of fire compelled the Saints to retreat.

Shit! Paul watched in helpless frustration as no less than six bridge-laying units appeared on the northern bank and began moving into position. If all those bridges got deployed, the rebels would get overrun in no time.

"Take out those bridge layers!" Paul shouted into the radio, "Destroy as many as you can, or we're **fucked!**"

A shell from a Southern Abrams annihilated one of the carriers in a plume of fire, before itself getting overwhelmed by a stream of AT missiles from Federal Bradleys and shoulder launchers. A rebel jet tried to destroy another but got repelled by a Vulcan anti-air vehicle. *Damn, I didn't know those things were even around still.* More artillery rained down upon the loyalist engineers as they scrambled to get their bridges set into place. A shell crashed onto one of the steel sections as the carrier began to extended it. Another layer got blown apart after a drone missile struck it from behind in the engine bay. Determined to protect their means of getting across the river, the Federals renewed their murderous torrent of fire, systematically neutralizing or suppressing every point of resistance as their fighters, drones, and helicopters started to win the bloody struggle for the skies.

In the end, the combat engineers managed to deploy three of the six bridges, and the loyalists began to pour onto the southern bank. Dozens fell to mortar or artillery shells and streams of machine gun fire, but soon the last resistance broke down as the rebels turned and fled. A drone without one of its wings spun out of control over the high school, sending Paul and everyone else to the deck as it sailed just above them and exploded on the football field.

"Everyone get the fuck out of here, go!" Paul bellowed, sending everyone into a scramble for the ladders facing away from the advancing Feddies.

A pair of Cobra helicopters bearing the Confederate Battle Flag unleashed their full payloads upon the southern bank. *Jesus, where's all this ancient shit comin' from!?* Despite their age, these flying relics savaged the loyalists who'd gathered there, buying Paul the time he and his troops needed to abandon the school. One of the helicopters got swatted down by anti-air missiles, while the other limped off to the south, leaving a trail of black smoke behind. Paul offered a prayer for all those who'd sacrificed themselves in this desperate effort as he made his way back down to solid Earth.

A rebel Bradley zoomed down main street, firing its cannon backward and simultaneously launching AT missiles. Trucks laden with rebel fighters and supplies flew across the tarmac at unsafe speeds as the steel groan of tank treads even louder. Paul controlled his breathing as he charged after a departing technical, doing his best to ward off panic as a Federal artillery shell obliterated an electronics store to his right. The driver of the technical miraculously saw Paul and slowed down just enough for him to catch up, but once he'd clambered into the flatbed the driver floored it and set off on their escape.

The technical's main weapon consisted of two .50 cal heavy machine guns with a Stinger missile launcher haphazardly attached to them. A man with a massive brown beard, and what Paul judged could be no more than five teeth, fired with reckless abandon at the numerous drones and helicopters now prowling the town for victims. Paul watched an entire five-man squad of Saints get shredded by an Apache as they tried to move from cover to cover, only for the Apache itself to get perforated by .50 cal rounds from the technical. All the while the radio broadcasted a cornucopia of anarchy. Overlapping orders, desperate pleas for help, coordinates for supporting fire that probably wouldn't come.

The outskirts of Fredericksburg faded into a blur for Paul as the technical took off down abandoned streets, diving between tall buildings as much as possible. Other vehicles of every kind joined alongside and behind them as they raced to leave the invaders choking on their dust. He knew that small handfuls of his comrades waited in concealed hideouts across the city, ready to ambush the Feddies later to sow more chaos and confusion. But Paul also knew that their purpose remained the same as his. Time. Stopping the Feddies seemed impossible, yet Paul knew it could be done. *If a bunch of Afghans could do it, so can we.*

CHAPTER 16:
UNCERTAIN TIMES

"Anyone who isn't confused doesn't really understand the situation."
— Edward R. Murrow

"I… I'm sorry, Captain. There was nothing more we could do…" Doctor Bowman explained to Alexander in a somber voice.

He stared down at the motionless body of his lifelong friend, unable to say anything. A tarp covered all below Derek's battered face, hiding a body that Alexander knew bore horrific wounds.

"You don't have to apologize for anything," he managed at last.

"I could… give you a moment if you'd like…"

"No." Alexander pulled the tarp over Derek's face with a trembling hand. "I'll take my moment somewhere that isn't in the way. How many others did we lose?"

"About three thousand in all," Bowman answered. "Apparently we took out around three times that many."

Alexander scoffed under his breath. *So what?* He turned to Bowman and tipped his sweat-stained cap, "Thanks, Doc. I'll let you know when it's time to pack up and move out."

With that he left the crowded medical tent, an expression of stone on his grime-covered face. Alexander had lost friends and comrades before, but Derek had always been there. He even seemed invincible at times, fearless yet cautiously optimistic. Now, Alexander would have to make it home without him, and get everyone else back too.

And of course, face down whatever had happened to America in their absence.

"American!" Alexander turned to find an irate Daskal storming toward him.

Fuck… "Something you need, Colonel?" the infantry captain asked.

"Indeed there is!" Daskal thundered back, "I've just received information that you have been keeping a secret from us this whole time!"

Alexander's face went slack, as he knew at once what Daskal referred to. "Ah yes, the Persian…"

"You have an officer of the Iranian Revolutionary Guard as your prisoner!"

"He has information we need, and from what I understand you've bagged no shortage of POWs yourselves."

"That isn't the point!" Daskal retorted. "You have kept a vital intelligence source hidden from us, and I demand that you hand him over immediately!"

Alexander's face hardened. "Prisoners weren't part of our agreement. And like I said, we need what he knows."

"What information could an Iranian officer possibly possess that would be any concern of yours!? You are still planning to leave, yes? What does it matter where he ends up!?"

"He knows about the attack against the states, and I want to learn everything that I damn well can about what went down there." Alexander stepped closer to Daskal. "We saved your asses, *twice*. You owe us."

Daskal scoffed. "If you believe anything the snake tells you, you're a damned fool! My superiors will not be happy about your refusal, they might even deny you permission to leave."

"That could be an issue," Alexander warned. "We made a deal, and I haven't broken it."

"You expect me to believe that you would let this bastard slip through your fingers were you in my position?" Daskal demanded, "You have your own fight back home, American, but ours rages on as soon as you leave."

The Israeli colonel stormed off with two of his officers in tow. Alexander sighed. *Well, shit. This is bad. I might have to wrack Farzan's brain before handing him over if the Israelis won't budge…*

"Captain Harris!" Price spoke up from behind Alexander, having made no sound on his approach.

Alexander whirled around in surprise to find the spook standing laptop-in-hand with filthy glasses and an exhausted face. "What, Price? What could it possibly be now?"

"Well... um..." Price stalled out.

"Stay with me, kid. Focus."

"The troops are uh, getting very... restless."

As Alexander calmed, he noticed the panic on the intel officer's face, and heard a clamor of shouts emanating from the docks. Without a word he began jogging toward the moored transport ships, Price following close behind.

As the duo approached the docklands, the sounds of chaos became louder. Rounding the corner of a bullet-riddled warehouse, they came face to face with a large mob of angry American soldiers, trying to intimidate or force their way past the U.S. Army military police and IDF soldiers guarding the transport ships. Americans and Israelis had gotten into numerous brawls, and both sides had taken to waving guns around and pointing them at each other. To top it off, an ever growing stream of soldiers—their rucksacks and duffle bags in tow—continued to amass, expectant, anxious, impatient, the crowd swelling and roiling more by the second. If Alexander didn't wade into this and somehow de-escalate the situation, he would have a disaster on his hands and end up either dead or stuck in the Holy Land for whatever remained of his life.

Alexander pushed and squeezed his way to the front of the throng with Price struggling to keep up. The desperate captain scrambled atop a steel transport crate and began waving his hands to grab everyone's attention.

"Listen up! We'll all be leaving soon, just return to your units and await orders to assemble back here!" Alexander tried to maintain a balance between sternness and appeal, trying to prevent things from getting out of control.

"Why!?" a female voice from the crowd demanded, "What is there to wait for!?"

The mass of soldiers grumbled in affirmation, showing no sign of dispersing.

"This place is still surrounded, we don't know if it's clear for us to make a break for it yet!" Not a lie, but not the whole truth either.

"We been killin' the rag-heads since my dad was in the army, and it ain't changed a fuckin' thing!" a hulking infantryman bellowed with the support of the crowd. "We wanna go home!"

The troops became more raucous by the moment, and larger numbers kept arriving as the disorder drew ever greater attention, until most of Alexander's force had crowded around the pier. MPs struggled to keep some kind of lid on the rapidly decaying situation. Standing on the precipice of disaster, Alexander made a decision. *Fuck this.*

"Okay, okay, alright!" Alexander shouted as loud as he could, waving his hands again. "Alright, everyone gets to load up **now**. But we do it orderly or this will be even more of a mess than it already fuckin' is. Everybody line up!"

Alexander jumped down from the crate as the clamor of U.S. troops began shuffling into a rough line with varying degrees of enthusiasm, a lieutenant of the IDF soldiers on the docks moved to confront him.

"What the hell are you doing, American!? You can't board these ships without authorization from—"

"Look around you. You think I can stop them from just taking these ships if they wanted? I'll sort things out with you superiors, just get them down here, will ya?"

Defeated, but also furious, the Israeli officer stormed off, barking into his radio in Hebrew. Alexander drew in a sharp breath, he'd bought a few minutes at least. Price came up behind him.

"Cap, what're we going to do with... *him*?" he whispered.

Alexander whirled around, holding up a finger to silence the intel man. "Bring him here, dress him up like one of our guys. He won't fight you if he knows we're getting him out."

"What about all our heavy shit? Tanks, artillery, heli—"

"Forget about it. Uncle sam has plenty more lying around and we don't have the means of getting it loaded up anyways. Besides, I don't know about you, but I've had my fill of this place."

Price just gave a silent nod after a brief moment of surprised bewilderment. The files of soldiers had begun shuffling aboard the battered old ships in earnest now, heedless of the tension that still permeated the whole docklands. Alexander paced back and forth, using his radio to inform everyone about the change of plans.

"*Aw come on, jefe! There's gotta be some other way!*" Escobedo pleaded.

"I'm sorry, Sergeant. But we either leave all the vehicles behind or we risk our necks by sticking around," Alexander explained.

"Copy that, boss. *Adiós querida, te recordaré siempre.*"

"See to it, Sergeant." Alexander switched channels, "Price, where are you, kid?"

"American!"

Fuck. Alexander craned his neck to find Daskal storming toward him. "Hello again, Colonel."

"So, it wasn't enough for you to have hidden information from us, now you are trying to twist my arm into getting what you want!?" Daskal hissed.

"I didn't do anything except prevent a bloodbath. These people are leaving, whether either of us like it or not. I'm taking my *one* prisoner and leaving *all* of our heavy equipment to you. Consider it an exchange, a donation, whatever. I just need to get things rolling before you have another marauding horde on your hands."

Daskal took a long gaze at the river of Americans making their way onto the various ships. He sighed, rubbing his brow. "Our ships will drop you off in Naples. That is as far as we can afford to send them."

"That will be fine."

Daskal gave Alexander a look from head-to-toe. "Good luck, American. You will need it."

Alexander watched with narrowing eyes as the Israeli colonel disappeared into the wall of humanity. *No way it was that easy.* Price emerged from the crowd with a trio of soldiers, one of them wearing a dust mask and goggles.

"Alright, here we are. Ready to bail?" Price asked with obvious anxiety.

Alexander scrutinized the masked "American" who regarded him with a silent nod.

"Yeah, let's get the hell out of here while we can."

"Not so fast, son."

Alexander whirled to find a tall blond man in a black coat and dark sunglasses approaching him, flanked by two bodyguards. Price's hand hovered near the pistol holster at his hip, but Alexander gestured for him to relax.

"I don't believe we've met, can I help you?" Alexander asked.

"It is we who can help you, Captain Harris," The Man in Black declared. "In fact, we already have. You may remember us from the ridge."

Alexander thought hard, with a hint of indignation. He hadn't seen any soldiers in black during the battle at all. Then it hit him like a thrown rock.

"The F-35s?"

The Man in Black grinned from behind his shades. "Bingo. I would've sent more, but we have many obligations and they were all that could be spared."

"They were enough, thank you." Alexander nodded. "But, what do you want in return?"

"I want you to do exactly what you planned on doing. Take your people to Europe and then make your way back home."

Alexander blinked about a dozen times in rapid succession. "You... do?"

"Oh yes. You may not realize it now, but you and your comrades, whoever they may be, will play a pivotal role in what is unfolding in America."

Alexander's eyes shot wide open. "What's going on back home? What the hell happened?" he demanded, trying to keep his voice down, only to realize everyone nearby seemed too busy loading onto ships to notice.

"It's better if you didn't hear it from me. But don't worry," he held up his hand, "You will have the answers you seek as soon as you arrive in Europe."

Alexander wasn't happy about that response, but could tell that protesting would be useless. So he just nodded his head in acceptance. Then the Man handed him a sealed folder. Alexander gave the featureless document a quick examination before giving the Man in Black a quizzical look.

"That in your hands is a list of everyone in European Command who will give you trouble, and everyone who will be sympathetic. I've already seen to it that your ships will be provisioned for the trip, your men have all the medical aid they need, and that they will be accommodated when they arrive."

"I… I don't… What?" Alexander stammered. All but speechless for the first time in years.

"You will understand soon enough." The Man in Black turned away from the bedraggled Captain, making his way back down the docklands. "You don't realize it yet, Captain Harris, but your country is going to need you more than it has ever needed any of its sons."

#

Emily awoke from her nightmares when a wave of lukewarm water crashed into her stinging face. She blinked and shook her head, stupefied. A brutal slap brought her into sobriety.

"Wake up, bitch!"

Emily managed to shrug off her stupor and shake the water out of her eyes, finding her hands bound in plastic cuffs. She groaned. "Fuck…"

"Right you are, miss. You have found yourself in one hell of a shitstorm," a mocking voice said in a sing-song tone. "Now, why don't you sit up so we can talk?"

As Emily rolled onto her back then leaned forward, she got a look at her new surroundings. A green military tent, Rob and Javier sat bound and bloodied on either side of her, surrounded by seven very pissed-off looking marines, all armed. *Why me?*

"There you go, now I've already talked to your friends here, but neither of them really wanted to share anything us. Maybe you're feeling a bit more helpful, huh?" the tallest marine, a man with blue eyes and red hair, asked.

Emily suppressed a growl upon seeing the bruised and bleeding face of her son. "I don't know anything you'd want to find out," she told them through gritted teeth.

"Well that's very strange," the tall marine stated in fake surprise, "because the three of you came runnin' down from the command post on that damn ridge, yet you didn't have any intel on ya. Sure you don't have it up here instead?" he asked with a grin while prodding Emily's head with the barrel of his M4.

"The commies don't tell me shit!" she snapped.

"Oh, and you ain't one of 'em!?" another marine demanded.

"Not before two weeks ago…" Emily stared into the ground, doing everything she could not to look at Rob, who seemed undisturbed. "We were just trying to warn some of the others—"

"Bullshit! She's lyin'," the shorter of the two female marines asserted, "This fuckin' nerd here's gotta know somethin'!"

"Well, technically yes," Rob spoke up. "Just not the information *you* want."

The taller marine responded by kicking Rob in the stomach with his hard boot, knocking him down.

"Hey! Fuck you! Aren't there rules for how you guys treat prisoners!?" Emily received a rifle stock to the face for her impudence, sending her back into the sandy dirt. Two of the marines wasted no time dragging her back up to her knees.

"Those rules don't apply to you scum-rakers," the tall marine said with a dire glare. "You spill your guts and maybe we'll consider it."

A side glance at Rob, and even through her blurred vision Emily could tell that he'd resigned himself to his end. But she hadn't made it this far to go out begging for forgiveness. Emily's eyes narrowed into a scowl as she steadied herself. "Burn in hell."

Before the crew of newly enraged marines could descend upon them, the tent flaps flew open and an weathered old veteran straight out of central casting marched inside. Upon seeing the state of the Red trio, the barrel-chested man rounded on the tall marine, who straightened.

"Didn't I tell you not to get too rough with 'em!?"

"Sorry, sir!" he replied in a tone that made it clear he wasn't. "The prisoners have refused to cooperate in any capacity, sir!"

The marine commander turned back to Emily, her son, and Javier. Rob had managed to sit himself back up with an irritated groan. All three returned the commander's scrutiny with an unbroken deadpan.

"Hrm, I wonder why…" he grumbled. "You two, guard them, and nothing else! The rest of you get the hell outside."

The commander followed his troops as they left, shooting the prisoners a final glare, which Emily ignored.

"Okay, so… we're still not dead. You guys okay?" Rob groaned, blinking some sweat and blood from his eyes.

"How are we defining 'okay'?" Javier rubbed the back of his neck, eyeing the pair of guards left behind, who regarded the three with disdain.

"Don't give up just yet, Rob." *Let's try something stupid.* Emily tasted the blood pooling between her lips and used her tongue to scoop it into her mouth before spewing it onto the boots of the closest marine guard, much to the astonishment of everyone in the tent. *Come over here, bitch…* The woman's face twisted from general disgust to anger as she lurched forward to strike Emily again, but her comrade pushed her back.

"Ah, come on, she—"

"Save it, Ramirez, you heard the colonel! And you!" He pointed down at Emily. "Why don't you stow the attitude, you're not helping yourself any!"

"You intend to kill us all regardless," Rob stated.

"Know that for a fact, do you?"

"Yes," Rob answered without emotion.

The marine shook his head. "At least wait until the big man comes back before you start waving yer crazy around, will ya?"

The female marine kicked some of Emily's blood off her boots and looked the bound former police officer in bewilderment. "What you said earlier, about bein' a cop, was that true?"

Emily sighed, glancing over at Rob. "Yeah."

"Then how in the hell did you end up here?"

"I didn't want to get lynched and have my family destroyed."

The marine scoffed, "Well that doesn't seem to have worked out too well, huh? Like the nerd says, this here is the end of the road for you traitors."

The male marine opened his mouth to speak, but Rob beat him to it. "We could say the same for you, mercenary."

The female marine laughed. "The hell are you on, kid? You really think you've got a chance of getting out of this?"

"Yeah, sorry, pal, but we won and you lost. We've got no reason to sweat your asses."

"Oh, we aren't the ones you need to worry about. I know you've taken us to the northern section of your camp, and I also know that you've found it empty and useless to you." The confidence on the marines' faces melted away as Rob spoke. Emily glanced between the pair and her son. Rob's own mask of careless joviality shifted into one of stone as he stared into the eyes of each marine in turn. "What, you think the idea didn't occur to us that we might lose? That the vaunted United States Marine Corps might break through our poorly-equipped and barely-trained forces? You haven't won anything."

The two U.S. jarheads exchanged an uneasy look.

"You don't scare us, commie. We fought worse than you, whatever scheme your masters come up with will just get more of you killed."

Rob's smile returned full strength. "Are you sure about that? We did stop you from breaking out to the city."

"That was just a feint, we always planned to come here," the male marine asserted.

"I wonder what the courageous defenders of San Diego would have to say about that?" Rob posited in mock concern.

Before the exchange could continue, the tent flaps again rustled open as the colonel and six other marines marched in. The six infantry troops paired up and dragged the three prisoners outside without a word, ignoring their struggles and protests. The dimming light of the California evening cast an eerie orange veil over the shattered, torched remains of a military base. Groups of marines stood around with their weapons slung, casting the occasional nervous glance up at the sky. Emily followed their eyes to find something that made her blood run cold.

Drones. Thousands of drones. More than she'd ever seen in one place. Circling over the base like carrion birds. The air resonated with the shrill cries of aircraft engines. Emily turned her gaze to Rob, who took evident comfort in the machines' presence, which could only mean one thing. Sure enough, the three soon found themselves at the facility's gates in front of a group of Marine officers and Reds, including a pair of familiar faces.

"Ah, comrade Bennigsen! I am thrilled to find that you are not dead! Though I see the empire's hospitality hasn't softened," Singh proclaimed, embracing Rob as soon as the marines released him.

Emily suppressed an instinct to shove the Red leader away from her son.

"I'm alright, did the rest of my troops…?"

"They are fine! These blowhards never made it onto the top of the ridge," Singh informed him with a wave toward the marines, who glowered back.

"Alright, kid. You've got your buddies back. Now it's time to keep your word," the colonel grumbled.

"Of course, Colonel!" Singh replied with courtesy that sent shudders down Emily's spinal cord. "Our transports stand ready to move you all to a recently liberated prison where you and your troops will be billeted until the conflict's end."

"And when will that be?"

"Who knows? Could be months or decades. It's all up to your employers, really."

The colonel sighed, scanning over the drone swarms and the numerous tanks on the heights, which Emily could now see. "I guess we don't have any choice…"

"You could always give me an excuse to murder you all and make this whole thing much simpler," Singh offered with a smirk.

The colonel mumbled. "Fine, let's get this over with."

Singh waved a group of gas-mask wearing Reds forward to collect the marines' weapons, before turning back to Rob as they headed over to the rebel vehicles. "Well, Bennigsen. Still feel the same about, 'leading from the front'?" he asked as the group climbed into an armored truck which lurched into motion the second the door slammed shut.

"We can't expect anyone to follow us if we don't share in their dangers, Singh."

"Nor can you be expected to lead if you're a bullet-riddled corpse."

"Can we save the philosophical shit for later?" Harper interrupted with folded arms. "You know that we got lucky, right? Those guys could have trashed us if the whole damn world wasn't stacked against them."

"Yes, of course," Singh acknowledged. "I had only hoped to bait them into doing something stupid. I'm fully aware of how dangerous they are under ideal circumstances."

"Good, now I wanna hear what your twisted-ass brain has planned for those marines. The *real* plan."

"Everything will unfold as I promised… at first. They will be taken to a nearby penitentiary—which is now a smoldering ruin—where they'll be led to what used to be the yard in groups… aaaaand… buried alive."

Emily's eyes shot open, taken off guard. Sure, the marines had beat and nearly killed her, but the fight was over now. Against all odds Singh had won. Now he planned to levy as much spite against them as anyone could conceive. Emily glanced sideways at Rob, who bore a resigned look in his eyes. In desperation, she found Harper's face, which reflected Emily's own shock and disgust.

"You crazy son of a bitch! At least you honored the other deals we've made, what changed this time!?"

"How exactly has the deal been broken?"

"You promised we would let them live if they surrendered!"

155

"I promised nothing of the kind. I said that, if they gave up, there wouldn't be anymore bloodshed. And there won't be."

"Oh... you little—"

"They're marines, Harper. They won't agree to help us except to trick us. We have nothing to gain by working with those cretans, and keeping them around as prisoners would be nothing but an extreme liability for us," Singh explained as he looked over a map of San Diego in a nonchalant fashion.

Harper snatched the map away to Singh's barely perceivable annoyance. "This isn't some dumbass game where you can just screw people over for not doing what you want, Singh. If no one in this war plays by any rules at all, then everything will just devolve into hell on earth!"

To Emily's discomfort and surprise, Singh didn't lash out in anger or become flustered. Instead, his gaze remained impassive. "Yes. Yes it will. Which is why we *do* have a rule, brutal though it is."

"What could that be!?"

"Simple! Surrender without a fight or join us, and you can live. Resist, and punishment will be annihilation," Singh explained, before gesturing to Emily, "With room for only occasional exceptions."

Emily blinked before looking away out the heavy armored window into the evening mountain vista beyond. She clenched her fist so tight she felt her joints crack and strain.

"So we're just going to live up to their worst expectations of us?" Harper asked.

"We don't lose anything by doing that, so... yes!" Singh answered with conviction.

"Hey," Rob's voice caused Emily to tilt her head his way. "We're *still* not dead."

Emily took a deep breath, stealing a venomous glance at the smoking Singh. "Yeah, for now."

CHAPTER 17:
THE SETTING SUN

"Necessity hath no law."
— Oliver Cromwell

Paul listened to the idle resonance of the water against his eardrums as he kept his head submerged for a long, surreal moment. He felt a strange itch across his back—someone approaching from behind—he pulled his head up and out of the sink, using his shirt to wipe the tepid water off his face, taking in a deep breath as he turned. A brown-haired woman in a hunter's cap carrying a pump shotgun stood at the bathroom doorway in a reasonable imitation of a soldier's stance.

"Captain Cunningham, sir! Lieutenant Mason is waiting to speak with you in the main lobby, sir. He said it's urgent."

Paul sighed. "That must mean it's time to get back to work." He grabbed his jacket and left the shattered restroom, following the private downstairs. The two squeezed their way past groups of Saints and refugees as they slid down the halls and stairwells. They may have escaped the main wrath of the hurricane, but they hadn't outrun the unending downpour. The old hotel quaked with the reverberation of thunder, raindrops the size of quarters battered the windows. The myriad smells of weather, sweat, and spent gunpowder permeated everything.

The lobby more resembled a fortified bunker now, overflowing with layers of corrugated steel and sandbags. Mason sat on a cheap couch left over from the room's previous furnishings, plotting something out on a map with his pen. He had a gauze bandage wrapped across his left cheek where a .50 caliber bullet had grazed him, taking a chunk of flesh with it. Paul nodded to the young private, who returned the gesture and went back to her own business.

"How's the face, Mason?" Paul asked.

"Painful," he answered, deadpan.

Paul nodded with a sigh, "Whatcha got?"

"Hm, what else? Trouble." He pointed to three locations on the map surrounding Richmond from north, west, and east. "They gettin' ready to move in on the city. All we been able to do so far is slow 'em down, but command wants us to hold this place. Said we can't fall back no more."

"Not for now," Paul clarified, "This whole thing was always going to be unconventional."

"Unconventional, meaning…?"

"Guerilla-style."

"Ah. So, our shit."

"Yeah, our shit." Paul chuckled.

"Good, we gotta get the drop on these soldier boys if we're gonna have a chance."

"Still can't let the Feddies up an' take the capital of Virginia like that. Our people might start thinkin' we're not too serious about this thing. Feddies might start thinkin' they can just roll over us without much of a fight."

Mason scoffed. "Great. We got any better chance of pullin' that off than last time?"

Paul shrugged. "We got five times as many guys as in Fredericksburg, half a year's worth of supplies, an' the Feds are havin' to deal with the hurricane way more than us now. God willin', we can pull it off. 'Least until a relief force can arrive."

For a while the pair just watched the lines of desperate people and disheveled soldiers shuffle down the drenched streets towards who-knew-where.

"Well, at least we done better than the last time anything like this happened…" Mason said after the long silence.

Paul did a double take. "You mean when Trump's guys sacked the capitol building back in 2021? Or do you mean the second time…?"

"Yeah," Mason answered with a laugh and a smile. "The second time."

"Jesus, those poor bastards." Paul shook his head, remembering way back when his uncle Spencer had been among those duped into marching on D.C. in the name of a spineless president who'd subsequently abandoned them to their fate. Then when a just over a decade ago, a disputed election ended up prompting a chaotic bloodbath in which the U.S. military tore itself apart.

"Think we'll end up the same way as all the others?"

Paul shook his head with a smirk. "There's so much shit piled onto the Feds, I don't think they can fix Humpty Dumpty this time."

Another quiet moment passed as Paul took a seat on a heap of salvaged electronics. Since the EMP had fried everything without heavy shielding, the Saints' leadership had decided to round them all up and have them recycled to build new components. Of course, this would have to take place far from the war front, so supply trains and trucks carried them further south after dropping off their payloads to the troops. Paul remarked on the speed with which people had taken to their own new enterprises and routines despite the inescapable calamity. He caught movement in his peripheral vision, turning to watch Mason pull a pair of cigars out of his army field jacket, offering one to Paul with a mock flourish. Paul raised an eyebrow.

"Hey, we did win for now," Mason pointed out. "Did better than *I* thought we would! We dun made it out alive, and with most of our homies to boot."

Paul laughed. "I guess we did. Now, we gotta put our faith in 'Maniac Jesus'."

With a depleted yet relieved smile, Paul accepted the tobacco wrapping and waited as Mason ignited his own before passing the still lit match. Paul drew the sweet-tasting smoke into his mouth before releasing it into the soaking air. He felt more at ease right then—sitting in a city that he knew full well would be under siege within a week—than he had in over a decade.

"What you think Conroy'll try to do with the place?" Mason asked. "Think there'll still be elections an' shit?"

Paul nodded. "Yeah he'll have to do something that at least *looks* like a democracy 'cause that's what everybody expects. How different it'll be from what we had before, I couldn't tell ya."

"Word is, most'a them politicians have signed up with either us or the Feddies. But they all just waitn' to see who'll win."

Paul shook his head. "I guess some things refuse to change."

"Yeah, for how long? I don't know that this new crop of wild men will be satisfied with platitudes and convenient loyalties."

Paul allowed himself the small sin of reveling in the potential downfall of others, seeing as, in this case, it felt richly deserved. "I guess we'll have to wait and see."

"Hear 'bout Texas? They gone their own way now. Won't join us either, though."

"Yeah, that sounds about right."

"And the west coast? They sayin' the lefties are takin' the whole place over, killin' everyone who gets in their way."

"No shit? God, I guess it's all turning upside-down for good, huh?"

"Hey, anything's possible in the brave new world." Mason grinned ear-to-ear, offering a toast using his cigar, which Paul returned with a smile of his own. The drumroll of thunder echoed through the streets of Richmond, vibrating the hotel's filthy windows. An Abrams tank crawled past with half a dozen Saints reclining on its turret roof.

"You think he'll bring back the old ways?" Mason asked.

Paul sat in silence for a while. "I don't think so. I hope not. But tell you what, if I hear anything nefarious, we'll both make a break for Texas. Should be safe enough from the crazy there."

Mason scoffed. "Might have to do that one way or another."

"Don't lose hope on me just yet, man. We've come this far."

Vocal music from outside drew Paul and Mason's attention back to the hotel windows.

"What the fuck?"

The two lurched over to the open door and watched a procession of robed men and women shuffle down the street, eyes down, hands clasped in prayer, singing hymns as the one at the head of their group led the way carrying a full-sized wooden cross. Bringing up the rear, a man waved around a Bible sealed in a plastic bag to protected it from the rain.

"Rejoice followers of Christ, for you are blessed in His light! We will not shrink before the minions of Satan, for the love of God shields us, and His unknowable might imbues us with strength! Let those without faith quail before the fury of the righteous!"

The crew of devotees went on by, hundreds of entranced civilians and rebels tailing behind them.

Paul stepped outside and watched them disappear into the shadows and rain, closing his eyes and breathing deep as the thunder rumbled through the biblical downpour. As Paul opened them again, gazing up into the tumultuous sky, he noticed something that took him aback. What started at first as small shooting stars, just visible amid the gloom, turned into huge tongues of flame illuminating the sky before flickering out into nothing. Paul stood mesmerized as he heard growing numbers of shocked and amazed voices cry out as Mason walked up to stand beside him. If only for a moment, the desperate city came to a serene rest, and watched the majestic spectacle unfold in the heavens.

"His angels come, fellow Christians! They come!"

#

Judith twisted the cap off her green plastic canteen and downed almost half its contents in a single great swig. She thanked the Lord that Eastern Oklahoma had trees to sit and relax beneath, unlike the open central plains. Zoey poured a bit of water into her hand and splashed it across her grime-ridden face. An Abrams tank with the Texas flag painted on either side of its turret rumbled down the road with a couple squads of National Guardsmen following in an old Deuce-and-a-half. Helicopters came and went every hour or so, vehicles and refugees clogged the roads at all times.

"I gotta admit, I'm glad I didn't stay back home, Jude," Zoey said out of nowhere.

"Despite all the shootin' an nearly dyin'?"

Zoey shrugged, "Well it would all be goin' on whether I was here to fight in it or not. An if I wasn't here then I'd just be a leaf in the breeze. Even more than we still are, that is."

"Yeah, you'd be at risk of becomin' one of them." Judith gestured toward the river of listless refugees.

"Not to mention, *you'd* be out here with nobody but them yahoos to watch your back." Zoey added.

"Aww, you're gonna make me blush, Zo."

"You know that a big battle got fought near this place in the last civil war?" Zoey asked, digging a nutrient bar out of her pocket.

"Nah, I didn't. Who told ya that?"

"Some of the Rangers on their way to Oklahoma City. The Battle of Honey Springs they called it."

"Well, what happened?"

"They said 3,000ish Union troops fought 'bout twice that many Southerners and Indians, but still won," Zoey explained.

"Geez. How'd they manage that?"

"Said the Northerners had heavy guns an' local help while the Confederates had wet gunpowder and a donkey for a general."

"Yeah, that'd probably do it."

The two just sat in unspoken communication, wondering in a shared moment if they would end up the same. Dead on some almost unremembered battlefield due to failures over which neither of them held any power.

"I've heard President Sutton just sent our guys into New Mexico and Colorado, all the way to the Rio Grande,"

159

Zoey said. "Both states'd just split in half along political lines, now we've got the one half with us on the east side of the river and the other half up in the hills on the west bank by their lonesome."

Judith shook her head. "Wait, what? Why'd we do that!?"

"C'mon Jude, the place would just be in chaos if we didn't move in."

"That's what the Washington Gang said about Iraq... and Afghanistan... and Syria... and Africa... and Iran... and Taiwan!" Judith continued, picking up steam as she went along. "What good is being our own country if we just run around makin' the same mistakes!?"

"Goodness, Judy, relax! It's not like we're tryin' to take over the whole damn world, or even the whole continent! 'Sides, that land used to be ours way back when anyways, before we got annexed. We're just takin' it back is all."

"That ain't how all the people livin' there'll see it! And ain't there some kinda socialist army out west? What if the others go to them for help?"

"We don't know who the hell is runnin' things out west," Zoey dismissed. "But whoever they are they'll have to deal with the Mormons before they can even think about comin' after us."

"I'm just sayin', it ain't a good idea for us to be—"

"What're you two bickerin' about so fiercely?" Taylor butted in, riding up to the sitting pair atop her black, white-spotted mare.

"Er— Nothin', Sarge!" Zoey blurted.

"Hmph." Taylor pivoted to Judith. "Travis, got some word for you on your family."

Judith shot to her feet. "You do!?"

"Don't tell me you'd given up hope already." Taylor chuckled as she handed Judith a rubber-banded file. "It's good an' bad news. Your brother Dean's with the division reinforcing Fort Polk, but your oldest brother , well..."

"What?" Judith's voice had fallen to just above a whisper.

"His squadron was escorting the Lieutenant Governor and the Gov—Ah, I mean President's wife from Oklahoma City to Topeka. But they've gone missin'. Don't fret though, we're already lookin' for 'em. Now try and keep it at the back of yer mind for now. Can't help 'im any if you get yourself killed, can ya?"

With that, the Sergeant rode off, leaving Judith standing amid swirling dust, holding a bundle of papers. Judith felt a hand come to rest on her shoulder, turning to find Zoey wearing her trademark expression of sympathy.

"We'll find him. Don't you worry."

Judith smirked. "Maybe, with any luck we'll be the ones they decide to—"

A disturbance from the twin refugee columns grabbed the two friends' attention. A woman in the west-bound column wailed while holding a motionless bundle in her arms.

"Oh, Lord..."

"Damnit!"

Shouts of outrage laced with curses flew back and forth between the two columns, followed by rocks. Judith, Zoey, and every other Texan around launched themselves into action, keeping the two sides separated from each other. Lines of riot shields along the road formed up to deflect projectiles. The voice of Taylor blared over the chaos through a megaphone, commanding everyone to cease the violence and keep moving. Judith, Zoey, and the other cavalry rode along the riotous mob, using their sheer mass to push the two groups apart.

None of the people with guns had used them thus far, but Judith didn't know how long that could last. Just as she felt the beginning of panic well up within her, a blazing orange light in the evening sky pulled her gaze around and upward. Judith's expression fell slack as she watched countless streaks of fire plunge through the atmosphere toward the earth, before they faded like shooting stars.

The already virulent spread of panic accelerated out of control. The confused refugees went from fighting each other to fleeing toward their respective destinations, creating a whirlpool of humanity, Judith and Zoey trapped in its currents. Judith grappled with Savanah's reins amid the chaos, trying to keep the spirited Bay under control as the refugees swarmed around them. Savannah's skittishness emanated into Judith herself as hands tore at her pockets, tack, and even at the rifle slung across her back. In frantic retaliation, Judith threw open her telescopic baton in a wide arc, sending a cluster of those to her right scattering. One woman rushed her and tried to snatch the baton away, getting a swift thwack on the nose for her trouble. As others tried to approach, Judith set to work swatting away anyone who tried to grab at her or Savannah. Another horse's terrified neigh grabbed Judith's attention just in time to see some guy with a Gadsden snake tattoo reach up to grab Zoey's reins and saddle. In slow motion, Blackjack reared up, throwing off the auburn-haired rider who disappeared into the swirl of humanity as the horse bolted. Judith watched her friend vanish like a ship sinking into the ocean, Blackjack trampling anyone in his way as he fled. The beating of her own heart became the only sound within her mind.

Judith maneuvered Savannah around, urging her ahead through the mass of people. Doing her best to maintain some semblance of composure, she nevertheless shouted and thrashed at those foolish enough to stand in her way. With herculean effort, Judith managed to force her own passage despite enduring numerous punches and blows from blunt objects. Judith charged on, her face streaked with sweat, caked in filth that adhered to her skin. Choking through the growing dust cloud, Judith kept her stinging eyes locked onto Zoey's location.

"Go on now, get!" Judith wrenched her leg from the grasp of a man in a baseball cap before kicking him in the face. Thinking she must've pulled a muscle in the effort, she winced as a searing pain shot down her left thigh.

Zoey had tried to climb back up on her horse, but kept getting yanked back down by those surrounding her. Without hesitation, Judith waded in, wielding the baton with deadly intent at anyone who moved against either her or Zoey. Judith managed to reach her best friend in the disorganized melee. Stowing the baton between Savannah's saddle and blanket, Judith grasped Zoey's arm, hauling her onto the horse with every ounce of strength she had left. Her leg throbbed in agony so brutal that it broke through the shroud of adrenaline fueled by her fight-or-flight response. The second she felt Zoey's arms wrap around her waist, Judith took the reins in both hands again and charged back through the crowd, making a break for the southern edge of the road.

The refugees remained in a state of disarray, but at least now they seemed more bent on getting away than cutting off each other's heads. As Judith and Zoey at last barged their way out of the scrambled horde, the irate voice of Sergeant Taylor boomed over the anarchy, issuing commands to National Guardsmen and civilians alike.

The rage-fueled battle came to a gradual end, people continuing to watch in unsettled amazement at the sky as they shuffled past. Judith could feel the tension wither away moment by moment, as the refugees wandered back to their respective roads. The air echoed with the sounds of engines and the sweeping winds, but few voices.

The wild light-show in the sky continued in a myriad of oranges, pinks, and reds as the pair gazed up into the heavens.

"What the hell is that?" Zoey asked with much trepidation.

"I dunno," Judith answered in a beleaguered voice. "Meteors or somethin'?"

"Well... whatever it is, for us its a lifesaver," Zoey said.

Judith looked around at the still defusing situation, the numerous wounded guardsmen and refugees now receiving the attention of medics. "Yeah, sure..."

"Hey, it could've been a whole lot worse," Zoey pointed out with sad smile.

"No kidding." Judith rubbed the back of her head, remembering the dismay she'd felt upon seeing Zoey get dragged into the abyss of enraged souls.

As Judith's adrenaline tapered off, the searing pain in her lateral thigh muscle radiated through her lower body, cramping her abdomen. She felt a warm wetness cascade over her skin and she winced when Zoey's hand traveled down to inspect the area.

"Judi! You're hurt!"

"It'll be fine..."

"No! It looks like you've been stabbed!"

"They just nicked me as I passed 'em…"

"Nuh uh! Head up to the squad camp, Mordecai'll patch ya up."

"Nah, I'm sure it'll be fine."

"Girl, we're goin'. NOW," Zoey insisted.

Judith, too exhausted to argue, complied.

Upon arriving at the makeshift med-tent, Zoey jumped off Savannah's back onto the dusty ground first, standing ready to help as Judith nearly fell out of the saddle. Judith would have collapsed the second her left foot touched the dirt, but before Judith could fall flat on her face, Zoey swooped in and caught the wounded rider in her arms. Judith embraced Zoey, trying to regain stability as they stared into one another's gaze, only inches apart. Judith looked away, feeling the warmth of a blush spreading across her freckled face.

Zoey's hand came up and cupped Judith's chin, raising her head to regain eye contact. Judith expected to find that familiar look in Zoey's eyes, the one she had always employed when she wanted to cheer her friend up. That look always came with a few words of encouragement and a benevolent smile. Judith had seen it hundreds of times. But here, in the darkening landscape, Judith instead met Zoey's blue eyes and saw something deeper. It only lasted a moment, not long enough for anyone to notice amid the madness, but for that brief stretch Judith felt the world slow to a crawl, the pain fading into the back of her mind.

The two women shifted as Zoey pulled Judith's left arm around her shoulder, holding her wrist as she slid her right arm around the wounded girl's back, clutching at her belt to support her weight. "C'mon, lets go get you patched up 'fore the sarge skins us alive for losin' a horse. I'll find Blackjack once we get you settled." Zoey beamed into Judith's astonished face, smiling, her eyes glistening with tears that seemed about to burst forth and roll down her cheeks.

Judith continued to hold onto Zoey as they shuffled toward the med tent.

"Stop Zoey, stop!" said Judith.

"You okay? What's wrong?"

"I just…"

"What!?"

Judith folded herself back into Zoey, "I don't know what I'd do without you…" she reached up to touch Zoey's face, "I don't know how I'd get through any of this without you."

"Well, don't worry. I ain't goin' anywhere." Without any further warning, Zoey took a hold of Judith's head and slowly drew her into a gentle kiss.

#

"Okay, things weren't looking good— but they *are* settling down now. But something's going on in the sky, it looks like a meteor shower," Yujing explained, doing her best to keep her voice steady as Jose pointed the camera up at the flame-streaked sunset. "I don't know exactly what's going on up there, but no one seems very interested in fighting anymore. The National Guard have been pretty aggressive about breaking it up. We're going to try and continue on our way west towards Denver, where we're going to try and meet up with our fixer who's *hopefully* going to get us safely into the West."

Jose took a long shot of the shuffling lines of refugees as they rode past in the flatbed of a west-bound technical. "Who is this guy, again?" Jose asked after switching the camera off.

"Roberto's brother. Apparently, the man moved there from California a couple years ago, and now he's got some connection to this 'Red Army' that we might be able to use."

"Then what the hell's he doing in Denver?"

"Red Army business, or so Roberto says." Yujing watched a Texan Apache helicopter thunder overhead toward the west.

"Eh, the Texans say they've got their own plans for that place."

"Hopefully it won't be bad enough to keep us out of the city." Yujing sighed, "Just wandering into the west like we did in the south isn't an option. That nearly ended in disaster, and if even half of the rumors we've heard about these 'Reds' are true… its a risk we simply cannot take."

"Yeah… are you sure you want to talk to these guys?" Jose ventured.

"Well, of course! Whoever they are, they're an important faction in this war and nobody knows a thing about them."

"I'll tell you who they are," a ragged, Kalashnikov-wielding refugee sitting across from them in the flatbed spoke up. "They're the only leftists in this whole fuckin' war who matter now. The Popular Front's gone," he said in a thick Brooklyn accent, showing them his red and blue armband, symbol of the now defunct organization. "All the schmucks in Washington are dead, and the poor fuckers in the midwestern cities are too outnumbered to do anything on their own. It don't matter what disagreements we got with the Reds, whoever they fuckin' are, it's them or total ruin at this point."

Yujing and Jose shared a worried glance, but they wouldn't back out now. And with that moment of resolution, welling up inside her, Yujing looked to the sky and saw something that resurrected a memory from when this whole disaster started. A memory of hiding, darting between the once grand buildings of Washington. A memory of being alone in the capital of a collapsing nation. A memory which generated simultaneous curiosity and dread in near equal measure. A lone black Osprey, just like the one she'd seen over the Jefferson Memorial and the White House.

And it was headed west.

#

Alexander gazed with unblinking eyes down into his half-empty styrofoam cup. The liquid inside looked like weak coffee, but it tasted like the best bourbon he'd ever drank. Sailors always kept decent booze aboard. He couldn't remember the last time he'd travelled on a ship. Maybe seven, eight years ago? The endless motion of the world around Alexander made the exhausted soldier nauseous. He took note of the garbage cans as he entered every room just in case he needed a receptacle to barf in. Nevertheless, he took another drink of whiskey. His head ached as he tried not to think about the dozens of faces and names of those he'd left behind. He tried harder not to think of the thousands he hadn't even known.

One of the heavy steel hatches swung open to reveal Price, looking just as disheveled and spent as Alexander felt. "Bad time?" he asked.

Alexander shook his head, gesturing for Price to take a seat across the table. "Won't be a better one."

"Fair enough. Wanted to see how you were holding up," Price explained as he sat down.

Alexander sighed. "Still holding."

Price grabbed the bottle of Jack Daniels from the table before it could slide off and poured himself a cup. "I'm sorry about Maxwell. I didn't really know him, obviously, but he seemed like a good man."

"He was a good man, and a great friend." Alexander smiled into his cup for a moment, then downed the last of the whiskey.

"Well then…" Price refilled Alexander's cup before setting the almost empty bottle down and raising a toast.

"To Derrick."

"And all the others."

The two drank.

Groans of steel reverberated through the corridors and rooms of the old freighter. The murmurs of distant, half-asleep voices echoed alongside them. Price drummed his fingers along the table, making it obvious he wanted to say something but couldn't decide which words to use.

"Shoot," Alexander prompted.

Price thought for a moment longer. "When we make it back home, assuming everything works out, what are we going to do?"

Alexander rubbed his hand across his blonde stubble of a beard. He'd avoided worrying about that until he had more information. But who knew when that would come? "I don't know yet. It will depend on the situation when we get there."

"Yeah, but we can only stick to that for so long. What if the government has gone mad? What if there's no government left? We still haven't heard a damn thing except for what Daskal told us," Price whispered.

"No we have not. And honestly, that worries me more than anything else."

"Will we end up fighting our own people?"

"...I've been praying that whatever's happening will have finished happening by the time we get there. But we both know that probably won't be the case. God... how did it come to this?"

"There could be several answers to that question," Price said, taking another sip of whiskey.

"Speaking of answers, have you had a chance to talk with our *guest* since we departed?"

"Nah, figured I would wait until you were ready before I dove into that."

"No better time than the present." Alexander finished up his drink, having intentionally avoided Price's earlier question, which the young man seemed to notice.

As they gathered themselves, a pair of sturdy-looking men in mechanic jumpsuits slunk through the room, heading deeper into the vessel. Alexander noticed with curiosity how both avoided eye contact, and after he thought for a moment, he couldn't remember seeing either of the crewmen before. Then a realization struck him, the service sections of the ship lay down a different passage from the one the men had used. The one which they **did** enter, led to Farzan.

"What do you think all the guys in Europe are doing?" Price wondered aloud.

"Hopefully getting their shit packed up." Alexander turned back around to Price with the intent of signaling to him that something felt off, only to find the intel officer already staring back with a suspicious expression. Alexander tilted his head toward the hall the mechanics had just entered, receiving a nod of affirmation from Price.

Without a word, both officers stood up and proceeded through the hatchway and into the rusted, narrow corridor leading down the length of the old cargo ship. Echoes of the sea and groans of the freighter's weathered hull rolled up and down the passage with such volume they almost smothered the two men's heavy footsteps. Alexander and Price increased their speed upon losing sight of the two suspicious characters, squeezing their way past the troops and crew they encountered. At last they arrived at the t-junction where the locked steel door to Farzan's room waited, a door that now sat slightly ajar... with an unconscious guard lying on either side. Alexander shoved it open and stormed in to find the chamber empty.

"Shit! Fuck!" Alexander hissed as he barged out of the room, head darting back and forth down both ends of the hallway. For the briefest moment, Alexander caught a glimpse of a boot heel turning the corner. Without a word, the Captain took off, the frantic Price hot on his heels. The pair flew up a staircase onto the deck level—though they remained within the superstructure—and through an open doorway.

Alexander stepped inside and just began to turn his head as a closed fist struck him in the jaw. Tasting blood in his mouth, Alexander whirled with raised arms as a large and furious man tried to deliver a gut punch, which the Captain managed to block with his leg. Alexander launched his own blow into the attacker's nose, sending the back of the man's skull into a steel bulkhead. Price drew his pistol and held it on the now stunned infiltrator, looking back up to find Farzan and the other intruder had disappeared down the corridor.

"You go, I got this one!" Price assured.

Shaking off the pain in his mouth and the taste of blood, Alexander surged after them, glancing around every corner this time. He burst out onto the main deck of the ship, slipping between exhausted and confused Americans. Searching the crowd for either man, Alexander couldn't see anything. Then he heard a loud, "Hey! What the hell!?" and turned to find a soldier knocked on his ass while two other men flew across the deck toward the ship's aft section. Charging across the steel deck as fast as his legs could propel him, Alexander grabbed his radio as he realized the imposter's goal.

"Intruder near the bridge tower! Lock down the lifeboats!"

The call sent everyone into a bewildered scramble as a multitude of armed American troops emerged from the rusted-out bridge and surrounded the area. Alexander rounded the bridge tower's corner just in time to watch a handcuffed Farzan get pushed into the back of a lifeboat by a "mechanic" with a drawn pistol. Not about to let this dude just sail away with his greatest intel asset, Alexander lunged forward, grabbing the back of the guy's shirt collar and yanking him out of the lifeboat, throwing him onto the roasting deck.

The infiltrator tried to raise his Makarov pistol at Alexander, only to get his arm pinned to the ground by the Captain in one swift move. Other soldiers appeared all around in a matter of seconds, scooping up and handcuffing the stowaway, then dragging Farzan out of the still docked lifeboat. Price appeared soon thereafter, seeming more than a little concerned as the second infiltrator got hauled to his feet. Farzan, on the other hand, looked like a man given a new lease on life.

"You seem pleased for someone whose escape just got thwarted," Alexander pointed out.

"Escape?" Farzan scoffed, "You call Mossad captivity an escape?"

"Wait, they're Mossad!?" Price jumped in.

"I would assume so," the Iranian answered. "They are not *my* people."

Alexander gazed at the handcuffed infiltrator who refused to meet his eyes, looking out to sea instead. The captain thought for a moment, then turned to Price.

"Put him and the other one in a lifeboat and send them off."

"W-what?" Price questioned.

Alexander gave him a raised eyebrow, to which Price nodded with some hesitance and gestured to the guards while giving the necessary orders through his radio. With that done, Alexander handed off Farzan to a bewildered Escobedo. "Would you kindly take him to the brig and station about a dozen guards around the door while you're at it?"

"Eh, sure thing, jefe…" the sergeant nodded as he took the grinning Farzan by his upper arm and led him back below deck. *So much for having him here incognito.* Alexander sighed, running a hand though his grime-coated hair while making his way over to the midship railing, just escaping as the ship's captain began kicking up a stink over ditching the a lifeboat.

The Mediterranean made every other sea on the planet look wrathful and insane by comparison, especially now with dozens of cities getting slowly consumed by the ever rising tides. Thinking about that brought his mind yet again to home, he missed the mountains and deep forests of southern Kentucky. He missed his family. He missed Samantha.

With barely a sound, Price came up to join him at the ship's railing. "You sure letting those guys go is a good idea?"

Alexander scoffed. "No. But I know that keeping them here is *definitely* a bad idea."

"You think Farzan will be any more cooperative now?"

"He'd better be. That slippery bastard is still the only…" Alexander trailed off as something in the early night sky drew his gaze ever upward. The heavens erupted in flame as thousands of meteoric trails plummeted through the clouds toward the earth. Voices all across the ship began to rouse in curiosity, surprise and panic.

Alexander's mind jumped first to the thought that these were missiles, but he soon realized they numbered far too many. He stammered, trying to make sense of the apocalyptic scene paying out before him. "What the… what are?"

"The satellites."

Alexander whirled around to face Price, who gazed skyward with a blank look of devastating realization. "What did you say?"

"It's the satellites. They didn't get hacked. They've been destroyed. All of them."

Those words just hung over Alexander's head, their weight crashing down upon him in slow motion. Those embodiments of the techno divinity of the US, the tools that gave its military near omnipotence over the battlefield. Gone. Not disabled, not taken over, gone. It couldn't be possible. Could it?

"How?"

"It's called Kessler Syndrome. It was one of those worst-case-scenario theories… until now. There are— or, I guess, there *were* hundreds of thousands of satellites in orbit above the earth, packed together, shooting past each other with dozens of feet to spare like some chaotic highway in the skies... so many we haven't been able to conduct astronomy on Earth's surface in years."

Alexander could with some effort remember hearing about that a while back, drowned beneath an endless tsunami of even worse news.

"You're saying somebody fucked up?" Escobedo asked, having arrived, whiskey in hand, alongside Bowman who stood mesmerized by the stellar extravaganza.

"Not quite," Price answered, his eyes still locked upon the thousands of fireballs as they either burned away into cinders or plunged into the dark sea. "You see, if an accident happened... **or** someone were to deliberately destroy a large number of satellites at once— like if, say, somebody destroyed all of our military and spy satellites— it would result in a kind of... scrap storm. An indescribably massive cloud of wreckage hurtling around the globe at thousands of miles an hour. Then it just snowballs. Nothing can withstand that."

"You're telling me we gotta send a shitload of new satellites into orbit?" Alexander questioned, knowing they could never afford such an expense on top of the already enormous military budget.

"Oh—oh, no. It's much worse than that."

A large group began to gather around the officers as they overheard Price's words. The S2 shrank at becoming the sudden center of attention.

"Worse, *how*?" Escobedo pressed.

Price cleared his throat. "Well, I mean, that scrap cloud didn't just go away. What we're seeing is... eh, *maybe*, eight percent of what's up there. The stuff that's closest to the Earth. Everything else, from chunks of space stations to bullet-sized bits of metal, is still swirling around up there, shredding anything. There's just no space to pass through, much less hang around in orbit."

"Well how long does it stay up there?" Alexander urged. "How long do we have to wait? Months? Years? Decades?" *Oh fuck. Price, Please, don't tell me it's going to take deca—*

"Centuries."

Alexander recoiled as though Price had just spewed a waterfall of bile from his mouth.

The whole deck surrounding the party fell silent. Escobedo's mouth twitched, around yet no words emerged.

Price swallowed, the sweat worming down his face visible in the pyre cast by thousands of dying machines. "I— It... The optimistic estimate, was that it would take over a hundred years for enough of it to either fall to Earth and burn up, or drift off into space. But realistically... it will take a lot longer than that. We're probably talking more like two or three centuries before humankind can travel into space again."

Gone. Forever beyond their reach.

"They sacrificed all of it... just to cripple us?" Alexander asked aloud to no one. "Heh, of course they did. What other choice did they have? Give up?"

"What about all our people up in space?" Bowman stepped in. "Surely some of them would've had time to get out before—"

"Dead," Price interrupted her, dragging all eyes back onto the shell-shocked intel man, whose spectacled eyes betrayed the dawning horror of realization taking place behind them. "They're all... dead."

#

Harper took long, measured breaths. Her gaze fixated upon the enormous concrete monolith which sat in the heart of the San Diego Naval Base, the Western Command Center built for running combined operations in the Pacific, Asia... and Western America. Now it stood battered, festooned with red banners twisting in the wind, smoke vomiting forth from a huge crater in its southern wall. All around Harper, Red Army troops staggered drunkenly, smoking, celebrating a victory that none of them had expected. They paid the general no mind as she stood in disbelief.

This wasn't how any of this was supposed to go.

They were never supposed to get this far without her.

They weren't supposed to be running wild just doing whatever they wanted.

She was supposed to decide what happened and when.

"Why the long face, General?" Singh's voice bludgeoned its way into Harper's mind. "Come! We have to secure the final victory! Can't have Bennigsen and the others getting killed by a bunch of imbeciles who've already lost, can we?"

He headed right for the building's entrance in a nonchalant stroll, Harper jolting ahead to reach him.

"How— how the fuck did your yahoos manage to take this place!? The automated defenses alone should've kept them out, let alone the robots!"

The few Rebels in the lobby made way for Singh and Harper as they rushed through.

"Patience, General," Singh said with a dismissive hand wave. "I assure you, the necessary introductions will be made at the proper time."

Singh ducked into an elevator, Harper right behind him. With the top floor button pushed and door closed, Harper used the opportunity to move within a couple feet of Singh, forcing him against the wall without laying a hand on him. Standing a full head taller, the general leaned forward until her brown eyes rested just inches above Singh's jade orbs.

"I'm getting *real* tired of hearing that," Harper ground out.

To her annoyance, Singh didn't seem afraid so much as irritated.

"Eh... okay." Singh's eyes darted all around the elevator, making Harper tense up. "But I'm still not going to tell you what happened just yet."

With that, Harper grabbed Singh by the collar of his jacket and lifted him off the floor until he had risen to her eye level.

"You were supposed to be some fucking joke! Some dumbass kid that I could brush aside like nothing! Who the fuck you think you are, upending everything and putting it all to the torch like it's your goddamn birthright!?"

"So happy... to disappoint you..." Singh ground out.

Harper's teeth gritted together as her world began to turn red. But as her grip began to tighten... the elevator dinged. Realizing the potential scale of her mistake, Harper slowly lowered Singh back to the elevator floor.

Singh kept his displeased eyes locked onto Harper's the whole way down, brushing himself off as he reached the ground. "Do try to contain yourself, at least for a little while longer." He glowered at her, straightening his coat. "Feel free to vent all your frustrations about how everything didn't work out just the way you wanted after we've made certain this place is secure."

The doors slid open and Singh disappeared between them, only to stutter to a halt after a few steps. Harper followed with a suspicious hand on her holster, only to find herself confronted by a horror scene. Before them stretched a long hallway, featureless and depressingly institutional in its design... smeared with blood streaks and pocked by bullet holes. At either side of the elevator doors and the closed entrance at the hall's opposite end, a pair of armed guards sat slumped against the shredded plaster. The bodies of five unarmed workers splayed upon the gore-smeared, pulverized tile floor. Standing amid the massacre, a pair of tall, burly Reds in armored coats, helmets, and those damned gas masks waited for their master, who waived them ahead after a moment. *Who are those guys anyway?*

Harper, no stranger to violence and death, had witnessed its victims before— terrorists, enemy troops, foreign civilians. She'd always thought of it as an unfortunate necessity... but now? She looked up from the dead to Singh, who did not look disturbed at all by the carnage rather; it fascinated him.

"Hmm... looks like it was over in seconds," he observed with great interest.

"How?" Harper growled.

Singh pointed to the ceiling as he began strolling down the bloody corridor. "Automated defense turrets."

Harper followed his finger to one of the six steel domes arranged in a zig-zag pattern across the ceiling.

"I doubt these unfortunates even had a chance to realize what was happening before they were bleeding out on the floor. Now come on, the command center is just through here."

Harper followed with the Sword of Damocles hovering over her, glancing between the retracted and inactive turrets. Her mind raced. How could Singh's guys have hacked into this place at all? Let alone the auto defenses? She knew he had to have some kind of computer whiz on his side with all the drones that'd gotten hijacked, but this represented something else... something more.

As Singh arrived at the blood-spattered steel door, he paused with a quizzical cock of his head. A handprint scanner jutted out from the wall to the right of the large doors and Harper saw one of the dead guards lying crumpled beneath it, a noticeably large blood pool surrounding him. As Harper arrived beside Singh, she noticed something else. A severed hand... sitting atop the print scanner. A severed hand with a note stapled to the back which read: "Use this." Singh glanced to Harper with a deadpan and a sigh before placing the chopped-off guard's hand onto the scanner and holding it in place for a few moments.

The twin steel doors retracted into walls, revealing the trashed remnants of the navy's vaunted command center. Singh moved to step inside, but stopped just long enough to place the door-opening hand back on top of the scanner. Harper closed her eyes and took several deep breaths before moving to follow Singh. The command center resembled Wall Street in the wake of a stock market crash, papers covered almost every surface, things broken or toppled over. More corpses lay strew across the floor, but most had gotten dragged off to the sides by Red Army soldiers who occupied every corner of the room.

To Harper's surprise, and secret relief, many of those working to get the command center up and running again had clearly come from the original navy staff. Their white class B uniforms and the fearful wariness with which they regarded both the Reds and the turrets within the ceiling gave them away in an instant. The man who she assumed to be in charge of these ex-sailors met her gaze, and in his eyes she caught a hint of... hope, perhaps? Singh ignored the commotion swirling around him and headed straight for the commanding officer's desk, sweeping all the papers into piles and taking a seat in the large chair. A Red officer in a peaked cap appeared beside Singh in an instant, but made no immediate move to grab the attention of his boss who continued to sink deeper into the office throne, much to the growing tension of the semi-circle which had formed around him.

"Maynen, why does this all have to be so complicated?"

"Because admission of failure is anathema to the American character." The older Red answered, shooting Harper and the naval officer a suspicious glance.

The navy man looked away and shifted in his boots, but Harper leveled a glare at this new stranger. "And you are?"

"Othias Maynen, Defense Commissar of San Diego," he replied without emotion. "I already know who you are."

"Why is it that most of the staff got wasted by the turrets, but some of them are still fine? Are the turrets off now or some shit?" Harper asked, seizing control of the conversation.

"They have not been deactivated," Maynen stated with a smirk. "The current crew have been aligned with us for some time now. Before the attack their IDs were removed from the staff registry, just before it was relabeled as a terror-watch list."

Harper turned to the bemused Singh, who shrugged. "If it works, it works."

"And just how were we able to do something that insane, huh?" Harper leaned down near Singh's head.

He glanced between Maynen and the security cameras, which focused in on the insistent general. Maynen too looked suddenly uncomfortable, but also irritated. Before the exchange could carry on any further, a loud repeating beep began pulsating from one of the consoles in front of the command desk.

"Ooo." Singh sat up. "That can't be good."

"It's an incoming communication," Maynen explained.

Even as he spoke, one of the navy personnel had jumped to the vacant station and put on its headset. Silence clung to the room for several seconds before the woman turned around, looking between the collection of superiors, unsure who to report to. Her eyes settled for a moment on the naval officer, prompting him to make a firm nod toward Singh, who waited with interwoven fingers.

"Yes?" he prodded through clenched teeth.

"Um, it's a transmission from sea, sir," the woman blurted. "A ship."

"Lots of ships," another voice inserted. A dozen heads pivoted to a Red Army officer standing behind another console where a bespectacled navy man sat hard at work. "We just got sonar back, there's a whole fleet headed our way due southwest."

"How many ships?" Singh queried.

"Can't tell yet, but its a lot."

"Well... fuck." Singh glanced up at Harper. "They're not supposed to be here yet." He turned back to Maynen. "Do we have Neptune up and running yet?"

"Yes, Comrade Singh, it was the first system we deemed vital to restore."

"Marvelous," Singh responded with a glint in his eyes, leaning back once again into the command chair. "Go ahead and play their transmission," he urged with a brushing off gesture.

The navy woman nodded and turned back around with much reticence.

With the turning of a dial, the console spewed a mess of static for several seconds before a message began to emerge. *"ccccchhhhhhh—of the USS Ronald Reagan contacting base command, do you copy? Over,"* came the unmistakable, gruff voice of a seasoned military man.

"We're looking at around 200 vessels," the sonar man reported. "They're moving very slow. Some are sailing in irregular ways, probably damaged."

Harper's head whipped around to Singh with wide eyes. "The whole Pacific Fleet!? They're supposed to be in Honolulu according to the treaty..."

"And yet here they are. Shocking. Truly shocking." Singh added. "Eh, at least they aren't in any better shape than us. Open the channel. Or... whatever it is that you people say."

"W—what?" the woman running the console asked.

"Ugh!" Singh groaned, rubbing his forehead. "Begin broadcasting our response," he elaborated, making several rapid rotations of his wrist.

The woman pressed a few more buttons, and a bright red light illuminated on the console's face. She stood up and held out her headset to Singh, which he accepted in a casual motion as he listened to the CO on the other end repeat his message.

"San Diego Base, this is Admiral Sobel from the USS Ronald Reagan contacting base command, please respond. Over."

At first Singh sat in deep thought, holding onto the headset earpiece, before at last raising the speaker to his mouth. "Hello, Admiral."

For a moment, only silence came through the radio.

"Who is this?"

"This facility has recently come under new management," Singh taunted. "And we must insist upon your immediate surrender."

"Who the hell is this!? Where's Admiral Forest!?"

Singh took his finger off the send button, a quizzical look on his face. "Maynen, where *is* the one in charge of this place?"

"Umm... she's right over there, Comrade Singh."

Both Harper and Singh followed the paunchy man's finger to the torso of a woman in a decorated white uniform, her glassy eyes gazing unblinking into the concrete roof.

A cold numbness washed over Harper.

169

"Ah." Singh again returned to the radio. "Unfortunately she's come down with a nasty case of... death."

"You goddamn traitors! Do you have any idea what kind of hell you're in for!?"

"I'm afraid so. Now... you will dock as usual and surrender yourselves into our custody. Should you refuse, we will be left with no choice but to initiate hostilities."

Singh pointed to the Red Officer running the Neptune missile defenses, who nodded before setting to work. Harper watched as the main screen, which had gotten hit with a couple stray bullets, powered up to reveal the missile targeting system focused in on a massive fleet of surface ships. The ping of an alert bled through the radio from the admiral's bridge.

"What in the Sam hell!? You can't do this!"

"Of course we can."

"Why!? We're your own people!"

"Are you now?"

"We swore an oath to defen—!"

"I am not interested in any of your pathetic excuses." Singh cut him off in the closest thing to a raised voice that Harper had ever heard him use. "The only thing I want from you is your immediate and unconditional surrender. And if you are not prepared to offer that we have nothing to discuss."

Harper glared at the back of Singh's head, but knew they had few options in this situation. Fewer still that could result in anything like a victory without further bloodshed. She also knew that reasoning with this Admiral could tempt him to take advantage of the situation, and maybe even try to disable the missiles.

"Listen to me, I've got civilians out here, you can't just open fire on us!"

"That is... unfortunate. But it changes nothing. Surrender or we will destroy your fleet."

"Did you not hear what I just said?" Harper could hear desperation creeping into the man's voice, *"We're carrying thousands of refugees from Taiwan, you fire on us and you'll be killing them too!"*

"I don't care," Singh stated. "Or to be more precise, I don't care enough to let you sail off into the sunset with one of the most powerful military assets on this whole forsaken planet."

"You're insane!"

Singh rolled his eyes. "I'm not the one using them as human shields. However, I can just nullify **your** human shields by ignoring them," he explained while lighting up a joint.

"This isn't happening!" the beleaguered voice on the other end uttered,

"Oh, yes it is," Singh insisted in a sing-song tone. "Surrender or die."

"I..." the Admiral sighed. *"Let me discuss this with my officers. Will you give me, an hour?"*

"No. I think not," Singh replied with a smirk, pulling a silver pocket watch from his long gray coat. "You have 30 seconds to decide, starting now."

"I—This is outrageous! It's in violation of every rule of war!"

"25 seconds."

"Even if you sink us all, we'll do a number on you too! I've got enough tomahawks out here to level that whole godforsaken base!"

"10 seconds."

"Others'll hear about what you've done, you son-of-a-bitch! You'll never get away with this!"

Singh held up his finger to the ceiling, then began to lower it in a slow arc toward the officer controlling Neptune. "Five... four... three... two—"

"Stop! Wait! Stop counting!" Came a frantic plea from the radio, halting Singh's finger in it's tracks as he waited in expectation. A shuddering breath came through the radio. *"We surrender. We'll dock at the port like you asked."*

"Splendid." Singh grinned in true contentment. "We'll be expecting you *very* soon." With that, he gave the navy radio woman the "cut if off" signal, tossing her the headset before turning around to face Harper. "Now that the revolution has a navy, perhaps we can see about satiating your ravenous curiosity, General. Maynen, I trust you can see to things here for now?"

"Yes, Comrade. We'll take care of all… this."

"You will do no such thing," the Man in Black commanded in his resonant voice, drawing all eyes to the doorway as he and eight of his spec-ops troops filed into the room.

This time the Reds reacted in a quite different way than when Harper saw them appear last. All of the armed rebel locked their immediate attention onto the new arrivals—most everyone else hunkered down behind whatever they could find for cover. Harper placed a tense hand on her own Beretta, ready to draw the pistol in a swift, well-practiced motion. The Man in Black pivoted his head toward her just a fraction. She would've locked eyes with him but she couldn't see past those damned shades. Harper unsnapped her holster, tightening her grip on the pistol, unwavering.

Singh's chair made a slow, almost lackadaisical turn to face the entrance of the room where the black-clad mystery men stood. He uttered a single word in contempt: "What?"

"You will refuel the Pacific Fleet," the Man in Black asserted. "Then you will send them back out to sea with us. They are now under our command."

For a moment, a near total silence reigned over the control room. Only the faint beeps and dull whirs of machines filled the air. Any of the Reds familiar with Singh knew this would never fly. The already palpable tension in the air became crushing as everyone glanced between the two figures. The G-man in shades and black trench coat, standing amid a cluster of bodyguards, and the young man in the gray coat and visored cap—sitting in the massive chair he'd effectively conquered, his face half-hidden behind interwoven hands as his narrowed jade eyes scanned the pack of wolves before him—stared each other down.

"Where will you be taking them?" Singh inquired at last.

Harper suppressed her initial shock. It couldn't be what it seemed, Singh had to be baiting the guy.

"It's none of your concern where they're going," the Man in Black stated in a domineering voice. "This isn't an option, Singh. You *will* let them go and hand them over to us."

"And why would I do something as *ludicrous* as that?" Singh retorted, his voice still an even deadpan.

"Because not only will your refusal mean an end to our assistance…" the Man in Black's voice echoed through the concrete chamber as dozens of eyes flew from one side of the room to the other. "It will also make us enemies."

"Well, I suppose we must be… enemies?" Singh shrugged, "Because we *aren't* giving you the fleet."

In the next heartbeat, the Man in Black raised his right hand and snapped his fingers, propelling his troops into action. With expert marksmanship they shot out all of the half-dozen auto turrets in the ceiling without breaking a sweat. By the time Harper drew her weapon and had it leveled it at the Man in Black's blond head, she had a Sig Sauer pointed at her own chest. The Man's bodyguards had their suppressed M4s now aimed at the horde of Red troops who surrounded them, a wall of various guns pointed back. The Reds had the dudes in black outnumbered, and the dudes in black had the Reds outgunned and out-trained. Everyone that is except for Singh's pair of mask-wearing bodyguards.

Satisfied that Harper and the others wouldn't fire unless fired upon, the Man in Black turned to Singh. "I get that you're riding high right now, and you think the whole world is ready to fall before you, but you need to take stock of where things stand. You're living in your own little echo chamber. The truth is, you are trapped on the edge of the continent, surrounded by a whole lot of country folk who do not like you, and a far-right regime's taken power in Washington. Without us… you have no chance."

Singh took a joint out of his coat and lit it as the Man went on. He released a cloud onto the concrete floor, causing it to spill out across the room. "If we truly have no chance of success without you, then what right do we have to exist? We managed to get far enough last time that you couldn't afford to ignore us."

Seeming to realize that Singh had made his decision, the Man in Black turned to Harper. The two remained locked in a direct standoff. "General, are you really willing to allow this?" He motioned toward her.

Harper blinked, not surprised but still irked at getting dragged into this herself. She caught Singh's dire eyes gliding over to her. "What do you mean? Why shouldn't I?"

"Singh and the rest of you controlling those ships will transform the dynamics of the war, and make *you* a major target," the blond man declared. "The Brotherhood and government remnant is focusing almost exclusively on the Saints and Popular Front right now, but that will all change if you seize an armada and go on a rampage that can't be stopped with anything but an equal or superior force. You are all about to dive in way over your heads."

Harper could see the others fidgeting, glaring back and forth. Not ready to dip, but ready to lash out like cornered animals. She glared back into the blank sunglasses. She may not have liked Singh, but still preferred him over these guys without question.

"They'll get around to trying to kill us eventually. Ships, or no," she retorted. "You just don't want us to have 'em, cause we'll rule the whole coast and you don't want that, huh?"

The Man's head cocked, his square jaw tensed. "You would sacrifice everything that you fought for? Let it all be destroyed by this lunatic and his thugs?"

"Everything that I fought for was a *lie*. And whatever of it may have existed was destroyed by *you*." Harper spat back.

The man grimaced, "We're not who you think we are, but I get it. Just think about all the sailors on those ships, men and women with families… are you willing to let them all die at this monster's hands?"

Singh scoffed after releasing another cloud and enduring a brief hacking fit. "No one was killed in the process, they will all be spared and expelled as is the agreed-upon policy."

"He promised that before, though. Didn't he?" The Man in Black reasoned, eyes still fixed on Harper. "Remember the marines? He lied to you."

"No. I lied to *them*. Not to her, you snake," Singh grumbled in indignation.

Harper couldn't help but smirk at the smart ass quip when she saw the fury buried under the Man's skin. "Besides," she spoke up, "this 'monstrous' 'lying' 'lunatic', is a guy who you all have been backing up till now."

"Yes, right up until they realized they couldn't use us anymore," Singh added with more than a little satisfaction. He knew Harper had no interest in betraying him for this guy and his ominous friends. "It doesn't have to end like this though. We could just go our separate ways, agree to disagree?" Singh offered, his hands held up like scales.

"You can't be serious." The Man seemed in disbelief now. "You've set out on an impossible mission. The whole country will never follow you. You will never be able to hold the entire thing together. There will be no United States of Communism."

For a long moment a sort of confused hush fell over the command center. The Reds looked between one another, uncertain of what the guy was talking about. Harper sympathized. Did this guy seriously think they wanted to overthrow Washington and conquer the entire continent? Did he really believe they were stupid enough to think such a scheme even viable? The apparent bewilderment of the Reds seemed to register with those in black. As a cruel grin started to spread across Singh's emaciated face, Harper's blood turn to an icy sludge.

"A wise man once said that: to defeat your enemy, you must first understand them. And you, my manipulative friend, have failed to understand *us*. I will ask one last time, what is your response to our obligatory offer of coexistence?"

Harper saw the Man's brow twitch ever so slightly beneath the rim of his sunglasses. "Not a chance. I made a mistake when I agreed to try and bring the lot of you into this. I won't make it again."

Harper's muscles had gone taut, and she had readied herself to shoot if—or perhaps *when*—things popped off. She saw the arms and hands of the black-clad bodyguards had done the same. The Reds around the chamber rested on a knife's edge of sweating tension, well aware of the fact they could die at any second. Harper drew in a deep breath, forced it out, her heart beating in her ears. She steeled herself, but then Singh spoke again.

"That is… unfortunate."

A beam of light came down from behind Harper, just above her head, and punched right through one of the Man in

172

Shades' troops and into the concrete floor. In slow motion, but faster than she could've perceived under normal circumstances, first dozens then hundreds of light shards zipped through the air at a downward angle, perforating the ground and kicking up clouds of concrete dust as all nine men caught in the eerily precise circle of death crumpled and withered beneath an unceasing monsoon of lead. Harper and the other Reds anywhere near the Men in Black leapt away in shock, as one would jump back from a spontaneous eruption of flame. Some made feeble attempts to shield their bodies, but on instinct brought their weapons to the ready once again.

The distinctive sounds of "bullet-proof" glass cracking like ice, then disintegrated amid the roar of chain guns. It took some time after the shooting ended to register in Harper's mind that the shots came from the windows as she surveyed the resulting carnage. The Reds swatted aside the whirling dust and smoke, revealing all eight spec-ops soldiers dead, reduced to mangled bloody heaps... the Man in Black still clung to life. Coughing, sputtering, unable to lift his right arm, he still held his Sig pistol, looking around as he knelt on his knees in a pool of blood.

Harper blinked about a dozen times, trying to process everything she'd just witnessed. A distinct mechanical whir drew her gaze about 13 feet up at a new pair of smoking holes in the command center's windows, glass pulverized and steel bars torn away. Through these cavities and the fractured remaining windows around them, Harper could see a pair of guardian drones with the letters SDPD on either side hovering in place like dragonflies. Each quadcopters' rotary gun continued to spool, making the general more than a little nervous. Even when they ceased, the machines still made a deep sense of dread well up within her. A dread she suppressed, frustrated at not knowing where it emanated from. *These things are just being flown by nerds behind computers. Right?*

A fearsome outburst of gunfire made it past the chopping of the drones' rotors, then got cut off by an explosion. The Reds' own radio squawked to life, a strange new sound from a strange new system.

"The courtyard is re-secured! All hostiles eliminated."

"Excellent work." Singh's voice drew Harper's attention back around to where the Man in Black still knelt, unable to do much of anything other than sit there and bleed. "Remain on high alert."

"Yes, Sir!"

Harper arrived at Singh's side, expecting to find a look of gloating satisfaction, but instead saw one of... curiosity? The cautious Revolutionary studied the crippled G-man like a scientist taking notes on the outcome of an experiment.

The Man in Black looked between Singh and his useless, bullet-riddled arm and chuckled. Using his still wounded but functional left arm, the Man in Black reaching into his long coat, provoking Harper and several others to aim their guns at him once again. Harper grumbled when the guy pulled out a large cigar case, placing the wrap between his teeth before discarding the case and taking hold of it in his trembling, bloodied fingers again. The Man in Black looked up to Singh, then down to a small matchbox on the cratered floor just beyond his reach.

"Well... kid, you got me." He placed the cigar back in his mouth, "Do you mind?" He gestured to the matchbox on the floor, "for old times' sake?"

Harper made a deep search of Singh's face, following his eyes to the Man in Black's left hand, which rested suspiciously close to the opening of his coat. Before she could say anything, Singh had already drawn and cocked his Python revolver, and the Man in Black had begun to lurch forward, hand burrowing into his own jacket. Then with a by-now familiar crack, it was over.

For an unfathomable moment, the Man in Black remained where he sat, the whiplash of the .357 magnum having scattered his shades across the concrete floor. Harper saw his icy blue eyes for the first time, as all energy began fading from them. Blood oozed from a gaping wound in his right cheek, as he slumped ever further forward, coming to a rest at last amid the ruined corpses of his troops. As he did, something clattered to the floor from his left hand, a knife. Harper identified the blade upon closer inspection, and her heart sank to her toes. She had only seen one a few times before, but she knew the make well. An Ontario MK 3 Navy Knife, the blade of the S.E.A.L.s.

"Come, let us leave this place," Singh prompted with disdain, slipping through the command center door and down the hall towards the elevator.

173

Harper followed, leaving the other Reds to clean up the mess left behind by the Men in Black, and doing her best to suppress the unease growing within her as she stole a final glance at the still hovering Guardian drones.

"Now wait just a goddamned minute," Harper demanded, bringing Singh to a stuttering halt. "What's going to happen to those refugees on the fleet? And the sailors for that matter?" Harper demanded, her eyes narrowed.

"There's no need for concern!" Singh brushed off, continuing back toward the elevator, "The naval personnel will be shipped to the Great Plains where they won't be our problem. And the Taiwanese... well..."

"We are not sending them back there."

"Don't be absurd," Singh scoffed, "Of course we are. The Chinese want them back and we want the war materials the Chinese have."

"Singh, you know they're just going to be killed—!"

"No. I suspect that only their leaders will be killed while the rest will likely be placed in some form of re-education facility. Regardless, it is none of our concern."

"None of yours, maybe. I'm not so discriminatory in who I give a shit about," Harper bit out.

"How noble of you," Singh deadpanned as the elevator doors slid open and a Red Army courier charged right up to the young warlord, extending an enclosed cardboard tube. Singh snatched it up with a nod, dismissing the courier before opening the tube and pulling out the papers within.

Harper tapped her foot in bitter impatience as Singh read through the documents, his eyes growing ever wider by the second. "What is it? The hell has happened now?"

Singh looked up at her like a man trapped in a dream, "There's an army corps moving against us."

Harper's face became a mask of stone. "That's a pretty serious problem, huh?"

"Indeed. But it gets more interesting then that," he held the papers out to her with a limp arm. "Air Force One has been shot down in the Sierra Nevadas."

Harper snatched the documents and read them over in seconds. A drone after action report, detailing exactly what Singh had said. She looked up from the curled papers as the elevator slid shut. "What the fuck is going on? It was *them*, wasn't it? Who *are* you?"

Quicker than Harper's mind could process, Singh lifted his arm to her eye-level, flicking his wrist as he did. Out from his sleeve emerged a compact pistol, which Singh had gripped in hand while Harper stood blinking, trying to comprehend what she'd just watched. In the end whatever arm-rig he had didn't matter, Harper now had a gun in her face.

"I take it this is a new perspective for you, yes?" Singh asked with, his head now craned in Harper's direction.

Harper said nothing, glowering down at the man who held all the cards over her despite being half her age.

"Not a very enjoyable position. Is it?" Singh stated as he leveled the pistol with Harper's forehead, gazing up at her with frozen eyes. "Do try and remember that, the next time you wish to vent your frustrations upon me." He slid away to opposite side of the elevator, collapsing the pistol-rig back into his sleeve as he did, "For I am an instrument of the universe." He made an outward, all-encompassing gesture.

"You're kidding me."

"I'm murderously serious," Singh declared. "If I die it will mean almost nothing. All that needs to occur for our triumph is already in motion. Whether it's you who leads our people to that end or Bennigsen, or Julian, or whoever, the potential is all there."

"Why shouldn't I just give that a try then?" Harper ventured, already knowing half the answer, but wanting to hear him justify his own existence.

"Because I can take care of all the things about which you know nothing, just as you are doing for me. Don' forget, this job is yours just as soon as I can find a way to squirm out of it. Unfortunate as it is, grand imaginative statecraft and military genius so rarely go in hand. It's much more likely to end in success if we play off one another, rather than try to be something which we are not."

Harper rolled her head around on her neck, cracking all its joints. She had to admit, she hadn't expected that answer. "Fine. I can keep tolerating you. But that doesn't mean that I have to like you."

"Tsk. You must learn to accept the nature of this rare cumulative event, and remember that we are merely its instruments. Nothing we have done would have been possible were it not for the incompetence, the complacency, the indifference, the *HUBRIS* of our former owners. The hordes of embittered prisoners now ravaging the land would never have been prisoners had it not been for the excessive laws that saw them exploited as virtual slaves."

The mismatched pair strode outside into light rain and distant gunfire, to where government stores of rations and medicine had become handouts distributed to the starving crowds of abandoned and homeless expelled from their cities at the start of the crisis. Armed horsemen rode through the streets, pouring into the base perimeter to surround the smoking wreck of a black osprey, surrounded by yet more black-clad corpses. Another pair of Guardians loomed over the scene, darting around like murderous hummingbirds as the horsemen prodded and looted the myriad of spec-ops corpses. Standing atop the roof of a police cruiser a Red orator with a megaphone addressed a mass of Red soldiers and civilians.

Singh pointed to this group, gripping Harper's attention once again. "The soldiers and police like yourselves—few as you are—who have joined us have only been willing to do so because of the blatant disregard with which *they* expend your lives and everything else." He gestured upwards at the police and official characters hanging all around, "The innumerable atrocities being committed in the streets are the result of so many systemic failures and callous decisions that I don't even have time to list them all off. And no one would have been desperate enough to do something this insane had *they* not literally pushed the world to the brink of utter destruction." Singh took a deep breath as his eyes fixed on the wild gray nebula swirling above.

"It doesn't have to be this way," Harper pointed out.

Singh released a long sigh. "No Harper, I could play this reprehensible game with kid gloves. But if you had done your homework, you would know that's bound to end in our defeat. And if we lose, not only will it mean utter death and destruction for all of us, but for the entire world in the long term. Our only chance of victory, depressing as it may be, is to chose a 'side' as it were and make ourselves the only ones who can save them."

"Well, we're sure on the way to doing that," Harper agreed in a bitter voice. "The Popular Front is evaporating in the East and after what we've done here, the cycle of escalation will only continue."

"Just as expected," Singh said with apparent resignation. "You really should read that book I gave you a while back, it explains so much of why this is unfortunately necessary. If it helps at all, Julian and Bennigsen are the ones who wrote most of it. My involvement was passing at best."

Curious, Harper dug the red book from her pocket and opened the cover. "It doesn't credit anyone."

"Of course it doesn't. We were all fugitives before a month and a half ago." Singh chuckled as the elevator opened at long last, and Harper growled. "The only clues we gave out were bait. It will be rectified very soon, if it hasn't been already. We have been forced to hide a great deal from the world, and you. Including our most... integral comrade."

Harper's eyes flew open as she followed Singh out of the elevator. "Well 'bout time! You talking about whoever's playing God with all the tech that didn't get roasted?"

"Yes. It is finally time for you to meet someone very important to our cause," Singh answered, gesturing for her to follow as he continued toward the waiting motorcade. "Then I have a vital mission for you to complete without my presence. Something I'm sure you will appreciate."

"But—wait, what about Air Force One?"

"Oh, I have another man who's perfect for that job."

A rising wave of panicked shouts spread throughout the streets like a plague. People pointed upward and ran for cover as the Red army troops readied whatever weapons they had and aimed them skyward.

"Oh, wondrous. What could it possibly be now?" Singh demanded of the heavens with irritable contempt.

As if to rebuke the young man for his impudence, an honest-to-god fireball sailed just over the rooftops before crashing into an already battered skyscraper. Soon there were dozens of flaming objects hurtling through the darkening heavens, then hundreds… then thousands. Singh and Harper shared a mutual look of puzzled confusion, each seeming to scan the other for some indication they held the answer.

"Aliens! It has to be Aliens!" Insisted an anomalous voice for somewhere amid the chaos

Singh rolled his eyes and scoffed.

"Well, what is it then, mister know-it-all?" Harper whispered with a wicked grin.

"For your information, keeping you out of the loop for this long wasn't even my—" Before he could utter another world, another fireball crashed into the roof of an adjacent building. It inflicted only moderate damage but sent a chunk of debris skidding across the street and into the opposite shopping center. Both Harper and Singh rushed over to the smashed storefront, which by some "miracle" had already been looted, and thus the falling mass had claimed no lives. But a mass of what? Upon closer inspection, Harper realized almost in an instant what lay shattered against a broken plaster and concrete wall before her. A U.S. Military satellite… or at least half of one. Complete with the air force insignia adorning the scorched steel.

Harper pivoted back to Singh again, who'd expression had gone from one of confusion, to that of unconcerned satisfaction as he lit a blunt.

"Aliens, indeed."

#

Emily's mind had become lost amid the swirling madness of the city streets. Trucks and armored vehicles rumbled past as squads of Red Army troops darted between and marched along behind them. The ever-growing cloud of drones flocked into rings which rotated in unceasing motion high above the last clusters of resistance within San Diego, swooping low on scanning or attack runs as they darted between buildings. Helicopters, manned and otherwise, prowled just above the rooftops as snipers—or at least Reds with rifles—covered the streets beneath. And atop one of these gutted skyscrapers, stood Emily Dawes. Disheartened, and at her wit's end.

Emily drew a deep breath into her exhausted lungs in spite of the dust-saturated air. Looking down into the streets she saw the now familiar corpses once again hanging from lampposts, windows, and just about everything else. Where once Emily burned with anger, she now felt only the chill of death's gaze over her own shoulder. She should've died so many times by now, but she refused to just let someone kill her. But that shouldn't have mattered given the odds stacked against her. God rejected her soul again and again, maybe the devil too. *What the hell have I done to deserve this? Why couldn't those bastards who shot the rest of my team have made sure I was dead? Why couldn't Singh have just had me shot instead of drafting me? Why couldn't those marines just kill me instead of taking me prisoner? Grabbing Rob made sense, but as far they knew, I was just some grunt who killed several of their buddies, so why not kill me!?* Emily took a seat on a dead AC unit, setting her grime-stained cap aside, wiping the sweat from her grungy brown hair, and pacing at the gruesome scab on her forehead which had only just begun to crumble away.

Emily heard footsteps on the gravel-covered roof behind her, provoking her muscles to tense up as her hand glided to the pistol lying beside her.

"Hey…" Rob said. "I'm sorry to bother you, but you said that you wanted to talk and this is probably the only chance we're going to get for a while."

Emily's eye flew open, forgetting the 1911 as she turned to face her son. He came to sit beside her. For a while the two just watched the setting sun as the battle below ground to a slow end, and a large fleet of ships began docking in the naval base. Mother and son sat alone, lost in the ambience of this bizarre moment of history, until Emily spoke the question which had bored a hole through her heart for over a month of insanity.

"Was it something… that I did?" she asked, choking back tears.

Rob smiled, clearly holding back his own. "It never had anything to do with you." He wiped his eyes. "Not really. You were just caught in the middle, and you didn't even know it. I hated what you were doing but I knew you *thought* it was right and that I didn't have the magic skills to convince you otherwise."

176

"You still could've told me."

"And then I would've ended up in prison, probably worse."

"I would NOT have turned you in," she hissed.

"If you had even just known, they would have found out eventually. I wasn't going to put that burden on your shoulders for my sake."

"Don't you tell me what burdens I can and can't handle! I would've done something—anything—to protect you, but *this*!" She gestured out at the chaos consuming the city. "Do you still think this was the best option? Do you think its right!?"

"I think its inevitable," Rob answered without getting upset, gazing back at Emily with crestfallen eyes. "I think that whether I, or Singh, or any of us were involved… And in whoever's name or for whatever reason it was done it would've eventually happened anyway. Being involved just gives me the chance to mitigate it where I can and, hopefully, make it worth something in the end."

"But you don't think it's all my fault?"

Rob laughed, a sound that brought a faint light to Emily's heart. "No, though I do wish you would've just quit. Would've made this all easier."

Emily sighed, wiping her eyes. "You know I couldn't just leave the others with everything going to hell."

"Yeah. I always admired that about you. Loyalty is priceless, even if I think it's misplaced. Sometimes I wish I found it as easy as you do."

"It's never been easy!" Emily retorted. "And I thought when things settled down more we could go back to the Sierra Nevadas and slip away from all this. I never wanted to stay with the sinking ship until in hit the bottom."

Rob had downcast his eyes, not wanting to argue with her. "I want you to know that I do regret all the lives I'm not able to save, and that I never directly betrayed your trust. I never used you to get secret information, and I never hacked into any of your stuff. We were just working on opposite teams. But I meant what I said a while ago. If you never want to see my face again once all this is finally over… I completely understand. I know I wouldn't want anything to do with me either."

Emily placed a hand on his shoulder, causing Rob to look back up. Before he had a chance to say anything, Emily embraced him. His initial resistance melted almost in an instant before he returned the hug, tears now rolling down Emily's face. "Don't you ever hide anything like that from me again," she commanded, giving him a tight squeeze to emphasize her point.

"Agh, okay, fine! No more secrets between us." He wrestled just free enough to look her in the eyes. "But you have to be willing to keep them, alright? We'll be like a team, unknown to anybody else."

"Deal." She let Rob go, leaning back against the AC assembly as an Apache flew past their tower toward the naval base. "I know you understand how likely it is that one or both of us won't make it…" That prompted Rob to look away again with a concerned expression. "So I want it to be just open and clear." Emily took a deep breath. "I forgive you."

Rob's blinking eyes zipped back up to meet hers as he stuttered. "W-what?"

"I forgive you. For everything you did. And I don't blame you for anything that you didn't do."

Rob embraced Emily again, this time in a more desperate manner, which she returned wholeheartedly.

"I love you, Rob," Emily said in a cracking voice.

"I love you too, Ma. And I forgive *you*."

Emily looked over her shoulder to check the roof access door and make sure they would remain undisturbed. Seeing it still latched shut, Emily's muscles relaxed and her eyes drifted closed as she held her son. Wishing for the days when she felt like her only job in the world was to protect him. When she felt like she had an actual chance of doing that.

"We're all that matters now," Emily stated, pulling back just a bit to look Rob in his eyes again. "You, me, Christina, and Zechariah are the whole world. We'll go with this plan of yours for now because it's the best choice we have. But the three of you are *all* that matters to me now. Understand?"

Rob nodded. "Perfectly."

An oppressive buzzing that Emily now knew well scratched at her eardrums as a tornado of the automated death machines pounced upon a far off skyscraper. The deluge smashed the glass and concrete pillar, sending it crashing to the ground in a bloom of flaming napalm.

Rob turned back to Emily as she watched the waft of smoke and concrete dust spill over through the streets as the cluster of drones responsible hurtled away, ascending back into the heavens. *The way they move...* She turned back to Rob. "We agreed no more secrets, right?"

"Y-yeah, we did," he answered, an evident dread dawning on his face.

"So then, what's the deal with all the crazy drones?" Emily asked with crossed arms and an expectant look.

Rob sighed, but gave her an exhausted—and wary—smile. "That... is going to take some explaining..." He drifted off, his gaze transfixed on something distant behind Emily.

She spun around... and became lost once again.

The sky had filled with shooting stars of countless sizes. Some of the blazing spheres even plummeting far enough to reach the ground and ocean, the little damage they caused going unnoticed by the fighters still battling for the last holdouts in the city. Emily mustered the will to turn away from the apocalyptic monsoon and turned back to Rob, who's face had become that of a statue once again. She realized after a tense moment, that he knew what was happening. *Put the drones and computers aside for now...*

"That isn't a meteor shower, is it?"

"No."